HOOK UP

A Novel of Fort Bragg

William P. Singley

WARRIORS PUBLISHING GROUP
NORTH HILLS, CALIFORNIA

A Warriors Publishing Group book/published by arrangement with the author

This is a work of fiction. Names, characters, military units, places, events, and incidents are either the products of the author's imagination or used in a fictitious manner. Any resemblance to actual persons, living or dead, or actual events is purely coincidental.

Edna St. Vincent Millay, "What lips my lips have kissed, and where, and why" from *Collected Poems*. Copyright 1923, 1951 by Edna St. Vincent Millay and Norma Millay Ellis. Reprinted with the permission of The Permissions Company, Inc., on behalf of Holly Peppe, Literary Executor, The Millay Society, www.millay.org.

Excerpts from "The Love Song of J. Alfred Prufrock" from COLLECTED POEMS 1909-1962 by T.S. Eliot. Copyright 1936 by Houghton Mifflin Harcourt Publishing Company. Copyright © renewed 1964 by Thomas Stearns Eliot. Reprinted by permission of Houghton Mifflin Harcourt Publishing Company. All rights reserved.

FOLSOM PRISON BLUES
Words and Music by John R. Cash
© 1956 (Renewed 1984) HOUSE OF CASH, INC. (BMI)/Administered by BUG MUSIC INC., A BMG CHRYSALIS COMPANY All Rights for the World outside the U.S. Administered by UNICHAPPELL MUSIC, INC.
All Rights Reserved Used by Permission
Reprinted by Permission of Hal Leonard Corporation

LITTLE DRUMMER BOY, THE
Words and Music by KATHERINE DAVIS, HENRY ONORATI and HARRY SIMEONE

© 1958 (Renewed) EMI MILLS MUSIC, INC. and INTERNATIONAL KORWIN CORP.
Worldwide Print Rights Administered by ALFRED MUSIC All Rights Reserved Used by Permission of ALFRED MUSIC

LONG TALL SALLY
Written by: Robert Blackwell, Entoris Johnson, & Richard Penniman
© 1956 Sony/ATV Music Publishing LLC. All rights administered by Sony/ATV Music Publishing LLC, 8 Music Square West, Nashville, TN 37203. All rights reserved. Used by permission.

MY SHIP (from "Lady In The Dark")
Lyrics by IRA GERSHWIN Music by KURT WEILL
© 1941 (Renewed) IRA GERSHWIN MUSIC and TRO-HAMPSHIRE HOUSE PUBLISHING CORP.
All Rights For IRA GERSHWIN MUSIC Administered by WB MUSIC CORP.
Rights for the World Outside of the U.S. Controlled by CHAPPELL & CO., INC.
All Rights Reserved
Used by Permission of ALFRED MUSIC

Poems by E.E. Cummings, "i sing of Olaf." Copyright 1923-1961. Marion Morehouse Cummings copyright 1972-1991. E.E. Cumming Trust copyright 1973, 1976, 1978, 1979, 1981, 1983, 1991

PRINTING HISTORY
Warriors Publishing Group edition/August 2014
This book previously appeared in significantly different form entitled "Bragg," © 2006, William P. Singley.

ISBN 978-0-9897983-3-4 Library of Congress Control Number 2014936946

PRINTED IN THE UNITED STATES OF AMERICA

10 9 8 7 6 5 4 3 2 1

The sky, much more than the sea,
Is most unforgiving for the slightest mistake...

Anonymous

He was crazy enough to be a good paratrooper.

James Jones: *From Here to Eternity*

This book is dedicated to
past, present, and
future paratroopers of the
82nd Airborne Division
and the rest of the world can
go to hell in a handcart.

DISCLAIMER

Hook Up is a work of fiction. Some of the characters are based on real people and some of the events actually took place; however, the names, dates, and events have been changed. Locations have been moved for convenience, and the dialogue reflects the moods of the times. There is no intention to cast aspersions on individuals, the military, or disrupt the geography of Fort Bragg and the Fayetteville area.

HISTORY OF FORT BRAGG

Fort Bragg—Home of the Airborne—is 50 miles south of Raleigh, North Carolina, and six miles northwest of Friendly Fayetteville. The post is nearly 200 square miles and was named in honor of General Braxton Bragg, a Confederate artillery officer. Originally an artillery installation—the first military parachute jump was from a observation balloon over Bragg in 1923—its vast firing ranges offered ready-made drop zones, so Bragg became the training site where all five WWII airborne divisions prepared for combat in the European and Pacific Theatres. Meanwhile, at Fort Benning, Georgia, parachute towers had been erected in 1932 and other airborne units including the all-Black 555th Parachute Infantry Regiment, known as the Triple Nickel, trained there, but Benning has always claimed Home of the Infantry. During the late forties and fifties, both airborne schools operated full time, feeding newly qualified jumpers into the airborne regiments at Bragg and Fort Campbell, Kentucky, the home of the 101st Airborne Division. The 82nd, the All-American Division, had returned from occupation duty in Germany in 1946 and set up at Bragg, where it later became part of the 18th Airborne Corps. Fort Bragg and adjacent Pope Air Force Base form one the largest military complexes in the world.

Acknowledgments

There is no way I can adequately express my gratitude to the officers and enlisted men with whom I served during four-and-a-half years of active duty. More than a few times I disagreed with their attitudes and orders, and just as often admired their courage, commitment, and trusted them with my life. I still consider most of them the finest individuals I have ever met. I am not the first person to say serving your country may be one of life's most dynamic professions—and the challenges of being Airborne make it more so. In particular, I thank former Eleven Bravo Specialist Fourth Class John Yeager of 'C' Company of the Five-Oh-Deuce, First Brigade, 101st Airborne, Vietnam, who assisted with historical perspective and military knowledge.

Preface

Along a circuitous route of my own making, I ended up in Vietnam as a public information specialist—more colorfully described as a combat writer/photographer—with the 1st Brigade, 101st Airborne Division. My greatest contributions consisted of one photo and two original stories. The photo ended up enlarged on the front page of *Stars & Stripes*, the military's traditional newspaper, and the stories validated two Medal of Honor recipients. At the end of my interesting—and sometimes exciting—tour, I returned to the states a different person, determined to write the great Vietnam War novel. The year was 1968. *Matterhorn*, *Chickenhawk*, and *The Things We Carried* were in the future. In the late sixties, no one was interested in Vietnam stories. Most of America just wanted the conflict to vanish. The war had divided our nation, and had devastated a nation struggling for survival. My literary efforts went unrewarded with some justification, and like many other writers I had to find another way to make a living.

Then I started sketches of my days in the 82nd Airborne rather than my time in Vietnam with the 101st. The handwritten notes grew from pages to paragraphs to chapters, and putting it on paper took most of my leisure time. Somehow, the book I had been looking for in Vietnam was born out of my days at Fort Bragg in the late 1950s.

At the time, I didn't realize what the stories were really about. It wasn't until the third or fourth rewrite that I discovered its true theme. The book wasn't a catalog of heroic tales. There were no ticker-tape parades down Broadway or grinding slogs up and down Hamburger Hill. The book was a pause, a respite between battles that allows today's readers to experience moments that have been lost. The story is the reverse of catastrophic moments and events. I wanted the reader to understand the everyday minutia of an airborne unit in a strict environment. The moments are small: KP, guard mount, parades, 'hurry up and wait,' and off-post adventures. *Bragg* is a book of survival, of opposition to the existing norms. It became history disguised as fiction. Every chapter digs deep into military details, the rules and regulations, the Non-Com harassment about haircuts and shined boots and inspections under blazing sun that melts the senses and, also, the revelations of juke joint and barmaid etiquette. In the epilogue, I took the liberty to imagine every man's future. Sadly, some of the characters will not fare well.

The novel recalls a time of innocence when rules were invented to justify a system that imposed itself on every 18-year-old American male: the draft—the Selective Service System that sent your friends and neighbors and you to fight wars.

In today's Armed Forces, about one percent of Americans serve on active or reserve duty. Whoever really talks or even sees a serviceman, or understands what the military is really about, except for what they see in movies like *The Hurt Locker*, Junger's *Restrepo*, *Zero Dark Thirty*, and small sterile obituaries in local newspapers? It has been this way since the draft was abolished in 1972, and the military went all-volunteer. The politicians listened to their constituent's demands—no one wanted *their* child drafted and sent off to unknown, strange-sounding places to face death for no understandable reason.

The military is now professional, with equipment and firepower never dreamed of during the Korea and Vietnam conflicts. Women and men enlist knowing their choices of training. Still, winning a war requires boots on the ground, and today's combat forces deploy back and forth every four to six months or longer and serve in some of the harshest places on the globe. There is no undercurrent of reluctant draftees mocking the operations and decisions. The troops know they will be there, and the new soldier is treated differently. There is nothing to polish; uniforms are dull camouflage and scuffed boots and harassment is lower than it's ever been. At home, military families have a multitude of support groups.

But it wasn't always like that.

During World War II, millions of draftees, along with men and women volunteers from all walks of life, served their country. After the war, most were discharged and enjoyed the benefits of the GI Bill. A draft was no longer needed—or so America hoped. However, arms rattled around the globe in places like Greece and Turkey, Berlin and China, and Southeast Asia as Communism expanded its sphere of influence. In 1948, the Truman Doctrine was initiated and the draft was reinstated along with desegregation of the Armed Services. The Cold War was on, and the American military machine needed to be oiled to march to the continuing threats.

Serving willingly, although an inconvenience to starting one's career, became a rite of passage during peacetime. An honorable discharge was a resume-enhancing document proving a person could follow and handle simple tasks. The Cold War was posturing between two mega-powers with policies of mutual destruction. While schoolchildren practiced hiding under their desks from the omnipresent threat of a nuclear attack, draftees of the day relished the opportunities to travel to *exotic* postings like Fort Polk, Louisiana; Fort Richardson, Alaska; or Thule, Greenland.

Meanwhile, Levittowns had sprung up around the country. World War II veterans had graduated from colleges paid for by the GI Bill and founded businesses and created steady employment. Flashy and affordable new cars, some sprouting keel-like fins and excess chrome, rolled off Detroit production lines while Little Richard and Bill Haley's Comets sounded the call of Rock 'n' Roll. Teenagers began to rebel against the old-fogy sedate parents living dull contented Ozzie-and-Harriet lives in suburbia. The kids emulated their heroes: they strutted like Elvis, sulked like James Dean, and imitated Brando's famous line from *The Wild One* when asked what he was rebelling against. "Whaddaya got?" he sneered. Young men grew ducktail haircuts with dangling pompadours and wore pegged trousers. Their girlfriends had beehive hairdos and wide skirts that came below the knees with sewn-on pony patches. For most young people, life was fun, cool, just a hot jukebox song except for the usual crises like no date for the prom and angst about acne.

Who cared about a canal called Suez or when an organization with the initials CIA fermented a coup in Iran? Or a backward place where millions of people suffered under the oppressive thumb of a dictator with the name that sounded like a dish on a Chinese menu: Mao Tse-tung.

Then, in June of 1950, Communist North Korea suddenly assaulted across the 38th parallel of the peninsula—the agreed-upon border from World War II—into democratic South Korea which was defended by United Nations troops, mostly American GIs undertrained and soft from years of mama-sans and garrison duty in Japan and Okinawa. The attackers rapidly pushed the soldiers to a toehold position at Pusan until the Marines landed in Inchon and pushed back. The Americans and UN troops chased the North's armies to the Yalu River, the dividing line between China and Korea, and then the Chinese, with blaring bugles and unlimited manpower, charged across in droves. A stalemate developed not far from the original 38th parallel.

Suddenly, for the first time since World War II, draftees faced a shooting war, not a dull cook's job in the humid mess hall at Fort Stewart, Georgia. They fought for their lives in a police action while some at home invented the serious science of avoiding the draft—to be perfected even more during the Vietnam era with escapes to Canada and even prison sentences. In 1952, when President Eisenhower came into office, he led the way to a cease-fire. The peninsula remained separated while the U.S.A. settled back into an era of prosperity and peace. Was there a better indicator of a good life when young people could wile away their afternoons watching Dick Clark's *American Bandstand* on the black and white TV while Mom prepared dinner and Dad mixed after-work martinis? The family had a Plymouth Fury in the driveway, a family dog, and annoying neighbors.

And the draft continued without a shot being fired, except a quick 1958 foray into Lebanon when the Marines assaulted the beach among sunbathing Arabs and American paratroopers flew over—primed for a combat jump, but instead landed like tourists at Beirut International Airport to settle the Christian and Muslim political dispute. At the time, no one could imagine what the Middle East would become.

Bragg reveals the late fifties and slices off bits of culture, events, politics, and—with some humor—places them in the context of a disciplined parachute infantry regiment where the proud veterans clashed daily with the draftees who believed in a different Bible. The Lifers' version was patriotic and proud, and their goal was to train the draftees to join the team. The draftees weren't used to orders and regimentation in their free-spirited lives, and the novel shows these conflicts up close and personal. Without a war to wage, military standards became shiny boots, gleaming belt buckles, and skin-tight haircuts. Few knew that a place called French Indochina was leaning toward America for help as the French, its colonial master for over a century, were losing a vicious war to a formidable peasant army.

Those halcyon days were numbered as the world's geopolitics progressed—or perhaps shattered—into the spread of nuclear weapons and the rise of Third World power struggles. Vietnam and all its ramifications were on the horizon, unseen by most Americans until the mid-sixties. *Bragg* is a jumping-off point which allows readers to make the connections between previous wars, the invasive draft of the fifties, and the social mores of the times. The book is a chance to take a breath and see the military before the Kennedy assassination, the rise of militant Islam, and most of all September 11, 2001.

Today's soldiers with their pounds of Kelvar armor, high-tech weapons, night-vision goggles, Humvees, GPSs, and drones might find *Bragg* quaint like World War I troops looking back to their Civil War counterparts or the simplicity of a rucksack, rifle, steel pot, and canvas boots of their Vietnam predecessors.

Drive across Bragg's expanse today and the division barracks of the fifties that symbolized regimentation and the Smoke Bomb Hill's World War II wooden barracks have vanished, replaced by dormitories with four-man rooms, parking lots, and low-slung corporate-style office buildings amid lofty trees. Fortunately, the classic three-story brick edifices on Main Post remain as a reminder of the fort's historic past.

In downtown Fayetteville, "Combat Alley" and the Hay Street bars have vanished, replaced by upscale shops, coffee houses, and health food establishments. It's become a popular Southern town and is occasionally selected as one of America's better cities to reside. Off-duty soldiers now scatter to fashionable brand-name shopping malls spread in the various suburbs, and spend more time with their iPads than killing six-packs in windy parking lots.

However, today, on the right day, if you drive out Longstreet Road winding through the tall Carolina pines, civilization vanishes and you can access the various drop zones and sit on the hood of your car or in the stark bleachers and watch C-130s cross over at 2,500 feet spilling platoons of paratroopers—little images at first, and then their chutes blossom to reveal a few hundred jumpers. You follow their descent to the rough red soil where they land then bundle up their chutes and hike to the assembly point. Lining up to turn in their gear, they are exuberant, grinning, kidding one another, and you will see it in the soldiers' faces and hear it in their voices, echoing jumpers from the past. Even you, as a witness, might hear the words, "This is what it's all about." Airborne.

Bill Singley

Chapter 1

Buck Sergeant Adrian Cooper, blue cadre helmet low on his forehead, found the small group of soldiers who had just arrived on the Vomit Comet, the regular bus service from nearby Fayetteville, standing by their new duffel bags on the replacement company's windblown street. Fresh from basic training centers across the country and wearing ill-fitting uniforms, they appeared to be lost souls waiting for an omen from the overcast skies to guide them away from the depressing two-story World War II-era wooden barracks that lined the street toward their brilliant military destinies. Sergeant Cooper was that omen. His first words were, "There's two things that fall from the sky—bird-shit and rain—and none of you 'cruits look wet to me. Form up in two ranks and follow me."

He led them to their temporary barracks and ordered them to leave their duffel bags on any bunk then marched them to supply where they drew their bedding: mattress cover, two blankets, two sheets, a pillow, and pillowcase.

Before they could make up their bunks, he had them standing in the chow line for noon chow or dinner in the Army.

Cooper, short and thin, tried hard to be tough on the men.

One of the new men pointed out the young sergeant wasn't Airborne qualified. He had no Wings sewn on his fatigues.

After chow, a few of them were finishing making up their bunks when Cooper stomped into the unheated squad bay and hollered, "Fall out! ASAP! Uniform is fatigues. You cherries are goin' to pick up parachutes."

Forty minutes and a cold deuce-and-a-half ride later, the new men found themselves staring at an immense sand and soil field.

Drop Zone Sicily: the biggest of Bragg's five DZs.

A dozen civilians, mostly women and children, huddled on the small set of bleachers; they were there to pick up their men.

"How many of you guys ever saw a jump before?" asked the young sergeant in charge of the detail. He wore the 82nd Airborne patch on the left shoulder of his field jacket, a black and gold U.S. Army label over his upper left jacket pocket with white cloth jump wings sewn above the Army label. Pinned to the center of his blocked fatigue cap were silver paratrooper wings on a background of blue and gold. His white and black nametag over the right pocket read 'Joyce.'

"I ain't ever been here before, Sarge," answered a gangly, pimply-faced man whose nametag read Mangiameli.

A few of the men laughed. None of them had been there.

"OK to smoke, Sarge?" asked Schmidt, a tall handsome young man who appeared older than the others and unfazed by rank.

The sergeant agreed, and while most everyone lit up, he explained since none of them had ever seen a jump, the detail would not be too bad. They would stand in the back of the truck and by the trailer to collect the mains and reserves of the jumpers. They were to make sure each kit bag had a reserve attached to the handles and the mains were inside.

"What's a main?" asked the smallest man in the group, a Cajun boy named DeFever.

A tall, baby-faced recruit quickly answered it was the parachute on the jumper's back, the one that opened. This was the recruit who recognized Cooper wasn't a jumper.

The sergeant confirmed the answer and advised they would work two lines leading up to the truck. It wasn't a big jump. About 180 men at most. "Are you guys mostly RA or US?" asked Sergeant Joyce.

Immediately, everyone asserted their status of being US, except the baby-faced soldier who knew about the chutes and the pimply-faced recruit, Mangiameli. They were RA which meant Regular Army and a three-year hitch as opposed to the US draft obligation of only two years. The baby-faced soldier added he was going all the way. "Thirty years for me. Some day you'll hear about Colonel Motz."

Most everyone snickered, admitting to liking the Army was like confessing a belief in Santa Claus.

"Two more months," bragged the young sergeant, "and I'll be back on the block."

Private Motz's eyes lit up. "You made sergeant in two years?"

"Three."

"RA, huh." Motz's tone revealed he knew it could not have been accomplished in two years.

Mangiameli asked how far it was to Detroit.

Joyce walked over to the nervous soldier with the bad complexion and looked at his nametag. "How do you pronounce that?"

Everyone expected the sergeant to bully the twitchy recruit or at least make fun of his hard to pronounce name.

"Man-gee-a-mell-ee."

Mangiameli fidgeted. He didn't like being the center of attention.

"Private Mangiameli," advised the Sergeant, "Detroit's about ten hours from here. Too far for a short trip."

From nowhere, one of the soldiers said, "Second star to the right and straight on to Never-Never Land."

Only Schmidt laughed.

The men were surprised. This sergeant acted like a regular guy.

"Are we really going to see a jump?" asked one of the few Negroes in the group.

"Right up there." The sergeant pointed to the gray early January sky. "This here..." he swept his arm toward the wide field "...is Sicily Drop Zone or DZ. If—and I mean *if*—you cats make it through Jump School, you'll see a lot of this place. Close up." Private Willie Patterson, shivering, asked if Jump School was as tough as they heard.

"Where in the hell's your field jacket?" asked the NCO.

The private's lips were icy blue and he could not conceal his tremors. Earlier, when Sgt. Cooper ordered them into fatigues, Patterson fell out still in his dress uniform. He had lost the keys to his duffel bag lock. Before Patterson could explain his story to Sergeant Joyce, the man called Schmidt told the NCO about them being rushed from the barracks by Cooper and some of them didn't have time to get their full uniforms. Patterson did not correct Schmidt's version and did not tell Joyce about Sgt. Cooper shouting in his face, threatening to give him an Article 15 for an improper uniform, Cooper's bloodshot eyes and raspy voice drilling forever into the private's memory. The NCO had chased Patterson into the barracks to find fatigues, even if he had to shoot someone for them. Patterson, stymied on how to open his duffel bag, accepted a last minute offer from a Mexican-looking guy coming from the latrine. "Like, man, you want me to slice open the motherfucker?"

He hitched his trousers and a switchblade appeared.

Patterson paused for a moment, stunned at the appearance of the knife and knowing Cooper waited specifically for him, nodded yes. The man—his name tag read Banuelous—expertly cut open the top of the bag. On his right hand, between his thumb and forefinger, there were small faded marks like a cross. Patterson didn't ask him about the rough marks as he pulled out his fatigues. Later, he learned it was a Mexican gang symbol.

Banuelous warned him not to mention the knife.

In the rush of changing and thinking about a Spic with a knife, he forgot his field jacket. Now there was a real live sergeant actually listening to him for the first time since he had been drafted.

"Hey, man," said Joyce, "wait in the cab. You'll warm up once we start working."

Patterson, too bashful to express his gratitude, headed for the truck, worried the others thought he was weak because of the cold, but grateful to get out of the wind. He hated the cold. A few seconds after he shut the door, another man joined him and produced a pint of Four Roses from beneath his field jacket. It was the man who made the comment about Never-Never Land.

"This'll warm you up, Cat."

Patterson took the offered bottle, aware he had never drunk straight liquor before.

The strong liquid warmed his mouth and throat then hit his stomach, executed an about-face and started back up. Patterson tightened his mouth shut and forced the liquor down again. His eyes watered.

"Another slug?"

Patterson waved off the bottle. "Ain't you afraid of gettin' caught carryin' around booze?"

"Hey, you can't do everything the Army tells you. You do that, you might as well become a tent peg."

He looked at his benefactor. The man was extremely pale with almost a shaved head and black eyebrows. His five o'clock shadow contrasted with chalky skin. In contrast to his dark eyebrows were brilliant ice-blue eyes. He looked immune to the world. Someone, unlike Patterson, not afraid to break the rules.

The man jabbed at Patterson's nametag. "You're Patterson, huh?"

"You must be Breslin." Nametags made it easy to ID everyone.

"Scott Breslin." He offered his hand. "I smell Irish in you."

"My old man is. My Mom's Dutch or somethin'."

Breslin sipped, then looked around to see if anyone outside the cab saw him. He tapped on the pint. "I'm practicing to become a priest."

"Yeah, I guess they drink a lot." Patterson's family went to Protestant services only on Christmas and Easter.

"I'm just kidding. This stuff saved my life on Jackson's rifle range. South Carolina's colder than a witch's tit. Made me shoot expert too." Breslin chuckled at the memory. "Want another taste?"

Patterson shook his head no. "I took basic at Dix."

"Oh, man, I wish I had. That's near Philly."

"I know. I'm from Downbeach at the shore."

Breslin lit up. "No kiddin'. I've been there. The infamous Jersey Shore. Me and some of my asshole college buddies went down a couple of times for summer weekends."

"You were in college?"

"A couple of years. Dropped out and drafted like that." He snapped his fingers and chuckled. "You sure you don't want another?"

Patterson wanted and didn't want it so he said, "Nah, but can I bum a smoke from you?" During basic at Dix, he had started smoking to keep warm. Breslin gave him a Chesterfield and kept one for himself. Patterson cupped his shaking hands around the match.

"Man, you really are cold."

"I hate it. There's no cold like Army cold. You can't escape it. I'd rather pull KP than be cold."

"I think we'll see a lot of cold around here." Breslin took a long swallow; his following sigh was that of a patient man waiting for a long journey to begin.

From his dramatic position standing on the fender of the heavy truck, the future Colonel Motz extended his arm toward the east end of Sicily and proclaimed, "There they are!"

"Get the fuck down, asshole," called Banuelous. Motz ignored him.

The planes appeared small in the distance. They came in a triangle of three. C-119 Flying Boxcars. Twin-tailed. Fat fuselages. Air Force troop carriers also know as 'Flying Coffins.' At first, the planes seemed like black insects against the overcast, but as they approached their silver wings and Air Force markings became apparent while the distant murmur of their engines became a low roar.

Patterson and Breslin came out of the cab in time to see the first indeterminate figures fall from the lead plane. In seconds, more bodies fell. No sooner had the first chute opened than a multitude of parachutes floated in the sky. Patterson was surprised to see the parachutes were green—he had assumed white. There was an unorganized symmetry to the hanging chutes somewhat in the manner of a sloping field full of flowers. It looked thrilling. A giant amusement ride. The new recruits knew they came to jump, but seeing it for the first time made some of them question letting their lives be held up by a few strands of nylon.

Could I do that, Patterson asked himself. *I could*, he hoped silently.

"You know," said Breslin standing next to a shivering Patterson on the tailgate, "looking at that from an objective perspective, you gotta be fucking nutzo to do it."

The planes passed rapidly, leaving the jumpers hanging in the sky like toys in a child's game. Gradually, they drifted toward the spectator area. The tiny bodies became men in uniforms.

One landed. Another. As the last jumpers hit the ground the first to land appeared on the edge of the drop zone, their field jackets and trousers soiled with red sand, carrying their deployed chutes in kit bags slung over their shoulders. In a few minutes, most of the men lined up in stick or chalk order, the order from which they jumped from the planes, and sat on their bags rehashing the jump and smoking. A few of the officers tossed their bags on the truck and left. Non-coms kept the stream of arriving jumpers in line.

A Negro sergeant called to Sergeant Joyce, "Hey, California, you ready to collect your trash?"

Joyce replied, "That trash just saved your worthless life, Sergeant Williams. Start 'em up. Stick order."

"Let's go!" boomed the Sergeant. "Move it out, lobcocks, and sound off like you got a pair!"

"Lobcocks," repeated Breslin softly and laughed his soft laugh.

The men shouted off their last names and chalk numbers as they dumped the kit bags onto the tailgate. Joyce checked off each name. On the tailgate, Patterson and Banuelous took the bags and tossed them toward the front of the truck where Breslin and Schmidt unhooked the reserve chutes and stacked them against the sidewall. Patterson saw the face of every man and was surprised at their youth, few matched the image of the battle-weary rugged paratrooper he'd seen in newsreels or the NCO who had recruited him at Fort Dix.

Working and the camaraderie of the men handing over the chutes warmed Patterson; he finally decided if they could jump, he could.

"Lobcocks," said Breslin again.

"Oh-oh," said Banuelous and looked at Patterson while making a jerk-off gesture. "Check out the sign." They had become friendly during their few days in Repo Depot because Patterson hadn't squealed about his knife. Banuelous saw the sign by peering over the cab of the canvas-covered 2-1/2 ton truck while everyone else nestled against their duffel bags along the wooden pull-down seats.

Patterson looked out the rear of the truck and saw the back of the sign framed in the arch of the truck's canvas roof.

It was a large sign, bigger than six by eight feet, painted white with dark blue and gold letters. It read, "You Are Now Leaving The 504ᵗʰ Airborne Infantry Regiment. The Best Damn Soldiers In The World." The regimental crest was painted on the upper left hand corner, a blue and gold shield with a winged sword across it. Written on the sword were the words "Strike Hold," the regimental motto. Another crest on the upper right corner showed a flag-draped devil.

The truck stopped in the middle of the asphalt street lined with modern T-shaped concrete barracks, the exact barracks Patterson had wished for the first day he arrived at Bragg and rode past them on the bus. New buildings had to be warmer than the dilapidated WWII barracks with sporadic hot water and heat he had endured during basic training at Fort Dix and the last few days in Repo Depot.

Corporal Craven, the Negro soldier who had picked them up in Replacement Company, formed them into a platoon on Grave Street, named after the Dutch city the 504ᵗʰ had liberated during the war and pronounced like 'brav' in bravo. Each man stood next to his duffel bag. Except for their small contingent, the winter street was empty. Small barren trees supported by posts aligned the sidewalks like scrawny sentries. A cold wind from the Great Smokies in the western part of the state swept past them on its way to the Carolina beaches.

Craven held another roll call to be sure no one had disappeared during the ride. Halfway through, a high rapid mechanical voice said, "Corporal Craven, is this a mob or a formation in the Five-Oh-Fourth Airborne Infantry Regiment?"

"Formation, First Sergeant."

"Make it look that-a-way, pronto."

First Sergeant Billy Martin had appeared from nowhere to be ten quick strides from Craven. The first sergeant was not a tall man. His white sidewall haircut showed beneath his fatigue cap and he wore Army-issue glasses. First Sergeant Billy Martin walked and talked like a machine. Intentionally, he did not wear a field jacket to impress the new men with his hearty endurance. On the right shoulder of his fatigue shirt was the black and white Indianhead patch of the Second Division. A soldier's combat duty patch always appeared on the right shoulder. The 82nd red, white, and blue AA patch adorned his left shoulder. Like Craven and every other jumper in the 504th, the Jump Wings on his blocked fatigue cap were pinned on a blue and gold background, the colors of the '04.

Craven called the men to attention and continued calling roll as the first sergeant walked among the new men reminding them they were at attention and to sound off like they had a pair.

"All present and accounted for, First Sergeant." He saluted.

Martin ignored the salute. "That's all, Craven."

Martin continued pacing silently in front of the formation as Craven departed in the truck. Every man's eyes followed the small sergeant. He stopped. Stared. Snapped. "What in the hell y'all lookin' at. Y'all at attention. Look straight ahead!"

Patterson wasn't sure what the others were thinking, but he knew he was in trouble; the NCO spoke so fast and with such a southern accent he couldn't understand a word.

"Men," he began, "that building behind me is Headquarters-and-Headquarters-Company-First-Battalion-Five-Oh-Fourth-Airborne-Infantry-Regiment. That's my company. I'm First Sergeant Billy Martin..." his hand rubbed his chevrons as if warming his fingers "...That's three up. Three down. And a diamond in the middle. If y'all can't read 'em, count 'em. I ain't yore mammy or yore daddy and y'all will address me as First Sergeant Martin. Y'all can thank yore stars y'all in my company. See those other buildings. Don't-turn-around! Y'all-at-attention! Those buildings are rifle companies. That's where real soldierin's done. Y'all in Headquarters Company are the pussy that helps their mission. The clerks and jerks. In this man's Army y'all are a necessary evil and I'm the mean son-of-a-bitch who has to baby sit y'all. Any of y'all fuck up in my company—even so much as step on the grass—only second lieutenants have permission to step on Oh-Four grass because they usually have their heads up their ass—I'll send you to a rifle company faster than chickens shit greased pebbles." He pointed along the street. "There ain't no typewriters there. Just M-1s. BARs and thirty-caliber air-cooled machine guns. The weapons of war…"

"First Sergeant Martin."

"Who said that?"

"Private Motz, First Sergeant Martin." The tall recruit had his hand up.

"What is it, Private, and it better be damn important."

"I'd like to go to a rifle company now."

"Y'all deem to interrupt yore first sergeant for a personal request? Get down and give me ten good Airborne pushups and sound off."

The men were speechless at Motz's audacity.

Motz dropped to the pushup position and began slowly, shouting the number as he finished each one.

"As I was sayin', this here's the Five-Oh-Fourth, the finest fightin' regiment in Uncle Sam's Army. History has proven that. The regiment has a proud tradition of discipline that y'all and me and every swingin' dick in it has to adhere to. This is the regiment the Germans called 'those devils in baggy pants.' Y'all can read about us in the military history books and y'all will buy the regiment book at the PX ASAP. It's required for yore footlocker display. Around here every time y'all see an officer I want y'all to salute him even if he's two miles away. Sound off and salute. I want to hear yore voice rock my eardrums. That's how things are done in the Five-Oh-Four. Private Motz, get up."

Motz had remained in the pushup position, knees on the ground, arms wavering from the strain.

"Yes, First Sergeant Martin." He did the best he could to get up quickly.

"Y'all slow and sloppy. Get down and give me ten more. Move!"

Motz dropped and attempted ten more. Slower this time. Again counting. His voice reflecting the strain.

The first sergeant moved to stand directly over the young soldier.

"Y'all think y'all makin' a good impression on yore first sergeant?"

"No, sir." Motz struggled, but he couldn't do more than five repetitions before going to his knees.

The short NCO said, "Don't call me 'sir.' I work for a livin'."

"Yes, First Sergeant Martin."

"Y'all want to go to a rifle company?"

"Yes, First Sergeant Martin."

"I'll send yore ass to a rifle company all right. Get up!"

Motz slowly got to his feet.

"Pick up yore duffel bag, Private. Go-on-pick-it-up."

The tall private shifted the bag to his shoulder. It hid his smile. He was getting what he wanted.

"See that building on the corner. That there's Charlie Company. Now y'all double-time down there and back. On the way I wanna hear y'all shoutin' 'I love Headquarters Company.' If I can't hear y'all all the way down and back y'all will do it again. Do-you-read-me, soldier?"

"Yes, First Sergeant Martin."

"Let me hear y'all say it."

"I love Headquarters Company."

"Louder, Private."

"I love Headquarters Company!"

"That's better. Move out! Move! Move! MOVE!"

The first sergeant ran several steps with Motz shouting in his face then turned to conduct his own roll call.

At 2200, the squad bay lights were turned off by the CQ runner.

Each side of the long squad bay had double-decked steel cots. Silence fell as men came and went to the latrine in the darkness, their shower clogs slapping on the linoleum floor. A footlocker lid banged shut. Someone farted. Someone else matched the fart. A man laughed.

"You know, you guys, that first sergeant can't be that bad."

"You mean First Sergeant Billy Martin. Three up. Three down. And whatever the hell he claimed," said Schmidt. No one could see his sarcastic grin.

Somebody shifted. Bunk springs creaked.

"He's the first person that ever said my name right the first time." It was Mangiameli.

Danny DeFever, perhaps the smallest man in the entire 82nd Airborne, pushed through the double doors of the squad bay. The hall light momentarily lit a path for him. At his bunk, he whispered to Mangiameli in the bunk above him, "That fucking Wise, man," he said in his Cajun accent that carried in the quiet room, "his prick's bigger, longer my leg is long. Believe that. I see it now."

"What'd you expect?"

"But goddamn, I'd like to have that big one for me."

Someone from the darkness advised DeFever he'd need a steel jockstrap to keep it from dragging on the ground.

"You saw too?"

"Like, how can you miss it?"

"Man, that's for sure one water moccasin." DeFever bounced into his bed. "It come after me I run like hell."

Schmidt asked everyone to be quiet. He wanted to continue the dream he had last night about starring in his first movie. In Replacement Company, Schmidt had let everyone know he was on his way to a career in the movies. In fact, when he was drafted he was on the verge of his big break. A gunslinger in a Western. Schmidt, tall and handsome, looked the part: he was the high school hero, Rock Hudson, Gary Cooper all in one. During the few days in Replacement Company, Sgt. Cooper's petty harassment never fazed him. He had stood up to Cooper by irritating him with questions like why they were not allowed to smoke and why weren't the barracks warmer and where was the enlisted men's club and why wasn't the sergeant a jumper and he missed his swimming pool back in Hollywood.

Finally, in frustration, as the new men climbed aboard the '04 truck, Sgt. Cooper had challenged Schmidt, "You volunteered for the Airborne. They're gonna love your ass in Jump School. Be sure to tell 'em about your fuckin' swimmin' pool, Private."

Breslin, on the bunk above Schmidt, said, "I'll say a prayer the dream comes back, lobcock."

The two men laughed like old friends. "Much obliged, Peter Pan."

Outside, the hungry wind rattled the vents of the wall fans at the end of the squad bay. Patterson shifted his back toward the light that came in through the small square windows of the squad bay doors. It had been a long day getting organized. When they were getting their bedding in the supply room, Banuelous and the mean-looking supply corporal almost came to blows. The corporal made every man do pushups on the stairs while waiting in line at parade-rest. Banuelous had given the NCO a hard look, and the corporal laughed and told him he wasn't scaring nobody. Before Banuelous replied, Patterson had dared to step in front of him. He shook his head and to his surprise it worked. Banuelous nodded. For the remainder of the day Banuelous seemed grateful. The men were so busy setting up their wall and footlockers Patterson had forgotten his first day wish when he had seen the modern barracks from the bus and had hoped to be assigned there.

Anyplace warm.

He fell asleep, unaware his original wish had come true.

"A little chilly this a.m., Sir?"

Second Lieutenant Seymour Margolin stood alongside the platoon of new Jump School candidates, flexing his arms and stamping his feet like the other men. He was new to Headquarters Company and trying to shape up. There wasn't any PT at the 90-day Fort Eustice, Virginia, indoctrination. The young officers there were paper pushers. He had been in the '04 for two months and had immediately started exercising after he arrived, running on Longstreet Road and doing pushups and chin-ups by the BOQ. He knew he needed a lot of work, so he often joined Wisnewski's sessions on the sergeant's invitation.

"Cold as hell, Sergeant."

The lieutenant hated exercise, but respected the platoon sergeant who had taken a liking to him. As a professional courtesy, Wisnewski brought Margolin under his wing while First Sgt. Billy Martin barely spoke to him since his arrival. The veteran platoon sergeant explained how the first sergeant controlled the company and did not appreciate second lieutenants. He showed Margolin how to conduct wall and footlocker inspections, rifle inspections, the way to handle guard mount, and pointed out regimental quirks, like only lieutenants walked on the grass. He introduced the young officer to colorful expressions like 'tighter than bark on a pine tree' and 'finer than frog hair.'

"If you let the cold get to you, Sir."

It got to the lieutenant. The cold and the whole concept of the gung-ho 82nd Airborne Division got to him. It was ramrod straight and buffed and polished and totally insane as far as he was concerned. Here he was in the division's strictest fighting outfit when he thought he'd be assigned to a paper-pushing job in the Adjutant General's Corps. After all, he had majored in business. Shortly, he'd replace First Lieutenant Stewart, the current acting commanding officer, who played tennis most afternoons at Lee Field House and let First Sgt. Billy Martin run the company. Stewart should be indoctrinating him on how to manage the company, but the officer did little more than shine his boots, drink mess hall coffee, smoke cigars, and sign whatever Martin put under his nose.

And play tennis. Lots of tennis.

On these cold mornings, Margolin always reminded himself he had volunteered for this craziness. His ROTC career had been set. He and his pals from San Fernando Valley State College were commissioned in the Adjutant General's Corps, the administrative portion of the U.S. Army. After indoctrination they expected assignments to NATO nations. Cushy desk jobs. Culture. No military *tsuris*. No first sergeants who disdained lieutenants. They had two weeks remaining before their assignments were given when the Airborne recruiting major appeared like Mars, the Roman god of war, and gave the 'speech.' The highly decorated World War II and Korean War veteran's cluster of medals screamed Manhood, Bravery, Balls and he demanded volunteers. He was searching for 'elite individuals.' "...men who wanted to be part of something proud. Men who dared to be different."

His best college pal Jack had looked across the row of nascent officers at Sy and held his nose. As young men, they had laughed at *goy* athletes and *schmucks* who drove their hot cars along Ventura Boulevard; they were the para-trooper types.

Without any rationization, Seymour Margolin, the nice Jewish boy from the Valley, took the dare.

Hook, line, and stinker, as his Uncle Ziggy, the family patriarch, might say.

He volunteered for something as *mishugana* as paratroopers.

Margolin would never admit to himself he volunteered because deep inside he was through being a pudgy Hebe. A guy who joked about himself with a father who never opened his mouth and a mother who never closed hers. In a flash, he saw a way to break the pattern in which he had grown up. He had been forced to work summers and after school in Uncle Ziggy's deli and listen to his cranky uncle tell everyone his nephew was going to be educated: a lawyer. Whenever Margolin asked his Dad a question he was referred to his Mother who always told him no. "You might get hurt" and "Nice boys don't go there…do that…say that" were her favorite answers. Between his mother and Ziggy, he had more than a few reasons to escape. He was not going to be Ziggy's deli lawyer handling lawsuits about slipping on the tile floor or hair in the soup. No more cleaning slicing machines, shaving ham, and purple-haired ladies complaining about stale bread after they ate half a sandwich. He was going to be different.

Live a life unfettered by a menu and a mother on his back.

But he did not say that when he told them of his decision while on holiday leave.

At the Hannukkah table there was momentary silence, then Uncle Ziggy summed it up. "So, Seymour, why this urge to jump from a perfectly good airplane?"

He didn't have an answer then and didn't have one now except he was freezing and angry with himself. Jack was in Frankfurt working nine-to-five and spending weekends in Paris while he performed PT in Grave Street in North Carolina where a good deli sandwich was as rare as tits on a tractor, as Sergeant Wisnewski might say.

"Exercise number five. The squat jump," announced Wisnewski.

The sergeant had selected DeFever to be the men's example of correct exercise posture. In front of the platoon, the private took up the fingers-laced-on-the-head, bent-knee position, looking like an ancient statue ready to tumble.

The troops groaned. Squat jumps were the cruelest of the daily dozen.

Margolin wished he was allowed to groan.

Sergeant First Class Richard Wisnewski had the small platoon stripped to their fatigue trousers, boots, and T-shirts for physical training. Their field and fatigue jackets were aligned in neat stacks. White nametags with black letters up. Caps on top with the brim facing front and touching the nametags. A person could walk among the folded jackets and read every name. They shivered and stamped their feet and rubbed their arms. No one could warm up, the wind chill from the Great Smokies never let up. Their raw-cropped heads added to the cold, a result of Sgt. 'Ski marching them to the barber shop in the basement of Foxtrot Company every two weeks and ordering white sidewalls for all of them.

The platoon sergeant did his best to pretend the cold didn't bother him; however, his taut blue lips and goose-bumped arms betrayed him.

"For that fuckin' attitude we'll do fifteen reps." Wisnewski waited for another complaint.

None came.

Since they arrived ten weeks ago, Wisnewski had taught them the PT formation and many more military activities like shining uniform brass, cleaning their weapons, and close-order drill. His standards were higher than what they learned in basic training because his mission was to prepare them for Jump School and introduce them to the ways of the Airborne infantry. They were destined for the adminis-trative areas of the regiment, not the infantry, so instead of hard-core squad and platoon tactics they learned the high standards of '04 spit and polish. Wisnewski's harsh gravel voice accompanied by foul language was their source of instruction. The sergeant's military appearance wasn't impressive, although his jump boots gleamed and his fatigues were tailored, starched, and pressed. He lacked the rugged recruiting poster look. He appeared to be a cynical high school teacher until he spoke, then his attitude became apparent; he was an exceptional soldier. He believed in himself and was determined to instill that belief in his charges.

"Attitude. With the right fuckin' attitude you can do any fuckin' thing you want. You fuckin' cocksuckers got to believe you can do it."

Their first morning in Headquarters Company. he woke them up at 0500 with his piercing NCO whistle worn by all non-coms and literally pulled Schmidt, asleep on his mattress, onto the squad bay floor and threatened to use the fire extinguisher to wake him up. Each evening he stood with them, saluting the flag being lowered at Regimental Headquarters, as the regimental bugler played *Retreat*. He liked to remind the small group that a flag descended everywhere there was an Army post every day and it was an honor to salute it. He knew the Airborne was serious business. He refused to allow the men a radio in the barracks because he didn't play. The squad bay was where a man learned to shape up: polish boots, belt buckles, and insignia. Do pushups. Memorize the 11 general orders. Buff the floor. Field strip and clean the M-1 Garand rifles they had been assigned. And read *Those Devils In Baggy Pants*.

They were restricted to the barracks area and only when they finished Jump School could they play the radio or go to town.

"Now," the Sfc. liked to say after *Retreat*, "I'm goin' home to my GI-issued bride and give her some close-order drill. You fuckin' cocksuckers better be squared away in the mornin'."

Behind his back the new men called him, 'Sergeant Fuckin' Cocksucker.'

"Ready, exercise!"

"One!" The men jumped up and reversed their bent-knee stance and shouted, "One!"

"Two!" Counted the sergeant. The troops repeated the motion and number.

"Three!" Again.

"Four!" And again.

"Two!" commanded Wisnewski to mark the second repetition and the men followed.

They were in their 11th repetition when Colonel Jack Steele and his Negro driver arrived in the colonel's shiny black Jeep with the '04 logos on the panels. No winter canvas cab on the colonel's vehicle. Neither man wore a field jacket and they appeared to ride at attention. The colonel's German shepherd, Strac, sat in the back at attention.

The two rigid soldiers watched the men exercise until Wisnewski halted them after the 15 repetitions. 'Ski ordered the platoon to the position of attention and turned to salute Steele.

"Good mornin', sir! How are you?"

"Never better, Sergeant 'Ski." The colonel dismounted. "Your men look half-way fit."

"They're still legs, sir, but they're shapin' up." A leg was a non-jumping nobody military type and the lowest form of humanity. 'Lower than whale shit,' according to Wisnewski.

"Let's take a look."

With Wisnewski beside him, Steele walked along the ranks. He spoke to a few of the men with no show of emotion. *Hard as a whore's heart*, thought Wisnewski as he walked beside him. 'Ski could see Margolin on the side, unsure what to do. When they passed to the second rank, the sergeant nodded for the lieutenant to come over. Steele continued looking over the men. The colonel stopped in front of Schmidt for a moment as if to ask him a question then moved on. Wisnewski gave the private the once-over to see what attracted the colonel's attention to his troublesome recruit and saw only Schmidt at his best position of attention. The colonel pointed to Patterson's belt buckle and told him to use more Brasso and elbow grease on it.

A shivering Patterson looked down.

"Don't look down," ordered Wisnewski. "You're at attention."

"Take my word for it, troop," advised the senior officer.

Patterson looked at the Wings on Steele's fatigue cap; it carried a small bronze star, the decoration for a combat jump, the paratrooper's ultimate glory.

As soon as the Jeep pulled up, Lt. Margolin knew he'd have to let the colonel know he was with the men. Without his jacket and cap, his rank did not show, and Steele hadn't noticed him. It would be good for him to be seen training with the troops, and he wished he'd gone right up to the colonel when he arrived.

On his first day in the regiment, Margolin had reported to Steele in '04 Headquarters and the colonel questioned him about his college and made a speech about the 504th being the best fighting unit in the USA. During the speech, Margolin reminded himself he was lucky he wasn't going to a rifle company and being in an infantry regiment was just temporary. Sooner, much sooner, he planned to transfer to an Adjutant General position or the Quartermaster Corps. He wanted to finish Jump School first.

The young lieutenant was not comfortable with the experienced career colonel. He suspected Steele did not like Jews. The colonel had seemed intrigued by his name, Seymour. He had grinned slightly and repeated 'Seymour' as if it was an exotic herb.

Margolin especially disliked the colonel's dog. It strutted as if cast in bronze for a heroic deed. An Airborne Rin-Tin-Tin.

He intercepted Steele heading for the front of the platoon. "Good morning, sir. Lieutenant Margolin reporting." Steele returned his salute and said, "At ease, Lieutenant. Good to see you working out with the men."

"Thanks, sir." He patted his mid-section and added, "I need all the training I can get."

Steele ignored the remark and called to Wisnewski. "Sergeant, we'll take the men for a run. Give them an idea of what to expect when they start Jump School Monday."

Every man's mind including the lieutenant's grasped the day of the week like free money. *Monday? This Monday?*

Motz jabbed Schmidt in the ribs and gave him a thumbs up. Some men held their breath. Eyes widened. *Yes, this Monday. Jump School starts Monday.*

"At ease in there! You're at attention!" commanded Wisnewski, and under his breath called the colonel a fucking cocksucker because he had stolen the sergeant's Sunday night diversion…getting the men ready for Jump School.

Steele stripped to his T-shirt and neatly folded his fatigue jacket on the front seat of the Jeep. He placed his blocked hat on top of the jacket. The older man's torso looked as tight as a leather-covered fist. Working his arms back and forth, he returned to Margolin and asked, "Lieutenant, what's your name again?"

"Margolin. Lieutenant Seymour Margolin."

"Seymour. That's what I recall. Seymour." The officer juggled the word as if trying to fit it into some mental parking place. "What do your friends call you?"

Because no one would be called a 'Seymour' thought Margolin and answered, "Sy or Mags, sir."

"Sy or Mags." Steele released a grin.

Was it funny? Sy or Mags. Comic strip characters? Should he be Mike or Spike or Butch?

Steele turned away from Margolin and asked Sergeant Wisnewski to order the men to stand at ease. He wanted to talk to them.

"Stand at ease! Listen up to the colonel." The men relaxed and moved in place to create some warmth.

"Men, I'm Colonel Steele, the commanding officer of the Five-Oh-Fourth Airborne Infantry Regiment, and as you start your careers in the regiment I want you to be aware that this is the finest fighting unit in the United States Army which makes it one of the best military units in the world. This is the regiment the German officer wrote about in his diary found at Anzio. It goes something like '…those devils in baggy pants are everywhere…' After Jump School you men will be those soldiers, those devils, and you're expected to meet the regiment's high standards. We believe in tough training. Strict discipline. Short haircuts. Starched fatigues. Spit-shined boots. You better have a sparkle in your eye and a hitch in your step that tells everyone you want to soldier. Are you ready for that?"

"Yes, sir!" the men responded in unison. Motz the loudest. He had been the first man to purchase *Those Devils In Baggy Pants* by sneaking to the nearby PX and reading it in the latrine after lights out. A few days later, Wisnewski had marched them to the PX to pick up the book and toilet articles.

"I can't hear you," challenged the colonel.

"Yes, sir!"

"Try again, troops."

"YES, SIR!"

Margolin shouted with the men and told himself *his* welcome speech had been better.

Steele turned to Wisnewski. "Move 'em out, Sergeant."

Strac jumped from the Jeep and stood next to his master. Ready to do or die.

Wisnewski commanded the shivering platoon to close ranks. They responded with unusual crispness due to the colonel's presence.

"Right-face!" They pivoted and faced down the street.

"Forward march!" sounded like 'horwarrd-haarch'.

Every left foot stepped off together as Wisnewski counted a ten-count cadence then announced, "We're takin' a little stroll with the colonel and I don't wanna see any grabassin'."

With a nod of the head, Steele signaled Margolin to join him in front of the platoon with Strac. Passing Sgt. 'Ski, Steele half-whispered, "Once around the division, Sergeant."

"Yes, sir. All the way, sir!" He picked up the cadence again. "Left. Your left. Your left-right-left. Double-time..."

The men, eyes straight ahead, raised their arms to a running position: fists closed, forearms parallel to the street.

"...march!"

They started a slow shuffle that became an easy rhythmic jog, their boots sounding loud against the macadam like a steady pounding drum. Whenever Wisnewski sounded off with an odd number, their left feet hit the ground. "One-two-three-four!" It actually sounded more like, "Hun-hup-rip-hore!"

They swung right on Wisnewski's 'column-right' command and began the downhill glide on Gruber Road. In the cold morning, their breath pumped with energy. A short run was how they usually finished the morning exercises. Every man looked forward to the run and the warmth of the barracks.

"Is everybody happy!" demanded Wisnewski.

With one voice the men responded, "Yes, Sergeant!"

"Is anybody tired?"

"No, Sergeant!"

In a normal voice, Wisnewski uttered, "Christ, I hope not, ladies."

Wisnewski turned and ran backwards alongside the platoon to watch the men in the rear. The blueness of his lips had spread into his cheeks. "Men..." he wasn't asking, he was telling, "...let's give the colonel and the division a little song. Are you ready?"

One resounding, "Yes, Sergeant!"

Ski used his best parade ground voice and began, "If I die on the old drop zone..."

"If I die on the old drop zone..." repeated the moving platoon.

"Box me up and send me home..."

"Box me up and send me home..."

"Tell my mama I done my best/And pin those Jump Wings on my chest."

They followed the sergeant line by line. The colonel joined in. Margolin was afraid not to chant; usually he simply mouthed the lines.

"Delayed, cadence. Count, cadence. Count, cadence count!" chanted Wisnewski, the words stretched out like a religious hymn waiting for the congregation's reply.

"One!" replied the men.

"Sound-off!"

"Two!"

"Sound-off!"

"Three!"

"Sound-off!"

"Four!"

"Break-it-on-down!" ordered the sergeant.

"One-two-three-four." Counted the men. "One-two! Three-four!"

"Can you hear these future troopers, Colonel?"

"Loud and clear, Sgt. 'Ski."

The shuffling men waited for more cadence, their boots sounding like one unending hammer.

"Two old ladies lyin' in bed..."

"One rolled over to the other and said..."

"I wanna be an Airborne Ranger..."

"I wanna live a life of danger…"

"Airborne!"

"All the way!"

"Gotta go!"

"Gotta be!"

"AIRBORNE!"

"I've got a gal who lives on a hill…"

"She won't do it, but her sister will…"

The formation stayed precise. Running. Chanting. In perfect step to their own rhythm. Steele and Strac sidestepped from the front of the small platoon and drifted back to join Wisnewski on the flank. Margolin stayed in front.

"Men, we're going to try another tune. Are you ready?" called out Steele.

"Yes, sir!"

"I said, are you ready?"

"Yes, sir!"

"Little louder."

"YES, SIR!"

Steele loudly complimented them for sounding better. Wisnewski drifted to the rear to monitor the usual slackers. He wanted to motivate them to keep up. Schmidt and Breslin were always on his list and he enjoyed berating them for their lack of enthusiasm.

The men ran quietly for a block.

Slowly, the platoon realized Steele was growling. A low growl growing with intensity. Strac, too. In seconds, all the men were growling, louder and louder, to match Steele.

Strac barked. The colonel stopped his effort.

The men stopped and everyone one of them noticed they were passing the street where Sgt. 'Ski usually turned back.

"Airborne!" whispered Steele in a heavy voice.

"Airborne!" repeated the men in the same voice.

"All the way!" continued Steele's whisper.

"All the way!"

Then, in a loud rhythmic sound of controlled thunder, Steele unleashed, "Lift your head and hold it high…"

"The Five-Oh-Fourth is passin' by…"

The colonel's timing was perfect; they were in front of division headquarters. "Let's rattle some windows and stars, men. Make 'em look!" He caught his breath and began again, "Lift your head and hold it high…"

"The Five-Oh-Fourth is passin' by."

"Strike!"

"Hold!"

"Strike!"

"Hold!"

"Standin' tall and lookin' good…"

"We should be in Hollywood…"

"Sound off!"

"One-two!"

"Sound off!"

"Three-four!"

"Break-it-on-down."

"One-two-three-four. One-two. Three-four!"

Steele picked up the pace to test the men. He was old school, a veteran of the frigid Korean War. Jump Wings were earned with sweat and blood. The tougher it was the more it counted.

Breslin fell out first. Literally.

He was acting as road guard, falling out and standing at parade-rest to block traffic at intersections they passed. Each time he ran to catch up, he felt every cigarette he had ever smoked glow again in his lungs. Who would believe he used to run the 400 meters at LaSalle College?

"Pick it up, Breslin!" commanded Wisnewski, who remained running behind the platoon.

The son-of-a-bitch! Breslin's head thrust side to side in his effort to breathe. His eyes were closed and he was suddenly too exhausted to follow Wisnewski's 'column-right' command so he kept going straight and tripped over a curb, sprawling on the red dirt in front of the 782ⁿᵈ Maintenance Battalion's civilian parking lot.

Even though he fell, stopping felt fantastic. Holy fuck. A miracle. God was looking out for him. All those mornings in the college chapel paid off; the Virgin Mary found a way for him to stop. He had quit school to get the draft out of the way, not to run himself into a frenzy. He pushed himself up to his hands and knees and started laughing at the preposterous idea that popped into his head—once he was through Jump School he'd go out for the Eighty-Deuce track team.

Then he threw up.

After the turn onto Ardennes Street, the border street of the New Division area, Steele and Strac moved in front of the platoon and picked up the pace even more. There was no more cadence, just the sound of boots on the asphalt and men breathing hard. Only the colonel and Wisnewski knew the way back was uphill.

Schmidt dropped out next.

The cocky private didn't know how far they were going, but he knew he wasn't going with them. He wasn't gung-ho and never would be. He saw through the military bullshit of being a man and blood and guts. It was all an act. The draft caught him late because he had moved so often, trapped him and dragged him from his Hollywood career. Being an Airborne trooper sounded interesting, so he raised his hand during basic at Fort Ord, but this running and exercising did not impress him. He intentionally lagged behind.

"Get back in there, leg!" Sergeant 'Ski would never allow him to go gracefully. He pretended to run harder. "You're fakin', Schmidt! I see you fakin' at everythin'!"

Schmidt intentionally faked even greater fatigue. "I swear to God, Sarge, on my mother's death, I'm trying." And he slowed even more.

Something about Steele bothered Schmidt. He couldn't put his finger ont, but something was there. Maybe just the man's impressive presence? A real man in Schmidt's usual make-believe Hollywood world? Schmidt grinned and slowed some more.

Sergeant Wisnewski dropped back closer to Schmidt. "You think quittin's funny, leg?"

Schmidt ran a little harder, but trying to look serious only made him laugh harder. *How*, he asked himself, *could anyone take this seriously?*

The NCO stayed close. "Duds like you always take the easy way. Everything's funny. That's the attitude that gets your buddies killed when the shit hits the fan." The sergeant left Schmidt to catch the next man who fell out.

As soon as 'Ski turned his back, Schmidt walked. Quietly he said, "Fuck you, Jack." Each block they passed another man or two with flushed looks of the beaten fell out.

Strac loped along. Grinning.

Steele's strides were long, and his expression one of determination. Wisnewski realized the colonel wanted to leave them all behind. The Sfc. would be a bald-headed chicken-fucker before a fucking officer out ran him.

Let's roll, he told himself. Wisnewski moved up close to Steele in the lead.

The increased speed caused Mangiameli, who had been happy with his effort, to stop and throw up his hands in disgust. He bent at the waist to catch his breath. DeFever, who had taken to staying close to Mangiameli to talk about their long-term girlfriends, stopped too. "That colonel, he too damn fast run for me."

"It's the fuckin' hill, Jim." Mangiameli started at an easy trot. "Come on, my balls are startin' to freeze."

"Your girl, no like they freeze."

"You ain't said shit, Jim."

The future colonel Harry Patton Motz was one of the last to fall out. He never actually stopped; his long skinny arms and legs worked hard against the incline as his baby fat jiggled beneath his T-shirt. The others just left him behind.

"Gotta go," he huffed for inspiration. His usually red cheeks were purple. "Gotta be. Airborne." He sounded like he was begging for alms. The more he slowed, the harder he called his own cadence. "Airborne. Gotta go. Gotta be. Like Steele." He finally walked, even though his motions mimed running.

A covered Jeep pulled alongside Motz. The canvas door opened on the passenger side. A youthful Pfc. with Jump Wings on his cap shouted into Motz's flushed face, "Quitter!" The door slammed shut and the Jeep of laughing men drove away.

Motz watched silently and continued his imitation running. Physical training was his weak point. His great fear was someone would discover he couldn't cut it and wash him out. He just needed time to train. To get stronger. He was still a growing boy. Motz pulled at his receding chin as if he could drag himself to catch up while making his jaw as formidable as Steele's. "Can't quit. Won't quit. Airborne all the way."

He jogged weakly in the wake of the few remaining men.

"*Nada!*" Patterson heard Banuelous spit out the word. He glanced over at his new friend. Banuelous ran with gritted teeth. He caught Patterson's eye and grinned as he strained to keep up. "*Nada!*" he repeated and waved Patterson to keep up.

Just ahead of Patterson and Banuelous were Margolin, Wisnewski, Steele, and Strac. Margolin seemed to be fading.

Private Willie Patterson, much to his surprise, had kept up. What had begun as a frozen nightmare for him turned into a delicious dream of discovery.

Just seven months ago, he was spray painting traffic signs in the Downbeach city maintenance yard, not caring one way or the other about anything except the fact he was out of high school and saving for a used 1955 Ford Thunderbird. When his draft notice arrived, there was no calamity in the family. All young men received draft notices, and he had requested his number to be moved up. His father was a veteran of the World War II Army Air Corps and counseled young Willie about his future. The Army was a good place to think things over. His sister wanted him to join the Navy; their uniforms were cuter. The day he caught the bus to the Newark induction center, his mother had cried.

He had never been away from home before. The truth was, Willie Patterson had never done much of anything.

He had grown up being careful. Maybe that was why he never had any real buddies at home. He was the son of the city comptroller, a political appointee easily removed if the mayor became displeased. His parents worked hard to please their benefactor and constantly reminded their children any outlandish behavior might cost their father his position. So Willie grew up a statistic, a perfect example for a *Life* magazine survey of the fifties. Average height. Average weight. Average looking kid-next-door. Average grades. Average upbringing. Average thoughts about girls, but not even average experience. The few girls he had dated had resisted his clumsy advances. He wasn't an athlete or a mechanic, but could do a little of both. He wasn't inquisitive. "Sort of an average guy," he'd say if asked to describe himself.

Basic training at Fort Dix had thrown him into a mixture of young men his own age and different races from the Northeast. Like actors in a play, everyone talked tough and joined in a mutual dislike for their situation. Patterson became part of the cast and, to his surprise, kept up. He could curse and smoke and pretend he was as experienced as those around him pretended. He excelled in marksmanship even though he'd never touched a weapon before: firing an M-1 was fun. He kept up on the long training hikes. A positive attitude developed. For once in his life he felt on his own. When the Airborne recruiting sergeant with a million combat medals addressed their training company and informed the new soldiers paratroopers were the best warriors the country had, Patterson listened. Airborne soldiers were different, better than the run-of-the-mill legs that made up most of the Army. Jumpers earned their Wings through tough training and bloused their trousers in glistening jump boots. Extra money, hazardous duty pay, was their reward as well as pride in being part of the best. Without any parental consultation or prodding from his peers and in what might be his first independent act, Patterson, along with several others, volunteered. It was too late to renege when, a week later during KP, the wizened lifer cook advised him never volunteer for jack shit in the Army, especially the Airborne which was nothing but chicken-shit and spit-shine.

Maybe the old cook was right, but that moment running along Ardennes Street, he knew something had happened. He could run. Run in the cold. Run with the colonel.

When the run extended past the usual turning point, he thought he'd be the first to drop out. His feet had felt like stumps. Frequently, he had visualized himself on the front lines of a Korean War winter he'd seen in newsreels, and he was the whimpering man who refused to come out of his sleeping bag because of the cold. Ashamed.

But today he had beaten the cold.

By the time they started up the hill, he was warm, running smoothly, watching the cool guys like Breslin and Schmidt quit while he kept up with the tough Mexican and the veterans Wisnewski and Steele. Patterson had never excelled at anything, and here he was floating along to an end somewhere ahead that only Col. Steele knew. With each step, Patterson grew more confident he'd be there with Banuelous as the two privates passed the struggling lieutenant.

The top of the hill did it to Margolin.

For a while he thought the enlisted men behind him would run him over then they began to slip away which fed his determination to set an example he didn't want to set.

He had never been a runner, an athlete of any kind, but now realized training on his own had paid off. He stayed close to Steele almost to the end, and then vowed to stay as close as possible even though he was falling behind. Hell, Steele might run them around again.

He made his struggle easier by imagining the psychotic colonel was trying to run him into the ground for being Jewish and daring to go Airborne. His relatives could be right: Jewish paratroopers were an oxymoron. Paratroopers were *goyim*. Seymours were not Airborne. Seymours were doctors, jewelers, lawyers, and deli men.

Today, he and Uncle Ziggy would agree. "Why run around in the cold in your underwear?"

They turned onto the company street with Margolin only 50 yards behind. The leaders stopped by the folded gear.

"Thank you, Sgt. 'Ski," said Steele. The colonel could not hide his fatigue.

Wisnewski saluted. "Anytime, sir." By slowly picking up his fatigue shirt and cap, he could keep his back to the colonel and hide his heavy breathing.

At his perfectly maintained Jeep, Steele slipped into his fatigue jacket. He called to Patterson and Banuelous. "Good job, troopers. You men won't have a problem in Jump School."

"Thank you, sir," they replied in unison. Patterson beamed, saluted, and knew Colonel Steele was America's greatest warrior.

Margolin had one arm up the sleeve of his fatigue jacket when Steele, ready to climb into the Jeep, called him over. Still panting heavily, Margolin jogged over. "Sir?" It took a conscious effort on the lieutenant's part not to turn away from Steele's penetrating stare. *Could the colonel read his thoughts?* The lieutenant saw a killer. A man who would line up his family and shoot them. Put them in an oven. For being a Seymour.

"A few more minutes you would've made it, son."

"Yes, sir."

"You should've hung in there. When the going gets tough. The tough get going." Steele climbed into the Jeep. Strac leaped into the rear seat. "That's all."

"Yes, sir." He'd dare not point out he lasted more than almost everyone. He knew the colonel lived by the 'no excuse' code.

Steele gave a perfunctory salute, and they headed up the street to the corner where Wisnewski had gone to harass stragglers.

Margolin held his salute to the departing Jeep. "Yes, sir. Yes, sir. Three bags full." He returned to his clothing and cursed himself for dropping back at the end. Just to spite Steele he'd…

"Some run, huh, sir?" Banuelous had finished dressing.

Margolin nodded as he tucked in his fatigue shirt. "They ran my ass off." He wanted to quickly walk away, but intentionally took his time, adjusting his trousers and shirt. No one would know how much Steele irritated him.

Patterson asked if it was true about Jump School Monday.

Margolin buttoned up his field jacket. "My understanding is we're all going. I believe the popular expression is, 'every swinging dick.' See you men there." Patterson and Banuelous laughed and saluted the young officer.

Margolin headed for the mess hall. He needed some hot coffee and one of Sergeant Potter's fresh Danish. Considering the pastry came from the mess hall, it wasn't half bad. *Maybe I could teach the mess sergeant to make a bagel?*

Staff Sergeant Davis Tate
Instructor Basic Airborne Course
82nd Airborne Division

Chapter 2

Just at dawn, Headquarters Platoon marched down Ardennes Road to start their Basic Airborne Course, a.k.a. Jump School. Every man carried a field pack containing a change of socks, a complete shaving set, and extra fatigues. Their canteens were full and their blankets were rolled up in their shelter halves and fitted across their packs. They wore dog tags and their fatigues were clean and starched with no buttons missing. Name tags and U.S. Army insignia were displayed and their shiny boots reflected the rising sun in a cloudless ice blue sky.

On their way, they were joined by other units.

The ranks grew and each unit counted its own cadence; their voices sounded inspired. With so many chants echoing off the modern barracks, the sounds seemed to be part of a massive religious ceremony.

In a way, it was a ceremony: all the men were preparing to leap from airplanes, to face death, and the question of whether or not they would actually jump.

Their repeated cadences, their precise marching, the looks in their young anxious faces indicated they were ready.

"I'm Staff Sergeant Davis Tate of the Basic Airborne Course. You people think you want to be paratroopers and I'm here to make sure you're sincere. So listen up and let's understand each other from the get-go."

The staff sergeant stood almost at attention in front of the second platoon. Everything about the sergeant's physique was designed for a big man: his head, wide neck and shoulders and trunk, but his stubby legs made him less than average height. A rough sculpture out of proportion. Tate's most impressive quality was his voice. Each word spewed from deep in his powerful chest, rising to spill in a deafening roar that would let no man forget he had been resoundingly addressed.

"One thing, the first thing you will learn now, not five minutes from now, but now, N-O-W! Every instructor here wears this black hat." He waved his cap to be sure there was no misunderstanding. "This here hat makes him God in every inch of Jump School. If you don't think so and want to challenge any of us, I promise you'll feel the wrath of the avengin' Lord. If a Black Hat tells you to shit, you better be askin' how much and what color while your Army issue drawers is descendin' your butt-tocks. You people understand?"

There was a murmur of agreement in the 100-man platoon.

"I asked, 'Do you people understand'?"

Most everyone now understood and shouted, "Yes, sergeant!"

"Lieutenant, your men ain't got no balls. Bring 'em to attention."

"Yes, sir," responded Second Lieutenant Seymour B. Margolin recently of San Fernando Valley State College who had been randomly selected to act as platoon leader of Second Platoon, Basic Airborne Course #33, Fort Bragg, North Carolina, March, 1958. Still wishing someone else had been chosen, Margolin executed an about-face to look at the men.

"Lieutenant, sir, don't ever call me 'sir' again. I work for a livin'."

"Yes, sir—Sergeant."

"Lieutenant, sir, are you thick as a brick? Get down in the leanin' rest and give me twenty-five good Airborne pushups. I wanna hear every one of them loud and clear."

Margolin dropped. Arms extended. Legs and back on an angle. Pushups were not easy for him; he carried extra weight and might do 15 tops. Tate took over. "Platoon, attention!"

The men braced. Tate walked along the front rank.

"When I ask you somethin' I want to hear a hundred pair of balls agree with me. Make no mistake people, if I tell you to eat my jockstrap you best be bringin' out the catsup. Now, do you understand?"

"Yes, Sergeant!" shouted the platoon.

"Do you understand?"

"YES, SERGEANT!"

Margolin slowly counted his pushups aloud and reminded himself, oh yes, he understood. Too well. He was a Jewish lieutenant in a Southern Baptist army and the platoon NCO planned to torture him into quitting.

"Nineteen!" he called out. His knees now on the ground.

Eating jockstraps! Margolin could not believe his ears.

As Tate moved among the troops, his powerful voice murmured a warning like a trainer calming a spooky horse. "Rock steady in there. Stand tall, troop. Rock steady." By the time he finished the 10 ten-man ranks, he had men doing pushups for scuffed boots, long hair, soiled fatigues, and unpolished belt buckles. One man was sent to the front of the platoon to dry shave with the razor from his field pack. Buttons from unbuttoned pockets were pulled off and handed to the culprits with the command to have the button sewn on tomorrow morning when he came through the ranks.

"Twenty!" There was the off chance he'd break a leg on a jump. That provided an honorable escape from this military madness.

"Twenty-one!" The extra $110 a month an officer made jumping wasn't enough to put up with the harassment, he reasoned silently as he waited for Tate to condemn him for not doing 25 perfect pushups.

"Twenty-two!" Didn't anyone in the entire division care that he had majored in Business Administration and…"Twenty-three!"…had been on the Dean's List three years in a row?

"Twenty-four!" Goddamnit, he had scored 1360 on his SATs.

"Twenty-five!" shouted the lieutenant, and he rose quickly off his knees to the position of attention to avoid Tate's wrath.

Tate and Sergeant First Class Leroy 'Brute' Barnes, a giant with a jaw of ebony muscle, led one half of the new class in PT while the other half ran. First the troops were herded through sets of pull-up bars. Each man was required to execute ten pull-ups under the intense scrutiny of the Black Hats. After pull-ups, they lined up at attention in rows across a sand and sawdust field and ordered to "Open-ranks, march!" Each rank stepped either back or forward until all were two ranks apart and an extended arm length between men. Everyone stared 'eyes right' with their left arms extended toward the shoulders of the men next to them.

Tate, on a stout log platform ten feet above and in front of the men, commanded, "Ready, front!"

Every man dropped his left arm and snapped his head to look up at Tate. Tate ordered the men to count off.

"One!" shouted the first rank. The troop's fatigue shirts were pulled out at the waist; it was too cold to strip to T-shirts. "Two!" bellowed the second rank and so on until the final rank shouted, "Sixteen!"

"Even numbers to the left, uncover!"

The even-numbered ranks took a large side step to the left giving each man space to exercise.

Tate announced Sergeant Barnes would be his demonstrator to ensure the men did them right. "And if you don't we'll be here all day doin' the Daily Dozen. Ready! Exercise Number One!"

Sfc. Barnes took up the starting position, which was attention.

"Side-Straddle Hop!"

"Starting position, move!"

Most of the formation did not move to the command, as they were already in the starting position. The few men who did drew verbal assaults from three or four Black Hats about how dumb and sloppy they were and ordered them to do duck walks and squat jumps while the others followed Tate and Barnes.

"Ready, exercise!" Class 33 was on its way.

Tate and Barnes led the men through the side-straddle hop, the turn and bounce, the trunk twister, squat thrusts and jumps. They concluded with the traditional four-count push-up. After PT, they ran two miles and then spent the morning learning PLFs—Parachute Landing Falls—from three-foot high platforms and stand-in-the-door positions in aircraft mock-ups. The afternoon was the same: PT, PLFs, door positions, harassment, and always cold as hell.

The second day of harassment began like the first, except every man now had an assigned number in white adhesive tape across the front of his helmet. Lieutenant Margolin's number was 101, which had no significance to him, but to wear the number 101 in the 82nd Airborne meant you drew attention to yourself. The 101st Airborne Division, known as The Screaming Eagles, located at Fort Campbell, Kentucky, was the Eighty-Deuce's traditional rival.

Tate immediately gave him ten push-ups for wearing the assigned number.

"Hurry up, Lieutenant, sir. We have work to do".

Margolin had to escort Tate for the morning inspections. He moved a step behind Tate and carried a small spiral notebook to mark down a man's number and his gig. A gig meant something was wrong: boots unshined, button missing, unshaven, or anything else Tate could dig up. In the middle of the second rank, they stopped in front of a man without a nametag on his field jacket. Tate turned to Margolin and asked why the man had no nametag.

"I don't know, Sergeant Tate. I've never seen the man before." The only men he knew were the ones from Headquarters Company, First Battalion, 504th. He recognized them as he and Tate passed among the troops. Schmidt, the vain dud. The Mexican Banuelous. Little DeFever. Patterson who finished the run. Wise, one of two Negroes in the platoon. Nervous Mangiameli. Future Colonel Motz, the gung-ho jerk-off. Breslin who seemed to just get by. The lieutenant hoped none of them would be singled out and envied their anonymity in ranks.

"You're the platoon leader. You should know."

"Yes, sir…Sergeant." Most of the platoon cringed for the lieutenant's mistake.

"Lieutenant, sir, are you tryin' to harass me by addressin' me like I was some kind of two-star, two-bit, ass-kissin' Pentagon sucker?"

"No, Sergeant."

Tate ordered him to the front of the platoon to take up the front-leaning rest position until the inspection was complete.

Margolin hustled along the rank and went to the front where he dropped into the 'up' position of the pushup and waited. As he strained to stay up, he consoled himself knowing the best thing about Jump School was that First Sgt. Billy Martin was not around to annoy him with his false courtesy. His thoughts distracted from his effort and he stayed up until Tate returned. The sergeant ordered him to move the platoon to the pull-up bars.

On the third day, they were introduced to the 34-foot tower. It was, literally, a ball buster.

The rough creosote-covered structure of telephone pole-size logs separated fools and idiots from the more cautious in life. The little hut on top of the poles had two doors on opposite sides like the tail end of a C-119 Flying Boxcar. The wide rounded doors were reinforced to take the stress of thousands of jumpers. Strung from each door was a heavy-duty cable that angled downward to an embankment 75 yards away. The tower was visible from every angle in the Jump School area. It was solitary, like a mystical Mayan temple or a cathedral on a Spanish hilltop. Thirty-four feet isn't all that high, but as high as a tall-building-in-a-single-bound if a man went out the door and fell ten feet before his static line snagged him and the harness crushed his crotch as he rode the descending cable. Years ago, some Army head-shrinkers reasoned if a man would not jump from a 34-foot tower he would never leap from a plane at 2,500 feet. They never attempted to jump. It was their professional conclusion after talking to men who did it for a living. And it beat riding up to over 200 feet and then dropping off the towers at Benning.

Lt. Margolin followed spastic Pvt. Mangiameli up the wide zigzag stairs, moving slowly in the line of helmeted men with reserve chutes snapped to empty chute harness straps that ran between their legs and across their shoulders to join at quick release buttons at their chests. Every harness had a static line attached. All the way up, the men heard the wires singing and men moaning and grunting from pain and surprise as the static lines cut off their mid-air descent and they rode the cable to the far end of the tower area.

Between each step up the candidates stayed at a modified parade rest, static line hooks in their right hands.

"Get in here, cherry!"

It was Sfc. Barnes. The huge Negro filled the interior of the hut and looked like he could knock the hut apart if he stretched out his arms. Mangiameli tripped and stumbled into the hut and backed away from Barnes.

"You 'fraid of me, cherry?" Margolin, at parade rest by the door, watched; he was definitely afraid.

"Yes...I mean, no, Sergeant." Mangiameli could not hold still.

Barnes' long arm pulled Mangiameli by his harness and he snatched the static line out of his hand and hooked it to the overhead cable. "This here static line will keep you from eatin' dirt. Get back over there and show me a good door position." He pushed Mangiameli backwards.

If he wasn't wearing a helmet, Mangiameli would have taken a moment to scratch his head to assist recalling the door and body positions they had rehearsed the past two days in the mock-ups.

"This ain't the post library, Cherry. You best get your ass in gear or I'll..."

Margolin wanted to help Mangiameli, but knew his officer status might bring him greater anguish for speaking out.

"I got it, Sarge!" Mangiameli formed the shuffle position and adjusted the static line in his left hand. His right hand touched the wall of the mock fuselage. He was ready.

"Stand in the door!"

Barnes gestured for the scared private to move toward the door, towards him. Mangiameli shuffled forward two steps and swung around to face the exit. He concentrated so hard on his body movements he forgot about being afraid. As his left foot came down, it landed on something not flat.

He looked down. His ugly GI-issue boot was on top of the spit-shined, sparkling Corcoran jump boot of Brute

Barnes. Mangiameli moved his foot. His eyes looked everywhere except at the sergeant who rose behind him like a chocolate volcano.

"Sarge, I'm sorry. I..."

"You are sorry, Cherry Number One-Forty-Two. I don't forget."

Barnes picked up Mangiameli, all 145 pounds and pimples, and tossed him head first out the door. He turned right around and faced Margolin. "You gonna stomp my boot, Cherry? Oh, a second lieutenant. God's gift to the fighting man."

Margolin, still listening to Mangiameli's painful yowl, replied, "No, Sergeant!" in his best command voice. In his life he may do many things wrong, but he would not step on that boot.

"Get over here, Cherry, sir."

Margolin shuffled as they had been drilled in the mock-ups and made sure when he turned to stand in the door he kept his boot wide of the instructor's. It threw him off balance. He teetered in the doorway.

"Cherry Lieutenant, sir, you looks like you're tryin' to piss through a straw." Barnes lifted his boot and gently nudged Margolin out the door.

The lieutenant gasped in surprise when the harness snared him. Riding down the cable, the sturdy canvas straps seemed to be sawing him up the middle. At the end, he unhooked and—still in the harness—doubled-timed to the instructor who sat in a tall chair below the tower door evaluating each man's performance. He stood at attention and shouted his number. "One-Oh-One, Sergeant!"

The stern Black Hat looked down and slowly said, "Sir, you're a walking gig. Just for having that number you'll never pass the tower. Get back up there!"

During this ascent, Margolin ended up in front of Schmidt and Breslin and listened to Schmidt as he whispered to Breslin he hadn't had this much fun since he jumped into a pool off a second floor of a Hollywood motel.

"Candy-ass coming through!"

The candidates on the stairs had to stand sideways to allow a tearful recruit descend the stairs accompanied by two Black Hats who loudly harassed him about his masculinity, courage, his future, and his lineage. Mangiameli, walking backwards to blend in, followed them down.

Margolin put out his hand. "Mangiameli, where in the hell you going?"

The private looked around and ducked between the lieutenant and Schmidt. He talked quickly over his shoulder as if someone would hear him. "That fuckin' deuce up there's trying to kill me."

Schmidt told him to relax. "He's throwing everyone out the first time."

"No, man. He keeps callin' my number. I stepped on his fuckin' boot."

"Fuck him, Tommy," added Breslin from behind Schmidt, "he can only throw you out for two weeks."

"My balls can't take it."

Margolin said, "Listen to your pals. Just pretend you're somewhere else." The lieutenant knew a million places he'd rather be, but he did not say that.

"This some kind of goddamn convention?" A Black Hat appeared from nowhere. "Get down and get ten. You. You. You. And you, Lieutenant, sir."

The four men spread themselves along the stairs among the others in line and did their pushups. The reserve chutes strapped across their chests made it impossible, but they bumbled through the punishment counting loudly and not in unison then rejoined the line.

Staring up to the hut, Mangiameli still talked. "He's gonna hurt me."

Schmidt, now ahead of Mangiameli, spoke over his shoulder. "Either go down the fucking stairs or jump, but shut the fuck up about it."

"That's easy to say when it's not your balls."

The same Black Hat from the landing below threatened with, "Keep it up ladies and I'll have you low-crawl to Fort Benning."

Barnes appeared at the top of the stairs. "Where's One-Forty-Two?"

Mangiameli tried to hide momentarily between his pals, then meekly confessed. "Here, Sarge."

Barnes' long arm and fingers pointed at Mangiameli like a lightning strike. "One-Forty-Two, I'm waitin' for you!"

The lieutenant was glad he wasn't being looked for.

With Margolin, Mangiameli, and Breslin watching, Schmidt looked at them, winked and said, "Piece of cake." He took the last step into the hut.

Barnes ordered Schmidt to hook up and stand in the door. Schmidt hooked the static line and shuffled toward the door.

Margolin and Mangiameli watched closely to rehearse their own second efforts. To their astonishment, Schmidt swung his foot down on Barnes' boot. Neither believed what they saw.

Sergeant Barnes did. He pulled Schmidt back and nearly off his feet. Schmidt was tall and hefty, but Barnes held him on his tiptoes by his harness against the side of the hut. "You ruined my shine, Cherry. That's the last shine you'll ever ruin. You got that? You got that, Cherry! You got that, One-Forty-Seven!"

"Yes, Sergeant!" shouted Schmidt in his best Army voice.

"'Yes, Sergeant' my ass!" And with not much effort, Barnes ran Schmidt out the door. On his way out, Schmidt looked back at Margolin and Mangiameli. Smiling.

"Lobcock," whispered Breslin from behind the lieutenant.

Lieutenant Margolin called the platoon to attention and, with a salute, presented them to Sergeant Tate for the Monday morning inspection. The second week had started.

"Follow me, Lieutenant, sir." Tate headed for the left end of the first rank.

At this point, jumping didn't worry Lieutenant Margolin. He might not get that far, and at the very least, if he did he could simply close his eyes and fall out the door. Most people went through life that way. Jumping from the plane wasn't courage; it was herd mentality. What bothered Margolin was Tate's effort to break him. He had started imagining the sergeant picked on him because of special orders from Colonel Steele. The previous Friday, the short sergeant made him perform squat jumps in front of the platoon because his boots weren't dusted off during noon chow break.

Sarge, he wanted to say and dared not, *did he look like the spit-shine type?*

No real serious gigs the first two ranks they inspected. He recognized the headquarters personnel. Motz looked serious. Patterson frozen. Schmidt ever confident. Man-giameli twitched as usual. Breslin seemed to smirk. Two bodies into the third rank, Tate stepped in front of a second lieutenant. Before Tate turned away, the lieutenant uttered the magic words: "I quit, Sergeant."

Tate stared. Margolin recognized the man from the BOQ. An enthusiastic type. Going all the way. Airborne. Ranger school. Survival training. The grueling stuff Margolin hated. The Airborne bullshit.

"You don't want to be Airborne?" asked Tate in a tone of voice that bordered on incredulity.

"That's right."

"Say it, sucker, sir!"

"I don't want to be Airborne."

"Say it louder!"

"I don't want to be Airborne!"

Nearby Black Hats, hearing the offending words and sniffing fallen prey, headed over. Margolin backed away as the other instructors crowded around the officer. What was this fool doing? The asshole left his logic in his footlocker. One didn't stand in ranks and quit. An officer could just call in, or he could have quit at the end of the day. It was almost as if he wanted to be punished.

Tate ordered him to drop and do pushups until he was ordered to stop—and the fool did it.

Margolin was amazed. The entire platoon remained at attention. Every man heard the drama. Some strained to peek from the corner of their eyes.

The quitting lieutenant started counting the pushups and Tate ordered him to stop. "No one told you to sound off, leg. It's an Airborne privilege."

"Legs have nothin' to say around here," added a Black Hat.

Fucking hyena, thought Margolin. *Why didn't the quitter stand up and tell these guys off? Why continue the game if you quit? Dumb goyim.* He wanted to step into the circle of Black Hats and tell the man to get up and walk away.

Another instructor added that lieutenants are always the first to go, and turned on Margolin, "Are you gonna quit, Lieutenant?"

"No, Corporal," replied Margolin.

The corporal instructor with his cap low on his forehead forced his jaw into Margolin's face. "That quitter has a little gold bar like yours. You should join him."

Tate stepped up beside the corporal and held his arm. "Never mix winners and losers. It spoils the blood lines. The Lieutenant here stays with me. He's a winner."

A winner? I am a winner? Margolin's mind blurred like a spinning carnival ride.

Tate had given him a seal of approval. There was no conspiracy. No intentional torment ordered by Colonel Steele. He followed the Black Hats to the front of the platoon as they escorted the departing lieutenant with shouted insults. Tate told Margolin to order the men to stand at ease.

The lieutenant did an about-face and ordered, "Stand, at ease!" In the last week, he had given more commands than four years of ROTC. It was easier than he imagined.

"Candidates," said Tate in his command voice, "that's a quitter who just left. He ain't ever goin' to be Airborne and have that rare privilege of standin' tall with the rest of you…"

Margolin faced the platoon, embarrassed he felt so good. He actually felt taller. Stronger.

"…at graduation." Tate paused as if he forgot what he was saying then loudly asked in his powerful voice, "Do y'all want to be Airborne?"

"Yes, sergeant," they shouted. Margolin one of the loudest.

"Let me hear it again!"

"YES, SERGEANT!!"

"Lieutenant, bring 'em to attention and move 'em out to the pull-up bars".

"Yes, Sergeant," he replied with a little too much enthusiasm.

"Platoon, attention!"

Their heels came together in a dull thud. Arms along the sides of their trousers, thumbs at the seams. Heads up. Chest out. Forty-inches-all-around. Standing tall. Looking good. And all grateful they had not quit.

"Left, face! Forward…"

The quitting lieutenant's humiliation strengthened Margolin's reserve to stick it out. There was no logic in being Airborne. No rationale. No one had to be a para-trooper to succeed in life. But he was going to make it. He'd find some *chutzpah*. Tate had called him a winner. Well, goddamnit, motherfucker cocksucker as Sergeant Wisnew-ski would say, he was a winner.

"…march!"

The second week introduced the candidates to the more complicated techniques of parachuting. The Suspended Harness or 'Suspended Agony' as some called it was a procedure where a man hung in a tight harness and learned how to check his overhead canopy for tears and slip or pull down a riser hard with both hands for some directional control. Tree and water landings were practiced as well. If a man was headed for trees, he simply chose to cover his face or his crotch or both. A water landing was different. More dangerous. The weight of a wet chute could drown a man already loaded with gear. Just seconds before their feet touched the surface, jumpers were trained to hit the single quick-release buckle, which held the chute's shoulder and leg straps. In theory, their weight would carry them free from the collapsing canopy. Next came the Swing Landing Trainer: a man hung in the harness and was swung back and forth five feet off the ground until suddenly the instructor dropped him to, hopefully, execute a perfect Parachute Landing Fall.

All of this was re-enforced with more strenuous PT and longer runs.

On Wednesday morning, they doubled-timed to the wind machine area. By Wednesday evening, the men hoped they never saw it again.

The class was titled Recovery from Drag. A man put on a full harness with the canopy spread out behind him and laid backwards on dirt worn hard by the task. Hooked across his gut to the harness D-rings was a reserve chute. On a signal, the machine-driven propeller cranked up wind. Black Hats held the billowing chute until the instructor shouted release. They let go and the would-be jumper, pulled by the chute, slid across the ground. The theory was he would reach over his head with both hands, pull hard on a riser, spin around, rise to his feet and run down the canopy and collapse it.

The instructor made it look as easy as strolling to his car in the parking lot and opening the trunk. The future paratroopers looked like circus clowns tripping and falling in the grand march around the big top.

Lieutenant Margolin, volunteered by the class instructor because he was a lieutenant, went first. He spun around and ended up riding on his ass like a man who forgot his sailboat. Banuelous rose quickly to his feet, fell face down, and rode the reserve until out of wind range. Patterson got to his feet and started running, but the reserve chute kept him from going fast so he angled away from the blast and Mangiameli, to everyone's surprise, stumbled to his feet, tripped, arms and legs going every which way, somehow reached the canopy and pulled it down. Schmidt shifted around in ranks and avoided the feat. Breslin simply never tried to get up; he slid on his back across the ground until the blast dissipated. Private Harry Patton Motz wanted no part of Recovery from Drag, but unlike Schmidt, his sense of honor kept him in line. At six-three and 180 pounds of soft baby fat, he had been the butt of jokes at Fork Union Military Academy because of his lack of athletic ability and enthusiasm for things military and love of history. Every day at the Jump School pull-up bars, he faked it, doing only two or three then dropping and joining the mass confusion of men rushing through the exercise. Here he was out in the open having to pull, jump, and run. He repeated to himself: pull, jump and run. Pull. Jump. Run. He tried. Got to his feet and with two Black Hats screaming in his face, "Run, numb nuts!" he fell face first, landing on his elbow, then scraped across the ground. Getting back in ranks for his second try he could feel blood congealing on his arm. He felt rugged. If this were war he'd have a Purple Heart.

Little Danny DeFever's effort was frightening. All 90 pounds of him was snatched off the ground the instant the canopy inflated. An alert instructor leaped at the chute and pulled it down or he might have floated away. Danny fell hard. For a long moment he laid there, then slowly rose with the crooked movements of a battered rodeo rider.

"You OK, boy?"

"Sergeant, yes."

"What in the hell you mean bein' no bigger than a hummin' bird's fart."

"I not so damn small…"

"Get down and give me ten for bein' too light." The instructor watched DeFever do the pushups to be sure he wasn't hurt. "You best start eatin' rocks, Private. You're gonna need 'em."

The Pit.

Two hundred and seventy-three men, more than half of Basic Airborne Course Class 33, stood in the cold gray morning in their long-sleeve winter underwear tops, boots, and fatigue trousers waiting to throw one another out of the wide four-log deep hole known as the Pit.

No rank was visible. Every man had close-cropped hair. They differed in size and color only.

"On my signal," explained Sgt. Barnes, "every swingin' dick better move into action. There won't be no pat-a-cake playin' with your sweetheart. We wanna see action. Blood and guts! Only one man stands at the end and he ranks as the meanest moatengator in the class. For being last in the Pit, he wins the right to be first out to face the Hawk on Monday mornin'. Are you all ready to face the Hawk?"

"Yes, Sergeant!"

Shouting helped warm things up. "Can't hear you!"

"YES, SERGEANT!"

Black Hats moved among the nervous troops bullying them in an easy manner. Their intensity had subsided. The men in the Pit had succeeded with ground school. One or two might freeze in the door. Maybe more. Maybe less. No one would know that now. They were as close to being paratroopers as they'd ever be. All they needed were five qualifying jumps next week to earn their wings.

And to survive the Pit.

"It will behoove you to know if you come out without a fight, me and my assistants will help you back in with a genuine Corcoran-jump-boot-swift-kick-in-the-ass. Get ready..."

The Pit concept had taken Margolin by surprise. He shivered in his winter underwear shirt, feeling even more naked without his gold bar. He was simply a chubby, not quite as bad as when he arrived, not-too-tall officer who had never been in a fight in his life, standing among a host of behemoths who might hate officers and want to get one. No one had mentioned the Pit among his fellow officers. Maybe it was because he wasn't close with his peers in the BOQ. He hadn't gone to a school with a football team and had few sexual adventures to share. On Sunday mornings, he wasn't hung over and he liked to read the week old Sunday *Los Angles Times* his mother sent him. *Now the truth would come out. I'm really not the winner that Tate had declared.* The Pit would keep him from being a paratrooper. *Chutzpah* be damned. This wasn't the Sermon on the Mount and there was no mercy for the weak. The two weeks training had him revved up to make the jumps, but now there was no place to...

"...Go!"

The arena filled with the sounds of flesh slapping against flesh, a cruel scary sound like a sudden unfamiliar noise. Men shouted and grunted as they jostled with one another. The wiser men linked up in small teams and went after individuals.

Lieutenant Margolin's fear was immediately realized from the initial command. "Sorry, sir," said someone from behind who knocked his legs out from under him and other soldiers were dumped on top of him. Looking up, he saw

Banuelous being pulled around by two bigger men until Patterson jumped on one of the men. Margolin struggled to his feet and went after the large man wrestling with Banuelous.

Suddenly free, Banuelous looked to see who had assisted. Thanks, Sir." He leaped past Margolin to tackle a man dragging Patterson toward the wall.

"Grab his neck!" shouted the Mexican and together they carried the now struggling man to the wall with Patterson squeezing the man's neck as if he was a huge snake.

"The lieutenant helped us," said Banuelous. "Where is he?"

They saw Margolin locked arm and arm with a man shoving him backwards until Margolin dug in his feet and held his own. The effort made the officer growl to maintain his leverage against the bigger man.

"Hold on, Sir!" Patterson took one leg and Banuelous the other and the three of them steered the surprised man toward the edge. Margolin growled like a diesel 18-wheeler going uphill until they dropped the man at the feet of Sergeants Barnes and Tate.

"I told you he was a blood and guts trooper," said Tate.

"The man sounds like a mad dog."

Margolin turned and looked. The sergeants, all starched in tailored fatigues and polished boots, were laughing at him. Mad Dog lieutenant. He was that. He had unleashed his *chutzpah* and no one was going to throw him anywhere.

As the numbers reduced and the struggle became more obvious, it also became more vicious. Some men now took the battle seriously as honor was involved. A prize. First out the door. Men were being pushed and thrown and wrestled out as the Black Hats shouted encouragement and watched for malingerers like Schmidt who got away with Breslin throwing him over the wall the first few minutes.

Back in the fray, Margolin stumbled and swung around in circles with someone on his back.

"Hey, motherfucker, get off our lieutenant's back!" Banuelous leaped on the man on Margolin's back. The three bodies collapsed. Patterson tried to unlock the man's arms around the lieutenant's neck as another man grabbed him by the legs. The body of interlocking men grew like a rolling snowball until there were about fifteen of them pulling and cursing, lifting and squeezing one another, from one side of the Pit to the other.

Margolin, deep in the middle, growled and managed to get his assailant off only to have another replace him. The mass of twisting bodies separated Patterson, Banuelous, and Margolin until they were individually fighting to stay inside.

Someone shouted, "Let's get rid of the wetback!"

Two men held Banuelous while another punched him in the stomach. From his helpless position, Banuelous called him a Gringo cocksucker. Margolin, alerted by the wetback, charged between the slugger and the men holding Banuelous and commanded, "Let go of that man; that's an order!"

"Order?" said the slugger. "Who in the hell are you?"

The weary soldiers relaxed, letting Banuelous go, and stared at Margolin. "Charlie, this is mob rule. There ain't no rank here," advised one of the slugger's supporters with a wise guy grin.

Charlie, the slugger, lean and as tall as a hard tree, said, "Go fuck yourself and your order—*Sir*."

From nowhere, Banuelous caught Charlie on the chin with a round-house right and hurt his hand. He bent over holding his fist between his legs and winced in pain. Charlie took the punch and called Banuelous a Mexican motherfucker and wound up to reciprocate.

No doubt Charlie had his application in to be king of the Pit.

Before Charlie uncoiled, Margolin growled and lunged to get inside the man's long, dangerous fists and drove him toward the wall. Patterson, now free, climbed onto Charlie's shoulders as Charlie's pals pressed against Margolin and Patterson to free their buddy.

"It's Mad Dog again," noticed Tate.

Most of 504th Headquarters Platoon, including Motz and Mangiameli, heard Tate and started chanting, "Mad Dog! Mad Dog! All the way! Get him, Sir!" Others picked it up.

Charlie and his pals swung wildly at their opponents. Banuelous flailed with his left hand. Margolin and Patterson, inexperienced, kept ducking and trying to pin their enemies' arms. The mass looked like a minor tornado snaking across the sawdust and red soil mix. Charlie dodged Banuelous and kicked a bent-over Margolin in the side of the head. Margolin went to his knees from the clean hit to the temple. He rolled over, and sawdust fell into his eyes. The sky blinked black and there was a dead silence. He seemed to disappear from himself then he was back, gasping for air, his head hurting like hell.

Patterson grabbed Charlie's leg and held on. Banuelous kept his left working, but Charlie was too fast, and without Margolin, Charlie's men managed to get Banuelous and Patterson out of the Pit. Then Charlie easily dispatched his cooperative buddies.

Margolin heard a distant whistle. *Who is blowing a whistle?* He rolled over onto his stomach and feared getting up, because he might not be able to stand.

Patterson and Banuelous, covered with sweat and sawdust, showed up at his side. "You OK, sir?"

He looked around. Slowly saw them. Saw Banuelous' swelling fist and remembered what happened. *Damn, I must've been knocked out. That's a first.*

Except for the headache it wasn't all that bad.

The struggle was over. The Pit had become a peaceful, relaxing place. It was as if he was in no hurry to pay the check after a good nosh of lox and bagels. He actually wanted to roll over and lie on his back a little longer. He hadn't felt as good since he outscored his high school pals on the SATs. *Actually,* he confessed, *this was better.*

"Right as rain," he replied. "We didn't do bad, did we?"

"If you dudes had stayed out of my way, I would've killed that asshole," said Banuelous and they laughed together.

For the first time in their young lives, the future para-troopers of Class 33 passed through the issuing shed to draw their T-10 parachutes, reserves, and kit bags. They assembled on the grassy slopes adjacent to the main taxiways of Pope Air Force Base and, using a buddy system, strapped one another into the restrictive harnesses. They checked one another and the Black Hats checked them more than once. Satisfied, they sat on the grass, using the chutes as backrests, and smoked, quietly waiting for their aircraft on the unusually mild morning. One at a time, looking like giant birds from a foreign sci-fi movie, the C-119 Flying Boxcars—with props semaphoring flashes of winter sun and powerful engines drowning out what little conversation existed— taxied slowly over the slight rise in the runway.

No one referred to the aircraft as Flying Coffins.

"Second Platoon! On your feet!" commanded Tate, clip-board jammed against his side, his black hat low on his eyes. The platoon was in the first lift of six aircraft.

Lieutenant Margolin stood near Tate and watched the men's reaction to the arriving troop carriers.

"Just like D-Day," muttered Motz who carried the secret he had never completed the ten pull-ups required by every man.

Banuelous had needed Patterson's help to chute up. His right hand remained painfully swollen, but he refused to show it to anyone in charge. They might recycle him. "This is it, Tony," said Patterson to encourage himself as well as Banuelous. Breslin crossed himself just in case and wished he had drinking-liquor in his canteen for additional fortitude. Schmidt announced to anyone near him that the jump would be like falling off a log. Mangiameli and DeFever knew their girlfriends would be proud of their Wings.

Margolin wished for a buddy, a fellow officer, to confide in, to confess his growing fear. "Scared as a hen in a fox house," Sgt. 'Ski would say or something like that. Scared shitless was more appropriate, although his bowels contradicted his thought. He did not want to get on the plane and if he wasn't an officer, he wondered if he would. It would be easy to stay behind. Just quit and walk away from the craziness.

Earlier, when they walked single file through the issuing shed, a spacious supermarket of parachutes, the lieutenant hefted the kit bag containing the main chute across his shoulder and took the reserve handed over by a smug-as-a-snake veteran rigger. From under the low-slung red baseball cap that covered most of his face, he said, "If it don't work, Lieutenant, bring it back." The standard joke for new jumpers.

One of the Negro riggers along the line talked repeatedly and loudly about the Hawk, the mystical force that plucked men in the air and sent them to their deaths through failed parachutes, mid-air collisions, high winds, and any airborne mishap.

Margolin felt weak-kneed. It had finally dawned on him: *I could die today*. And all during training, he had believed he wouldn't be scared.

He did not have the courage to refuse to board the plane. Like a man accepting the firing squad, he moved along and climbed up the short ladder into the Flying Coffin.

Tate checked off names while his assistant jumpmaster, Corporal Adams, helped the men with their unfamiliar burdens scale the ladder. The interior of the aircraft was functional. Stark. Uncomfortable. Pipes and colorful wires ran parallel along the sides and overhead like an unfinished building. Canvas pull-down seats lined each bulkhead and faced matching seats in the middle. The aircraft carried 60 jumpers. Two chalks of 30. Immediately, the men felt strong vibrations through their boots and posteriors. No one had alerted them for this sensation which demonstrated the planes meant business. The future jumpers were strapped in their seats by a long canvas strap running forward to aft by the stern-looking aircraft crew chief sergeant who wore a headset.

Slowly, ever so slowly, the aircraft taxied. Increased horsepower rattled the men more. Most tried to appear nonchalant. Everyone knew there was only one way down— out the door with the chutes on their backs.

The engine pitch increased. Thrust pushed the men rearward, closer together, as the aircraft rolled down the runway. The noise and vibration increased until it was almost painful.

Liftoff! The vibration vanished and the noise reduced. It felt better. Safer. And they were finally flying.

As one plane lumbered into the sky, another began its run. Within five minutes, all six aircraft leveled off at 5,000 feet, forming into triangles of three. Class 33 was Airborne.

It was colder in the planes. They tried to stay warm by leaning on one another. Each man wore his steel pot with his Jump School number taped across the front. Chin straps extra tight. Men tried to smile, not wanting to believe they were simply like creatures in Noah's Ark. Most stared straight ahead, avoiding the open doors at the rear. A few feigned sleeping as they rocked with the gentle floating motion of a boat on a peaceful sea. A couple of men read Bibles.

All were destined to abandon ship.

The Air Force crew chief nodded in response to something being said in the cockpit. Margolin leaned forward to look toward the rear open doors. Tate and Adams, now wearing B-12 chutes which were free of static lines and allowed movement inside the aircraft, stood by the door discussing the landscape below. The lieutenant was glad he wasn't sitting where DeFever was. The little private from Louisiana sat across from the open door, his feet barely touching the deck, his view nothing but empty sky. *Was the Hawk waiting out there?*

Cpl. Adams walked the length of the aircraft, releasing the long tie-down straps on both chalks. He rolled the straps up and stowed them in a gearbox at the rear of the fuselage.

Tate looked up from checking his watch to see most everyone's eyes on him. He laughed, took a second look, and noticed Margolin squeezed in the middle of the stick. He balanced himself with the overhead anchor line cable and made his way to stand in front of Margolin. "Sir, come with me."

Second Lieutenant Seymour Margolin did his best who-me look. Tate pulled him up by the arm. A moment later, he was sitting next to DeFever, staring out at the empty sky.

Tate acknowledged some information from the crew chief. He kept a vigil on his watch, then planted his feet firmly on the steel deck, extended his arms straight out, palms up, and ordered, "Get Ready!" The assistant jumpmaster did the same halfway down the interior.

Every man sat up straight and held up his static line hook. They could have been robots in a bad movie. All eyes, and they were big eyes, gaped at Tate by the open doors.

"Stand up!" Tate dipped and slowly raised his outstretched arms as if to lift the men himself. The men could not spring up; their equipment forced them to push off one another and the fuselage to get to their feet.

"Hook up!" Tate grinned as he gestured for the men to hook up to the anchor line cables that ran seven feet high along the both sides of the aircraft.

"I'm not really here," Margolin said aloud knowing the words were hidden in the engine noise.

Volunteering for this and actually doing it were two different things. He wasn't supposed to be there. *It was a mistake. A bad joke.* A cruel joke on himself. He and his parents and Uncle Ziggy had spent a lot of money on his education and it could, in just a moment or two, go out the door to oblivion. *They'd never forgive me.*

"Check your equipment!" A flurry of movement passed through the troops as they twisted to check one another's chute packs and straps. A static line inadvertently running beneath a shoulder harness of the chute would prevent a canopy from deploying and keep a man attached to the aircraft. The anchor line cable hummed as men pulled hard on their static line fasteners to insure they were fixed correctly.

Margolin saw only the horizon as DeFever checked his backpack. *The hell with it.* He wasn't going to jump and kill himself over a little pair of Wings. He'd just step aside and let DeFever lead the way. The rumor existed that any man who did not jump was shipped out within 24 hours.

Europe. Desk job. Here comes Second Lieutenant Seymour Margolin.

"Sound off for equipment check!" Like an electric current, the butt-slapping ritual learned in the mock-ups started at the rear of the stick and worked its way back to the doors as each man shouted his stick number and confirmed he was OK. The assistant jumpmaster moved among the men correcting their stances, pushing them apart while shouting to give one another room. They leaned out past one another looking toward Sgt. Tate for the next command.

He did not let them wait long. "Stand in the door!"

Margolin, still convinced he would never jump, swallowed hard and automatically swung into the door position as he had been trained. Over his right shoulder, the jump command light glared red.

He was there. Head erect. Not looking down. Outstretched palms pressing against the doorframe for leverage. Legs bent in a swimmer take-your-mark position. The metal was cold. Heat and exhaust blasted into his face. The engines screamed a powerful chorus warning him not to jump.

Tate shouted in his ear. "Rock steady, Mad Dog! Don't look down!"

The lieutenant hardly heard him. He stood stunned. Frozen internally and externally. Margolin's mind searched rapidly for a reason to step aside. *There was still time. A headache? Throw up?* He tried to discover something. Anything. *Step back. Do it now!*

The light went green. "Go!" Tate smacked the lieutenant hard on the ass.

Margolin, confused in his search for an excuse, went, falling more than jumping, letting gravity do the work as his mind refused to push his muscles.

DeFever shuffled into the door. Gone. Another man. Both doors emptied bodies into the winter morning as Tate and Adams shouted, "Go! Go! Go!" Then the plane was empty except for the jumpmasters and the crew chief.

The instant Margolin fell, the full force of the hot engine blast smashed into him with a supernatural power, lifting his legs high over his head until he felt he was upside down. There was no sense of direction. He could not tell if he was falling or blowing across North Carolina. With his eyes tightly shut, he saw no ground, no sky.

A ripping sound, a loud snap, and somehow the brakes came on. He opened his eyes and discovered he was swaying back and forth in the sky. Instinctively, he raised his arms and looked up to check the canopy.

The fucking thing opened. He was alive.

The noise, the exhaust, the helplessness disappeared with the airplane. The jump had been a tunnel of confusing thoughts and fears and unknowns that locked his mind until this moment. This ecstasy of freedom.

Alive and kicking and swinging in an unhampered sky. No noise. No cramped space. No earth on which to rest his feet. He could see across the countryside; it was his personal universe. He had faced the Hawk's power and survived. It was the most magnificent feeling he had ever experienced.

Second Lieutenant Seymour 'Mad Dog' Margolin, without reservations, was fucking-A number one Airborne. All the way.

The second jump that afternoon wasn't much different than the morning blast except the troops were more aware. Many kept their eyes open and charged out the door. Many more lied and said they did. The following morning, an even milder North Carolina winter day, they made their third jump.

They jumped Wednesday afternoon and Thursday morning in full combat gear.

Sgt. Tate poetically briefed his platoon on how to land with the extra gear. "Hope for the best—and do a PLF."

Walking with two chutes on made a man feel like an overloaded donkey. Adding a full-field pack, a gas mask, and an M-1 rifle created lumbering, struggling creatures who felt they were personally carrying blocks for the pyramids. Those who had previously leaped out the door now simply fell forward or were pushed by the anxious men behind. Danny DeFever appreciated the extra weight. Motz fantasized again he was dropping into Normandy. Margolin, no longer frightened, accepted the challenge of the extra gear. Jumping was natural. The reward for all the hard training and harassment. Hawk or no Hawk, it was a big kick in the ass.

And he carried only a .45 pistol.

After the fifth jump, riding back from Sicily in the big, open semis called cattle trucks, Pvt. Breslin said it best. "It's like being born again."

Chapter 3

The Basic Airborne Course (BAC) Class 33 graduation took place on an mild winter Saturday morning. The brass—captains and majors, in their formal Class A uniforms—aligned the low stage and the division band inflicted the small audience and new paratroopers with the standard military melodies.

At the microphone, the Jump School Commandant Major Mahoney called the formation to attention, his command echoing among the platoons and squads. The formation sounded as one large snap as the men obeyed. The major then announced to Major General Harold 'Howl' Busby, the division commander, that the men were ready to graduate. The general, looking fit and tan, stepped smartly to the microphone. "Stand at ease, men," he ordered.

As one, the formation shifted, every man's left foot out and his hands clasped behind his back, heads held high, and waited.

His words caromed off the loud speakers set up off the side and rear of the troops as he welcomed the newly qualified jumpers to the 82nd.

Major General Busby proceeded to remind them were now part of the proud airborne fraternity of troopers who spearheaded invasions across Europe and that tradition was maintained during peacetime by discipline and hard training. "Don't falter, men. Don't let your proud history grow dull with complacency; add to it by being the sharpest troopers in the United States Army. Take pride in yourself, your unit, and the division. We're America's Guard of Honor.

You're All-American now. March proudly. Congratulations, and Airborne all the way."

"Airborne all the way," echoed back from the other speakers to the crowd as the general saluted the formation and took two steps back from the microphone.

The brass along the rear of the stage looked at one another and nodded approval the the general's speech. He knew it by heart because he gave it every second Saturday of the month.

"Honor graduate Second Lieutenant Seymour Margolin..." Major Mahoney looked up from the microphone in anticipation of the honored officer.

Margolin, standing in the front of second platoon, could not believe his ears. 'Who, me?' almost blurted from his lips. He had been daydreaming about the ceremony and the orderliness of the military compared to the wild brawl in the Pit. Slowly, he was beginning to understand the need for regimentation, orders, duty—and slowly discovering he liked being a paratrooper.

"...front and center."

Standing three paces behind him, Sgt. Tate whispered, "Go kick ass, Mad Dog."

Margolin suppressed a grin and marched at right angles to face the major. On his way up, he couldn't believe it was really true. There had been a BOQ rumor he was up for it. So were other new young officers. His ROTC pals would never believe this. Uncle Ziggy would say, "Honor, Schmonor; make some potato salad." It was all he could do to keep from running up and grabbing the mike and shouting, "Make no mistake, people!" He was an ass-kicking, hard-core Jewish paratrooper.

The major and lieutenant saluted. Major Mahoney read the official order. "By Division General Order Four-Fifty-Six, it is with great honor the Basic Airborne Course Committee hereby selects and recognizes Second Lieutenant Seymour Margolin as the honor graduate student in acknowledgement of his outstanding leadership and initiative in Basic Airborne Course 33. His constant alertness and unselfish motivation stands as an Airborne example for Class 33 and future classes. This graduate embodies the true meaning of the Airborne soldier. He has earned this cup of distinction with his sweat and spirit. Congratulations," the major smiled and added, "Lieutenant Mad Dog."

General Busby handed the engraved silver-plated cup to Margolin. The junior officer saluted when he should have reached for the cup and the general almost dropped it. Flashbulbs popped. The general handed it again to the lieutenant. They shook hands. More flashbulbs.

The general pinned on his Jump Wings and they shook hands again.

The lieutenant turned and started off the stage. He realized he had achieved something he had only dreamed about. He was a winner just like the high school jocks he envied and ridiculed. The *goyim* lettermen with the *shiksas*. *Now, I'm a winner in a more important game. I beat the tough cadre, the course, the whole* schmear. He felt...

"Lieutenant?"

Colonel Steele stepped up. He looked Margolin up and down. A serious up and down.

The lieutenant's enthusiasm waned. *What does he want*?

"Congratulations, Lieutenant," Steele said in a monotone as he offered his hand. Margolin gave him a firm handshake and reminded himself that the colonel did not know how to be civilized—spit and polish were the only concepts he understood.

"What was that the major called you?"

"Mad Dog, sir."

"Mad Dog?"

"Yes, sir."

"Why's that?"

Margolin sensed his moment of triumph was being chiseled into ruins. "I growled a lot in the Pit."

"I see."

Did he? He looked like he had drifted off, maybe to an imaginary war. No matter what, the lieutenant knew *he* was the honor graduate.

Steele looked Margolin in the eye. "Remember, Lieutenant, in my regiment it takes more than growling to be a top-notch officer."

Margolin wanted to ask if the colonel said that because he was Jewish. Instead, he replied he intended to not only be a good officer, but "...an outstanding officer."

"That's all."

They saluted one another. Margolin did an about-face and retraced his steps to the platoon. Each step made him dislike Steele more. The man had knocked him flat with a cold stare and three or four words. The *schmuck* wanted him to feel inadequate, feel as if he did not belong there.

Goddamnit, I do belong. His pals and Uncle Ziggy were not going to be right. He was an Airborne officer, the honor graduate of Jump School, and he was staying.

While the band played a series of martial songs, various unit commanders moved among the enlisted ranks pinning on the new Wings. Gen. Busby did the honors for the officers' platoon. Before Steele reached the headquarters men, Sergeant First Class Wisnewski, who came to assist in the medal awards, walked among the ranks with the tray of Wings and quietly, in his special harsh tone, reminded the men Col. Steele was just a man. "Don't let him scare you. He puts on his drawers like the rest of us fuckin' cocksuckers."

Steele met Tate and Margolin in front of the platoon. Wisnewski stood at the first rank. Margolin saluted and announced, "Second Platoon ready to be decorated, sir."

Steele, with Sgt. 'Ski, Margolin and Tate trailing, went through the ranks pinning on the Wings. Each man was questioned by the colonel on his status as either Regular Army or US draftee. Draftees were offered a 30-day leave to become RA and add another year to their obligation. It was re-enlistment on the spot. Few were interested. Breslin declined with a brisk, "No thank you, sir." Patterson and

Banuelous did the same. Motz proudly announced loud and clear he was already RA. Mangiameli, squirming all the while, confused the question and the colonel when he declined another year even though he was already RA. Wisnewski hid his grin. When the colonel stepped in front of Schmidt he paused, "Soldier, haven't I seen you somewhere before?"

"You ran us one day when we were training for Jump School."

Wisnewski leaned into Schmidt's face, "You ran us one day *what*?"

"You ran us one day, sir." Schmidt's military voice sounded strong. Official.

Steele pinned on the Wings, shook Schmidt's hand, and offered, "We're giving thirty days leave to the men who re-enlist today, trooper. Are you RA?"

"US, sir." Schmidt was uncomfortable with the colonel's attention like he was the morning of the run. Something bothered Schmidt. Something familiar, but he couldn't put his finger on it.

"In three years you look like you could make sergeant. Couldn't he, Sergeant Wisnewski?"

"Yes, sir," said Wisnewski. Over his dead body.

The man's weird, thought Schmidt. "I'll do them two at a time, sir."

The colonel moved on. Finally, he made the offer to Private Danny DeFever, the last man in the platoon due to his size.

"When I go home?"

"When do I go home, sir," reminded Sgt. 'Ski.

"When I go home, sir?" repeated DeFever.

"Tonight," replied Steele, "as soon as you get back to the company."

Lieutenant Margolin held his tongue. DeFever should not do this. The ceremony and officer were intimidating him. DeFever should wait, learn more about the Army then decide. *Don't, Danny, don't.* His thoughts were shared by most of the others. No one dared say a word.

"Yes, sir. I do it. I'm Airborne soldier now. I marry my girl on leave."

Steele nodded his approval. "Son, we're proud to have you in the 'Oh-Four."

"I'm best damn soldier for you."

"Airborne, trooper."

"All the way, sir, yes."

Following their Jump School graduation, the men of Headquarters Company were authorized their first pass to town. As they were changing into their civvies, Sfc. Wisnewski walked into the squad bay and warned, "You assholes best not try any PLFs off the Fayetteville bars and do not—repeat—do not earn a DR from the raggedy-ass MPs. They love to crack the skulls of new jumpers who celebrate too much. And be sure you fuckin' cocksuckers are back here for Monday morning reveille. No one goes over-the-hill in my platoon."

After two months of squad bay living, close-order drill, guard mounts, KP, and Jump School training, the undisciplined time seemed like early retirement.

Schmidt, Breslin, Patterson, and Banuelous had a serious discussion on wearing the GI-issued low-quarter shoes and appropriate civilian clothes. According to Banuelous, no cool cat would ever wear low-quarters. Patterson and Breslin were not cool cats. Motz and Mangiameli actually wore their uniforms, inspiring Schmidt and the others to hide from them and catch the next bus into Fayetteville. During the ride, Schmidt stood apart from his buddies as if their mismatched dress and low-quarter shoes would contaminate his collegiate look of tan bucks and imitation London Fog wrinkled raincoat.

Across Bragg at the Main Post BOQ, Lieutenant Margolin did not call his parents about the award. He wanted to revel in the accolade without doing a lot of explaining. As his peers congratulated him, he experienced a sense of belonging and secretly wondered how the award might assist in his efforts to find a woman. He had been to town often and knew the bars were filled with too many enlisted drunks and hard case females, had been to the Zebe House at North Carolina State in Raleigh, the Charlotte campus, Wake Forest, and Greensboro Women's College as well as every officer's club on Post. He had yet to find a decent female. Or sandwich.

It was as if North Carolina had never heard of pumpernickel or women without pimples and pencils stuck in their hair after they took your order.

So instead of chasing women or food, he took all his fatigues to the tailor on Yadkin Road and had his Wings sewn on, then slept away the afternoon with the hope of dreaming of a beautiful girl. Or sandwich. Either would do.

Breslin refused to allow his pals to enter the first bar by the bus station. With information gleaned from Sidney the headquarters cook, a self-described stud, he knew the most sophisticated waterhole in Fayetteville was the Canopy Lounge on Hay Street, Fayetteville's Great White Way. The four young soldiers hunched against the cold wind as they walked from the bus station past the Gillespie Street bars—known as Combat Alley—to Hay Street. On paydays, Combat Alley lived up to its reputation; it could be described as a father's vision of hell for his teenage daughter. Soldiers in civvies wandered drunkenly from bar to bar. Fights started with no more excuse than a glance or wise remark. There was the Gillespie Street Drive-In where biker soldiers lounged and executed spin-outs on BMWs and

Harley-Davidsons in the surrounding gravel parking lot. Newer troops frequented Sam's Place, the Arena, or the Red, White, & Blue Bar. These were the joints where a trooper downed his last beer before climbing aboard the Vomit Comet. The general neglect of the street with its potholes, broken curbs and sidewalks, trash-filled vacant lots, and run-down storefronts added to the other-side-of-the-tracks ambience.

To avoid the wind, the four soldiers cut onto a side street. About four stores down, they passed a wine shop. Breslin peeled in before they noticed he had slipped away and caught up with them carrying a bottle of Catawba pink. "It's cheap," he pointed out, "and brewed right here in good-old-boy North Carolina. Sky soldiers, this will warm our cockles until we find better."

Sheltered from the wind in the Sears parking structure, they opened the bottle and took turns sipping. Schmidt educated them on the screw cap; good wine was corked. He preferred scotch. Banuelous needed tequila. Breslin really wanted Guinness. Patterson, legally able to drink for the first time, enjoyed the warmth of the sweet wine and asked, "What do you think our company assignments will be?"

"Who gives a fuck?" replied Breslin. "We're living for the now." He took a huge swallow.

Banuelous, after several sips, backed away, snapping the fingers of his good hand as his right hand had not healed from the pit brawl. "Like, fuck you cats." A cigarette hung from his mouth. "What're we gonna do? Drink piss-poor wine in a parkin' lot all day and freeze our *cojones* off." He took the cigarette out of his mouth and flipped it aside and started toward Hay Street in an exaggerated strut. "I wanna swing, *ese*. Get cool. Dig it, cat."

His pals, grinning, followed close behind. Breslin concealed the wine under his jacket.

Banuelous continued his strut on the main street, rudely looking at people as they passed. "Gotta go. Gotta be, you know what I mean, *ese*. All the way, moatengator."

The moment before they opened the door of the Canopy, Schmidt stepped in front of them and entered the crowded bar as if he had been there since Hitler was a painter. Every booth was taken. Overhead, an enormous red and white cargo chute hung across the ceiling. Presley shouted from the jukebox that he was stuck in *Heartbreak Hotel*. Bar girls circulated with orders. Schmidt anchored the only open spot at the bar and ordered three tall-boy Budweisers and a glass of red wine. His pals remained standing, looking around like rubes.

"Keep an eye out for a booth," Schmidt said as he passed them the beers. "I'll hang here."

Patterson hadn't yet swallowed a sip of beer when he saw a tattoo on one of the waitresses. "Tony, you see that girl?"

"Which one?" asked a puzzled Banuelous. Breslin looked too.

"She's got a real tattoo. A girl."

"Hey, in TJ, I've seen 'em gettin' 'toos."

Breslin said it reminded him of concentration camps and looked for a booth. "Here we go!" He pulled Banuelous by the arm and they moved to a spot where the inhabitants were collecting their cigarettes and change. They slid in just behind the last man leaving. Patterson followed. Schmidt stayed at the bar talking to the older woman who seemed to be the manager. Settled in the booth, they took quick sips of wine to knock off the smuggled bottle.

When they ordered their next round, their unattractive waitress wanted to know if Patterson was old enough to drink. Eighteen was the legal age for beer and wine in North Carolina.

Without a word, Patterson flipped out his wallet and pushed his military ID towards the waitress. Breslin said, "Good looking, I wouldn't have brought him in here if he wasn't legal besides being a big stud from New-goddamn-Jersey."

"Just bring on the beer, baby," said Banuelous. The waitress returned Patterson's card and went to fill the order.

Being the center of attention embarrassed Patterson; however, he liked being a big stud from New-goddamn-Jersey. It would be cool to talk to the girl with the tattoo. Something warned him he better practice first.

"Like, man," said Banuelous watching the vanishing waitress, "Horny as I am I couldn't fuck her."

"I couldn't watch you fuck her and I wouldn't let Willie watch me watch you fucking her," claimed Breslin.

Patterson laughed and choked on his beer. His eyes watered. People never said things like that where he came from, or if they did he never heard them.

"Let's toast Jump School," suggested Breslin. "It's over. We made it."

They held up their tall boys. "Down fast," coached Breslin. "All the way. Airborne. Ready?"

Patterson couldn't finish his bottle. The others did. Gradually, he felt like he thought a paratrooper should feel. Cocky. Smart. Tough. He lit a cigarette and looked for the tattooed girl.

The waitress returned with their beers. "Your buddy at the bar says he's goin' to stay over there." Schmidt was leaning across the bar deep in conversation with the older woman. The bar grew more crowded. Patterson watched how the other guys operated. The off-duty soldiers were loud. Showing off. Competing for the attention of the barmaids. There was a short line at the jukebox. Then, the waitress was there with three more tall boys.

Breslin told Patterson it was his round. As Patterson took out his money, the tattooed girl passed. "Hey!" he called to her as he placed two dollars on their waitress' tray. "Keep the change." Big studs said those things.

The tattooed girl approached their table as if she alone in the world knew what was coming. As if the music stopped and the spotlight showed only her. As if she knew she wasn't a beauty, but knew she didn't have to be. Patterson had never seen such confidence; it was more than he could ever conjure up. Closer up, he realized she had seen and done more than he would ever dream of in a lifetime. To avoid her eyes, he fixated on the tattoo.

She waited for a smart remark. Bored. "My colleagues and I," said Breslin, "are doing a survey for *National Geographic*."

The tattoo was a rosebud. Dark red. It looked like it covered up a name. "I like your tattoo," admitted Patterson. "It's pretty."

"Y'all want somethin' else to drink?"

Breslin ignored a follow-up on the *National Geographic* line realizing she didn't know the *National Geographic* from a Dick, Jane, and Spot reader.

Banuelous stared back at her. Cooler. Defiant.

"Don't you care its pretty?" asked Patterson.

"Y'all better watch your friend. He's drunk." She didn't move. A challenge.

On the jukebox, Johnny Cash kept a close watch on his heart and walked the line. "The truth is," said Breslin, getting up, "he's intoxicated with your beauty," and headed for the bar.

"Why couldn't I think of that?" asked Patterson aloud and added, "What's your name?"

"Y'all writin' a book or somethin'?"

Banuelous finally spoke up. "You know what you need, baby?" He started up as if to slug her. She grabbed Breslin's empty beer bottle and expertly held it like a club.

"Jeeze!" Patterson half rose from the booth, reaching to stop Banuelous' swing.

"A kiss on the cheek." Banuelous leaned toward the barmaid and pursed his lips, making a smacking sound. Patterson slumped down. Embarrassed.

"Funny." She slammed the bottle down and walked away.

Banuelous laughed. "We were just leavin'," he called after her. "Come on, Willie. This place is a drag."

Patterson claimed he liked her. It was cool to be that close to a girl with a rose tattoo. He rested his head against the back of the booth. It felt good to close his eyes and think about her. His fresh beer untouched.

"Man, you know how I cry about waitresses." Banuelous tested his bad fist into the palm of the good hand. "Let's grab those guys and hat up."

"Where?" Patterson felt too woozy to move.

"Anywhere. Who cares?" Banuelous bent over and placed the empty wine bottle on the floor.

"I want to stay here." Patterson's eyes remained closed. "I like her."

"Sure, *ese.* Take her to the fuckin' opera. Come on, let's get those guys." Chuck Berry offered a musical demand for Beethoven to roll over.

Breslin, Banuelous, and Patterson huddled in the doorway of the Canopy while they zippered their jackets and lit cigarettes. Schmidt stayed inside talking to the woman who he had introduced to Breslin as Margie the manager.

Banuelous, jealous, complained, "That son-of-a-bitch has somethin' going on." They walked along the street just to warm up.

Breslin said, "He's talking the old broad's drawers off. She thinks he's a captain just back from on a secret mission behind the Iron Curtain and we're his men."

"No shit!" Patterson thought that was neat. "He really is Hollywood. Captain Hollywood."

They crossed the Atlantic Coast Line's tracks on Winslow Avenue. The open space allowed the wind stronger bites at their ears and cheeks. They pulled up their collars and walked faster. In the next block, they stopped in front of the Seven Dwarfs Bar, the last bar on the last block of Hay Street.

"Here," asked Breslin, "or across the street?" The Turf Club beckoned, the final stop on that side of the street. Breslin never missed a bar.

"I can't go in," confessed Patterson, "I feel like I'm on the deck of a sinkin' ship. Another beer I'll drown."

Breslin pointed out he could not just stand out in the cold.

Patterson wasn't sure what to do, so he offered to take a walk. They agreed to meet in an hour back at the Canopy. Breslin and Banuelous went in. To get out of the wind, Patterson crossed to the other side of the street and walked past store fronts, doing his best to walk straight as an arrow, adhering to Sergeant 'Ski's warning about the MPs. Hay Street was busy. The shops and bars were a step or two above Combat Alley's. There were two movie theatres, the Prince Charles Hotel, a Sears and Woolworths, and several jewelry and clothing stores.

A police siren sounded.

Farther down Hay Street, he saw blinking lights headed towards him. An MP Jeep raced toward the approaching blinking police lights.

Were they after him? Jesus, he had to get off the street.

He looked through the window of a military souvenir shop. *Was that Motz?* He went inside. The shop seemed like an exaggerated dream of a military warehouse. There were display cases of cheap engagement rings, watches, knives, bracelets, military medals, and insignia. Gold-plated belt buckles for truckers and motorcycle riders were available and an unending display of silver and gold parachute Wings for master and senior blasters in all shapes and sizes.

The sirens passed.

A pretty girl followed along with Patterson who had forgotten about Motz as he gazed at all the paraphernalia. He reached the armament section. There was everything from brass knuckles, blackjacks, and K-bar knives to .22

pistols, 30-06 rifles, and shotguns. She refused his request to look at the 30-06. Instead, she offered the opportunity to have his portrait superimposed on a descending solo parachutist silhouetted in a sunset. In color. All the new jumpers do it, she assured him. He didn't ask how she knew he was a new jumper.

"Willie, how do you like it?"

Patterson turned around to find Motz standing in front of him, wearing a black stadium jacket with the large 82nd patch sewn on the right chest pocket and a giant pair of Wings on the left pocket.

"Harry, I had too much beer to know if it looks good or not. We've been..."

The tall man turned around. Sewn across the back circling a giant pair of Wings were the words:

When I Die I'll Go To Heaven
Because I Served My Time In Hell
82nd Airborne Division
Fort Bragg, N.C.

Patterson leaned against the counter for support and laughed. "That's great, Harry. Buy it now. Right now. You ain't got the balls—I mean guts."

"You're right, you're too drunk to make any sense."

"No, buy it. I'll lend you the money," goaded Patterson.

Motz headed toward the clothing area. "Not this time, but I might if I feel like it later."

Patterson followed him. There were complete uniforms of every service branch on hangers. Shoes and boots were aligned toe to heel. Service caps, overseas caps, fatigue hats, overcoats, sweaters, and sweatshirts with unit designations were displayed. Unfurled from the shelves were scarves painted with scenes of C-119s bursting through sunrises with the words to "Beautiful Streamer" and the "Paratrooper's Prayer." A guy could buy a pillow for his Mom or sweetheart with the same scenes. There was a special area for feminine articles. Jewelry. Soap. Lingerie like Patterson had never seen. Padded bras and panties. Crotchless panties with suggestive sayings and other things too dainty to wear.

"I've never seen so much sh...crap. Sorry."

Patterson wasn't comfortable looking at the special feminine lingerie with the salesgirl right there.

Motz, back in regulation uniform, asked, "Were you lookin' for me?"

"I'm tellin' you, Harry, buy the jacket." Patterson imagined him wearing it in the squad bay and the others making fun of him. "Hey, where's Tommy?"

"He hiked out to Bragg Boulevard to look at used cars."

"I want something," said Patterson, "but I don't know what." The patient sales girl asked what unit they were in.

They responded simultaneously. "Five-Oh-Fourth Airborne Infantry Regiment."

"Best damn soldiers in the world," added Motz.

"I've got something up here," she said and walked toward the front of the store.

They followed her. Motz elbowed Patterson and pointed at her ass. "I know," said Patterson, "if only I could." Neither man would admit they really wouldn't know what to do or that she watched their reflection in the plate glass window. From a display case, she produced a Zippo lighter. On one side was the regimental Strike Hold crest and on the other side was the image of the 504th Devil. It was $4.98.

Patterson immediately bought it even though he thought it was expensive for a lighter. The girl gave him change and took a minute to fill the lighter.

"What's your name?" asked Patterson.

"That doesn't come with the lighter." She spun the flint. It worked. "Here."

He stepped back. "Tell me your name or I'll take my money back." He felt in control like a veteran paratrooper should. She pointed to the small sign on the back wall behind the cash register among the playing cards and religious articles. It read, "All Sales Are Final."

"Suppose," said Patterson, "just suppose I don't want the lighter without your name."

She shook her head, crossed her arms, and moved back from the counter.

Motz pulled Patterson by the arm. "Willie, let's chogie."

"Her name won't hurt nothin'."

"She ain't listenin', man." Motz pulled him toward the door. "Outside you got to rock steady. The Pees are in full force." The thought of the MPs distracted Patterson from the salesgirl. Motz opened the door and they stepped into the cold night. Patterson explained he should meet Breslin and Banuelous back at the Canopy.

"Come on, it's freezing. Double-time, march!"

They jogged across Hay Street to Motz's cadence, past the front of the Miracle Theatre, then walked the rest of the way to the Canopy. Patterson, now the veteran boozer, ushered Motz into the bar.

"War suit!" someone immediately shouted in a reference to Motz's uniform. Uniforms were not appreciated in the bars. Only MPs wore them.

They found two seats at the crowded bar. Right across from them were Banuelous and Breslin, who looked like they were hiding their faces from Patterson and Motz while talking to the bartender.

"Tony!" called Patterson loudly without thinking. Most of the patrons around the bar looked at Patterson and the guy in the uniform. The bartender turned around and came towards them.

It was Hollywood Jack Schmidt.

The two-tone green, two-door '54 Chevy with white walls moved slowly under the streetlights lining Gruber Road. It was the solitary vehicle on the main street of the 82nd Airborne Division in the early morning hours. At Grave Street, the Chevy turned right and stopped at the end of the street outside Headquarters and Headquarters Company.

Loud voices sounded from the car. "You can't, Hollywood. You can't walk out like that. They'll hang your ass out to dry." Motz leaned against the front seat nearly shouting his warnings in Schmidt's ear against missing reveille.

"Like, whadda you care what he does, *ese*?" asked Banuelous who sat next to a half-asleep Patterson in the back seat.

Schmidt sat behind the wheel. Next to him was Margie, the owner of the Canopy and the car. In the front passenger seat by the door Breslin sat, silent, staring straight ahead. All of them had continued drinking since the Canopy closed. Their take-out empties, courtesy of Margie, made footing difficult in the car. Margie didn't seem to mind as long as Schmidt kept touching her and talking softly.

"I like Hollywood. He stuck up for Tommy in the tower and he ain't afraid to speak up like the rest of us. He goes, he spends..." They recalled for Margie's benefit and their own entertainment when Schmidt intentionally stepped on Sergeant Barnes' polished jump boot. "...the rest of his life on the run. Maybe gets a dishonorable. Shit, they might even shoot him," declared Motz over the jump boot story.

Patterson wasn't too drunk to understand what a dishonorable discharge was. It was a black mark against a man who could not adjust to military life. *A symbol of failure. Hell, if a person couldn't hack it in the Army where could he?* Patterson stirred enough to add, "Hollywood, stick around. I need someone to teach me about broads."

"For sure, *ese*," agreed Banuelous.

Schmidt calmly replied he had never said anything about leaving. He had simply asked for them to not tell Sgt. 'Ski where he was if he did not show up at reveille Monday morning. "Can I count on you guys for that?"

No one answered. They swam in their own thoughts about not showing up.

Margie pointed out, "Jackie, it's getting later and later."

Finally, Breslin broke his silence. "Yeah, it is late." He cracked open the door then looked across Margie at Schmidt. "You really gonna go?"

Schmidt shrugged his shoulders.

"I wish I was going with you." Breslin got out and held open the door. Cold air stole the car's warmth.

Banuelous pushed up the front seat. "Come on." He pulled Patterson by the upper arm to urge him out. Patterson repeated his need for someone to show him how to find quiff, coo, bush, beaver, snatch, and gash. He loved saying those words he had recently learned and in the presence of female.

"Put that in alphabetical order, Willie," joked Breslin.

"Hollywood," said Motz as he stuck out his long legs to exit, "you're a natural for O-C-S. You and me could take over this Army in the next ten years."

Schmidt slipped his arm around Margie. "I swear to God I'm not going anywhere except maybe back with Margie. Right, baby?" He ran his thumb lightly down her neck. She gave him a look of impatience the others couldn't see. "I'll see you cats Monday morning. Maybe."

Banuelous, shivering, spoke up. "You ain't comin' back."

Breslin leaned into the car. "Hollywood, you make me feel like I'm sinning by staying. My main bitch is you're gonna leave me with assholes like this."

They looked at Patterson chattering from the cold and tilted to one side. Motz's overseas cap was on backwards, and his poplin shirt hung out from under his Ike jacket. Banuelous shook his head back and forth and squeezed his sore fist like a boxer warming up.

Hollywood Jack Schmidt grinned his championship smile and said, "As we say in the business, don't call me."

"Later, man." Breslin shut the door.

They watched the car move down the street, its white exhaust fluttered in the darkness. The brake lights glowed for the stop at the corner.

"They'll hunt him down like dog," predicted Motz. "The Army never lets a man walk away."

The car looked small as it turned at the end of the street.

"'Olaf (upon what once were knees)/ does most ceaselessly repeat/ There is some shit I will not eat...',," said Breslin.

Banuelous asked him what he was jiving about.

"A buddy of mine, Eddie Cummings, said that once, '... he was more brave than me: more blond than you...' Olaf couldn't hack it either."

Without anyone suggesting they run, they did, sprinting hard for the barracks. No one whooped it up; it was as if they were running from the loneliness and foolishness they had witnessed. And maybe they ran because they were tempted to leave, too. They ran across the grass for the first time since arriving in Headquarters Company and being warned by First Sgt.Billy Martin that only second louies could walk on the grass.

Patterson felt something in his jacket pocket. He stopped and pulled out the lighter. Where did...he remembered. He squeezed it in his hand and ran to catch up, deliberately treading hard on the sacrosanct grass, too drunk to worry about being caught.

Chapter 4

Early Monday morning, a still dark and cold morning, the only lights burning in the division were the 504th's. Col. Steele, outlined in the doorway of regimental headquarters, listened as the responses from the squads, platoons, and companies verified the troops were all present and accounted for.

Steele never tired of the daily ceremony dating back to his days as a cadet at West Point. Events like reville and the chain of command were the foundations of the military unit. Men training together, experiencing hardship, sharing the bond of attacking from the sky. If he had his way, he'd lead the division on an exhilarating daily run around the entire area, but he was only a colonel, not the commanding general. Yet.

He watched the major in the parking lot salute and report, "Regiment, all present and accounted for, Sir."

Steele paused, then ordered, "Regiment!"

As he remained in the doorway, he could hear his command running back through the ranks where the troopers waited—cold, tired, hungover, unshaven. Some still pursing interrupted dreams. Others counting and re-counting their days until discharge. Few stood with the colonel's enthusiasm.

The colonel waited until there was silence across the regimental streets and then ordered, "Dismissed!"

Again, the command traveled down the battalion streets until the troops fell out.

Just an inkling of dawn appeared in the eastern sky.

After Headquarters and Headquarters Company broke ranks, Sfc. Wisnewski took his platoon on police call around the company. "All I wanna see are assholes and elbows," he commanded. "Pick up everythin' that ain't growin'. If you can't pick it up, paint it. If you can't paint it, piss on it." He followed behind Breslin, Patterson, and Banuelous. When he dismissed the platoon he had them wait.

"Where the fuck is Schmidt?" Sgt. 'Ski's frozen breath leaped at them.

The four soldiers walked slowly toward the mess hall. After a long silence Breslin said, "Got me, Sarge."

"You guys are asshole buddies."

Patterson worried Wisnewski would ask him directly. He did not want to lie.

Banuelous did lie. "He went off on his own once we hit town."

"Mox nix to me if you cover for him. It's the first shirt who hates AWOLs. They stain his duty roster like a wet dream in a fart sack. Personally, I hope he never comes back. He's a pure dud, but tell him if he gets his ass back here in a day or two I can probably get him off with some hard labor up at regiment. He goes more than thirty days there ain't nothin' nobody can do. Six months and a D-D is all she wrote. Make no mistake, if he was my buddy I'd tow him back by his balls and be doing him a favor. Uncle Sammy don't like his troops going A-W-O-L."

They stopped by the dumpster to discard what little trash they had picked up. Breslin said, "Sergeant 'Ski, I guess he doesn't like the Army and had the gonads to do something about it."

"A lot of fuckin' cocksuckers don't like the Army. You come up with a better way to protect your country let me and Ike know about it. Now get your asses to the orderly room. Martin wants to ask you the same thing I did. I pity Schmidt if Martin catches him."

This Monday morning, First Sgt. Billy Martin was not pleased, not pleased at all, by God. There was a man missing from his company. A body. A number. A slot unaccounted for. And no reason for that man to be missing. It was standard SOP to cover a man for a few days, but after that he would be officially recorded as absent without leave or AWOL.

No, sir, that did not please him one little bit.

Martin's desk faced the orderly room entrance. No one could pass in the hall without being pricked by Martin's rapier glance magnified through plain GI-issue glasses.

The orderly room was aptly named. It was as neat and clean as a drawer full of nun's underwear. A work of art in exactness. The linoleum polished enough to reflect the overhead lights. Pencils sharpened just so. Pictures of President Eisenhower and Secretary of the Army Bruckner aligned on the wall and dusted nightly. The two blonde mahogany desks, Martin's the much larger one with six drawers and the company clerk's with three drawers and a typewriter well, shined from constant polish applied by troops on extra duty punishment. There were always a few bodies for that. The two matching wooden swivel chairs with arms shone as well.

"Morning, First Sergeant."

"Mornin', gentlemen." Martin barely looked up from his duty roster, which he inscribed daily with artistic intensity. The visitors were only lieutenants and his commanding officers. First sergeants paid little attention to lieutenants. Martin's respect for military courtesy didn't kick in until a major appeared.

"Everything copacetic?" asked First Lieutenant John Stewart who was company commander as he and Second Lieutenant Margolin, the Executive Officer, passed into the adjacent CO's office. They dared not linger in the orderly room.

Nobody ever lingered, especially when Martin worked on his rosters.

Hanging from brass hooks on a dark-stained oak one-by-four screwed into the wall at eye level, if one sat in Martin's chair, were six large 10 x 16 clipboards holding legal-sized documents. Each clipboard veneer had the Strike Hold shield-and-sword symbol of the 504th as well as a small '04 devil sticker in the lower right corner. The first clipboard was the Tables of Organization and Equipment—or TO & E as the stencil read. Recorded on these pages were the locations of every Jeep, three-quarter ton truck, deuce-and-a-half, weapon, and typewriter; anything with a serial number that made up the company gear. The second clipboard, the one closest to Martin's heart, was the duty roster. In his mind, he could see the chart without even opening it up. This was the cornerstone of Headquarters Company's manpower. Every man's name, date of rank, serial number—including his own—was recorded. From this list, Martin ruled like a spoiled despot. He sent men on guard duty and KP. Special details like cutting the grass on the officer's golf course and funerals were created off the pages. The form was the basis from which he filed the daily morning report to regimental headquarters. Entries revealed who was present and who was absent and where they were if they were absent. There was a special column for AWOLs and Martin intensely disliked an AWOL entry. He felt it blemished the company, insulted his ability to control his troops. And today Schmidt had insulted him.

The Army Regulations clipboard held all the special orders from the Department of Defense, Third Army Headquarters, 18th Airborne Corps, 82nd Airborne Division, and regimental and battalion headquarters. Next to it was the Regimental Schedule clipboard. With a glance, one could see the commitments of the regiment and number of men needed 90 days in advance: ten men for an honor guard at a high school baseball game, 12 for regimental guard duty, the entire company would police up Yadkin Road on a Wednesday morning. There was the Sick Call Clipboard, cross-referenced with the duty roster. Anyone could quickly note a pattern of malingering if a man went on sick call more than a few times a year. As far as Martin was concerned, paratroopers were not authorized to get sick.

The Motor Pool had its own clipboard that matched the TO & E vehicle roster. This was more detailed; it carried driver assignments and maintenance schedules.

The final roster was Troop Information. This carried Orders of the Day back to the beginning of each month, as well as regulations on hair cuts, phone calls from the Red Cross, and pamphlets on venereal diseases.

The clipboards hung, fingerprint free, beaming the reflection of anyone standing in front of Martin's desk. They were his guides, his bibles, his constitutions with which he ruled from laundry marks on the men's underwear—first letter of last name and last four letters of the individual's serial number—to who would have the honor of carrying the company's guidon in the Armed Forces Day parade in Washington, D.C.

"Right as rain, gentlemen," replied First Sgt. Billy Martin without looking up. He did not share his concerns about the AWOL with the lieutenants.

Since his arrival in the unit, Lt. Margolin had shadowed First Lieutenant Stewart, the acting company commander. His position was executive officer until Stewart departed and a captain arrived to command the company. Margolin's intimidation by Martin had been assisted by Stewart's deferential attitude toward the first sergeant. Stewart never questioned the senior NCO and simply let him run the company while he played tennis on Main Post most afternoons. Now, with honor graduate on his record, Margolin believed he should be more assertive within the company, but he wanted to wait until the first lieutenant departed for law school at the University of North Dakota.

Every morning, they breezed through the first sergeant's office and barely received an acknowledgement. They took their respective, barren desks in the Company Commander's office and touched up their boots while reading sections of the *Fayetteville Observer*. A picture of President Eisenhower hung on the wall behind Stewart's desk and a framed copy of the *Pledge of Allegiance* hung on the sidewall. An American flag the size of a tall man stood in a corner along with the company guidon. Next to the flag was a four-point coat rack where the officers hung their field jackets and dropped their gym bags—Margolin's for handball, Stewart's for tennis. Their desk drawers contained little material: rubber bands, letterhead, legal-sized writing tablets, and Stewart's boot shining gear. There was a single leather-covered book on top of the bookshelf—a bible-like copy of *The Uniform Code of Military Justice*. Aligned on the lower shelves were yards of Army Regulations in three-ring cloth binders.

The two lieutenants had little in common. Stewart thought Margolin was too much an idealist and oddball. Not only was he serious about being a good soldier, he was Jewish and from Southern California and didn't play tennis. Margolin saw Stewart as taking the easy road in executing his duties. He spent too much time playing tennis and existed only as a figurehead commander to Martin's tight grip on the company. And it was difficult to reconcile tennis with North Dakota.

"John?" Second lieutenants could be on a first name basis with first lieutenants. Never a rank higher.

Stewart, using the bottom left hand drawer as a footrest for shining his boots, looked up from his brushing.

"I haven't said much in the past weeks. I've been waiting to get these." Margolin touched the new Wings patch sewn above the U.S. Army label over the left breast fatigue pocket. "But what in the hell am I supposed to do?"

Stewart grunted slightly as he finished buffing his boots and sat back. He dropped the brush in the drawer and shut it with his foot then leaned way back to raise his feet carefully to the corner of the desk and replied, "You're catching on too fast. I didn't ask myself that question until I'd been here for a year."

Martin's staccato voice penetrated their office as he answered the phone, "Headquarters-and-Headquarters-Company-First-Sergeant-Billy-Martin-speakin'."

Margolin nodded toward the door to the orderly room. "I'd like to be part of what goes on." He didn't say he'd like to be more than a shoe brush in a desk and a robot signing papers. He wanted to soldier. He had a degree in business. He was the Honor Graduate. He wanted to run things. Make decisions.

"Here? The company?" Stewart's words carried a tone of incredulity.

"That's my assignment, but all we do is drink coffee in the mess hall, sign whatever he puts in front of us and be-gone-the-rest-of-the-afternoon."

Stewart lifted his hands behind his head, raised his eyebrows, and leaned back as if to say, *What's wrong with that?* "I mean, you can always inspect the mess hall if you get too bored."

Most days after lunch, dinner in military terms, the two officers came back to the office. Stewart would light a huge cigar and re-read the paper. Cigars were popular at the BOQ too. Margolin could not stand them and passed off their presence as another attempt at ruggedness for young officers. He usually read the *UCMJ* and parts of the Sunday *Los Angeles Times*. After a decent interval, Lt. Stewart would say, "Come on," and stand up, stamp his feet to allow the trouser blouse to settle over his boots, and, cigar in hand, walk past the first sergeant's desk and advise the senior non-com he and Margolin more than likely would be gone the-rest-of-the-afternoon.

"Yes, sir," Martin would reply, usually with his hand covering up the phone to show he was really too busy to talk, but before they left would they be kind enough to sign those papers. He'd point to a pile on the desk.

Stewart signed anything, anytime, and did not read a line. Margolin had no choice but to follow along.

Once in their separate cars, Stewart went for tennis and Margolin, who had spent time getting in shape for Jump School, looked forward to handball with anyone he could find at the courts. But he didn't want to play handball every day.

"There's not a damn thing wrong with having the afternoon free," replied Stewart who sincerely felt mornings went too slowly.

Margolin didn't disagree. However, he believed they should be more aware of what goes on in the company.

"Sy, Martin takes care of the day-to-day bullshit and, to be perfectly frank, I could care less. I'm out of here in a month."

"John, I've got eighteen months left and I don't want to spend it signing what *he* tells me sign."

Stewart swung his feet off the desk. "You're new. Gung-ho. Jump School honor graduate. Relax. This is the Army, not General Motors."

"I wish I could, but I've been thinking. When you leave some ambitious captain will come in here and ask me what's going on and I won't know."

"Then you roll out First-Sergeant-Billy-Martin," Stewart said, "and turn him on."

"I hate to admit this, but he scares me."

Stewart laughed. "Why do you think I leave after chow? He's a major pain in the ass." They laughed together for the first time with their mutual assessment of the older sergeant.

Lieutenant Margolin experienced a bit of relief.

"You want to do more? If I was a Lifer I might, but here's what you can do." Stewart lowered his voice. "Keep the door open between the offices for an opener. Tomorrow morning, ask to see the morning report and duty roster before he sends it up to regiment. Hook up this phone and start answering it yourself. See what reaction you get from good-old-boy-First-Sergeant-Billy-Martin then take it from there."

"You wouldn't mind?"

"Be my guest, but don't walk around too much. He gets upset if the floor is too scuffed up at the end of the day."

"You mean, like this?" Margolin got to his feet and did a quick tap dance step.

The door opened quickly. First Sgt. Billy Martin took a step into the room. "Yes, sir?" His eyes darted, searching for the source of the noise.

Margolin felt like a third-grader caught stealing crayons. He made himself ask, "What's up, First Sergeant?"

"I thought I heard somethin' fall, sir. I worry about my lieutenants." He appeared to be waiting for an explanation.

Margolin was not going to be his lieutenant anymore than he had been his uncle's obedient nephew who hadn't gone to law school.

Lieutenant Stewart stood up. "That's nice to hear, First Sergeant. We'll be in the mess hall if you need us."

Martin turned back into his office. The officers followed him into the orderly room where Pvt. Harry Patton Motz stood at attention. Standing by the hall doorway, looking as if they were on their way to Devil's Island, were Patterson, Breslin, and Banuelous.

Margolin knew they were in trouble. He had already equated the orderly room to a high school principal's office. He asked Motz, "What're you doing here?"

Motz is his best military voice replied, "Sir, I think I'm gonna work here, sir."

Martin, standing behind his desk, leaned forward as far as possible. "Whadda y'all mean 'I think?' Y'all ain't here to take a three-day pass. Y'all are my new clerk and jerk. Take charge of that desk, Private."

Motz's expression was not happy, but he dared not say anything. He swung around behind the desk and sat at attention. Margolin knew from their Jump School talks the ungainly private wanted infantry training, not pushing papers. *Why did the First Sergeant sound angry?*

Because he, a mere second lieutenant, had risked life and limb to speak to someone in *his* orderly room? Margolin pushed his luck and asked about the men waiting in the hall.

"I'll take care of them, sir," he replied as if a lieutenant would never comprehend what to do. "Their bunkie's gone AWOL and I'm goin' to find out where."

Margolin heard himself ask if Martin would mind if he stayed and listened. He should have just stayed and declared he wanted to hear all about it.

"Suit yourself, sir, but it ain't necessary."

Stewart, grinning, advised Margolin he'd see him in the mess hall and departed. First Sgt. Billy Martin ordered the three men to enter. "Last man in shut the door and y'all stand at attention."

Motz watched from his ramrod sitting position. Margolin leaned against his office door, then decided to stand at a casual parade-rest to prevent the first sergeant from ordering *him* to stand at attention.

Martin came around his desk and went to the bookshelf where the company passbook always rested. "Y'all listen up." He flipped the passbook pages. "It's right here. Schmidt, J. Signed out at thirteen-fifty. Destination, Fayetteville. Banuelous, A. Destination, Fayetteville, thirteen-fifty. Breslin, S. Signed out at thirteen-fifty. Destination, Fayetteville. And Patterson, W. Signed out thirteen-fifty. Destination, Fayetteville."

He slapped the passbook shut, went to his desk and pulled his copy of the *UCMJ* out of the bottom left drawer then walked among and around the three enlisted men, staring into their young faces. They could feel his magnified eyes judging them. "My experience as a first sergeant in this here man's Army for more 'an ten years tells me y'all are headed for trouble. To save yore asses down the road I want to know the whereabouts of Private Schmidt and I want to know now."

He slammed the book flat against his desk and kept his icy stare on the three men.

Margolin saw what the first sergeant saw. Banuelous remained stoic. Breslin suppressed a grin. Patterson worried.

Martin stepped close to Patterson. "Private, are y'all gonna tell me where that AWOL is? That individual y'all went to town with and is now violatin' the Uniform Code of Military Justice?" He held the black book in Patterson's face.

In all honesty, Lt. Margolin didn't care if Schmidt was gone or not. The man had always been too arrogant for him the short time he had known him, but they did share the bond of Jump School.

Patterson involuntarily wiped his mouth. Martin roughly pulled Patterson's hand down. "Y'all at attention. Snap to. All of y'all!" The three young soldiers adjusted to a sterner rigidity.

Martin stepped back behind his desk and again smacked the book down. It sounded violent in the quiet room.

Margolin did not like Martin yanking Patterson's arm. These were the soldiers who helped him in the Pit. He found himself siding with them as if he was still in ROTC summer camp and in trouble with his pals. Schmidt was missing, but it wasn't the end of the world. He might be back tomorrow. Margolin dared not say a word.

"It's all there in yore own writin'. All of y'all were with him." Martin took off his glasses and gently placed them on the desk. His voice softened and he leaned toward the men. "Men, y'all are soldiers together. I understand that. Today was the day y'all get yore company assignments. It would behoove y'all to tell me where Schmidt is, where y'all think he is, and nothin' else will be said. Yore first sergeant can let a lot of water go under the dam." He stood back to give them a few moments to think about his deal.

Margolin watched them remain unmoving at attention. He imagined Patterson acquired some resolve from his pals' silence.

Martin put his glasses back on. "If y'all don't tell me, I'll personally make sure yore life in Headquarters and Headquarters Company is a livin' hell. Yore first sergeant can do that." He came from behind his desk to stand in front of each man for a moment. They did not move.

Martin started back toward his desk, suddenly whirled around. "Private Patterson. Where in the hell is he?" Patterson looked stunned.

"Y'all better answer, Private, or yore ass is goin' up to regimental headquarters to explain to Colonel Steele why..."

Patterson spoke quickly. "We...we took the bus to town..."

Margolin silently urged Patterson to hold on. Martin could do nothing to him. *Hold on*, he wanted to say aloud.

"...had a couple of beers and he was gone."

"As sure as y'all are goin' to the stockade for aidin' and abettin' a fugitive from military justice, he just as sure told y'all where he was goin'. Now, Private, what'd he say?"

"Nothin', First Sergeant," interjected Breslin.

"Nothin'," Patterson added quickly.

"I ain't buyin' it. No, siree bob. No way in hell y'all are gonna make me believe that." Martin went behind the desk.

Margolin said, "Excuse me, First Sergeant."

"What-in-the-hell-do-you-want? Oh, excuse me, Sir."

Motz, deadly silent at his sitting position, enjoying the process because he wasn't involved, let out an audible breath and raised his eyebrows. Enlisted men did not speak to officers that way.

"I'd like a piece of scratch paper, First Sergeant." Margolin found the courage to stand in front of Martin's desk.

"Lieutenant, I'm in the middle of a critical investigation in the whereabouts of an AWOL in the United States Army and y'all want yore first sergeant to find y'all scratch paper?" The NCO sat down and spread his hands over his neat desk to show there was no scratch paper.

Margolin felt like the man at the cocktail party discovering his fly open. "I want to write down a suggestion."

"Speak your mind, Lieutenant. This ain't no college dormitory where boys and girls pass around love notes."

Margolin knew he did not have to listen to Martin's rudeness and also knew he should not disrespect the first sergeant in front of the men just as Martin should not have been disrespectful to him. *How could he stop Martin? No enlisted man had ever spoken to him like that since he had put on his gold bar.* Momentarily, he was lost for words. His face flushed, but he managed to say he thought it would be a good idea to question the men separately to see if their stories matched.

"Beggin' the Lieutenant's pardon, it don't make a hill of beans if their stories match or not. They knew he was gonna go and they know where he is." Martin pushed himself out of his chair and came around the desk. "They're gonna spend a lot of time in the mess hall thinkin' about where their bunky is."

He poked Breslin hard on the shoulder. "Report to Sergeant Potter ASAP."

Breslin turned and winked at Motz as he left.

He tapped Banuelous with the same hard fingers, daring him to react. "Y'all do the same, Private."

With Banuelous gone, First Sgt. Billy Martin faced Patterson. They were both of average height. Martin was acquiring a middle age spare tire. He put his hand gently on Patterson's shoulder.

"Ain't nothin' gonna happen to y'all, son, if y'all just let yore first sergeant do his job. All I wanna know is what Private Schmidt said."

Margolin silently promised himself if Patterson fell for that blatant soft soap he'd add him to his rapidly growing shit list topped by First Sergeant Billy Martin.

"First Sergeant…" Patterson swallowed hard. "…we rode the bus and had a beer. He said…" Patterson's voice cracked. "…he didn't like our Army-issue shoes and left us."

Martin swiped the *UCMJ* book off his desk and held it close to Patterson's face. He opened it and waved it. "This is the page, Private. This is the page that puts y'all in Leavenworth for harborin' a fugitive from military justice. Lemme see."

He walked behind Patterson and pretending to read, said, "Known perpetrator will receive no less than five years of hard labor in the United States Army Prison at Fort Leavenworth, Kansas." Martin's voice grew more strident. "Do y'all want five years of breakin' big ones into little ones? Do y'all, boy? Five long years away from your Mama's cookin'? Y'all be an old man when y'all got out. Do y'all want that? Answer me, Private!"

Motz looked at the lieutenant with a pleading expression. Both knew Martin was lying and over-reacting. Margolin knew Motz wanted him to intervene.

He didn't. He did notice Patterson's eyes watering.

"No, First Sergeant, but I can't…"

"Can't tell me. See, there is more. Y'all afraid of yore asshole buddies thinkin' y'all told on them. What y'all would really be doin' is protectin' the U.S. Army from malingerers and reprobates who deserve the barbed-wire hotel. Y'all be savin' Headquarters and Headquarters Company from having to file an AWOL report and have the regiment come snoopin'…"

The first sergeant's threats had turned Patterson to stone. He couldn't have responded if he wanted to. His fear of saying the wrong thing kept him silent.

"…around why a man was missin'. No one goes AWOL from my company. No…"

Patterson blurted, "First Sergeant, I don't know no more than what I said." His words as hurried as Martin's. His effort to overcome fear obvious.

Congratulations, Patterson, thought Margolin. The young man had more courage than he had been giving him credit for. More than the officer had; he wasn't standing up to protect the enlisted man.

"Y'all talkin' back to me, Private?"

"No, First Sergeant."

Patterson's watery eyes had cleared. His voice sounded stronger. At some point he realized he had to stand up or he'd lose in so many ways. The biggest loss would be facing his buddies if he cracked.

"Y'all report to the mess hall and y'all tell Sergeant Potter to keep y'all on pots and pans 'til I deem it unnecessary. Move-out!"

Patterson nearly ran from the office.

"Any fool can see that boy is lyin'. If I have my way those three will be pullin' KP 'til the world ends. Motz, the first thing a man has to learn in my orderly room is to never speak up when I'm talkin'. Oh...Y'all still here, Sir?"

Margolin, bolstered by Patterson's valiant effort, replied, "I sure am, First Sergeant, and I intend to be here for a long time." He did not wait for a reply.

On the way to the mess hall, he rehashed their confrontation: his should've saids, and who said what, and this meant that. But it wasn't really complicated. All he had to do was stand up to the little *schmuck*.

Damn, Sy, show some chutzpah.

Before he reported to the mess hall, Patterson went to the squad bay to change his shiny new Corcorans for the worn Army-issue basic training boots hidden in his laundry bag and used for dirty assignments. For a moment, in ranks that morning with his fresh Wings sewn on his fatigues and field jacket and metal Wings pinned on his fatigue cap, he'd been proud and anticipated receiving his company assignment. *Now I'm in trouble and facing pots and pans for who knows how long.*

Banuelous and Breslin were cleaning the chow line when he walked in. A glance back to the big sink showed a Negro already on pots and pans.

It was a jig's job, thought Patterson. He had KP in basic one time: pots and pans.

You say anything, *ese*?" asked Banuelous.

"Same story." Patterson acted casual. It was easy away from First Sgt. Billy Martin's glaring eyes.

"K-K-K-Ps don't grab ass he-he-here. They work." Sergeant First Class Todd Potter had come up behind them.

The mess hall of Headquarters and Headquarters Company of the First Battalion, 504th Airborne Infantry Regiment of the 82nd Airborne Division was the best eating establishment on Fort Bragg. Month after month, year in and out, the mess hall won Best Mess. There was a single reason for this consistency: Sergeant First Class Todd Potter.

Potter was a chunky Negro, the extra weight an occupational hazard, who appeared shorter than he was. On the right shoulder of his fatigues he wore the combat patch of the First Cavalry, a large triangular insignia of yellow with a black diagonal stripe and a horse's head. Potter had seen the worst of the Korean War during the early months when the North Koreans overran the rapidly inserted, poorly trained American troops who had become soft from garrison living in Japan. He was part of the cooks and clerks brought in to stem the advance until replacements arrived. The terrifying fighting inspired him to remain a career cook in the U.S. Army—after all, a man could get hurt when and where bullets were flying.

Each morning, the cooks knew the eggs better be shelled and waiting to be cooked to order. No powdered eggs in Potter's mess. The bacon had to be yipping on the grill like quarreling Pekinese. Cold cereal, fruit, and pastry made early every morning were a must. Potter personally checked the cooking as well as the cleanliness of the serving line without fail.

No one entered until the Sfc. gave the OK.

Potter lived a solitary life. He was the only career NCO who lived in the barracks and seemed to be there for every meal, even on Sundays. And Potter stuttered. But he easily made himself heard and understood when he gave KPs and cooks directions.

Potter had no favorites when it came to KPs. If a man did his job he'd be finished after 12 or 14 grueling hours. If he didn't, he'd be ordered back the next day and the next. A week of KP was standard company punishment.

All day long the KPs heard, "Cl-cl-clean it again, sol-sol-soldier." "Mop th-th-the floor A-A-A-SAP." "On yore your feet, KP, th-th-this ain't no-no-re-re-hotel." KPs did not like Potter.

"Maybe," Breslin had said after his first stint in the mess hall, "the starving children of China might like 'Pee' with Potter, but I don't."

"He ain't so bad," countered career soldier Motz, "and the food's great."

"I'd rather have polio," advised Schmidt before he took off.

Patterson reported to the Sfc. who sent him to Sidney the Cook who directed him to help the big Negro at the pot and pan sink, the toughest of all kitchen chores. The heavy pots, pans, and roasting trays had to be cleaned and re-cleaned all day long in water too hot to touch.

Patterson approached the man who was singing, " 'You're the cutest thing that I did ever see/ I really love your peaches/ Wanna shake your tree/ Lovey Dovey/ I can't get you outta my mind...' What's up, young blood?"

Patterson explained his sentence of pots and pans until further notice.

"Good training for you. Pots and pans puts hair on a cat's chest and jit in his cannon. Jump in here while I make the rounds. When ex-Corporal Brookesie works the big sink no one can keep up with him."

Brookes left Patterson standing in front of several cake trays encrusted with the coffee cake residue. Clean, steaming hot water filled the sink. Brookes must have just changed it, a frequent necessity to keep water grease-free. Continuing his rendition of "Lovey-Dovey," Brookes circled throughout the kitchen collecting dirty pans and utensils scattered here and there. Before Patterson even finished one cake pan, Brookes returned with two roasting pans and a pot used for mashing potatoes.

"Say, young soldier, you best turn your belt buckle around or you'll ruin it against the sink," advised Brookes. "Now, let's knock this shit off."

For the next two hours, Patterson and Brookes scoured pans, changed water, cleaned the sinks, mopped around the sinks, scrubbed the parts of the peeling machine, and soaked knives, ladles, and spatulas. They were so busy, Patterson forgot about Breslin and Banuelous across the kitchen cleaning dining trays and dragging out garbage cans. Several times Sidney the Cook stopped at the sink to drop off a pot or large utensils. When he did, he and Brookes would harmonize for a moment on songs Patterson had never heard like "Lovey-Dovey."

Brookes showed Patterson how to steal cookies from the pantry by pretending to mop the floor and coached him how to stay ahead on the pots and keep the water hot and clean. "Anytime you want to fuck off, just mop the floor," advised Brookes who seemed unfazed by KP. Patterson learned Brookes had KP every day and he was the guy living in the pup tent on the company lawn. He had been AWOL for 30 days because he had sideswiped a car while drinking in Raleigh. The cops didn't like his northern, big-city attitude, so they beat him up and charged him with resisting arrest and punished him with 30 days on the chain gang. The Army knew where he was, but he wasn't where he was supposed to be, so under military logic he was AWOL. Living in the pup tent was normal company punishment while awaiting court-martial.

Brookes had been one of the best NCOs in the company. He had been a corporal in charge of the communications platoon, ready to make sergeant, and wanted a career in the Army. Now, he was just killing time until he went back on the block with a dishonorable.

Working together, they had spare time, so they went on the back porch to smoke. The cold winter air felt like a fresh shower after a morning of leaning over the deep hot sinks.

"I've never had extra time workin' pots and pans," said Patterson. "You make it look easy."

"After thirty days on the gang, this is a piece of cake."

Patterson told Brookes about Martin's threat of five years in Leavenworth. Brookes laughed hard and long. "They can't touch you except to scare you, and that worthless motherfucker couldn't send Dillinger to a bank. The man's a psycho. Martin's a fuckin' homesteadin' midget. Homesteaders are the dudes who volunteered to go Airborne to avoid Korea. That Indian Head patch he wears is bogus. He was a fuckin' company clerk in Korea for a month and went Airborne to come home. Bragg's full of 'em."

Patterson asked Brookes if he was afraid of his pending court-martial.

"Afraid?" As Brookes stubbed out his cigarette on his boot, he said, "Let me explain the Army, young blood. It's like this: no matter how good you are, and I was one of the best, when you step on your dick, watch out." He tore the paper apart, scattering the remaining tobacco into the wind. "There ain't no mercy in the Eighty-Deuce. 'No excuse' is what they say." He rolled the torn paper into a tiny ball he put it in his pocket. "These motherfuckers jump in your shit for any little two-bit thing. Division. Regiment. Battalion. The company. They want your blood like you poopchuted their old ladies. This, they want everyone to see, is what happens when you fuck up. And you know what, with all that they ain't never laid a hand on me. I'm back in the world after my trial and these fuckers have to stay here waitin' their turn to fuck up."

Sidney the Cook stuck his head out the door. In his hand was a pitcher of steaming coffee. "Anyone have to piss?" Patterson didn't know what to reply.

Brookes did.

He hopped off the railing and went inside with Sidney the Cook. Patterson followed them to the pantry. Brookes told Patterson, "You stay here. Anyone comes cough like hell."

Patterson stood outside the pantry and watched Brookes piss into the coffee pot Sidney the Cook held. Obviously, they were experienced at it.

Patterson didn't know Sidney the Cook. The short, wiry young man was a Specialist Fourth Class or Spec/4 or Speedy-Four who cooked to have odd hours to avoid inspections and fuck the wives of soldiers who worked regular hours. The Army was his chosen career because he loved to jump from planes and get laid. He treated KPs fairly and worked hard when on duty. The candy-apple '53 Olds coupe with five coats of lacquer in the enlisted man's parking lot belonged to him. It came in handy as a female lure. "If they're old enough to pee, they're old enough for me," admitted Sidney the Cook, the original 'fuck-a-snake-if-it'd-hold-still' kind of guy. And he'd tell you that.

Patterson thought his tattoos and long hair hidden under his cook's hat made him look evil.

"That's enough, for Christ's sake!" Sidney the Cook pulled away the pitcher and the spray hit the floor. They all started laughing. Brookes went to the latrine while Patterson mopped up. He heard Sidney the Cook call, "Hot coffee comin' up! DRO!"

The Dining Room Orderly turned off the floor buffer—the floor was buffed after every meal—and carried the pitcher back to the NCO section where there were several NCOs on break and Lieutenants Margolin and Stewart.

While mopping up, Patterson reflected on what Brookes told him.

The man had the right approach to the Army. Patterson now realized Martin had picked on him because he appeared to be the weak link among the three of them. *The way to get along was to not let anyone know they were getting to me.* He would never tell on Schmidt and there wasn't anything Martin could do. Put him on more KP; he'd handle it like Brookes. Work hard, laugh a lot, sing some songs—he needed to learn cool music—and never give them the satisfaction of thinking they were winning.

Brookes was a sharp cat, even if he was a spade.

After noon chow, Motz, in his new position of company clerk, came for Patterson, Banuelous, and Breslin. They were to report to their new jobs: Patterson to the supply room, Breslin went to the chapel down the street as the chaplain's assistant, and Banuelous reported to regimental headquarters where he was assigned to ration breakdown.

Their question to Motz was, did Martin plan anything else to force them to talk?

He replied the first sergeant had been bluffing. "Besides, I've got a royal case of the ass. I should be in a rifle company with a machine gun. I'm stuck here pounding a typewriter like a genuine candy-ass, rear-echelon mother-fucker."

From the moment Patterson walked into the supply room, Sergeant First Class Andrew Webster treated him as if he was his solitary student of world affairs, not a supply clerk. Sgt. Webster was a Jamaican who had built a career in the U.S. Army. He was blacker than burnt ebony, lean as beef jerky, never without a toothpick, and spoke the Queen's English, emphasizing his accent whenever he quoted Kipling. He had been educated in one of the best private schools in Jamaica because his mother worked in the cafeteria. At first, Patterson suspected Webster's mannerisms were too polite. He appeared a sissy compared to rough individuals like Wisnewski and First Sgt. Billy Martin. Some men in the company who did not know him considered him a pansy. There were not many sergeants first class who used an ivory cigarette holder and spoke like an English earl. What most men in the company did not know was Webster had been wounded twice while serving with the 17th Infantry Division in Korea. After he warmed up to Patterson, he explained, "I was foolish then, Private William. A young Danny Deever whose sword would save humanity from the Communist chains of oppression and proudly served my adopted country. And, by God and queen, my black face scared the hell out of the Chinese. After I was wounded the second time I retired to supply. It's a gentleman's game. Barter. Trading. Give and take. Lend out a few shillings to my colleagues."

Webster was the company shylock. He had no love for First Sgt. Billy Martin; the bloke didn't play cricket.

The other person in supply was Corporal Marcus Broomfield, whose physique and countenance inspired brave men to flee. He boxed for the division at the middleweight level. If Webster needed to collect a loan, he simply had Broomfield stand behind him. Errant debtors could not pay fast enough.

To Patterson's surprise, Broomfield proved to be a kind and gracious—if unschooled—individual. The corporal never cursed or smoked and prayed on his knees with a Bible. His only mistake in life might be linking his star to Sfc. Webster's numerous shady enterprises.

Patterson quickly realized his good luck with the supply assignment. The reality was his new job wasn't much different than working in the Downbeach city yard where he drove a pickup and spent a lot of time erecting and taking down city holiday decorations and cleaning up after serious winter storms. The supply room job proved to be better than his civilian job. His father had not pulled strings to get him work and he wasn't treated as special. He was making his own way.

If he felt like it, he could take the three-quarter ton truck on a laundry run to Main Post and squander more than a few minutes in the popular cafeteria sipping hot chocolate and munching a glazed doughnut while admiring the civilian secretaries and WACs on break. Sometimes he'd stop by the regimental chapel and take Breslin with him.

In one of those weird military twists of fate, Private Scott Breslin, Roman Catholic and draftee, ended up as the chaplain's assistant to the Protestant Chaplain, Major Nathaniel Byrd, a spit and polish career man who craved neatness and cleanliness for his chapel. It was highly unusual for the military to assign someone a job he wanted. In military circles, the chaplain's assistant was known as an easy gig. A piece of OD cake. And Breslin embraced it. He polished the wooden pews, vacuumed the altar carpet, dusted everywhere, and stole sacramental wine. The toughest part of his assignment required him to stay awake while suffering a hangover during the seemingly endless Protestant and Catholic Sunday morning services in which he sometimes served as an altar boy for the priest.

His large Irish Catholic family back in Narberth, Pennsylvania, expected him, the last born male, to become a priest since the first-born chose not to. He served as an altar boy, attended LaSalle High School, and had two years of college. He considered the priesthood, but before he made any decision, he decided he needed some real life experiences just like Saul Bellow in *Augie March* and Kerouac's *On The Road*. He quit school, and within two months he was drafted. The reality he found wasn't exactly what he had in mind, 24 hours a day of regulations.

The Army, he liked to say, gave him a perspective, so therefore the all-volunteer Airborne gave him an even greater perspective.

On their trips to Main Post, Breslin kidded about wanting to hear Col. Steele's confession. The colonel went to the regimental chapel every Sunday for the 0900 Catholic Mass. Breslin thought the confession would go something like, "Bless me, Father, for I have sinned. My last confession was two weeks ago and I have sinned by not driving the regiment harder, not court-martialing enough men, and most of all, Father, I have sinned by not starting World War Three."

All of the new jumpers of Headquarters Company fell into work-a-day patterns. Motz, much to his chagrin, stood tall in the orderly room every morning. His only solace was the easy access to numerous U.S. Army manuals. Private Tommy Mangiameli ended up in the motor pool dispatch shack where he immediately designed a scheme to steal gas for his long drives home in the '48 Buick he purchased with money loaned from Sfc. Webster from a Bragg Boulevard used-car dealer. During the week, he used the car to drive soldiers to town for bus fares to support his weekend trips. Private Danny DeFever, who had taken the Jump School re-up leave, never came back and was now carried as a deserter on First Sgt. Billy Martin's beloved duty roster.

Martin knew they'd never find DeFever in the Louisiana bayous, but Hollywood Jack Schmidt was another story. Schmidt was so close Martin thought he could smell him and said that more than once to Motz and Sfc. Wisnewski. The first sergeant wasn't wrong.

Hollywood Jack Schmidt, the new bartender at the Canopy Lounge, grew a moustache and longer hair. His speech acquired a slight North Carolina drawl. The role came easily to him and he played opposite Margie's bawdy heroine. His attention made her more pleasant to her barmaids and she bought herself nicer clothes. She did Schmidt's laundry, paid his salary, and let him use her car. Hollywood kept the barmaids at a distance and in line which Margie liked even more.

Meanwhile, Patterson and Breslin kept telling him to come back before he's officially a deserter. They assured him Sgt. 'Ski would help him. "I don't need a lifer to look after me. I'm a grown boy. A cad with ambition."

"You'll be a cad in the stockade if they find you," warned Breslin. Their entreaties failed.

One of the Canopy's best and newest patrons was Tony Banuelous. During the week, he worked the regimental ration trucks that ran from mess hall to mess hall delivering rations. A very un-military occupation. Everything served in the mess hall came off the truck except for beef and dairy products, which were delivered cold. He became good pals with the ration truck veteran—Spec/4 Nicky Lazor, a cool cat from Calumet City, Illinois, who owned a 1951 white Cadillac that had 'Moonlight Gambler' scripted along both rear fenders. Lazor came from Division Artillery—known as DivArty—and knew the Fayetteville bar girls. He took Banuelous under his wing and taught him the ropes of ingratiating themselves to bar owners with stolen food. The two men spent a lot of nights at barmaids' apartments, barely making reveille each morning. They dressed in near zoot-suit style and grew their hair long for ducktail combing. Wisnewski enjoyed pulling off Banuelous' fatigue cap and ordering him to the barbershop.

Since Lazor was assigned to DivArty, Sgt 'Ski couldn't touch him.

Sometimes they'd all meet in the Canopy and knock back the tall boys. Usually, like most soldiers off duty, they griped about the chicken shit '04.

Gripe about events like the spring regimental full field inspection. A full field inspection affected everyone in various ways.

The night before the inspection there was no lights-out. The men worked late ascending and descending the florescent-lit concrete stairwells, carrying armloads of gear to be displayed on the company lawn. As dawn approached, the usual inviolate lawns of the 504th were dotted with tents of all sizes: Company mess tents with outdoor ranges and water heating units. Command post tents small, medium, and large. Medical tents. Latrine wall shelters. Field desks from orderly and supply rooms. And the personal displays of 1,500 troopers.

Each man laid out his shelter-half and on it displayed his mess kit, entrenching tool, tent pegs, poncho, web belt with canteen, ammo pouches, and a first-aid packet. There was a change of socks and underwear in the knapsack and the M-1 rifle field stripped into the trigger, barrel, and stock groups.

As Patterson and Broomfield carried the final footlocker of salvaged gear up the outside stairs, Broomfield griped, "Just once I'd like to carry somethin' out of supply knowin' I wasn't gonna be carryin' it back down."

Motz slipped behind Patterson and said they had to talk. Fast.

He whispered to Patterson while the two men stood holding the footlocker at the top of the stairs, "Someone called the first shirt. They know where Schmidt is. You gotta warn him. He's callin' the Pees now."

"You don't want me to hear, Private?" asked Broomfield, a corporal Lifer and therefore the enemy.

Patterson shook his head. "It's nothin', Broom. A car thing."

Motz strode back to the orderly room. Patterson and Broomfield continued their journey to the supply tent. On the way, he tried to think of what to do. As soon as they put down the footlocker, Patterson told Sergeant Webster he had to take a wicked dump and ran back into the building, out the opposite side, around the mess hall and started trotting up Grave Street toward the chapel with his fatigue hat in his hand.

Breslin could call Schmidt and...

"Soldier!" The powerful God-like voice stopped Patterson dead.

Less than 20 yards behind him were Col. Steele, the Regimental Sergeant Major Kaley, and a general from the 18th Airborne Corps on Main Post: the 82nd was part of the 18th Airborne Corps which was part of Third Army.

Patterson came to attention, saluted, and half-shouted in his best military voice, "Good mornin', Sir!" When he saluted he realized his hat was in his hand. He quickly shoved it on at an odd angle, saluted again, the crooked cap making him more uneasy.

"Where do you think you're goin'?" asked the sergeant major in a threatening tone, advancing on Patterson, his swagger stick tapping his thigh.

"The chapel."

"He's going to the chapel, sir," said Kaley as if Steele was deaf.

Steele asked, "Doesn't that soldier know we're having a full field inspection, Sergeant Major?" The NCO repeated the colonel's question.

"Yes, sir. I'm squared away."

Why? Why? Why was he going to the chapel? Why? "The company clerk said there's a letter from my Mom there, Sir."

Be worried. Christ, he was. And scared. And he wasn't used to lying and feared being caught. The sergeant major might be reading his racing mind.

"Sir, he says he has a letter from his mother over there."

Steele ignored that remark and asked what company Patterson belonged to.

The sergeant major repeated the question, this time using Patterson's name thanks to the black and white U.S. Army nametags on outer garments.

"Headquarters, sir."

"Headquarters, sir."

Sgt. Maj. Kaley pointed his swagger stick at Patterson's chest and said in a low voice, "Don't call me 'sir.' I'm the regimental sergeant major." Senior NCOs took great pride in not being officers.

Steele issued the decree they were headed there now and when they inspected he better be in ranks.

"You heard the colonel?"

"Yes, Sergeant Major. I'll be there."

"With your cap on correctly," warned the veteran and pointed the swagger stick at Patterson's head. "Dismissed."

Patterson adjusted his cap, saluted, and ran toward the chapel. A fine cold mist began to fall.

Breslin came out of the chapel door as he ran up. In a moment, Breslin was on the chaplain's phone to Schmidt as Patterson ran back to the company. In the few minutes it took to get back in ranks for inspection, it started to rain. A slow, cold spring rain.

Lt. Margolin and Sfc. Wisnewski, acting as the company first sergeant because First Sgt.Billy Martin was too busy with his rosters for any chicken-shit inspection, stood in front of the company talking. The lieutenant had unofficially become company commander since Lt. Stewart departed to play tennis in North Dakota. Wisnewski ordered the men to put on their ponchos, and then Margolin called the company to attention. The platoon sergeants repeated the command, as did the squad leaders.

Steele and the general arrived in front of Headquarters and Headquarters Company to inspect. Behind them, three official paces, walked the sergeant major. Margolin announced that the company was ready for inspection and the three officers, the sergeant major and Sfc. Wisnewski walked along the ranks without really looking too hard; the ponchos covered any sloppy uniforms and the exposed gear had become soaked.

Patterson watched from the corner of his eye to see if there was any discussion about him. The inspection party came down his rank. They went past Patterson, and he thought he had made it until the rugged sergeant major stopped and asked if he was the man in the street without his cap on.

The group stopped and looked. "Yes, Sergeant Major."

Patterson felt his legs shaking under the poncho and forced himself to stare at the sergeant major who grinned like the cat who had caught the canary.

Rock steady, whispered Patterson to himself, repeating the strong command of Jump School instructors. *Rock Steady.*

"The rain bother you, son?" asked Steele.

Patterson, surprised Steele had spoken directly to him, replied in a quaking voice, "I...I don't like it, Sir." He didn't like his voice. He wanted to sound sure of himself. *Would they ask about the letter from my mother? If they did...goddamnit, rock steady.*

"Always remember, soldier, it's raining on the enemy too."

Patterson replied with a firm, "Yes, Sir."

The group moved along. Wisnewski stopped at Patterson. "What were you doing in the street without your cap?"

As quietly as he could, he answered he was running to the PX for shaving gear and soap for the inspection when they stopped him. No one heard his lie.

Wisnewski wrote Patterson's name in his little spiral notebook. "See me for some extra duty."

"Hup, Sarge."

Wisnewski hurried to catch up.

Patterson shivered in the rain, but smiled. Maybe Schmidt would make it. And it did rain on the enemy and there they were: Steele, Kaley, Margolin, and Wisnewski. Yet in the order of things, they were supposed to be on the same side.

Chapter 5

The major spring maneuver carried the designation 'All-American.' The last big operation was the previous fall, when several companies from the 504th, had flown to Nevada and sat in ditches on Jackass Flats while an A-Bomb was detonated five miles away; it was called Operation Smoky. The men hiked through the fallout to see how troops would react. Ongoing maneuvers like that were theoretical proof the Army could have the 82nd anywhere in the world within 24 hours.

And be ready to fight even if an A-bomb fell.

During All-American, the 504th acted as the attacking regiment. Fifteen hundred men convoyed to Shaw Air Force Base near Sumter, South Carolina, where they marshaled for three days preparing Jeeps, water trailers, and 105 howitzers for heavy drop. With three days C-rations in their field packs, the '04 would parachute onto Bragg which was defended by 77th Special Forces and the 502nd Airborne Infantry Regiment from the 101st Airborne Division based at Fort Campbell, Kentucky.

For many of the 504th troopers it was their cherry blast, the first jump with their regular units. During the flight, the new jumpers were surprised to be allowed to smoke on the planes, and when they stood up and hooked up, the veteran paratroopers acted like rampaging commuters—shouting, cursing to get off the train. With the flash of the green light, there wasn't any orderly shuffle toward the door and swinging into good door position like the training jumps. The heavily loaded troops surged toward the rear doors of the C-119s, challenging the Hawk to grab them, cursing the men in front of them to move faster.

"Go!" "Go, Goddamnit!" "Go, Motherfucker!" "Go!"

In moments, the sky over Drop Zone Salerno filled with 1,500 men from 20 lifts of Flying Coffins. Men drifted across the balmy April sky calling one another, feeling like they were attached to anvils with their heavy field packs dangling between their legs, their reserve chutes across their chests, and their M-1 carriers hooked to their jump harnesses. Some men just fell out the door, letting the weight pull them. Everyone worried about getting trapped in the risers of another chute and losing their air. Jumpers died when chutes tangled.

There were jump delays in a few planes when gear came unstrapped, men tripped, and others waited too long in the door. Men continued jumping even after the red light flashed. They found themselves drifting past the DZ, landing in trees, accumulating bruises from bouncing off the thick lower branches. A Spec/4 in Dog Company refused to go out the door and a massive heavy drop cargo chute for a Jeep failed to deploy, turning the Jeep into a squashed metal bug buried three feet deep in the drop zone.

All in all, the mass drop went as usual, with several assorted broken bones from jumping in full combat gear.

An unexpected spring freeze dropped the temperatures to single digits the second day of the mock invasion. It stayed below 15 degrees for four days. On the third cold day, Third Army Headquarters and XVIII Airborne Corps cancelled the maneuver. There were rumors that five percent of the troops suffered frostbite and a few even lost some toes and ear tips.

Winter sleeping bags had been forgotten.

Operation 'All-American' became the barometer by which all future maneuvers were judged for degree of difficulty. No operation below the Mason-Dixon Line would ever be as cold.

During the convoy to Shaw before the jump, the unofficial commanding officer of Headquarters and Headquarters Company, First Battalion, 504th AIR, Second Lieutenant Seymour Margolin, shared the canvas-covered headquarters Jeep with First Sgt. Billy Martin. Their driver was newly promoted Private First Class Harry Patton Motz. When the time came to load up, Martin had held open the flimsy canvas front passenger door and waved Lt. Margolin into the hard-riding rear seat jammed with field packs, a PRC-10 radio, and orderly room paraphernalia.

Military courtesy called for the highest-ranking individual to ride in the front passenger seat. The slight wasn't lost on the young lieutenant or the new Pfc.

Tennis playing Lt. Stewart's departure ostensibly left the ranking officer in charge: Lt. Margolin. But he had not been officially notified and the lieutenant accepted the fact he did not have the courage to declare that status. It was really up to regiment to dictate who was in charge.

Margolin stared at the first sergeant's high-shaved neck visible under his steel pot and his dislike for the man increased with each passing mile as they barreled along in the Jeep, weaving among the deuce-and-a-halves—6x6s— and three quarter-ton trucks—4x4s—pulling mess and supply trailers. He quietly fumed as Martin worked the radio mike and ordered Motz to speed up or slow down. Their convoy call sign was Striker Three.

When Stewart left, Margolin had moved his personal gear into the CO's desk and hung his diploma from San Fernando Valley State College on the wall beside his certificate for being the Honor Student of Basic Airborne Course Class 33. His boot shining gear, polish and rag, went into the bottom left hand desk drawer. Cigars—he now attempted them on occasion—were kept in the upper right-hand drawer. His handball gear stayed in the gym bag he kept under the coat rack in the corner. The Jump School honor had led to social invitations he hadn't experienced previously. Regular handball matches were part of that, and he wasn't half bad since he had turned to exercise and lost weight.

There had been no further embarrassments like the morning Martin had spoken back to him during the interrogation of Schmidt's friends. In fact, First Sgt. Billy Martin had been 'yes, sirring' and 'no sirring' him by the book as if he realized he had been out of line.

But it was all by the book, never a word more than necessary and no courtesy, for example, like the seat in the Jeep.

Margolin argued with himself every morning about not taking any bullshit from the first sergeant as he drove his black '51 Chevy coupe from the BOQ on Main Post to the 504th area. He worried if he stood up to a veteran like Martin, he'd be disrespecting the man or overly pushing his officer status. If Martin treated him like dirt in front of the men again should he call him out? *As usual, I don't know what to do, but I haven't forgotten First Sergeant Billy Martin's arrogance that morning in the orderly room—and here it was again with the Jeep seat snub.*

So far, his big triumph had been keeping the door open between their respective offices and hooking up the phone. The victory was short-lived; now he had to listen to Martin bray and badger and snap at the troops every day: "Don't ever set foot in my orderly room unless yore mammy's dyin'. Y'all understand, troop?"

"My mother's dead, First Sergeant."

"Tough tittie and no excuse. Get out-a-here!"

Everything was *his*. His hallway. His orderly room. His mess hall. His vehicles. From Margolin's point of view, the first sergeant never worried about the men. They were the easiest to replace.

Margolin's small encroachment on Martin's territory—keeping the door open—may have signaled the first sergeant to be on the alert. More than a decade as an enlisted man had not prevented him from learning a trick or two in dealing with uppity second louies. When Margolin used the officers' latrine across the hall from the orderly room, Martin would enter, whistling, and then yank the locked stall door. Margolin never came up fast enough from reading his Sunday *Los Angeles Times* to warn the NCO he was there, although he knew First Sgt. Billy Martin knew he was there.

"I'm in here, First Sergeant."

"Didn't see you, sir." Martin would reply then fart loudly, wash his hands, and leave. Margolin never brought up the fact it was the officers' latrine. Defiance did not come easy to him.

The two men, the veteran and the novice, were at war. A false war perhaps, an undeclared war, but nevertheless a war.

Margolin planned to win the war, but he wanted to win without pulling rank, he wanted to win Martin's heart, if he had one. A fool's errand, he knew, but he still wanted to try. *My Uncle Ziggy would have advised me to sue.*

Their part of the convoy pulled into a Texaco station on the outskirts of Laurinberg, just above the South Carolina border. "Gas up and piss break," announced Sgt. Wisnewski in the parking lot. He rode shotgun in the deuce-and-a-half that Pfc. Mangiameli drove. In the canvas-covered back were CP tents, duffel bags, and about ten headquarters troopers. A line formed at the rest room. Some of the men wandered over to Clyde's, an unpainted roadside café, where pecan jelly and candy appeared to be specialties.

Second Lieutenant Seymour Margolin uncurled himself from the cramped back seat and followed Martin toward the café. Motz stayed with the Jeep to gas up. He turned down Margolin's offer to bring him something.

Margolin was a step behind Martin as he opened the screen door. They both heard, "What in the hell you mean you ain't servin' him?"

"Y'all heard me right, boy."

Banuelous had asked the question. He stood with Breslin and half a dozen other soldiers. In between stood Wise and his pal Carter, the only two Negroes in the place. Wise had his fresh Pfc. stripes on. Carter was a veteran Spec/4.

"You want us to turn this place into a disaster area, old man?" Banuelous worked his shoulders like a boxer warming up in the ring.

"Y'all go do what y'all like. I ain't supposed to serve no one my boss don't want me to."

Wise looked around and suggested they forget it. Craven and some of the other Negroes who had more experience on the North Carolina highways had not bothered to come in. They used the rickety vending machines at the gas station.

Breslin stopped Wise, "Wait, man." and asked for the boss.

"He ain't here."

Martin pushed his way forward. "What-in-the-hell's-goin'-on-here?"

The group loudly protested the man refused to serve Wise and Carter. Carter didn't say a word, he just stared at the man refusing him service.

"At ease!" ordered the first sergeant. They shut up.

Martin moved next to Wise. He glanced around and stared at the red-faced older man behind the counter who, he realized, was holding a knife. "Y'all don't want to serve these two soldiers?" Some of the men grinned. They anticipated Martin jumping into the cat's shit.

"I can't. Boss's orders."

"Y'all just followin' orders?"

"That's right, Sir."

First Sergeant spun around in one of those mechanical moves he did so well in the orderly room and announced, "This man's only doin' his job. Same as y'all." He turned to Wise and Carter. "Y'all have someone bring somethin' out to y'all." Settled. He pushed his glasses back on his nose and waited.

The men were silent. Carter nodded in affirming what he expected. Breslin said he wasn't hungry.

"That's enough, soldier. Everyone get what they want and clear out." Martin moved toward a stool.

"No, that's not enough, First Sergeant."

Margolin had seen enough and knew about bigotry and it wasn't going to happen to his men. *His men*, he said to himself for the first time. His anger made him speak out without thinking, worrying, and weighing options.

The men looked at the lieutenant standing at the screen door. He felt the pressure of their desire for some better solution. "If Pfc. Wise and Specialist Carter can't eat here, none of us will."

"Cool," said Banuelous among the murmuring of agreement.

Margolin stepped toward the counter. "Are you going to serve our fellow soldiers? Soldiers in your country's Army?"

"I can't, mister."

"You've just been put off-limits. No one eats here and tell your boss he's being permanently put off-limits to all military personnel. First Sergeant, move the men outside." Margolin went to the door wondering what he'd do when the first sergeant took a seat and ordered a Nehi.

"Y'all heard the lieutenant. Move out!" The anger in Martin's voice was not directed at the counter man.

All the way to the Jeep, Margolin grinned. *He did it*. And now, if necessary, he was prepared to argue over the front seat like high school kids preparing to cruise Ventura Boulevard on Friday night. The rules were on his side. Martin had to obey him in front of the men if he wanted his own orders met. He would practice this more often.

Motz, unaware of what just happened, sat behind the wheel of the Jeep. When Margolin opened the passenger door, the Pfc. reached to pull back the seat.

"It's OK, Motz. The first sergeant's going in the back." He sat on the seat and kept the door half open. Motz didn't say a word; the first shirt would go rammy if the lieutenant tried this.

The first sergeant settled with the Texaco man and returned to the Jeep. *His* Jeep.

The moment the first sergeant reached the door, Margolin pushed it open and climbed out and pulled the passenger seat forward for Martin to squeeze in the back.

"Sir, if y'all gonna take my seat I'll ride on one of the trucks."

"Suit yourself, Sergeant Martin," replied Margolin and for the first time not using his rank when he addressed him. "We both know this seat goes to the ranking man."

Martin nodded, his mouth in a sour twist. "Rank before age and experience." He saluted and walked over to Wisnewski's truck and banished Mangiameli to the back. He climbed behind the wheel and said three words to Wisnewski. "Jew boy lieutenant."

Inside the Jeep, Motz failed to hide his ear-to-ear smile. "Should we go to the front of the convoy, sir?"

"You bet your ass we should," replied Margolin and hit the call button on the mike. "Striker One, this is Striker Three. Headquarter's element fueled and back on the road. Over."

The weekly Saturday morning inspection ritual was over. Men turned in their weapons and headed for the noon chow line. It was the end of May, and not too many men hightailed it off post. Payday was the first of every month and few soldiers had enough money to last the month. A private first class drew $99.23 a month. Jump pay added another $55. An individual's uniform cleaning bill could run as much as $20 a month or more unless a man was like Mangiameli who seldom 'changed the oil' in his fatigues. He hid out in the motor pool dispatch shack and saved every cent for his desperate weekend drives of 11 hours back and forth to Detroit.

Patterson locked the arms room after making sure every man's weapon was returned after inspection. On May First in northern hemispheres, the U.S. Army changed to summer khakis. Patterson's were tailored to fit his trim body. A Presidential Citation with cluster, awarded to the 504th in World War II, was pinned over his right breast pocket. Over the left pocket were his National Defense ribbon and Expert M-1 Badge. Centered on top of those were his Jump Wings. New Pfc. stripes on both sleeves. Over his shoulder and through the right epaulet, he wore the light blue braid that signified infantry.

A loud voice from the anteroom on the other side of the closed counter doors called, "Who's the M-M-I-C around here?"

Patterson opened the Dutch door top to find a stocky Pfc. in tightly tailored fatigues with half an unlit cigar stub in his mouth leaning on the counter as if he lived there.

"What's up, man?" asked Patterson.

The man slapped the counter. "Need to draw me some linen and field gear. I've just been railroaded out of the 'Oh-Five to this route step outfit." The name on his fatigues read 'McBride.'

"You're in the right place." Patterson nodded for McBride to follow him inside the supply room. Patterson produced the DA-121, the field gear issue form and the company bedding form, and moved around to collect the items. McBride said he didn't need all the field gear—helmet liner, web belt, canteen and cover, first aid pack. He had his own which he used for guard mount, and he then declared himself the sharpest soldier in the entire 82nd Airborne if not all the Armed Forces of the free world. Patterson found the man entertaining and likeable.

McBride explained he was the best machine gunner in Hotel Company of the 505th Airborne Infantry Regiment and could not understand coming to the 504th with all that devil-in-baggy-pants bullshit. And on top of it all: "They put my STRAC ass in a headquarters company where they soldier like a truck load of dead babies." It was going to be fun watching the first sergeant shut him up.

Patterson asked, "What's M-M-I-C mean?"

"Main-Motherfucker-In-Charge, Pfc. How long you been in the war? All day?"

"What platoon you in?"

"Sergeant 'Ski said Headquarters." Before Patterson could finish issuing the gear, they heard shouting outside; it sounded like a fight.

Patterson led McBride up the rear supply stairs to the mess hall entrance. On the porch, two men were going at each other. Banuelous and Broomfield.

It had been a long time coming. Banuelous had wanted to try Broomfield from the first day they had gone to supply to draw their bedding and Broomfield had pulled new-guy chicken-shit stuff on them. Patterson persisted in telling Banuelous what a good guy Broom was, but Banuelous always cracked on Broomfield being a boxer. A tough guy. Broomfield, too polite, usually smiled and waved him away.

Not today.

Banuelous danced and feinted around a stoic Broomfield. Each time he threw a punch, Broomfield flicked it off like a horse's tail sweeping its rump. Broomfield's overseas cap remained on his head.

Patterson and McBride joined the crowd. The majority shouted encouragement to Broomfield. Most men were too cautious to root for Banuelous. Broomfield might hear them.

Patterson joined Mangiameli and Breslin and asked how it started. Mangiameli explained, "Sergeant Webster came up to me in the chow line and tells me I missed last month's payment. I says, I couldn't help it. Webster says, you know how he talks, I don't want to turn your knickers inside out or some shit like that."

Banuelous attacked with a fury of blows. A surprise left stung Broomfield in the throat. He actually backed up and the crowd held their breath. Banuelous paused then swung again and again, the blows falling on Broomfield's thick forearms and shoulders. The corporal's overseas cap did not move.

Mangiameli continued his explanation. Banuelous told Webster and Broomfield to leave him alone. He'd pay them when he had the money. Webster said something like, "'You're missing the point, old chap.' and Banuelous replied, 'I ain't missin' dick-shit.'"

And it started. "Let's break it up!" shouted someone.

Patterson realized it was McBride. That took a lot of guts for a new man to shout, then he realized McBride was joking.

"Go ahead," encouraged one of the many diners who had left their meals to come out and watch. The KPs were there. Sidney the Cook. Men across the grass at Able Company watched. Former Corporal Brookes who lived in the pup tent between the buildings wasn't there. He had been dishonorably discharged six weeks earlier.

The only company officer—Lt. Margolin—and the first sergeant had left immediately after inspection. The mess sergeant was on pass, so Sfc. Webster might have been the ranking if not the only senior NCO around. He should have been breaking up the brawl, but he looked at the fight as a business opportunity and to inspire those who borrow from him to pay back promptly. The supply sergeant offered two-dollar bets that Banuelous would not last another minute. He checked his watch, looked up, and announced, "Starting now, gents." There were no takers.

Suddenly, Banuelous looked tired. His arms dropped and he stepped back. Broomfield ducked right, weaved left, and shot a left cross from nowhere to pound Banuelous' temple. He fell backwards, but caught himself against the railing. Broomfield gave him a moment to think about the punch. Banuelous recalled Patterson warning him more than once not to rile up Broomfield, he was a great guy, but he might just rip out Banuelous' heart.

Banuelous made up his mind: if he was going down, he was going down swinging.

Banuelous stepped forward and raised his fists. He swung. Again, Broomfield endured the punches, which no longer carried any force. The cap, undisturbed, stayed low on his forehead.

Banuelous looked at his right hand and shook it as if checking to see what wasn't working. He then came in close and tried to knee Broomfield.

Broomfield pushed him backwards with one hand then followed with a right hand that caught Banuelous in the center of the forehead. He reeled backwards. The men on the stairs did not catch him, but parted to let him stagger, slip, grab then fall over the railing onto the grass and land on his ass.

He sat, legs spread, head in hands, and did not try to get up. Blood from his nose seeped through his fingers onto his sleeves.

At the top of the stairs, Sgt. Webster took Broomfield by the arm. "Easy, Broom. You might harm the lad." Everyone laughed.

Patterson worried Banuelous' knife might appear. Banuelous rose slowly. No knife, but he pulled off his web belt and said, "OK, motherfucker, here we go." Patterson knew the religious Broomfield did not especially appreciate that particular expression.

Banuelous wrapped most of the belt around his right hand, leaving the sharp buckle free.

Broomfield pulled away from Webster. "Start saying your prayers, sucker."

"Come on, chump. I'll cut you a new asshole." He swung the buckle and charged, slashing, trying to catch Broomfield mid-step on a stair.

The buckle disappeared into Broomfield's fist. With it, he lifted Banuelous up then forced him to his knees like a disobedient dog. Holding onto the buckle he hit him twice. Banuelous slumped, only Broomfield's hold on the buckle kept him up. Slowly, the belt unwound and Banuelous went to his knees. His loud moan announced he was finished.

Broomfield bent over and wrapped the belt loosely around Banuelous' neck, then stood up and said, "If you ever talk like that again I'll hurt you."

Webster and Broomfield went down the supply room stairs. On the way down, Broomfield straightened out his cap.

"Ten more!" called the Charge of Quarters who resumed his responsibility for the chow line. The men reformed and began entering ten at a time.

Banuelous, uniform stained with blood and grass and holding the railing for support, looked around, wiped his nose on his sleeve, and smiled. It was a grin of celebration. He bragged, "In a real fight I'd kill him."

"You're fuckin' nuts, Jim," said Mangiameli.

"Sure you would," encouraged Breslin, "and I'm meeting Kim Novak at the Canopy today."

Banuelous flexed and shook his right hand. "I hope I didn't break it again. The fuckin' dude's made of cement."

"Hey," called Patterson, "catch this." He held up Banuelous' buckle; the heavy gauge brass was bent like an opened bottle top.

Chapter 6

Parades were the division's June objective.

Instead of the usual Saturday morning inspections, the division hosted the retirements of several generals. A general deserved a parade even if no one ever heard of him and he wasn't a paratrooper; it wasn't like Jumping Jim Gavin or Max Taylor were retiring. Parades for those Airborne heroes would have been welcomed.

The regiments marched on the hot asphalt down Ardennes Street and Gruber Road, sweat darkening their starched tan khakis. Polished OD helmet liners, web belts with bayonets, and full canteens added to the heat. They stood in large battalion formations at parade-rest or attention for hours under cloudless Carolina skies while nameless generals droned on. Their ranks simmered across Pike Field like scorched wheat on a parched Kansas prairie. The magnified sun burned the metal parts of their weapons, making barrels and trigger housings too hot to touch.

Men grew thirsty. More than a few fainted. Those who did not faint during the ceremony had ample opportunity on the return march. It was a long sweltering uphill.

By the third parade, the speeches sounded identical. Some men tried surviving the potent heat by putting cold beer in their canteens. By the time they had a chance to drink, the beer was warm and they became sick. Once one man threw up, another would. And another—then pass in review.

Wide ranks of men, squads, platoons, companies, were commanded right-face. Guidons in front of every company rose and fell with each command.

Sousa's *Washington Post* played; the standard of the military and football music America cheers.

"Forward, march!"

The entire division stepped off in one motion. They headed for the first far corner of vast parade ground where they executed a left-turn—column-lefts do not work with such long ranks—then continued 150 yards where they made another left-turn. This maneuver put the men in a straight line past the reviewing stand. As the final left-turn started, some troops still hadn't completed the first left-turn. Those men, usually the shortest men in the companies because parade formations always had the tallest men to the front, ended up running to catch up, weapons at right-shoulder-arms, bayonets flapping against their legs, helmet liners bobbing or falling off. A few tripped, sprawling on the dusty field, and were run over by the following ranks.

The spectators never noticed this crack-the-whip chaos, but it was very noticeable to the NCOs in ranks who shouted continually, "Close it up! Close it up, goddamnit!"

At last, the columns straightened out and the men paraded past the reviewing stand, snapping their heads right on the eyes-right command as they passed the American flag and the retiring general of the day to the tune of "All-American," the division's theme song. They marched right off the field and headed up the incline of Gruber Road, their M-1 rifles feeling like burning railroad ties. More men fainted or dropped out. Slump-shouldered stragglers walked slowly behind the formations, rifles held casually in one hand, the fading cadence of those still marching reminding them they could not keep up.

At various points along the street, regiments peeled off to their respective areas. And then the Saturday parades stopped as quickly as they started.

The day before the Fourth of July weekend, the entire division went on alert. Cots were set up in the day rooms for the enlisted men who lived off-post. The troops were restricted to their unit areas. No TV or radios allowed. No phone calls. The barracks regulars suffered; the NCOs who normally went home at night stayed around to order them into another GI party or inspection or police call.

Headquarters platoon spent most of the holiday weekend rigging heavy drop in the motor pool under Master Blaster Sfc. Wisnewski's critical eye. Sgt. 'Ski bragged he'd attended every Airborne school the Army had. If necessary, he liked to state, he could rig, "fuckin' sand in a fuckin' sieve."

It was Breslin who noticed the gear they were piling on pallets was not the usual ammo boxes filled with sand. It was real ammo and real medical equipment. Was the alert genuine? Rumors flew.

McBride figured they were on their way to China to take back the mainland. Motz predicted an attack on Algeria to help DeGaulle. The two men argued their points while no one paid attention. Motz had not been happy since McBride joined the platoon; the outspoken Pfc. draftee knew as much or more about the military and always let Motz know when he was wrong. It started when McBride questioned why Motz always carried the company guidon; that honor belonged the sharpest soldier. Motz pointed out he was the sharpest soldier as well as the tallest. McBride questioned how a company clerk could be qualified to head any formation other than a pencil-sharpening brigade. He should be the guidon bearer since he was the best ex-machine gunner in the Eighty-Deuce.

From that moment, there was no peace between the two men. Motz nicknamed McBride 'Horsecollar,' meaning he was a zero. The others became bored with their military competitiveness.

Breslin's choice for action was Cuba. They were going to help Castro.

Sergeant Wisnewski, sitting and sipping PX beer with the men along the thin strip of shade thrown by the maintenance building, didn't care where they went as long as he could make a combat jump and earn some medals. He had grown up regretting being too late for World War II and too young for Korea.

Mangiameli knew he was being screwed out of the long holiday weekend by the alert. "Jim, I want to go to Detroit City, that's what I want."

If they shipped out, Patterson hoped it would be warm. The chill of "All-American" remained deep in his bones.

The men predicted and guessed and bet and waited as they rigged pallets, cleaned trucks, Jeeps, and weapons; packed and un-packed, rushed to sit for hours by their deuce-and-a-half trucks along Grave Street in full combat gear. Smoking and waiting. Hurry up and wait.

When the chaplain showed up with his driver, Pfc. Breslin, to lead the men in Sunday prayer on the street they knew they were going. They went. Back into the barracks to hurry up and wait. And they waited two more days.

Late on the fourth night, after lights out, McBride took Breslin's, formerly Schmidt's, cheap radio into the latrine and listened to the news. The U.S. had invaded Lebanon the day they prayed on the street.

Much to Motz's chagrin, McBride turned on the squad bay lights and revealed the event. The next morning it was announced at reveille and a stand-down was ordered. They would not be needed. The invasion had gone peacefully.

All during the hot weather, while sweating through their backbreaking details, the men talked about getting away. Patterson convinced everyone they should head for the ocean—he had never been away from the ocean during the summer, and his descriptions of salt water's healing effects, a liquid designed to wash off the military stench and clear the mind of military thoughts, would make them new men. Like a baptism, added Breslin.

All they needed was a car.

"Jim, before I put this motherfucker in gear, I want two bucks a man."

"He's a goddamn Jew," accused Patterson.

"That's more than Judy charges niggers."

McBride elbowed Banuelous in the side. "Hey, Tony, she stopped fuckin' spades."

"Not more than two at a time."

They wore civilian Bermuda shorts, bathing suits underneath, T-shirts, and brought their shaving kits. The six young soldiers were squeezed into Pfc. Tommy Mangiameli's Buick in the enlisted men's parking lot, attempting to depart for Myrtle Beach. Mangiameli wasn't persuaded by the others' hopes of women and booze. Money was his motivation. Initially, he had wanted three dollars a man. Breslin convinced him two was a fairer price. He accepted that and now waited for the money to arrive in his hand.

"Come on, guys, we'll let the pimply jerk-off drive us around." Breslin pulled out his money. Patterson joined him and remarked it better be a round-trip fare. Patterson looked forward to the beach and the chance to see a few quiff. Sidney the Cook had advised him if a dude couldn't get laid there, he'd never get laid anywhere.

Motz, always frugal, suggested Mangiameli use the gas from his stash in the boonies.

"That's my Detroit juice, Jim," he replied as he finally received the tolls from Banuelous, McBride, and Motz.

They were almost on their way, then remembered to stop at the EM Club at Charlie Company, where they picked up a case of beer and two bottles of cheap wine. Now they were on their way.

The Buick swayed as it cruised along two-lane Highway 87 toward South Carolina. The swaying came from the car's odd alignment and Mangiameli's need to turn his head to look at anyone who talked to him. Every time he turned his passengers shouted to watch the road.

"I am, Jim, don't sweat it. You're nervous from the service."

"Tommy, slow down when you pass this car," demanded McBride who sat in the front passenger seat, a position he vehemently argued for with Motz who wanted the seat for his long legs. McBride reasoned he alone would attract women. A coin flip had settled the crisis.

The Buick pulled alongside the four-door '52 DeSoto carrying four older folks dressed up for a weekend visit to relatives in Elizabethtown. Banuelous, squeezed between Mangiameli and McBride, turned up the music as McBride leaned out the window into the warm breeze. A wet stub of a cigar hung from his mouth. He banged the half empty bottle of wine against the side of the Buick and announced, "Just paratroopers, good citizens, protectin' you from the dirty Commies!" and took a long swallow of wine, intentionally allowing some dribble down his chin. The occupants of the DeSoto stared straight ahead.

Motz stretched over the seat to pull McBride in. "You asshole! You're gonna give the division a bad name!"

Patterson, stuck in the middle of the backseat, may have been the only person to see the approaching truck in their lane. He bent over and picked up a can of beer, staying down, calculating the three bodies in the front seat would keep him alive.

McBride, laughing, allowed himself to be pulled back. "Give it a bad name! What the fuck you think it has now? We ain't in the Salvation Army, you know."

Mangiameli swung the Buick in front of the DeSoto as the truck passed, leaning slightly to the right. Patterson looked back; the truck carried watermelons. He used the church key to quickly punch two holes in his beer can and hissed in relief along with the air from the can. "Anyone see the truck?"

"What truck?" asked Mangiameli, turning as if it was coming up behind them.

"Kill me, Tommy, and I'll piss on your grave." threatened Patterson.

Breslin leaned against the front seat. "Please, please, turn down the radio and get some news on. Let's find out what's been happening in the world."

Banuelous considered himself in charge of the radio. He adjusted the dials to find Elvis Presley begging to be somebody's Teddy Bear, but he didn't lower the volume. Breslin reminded everyone Elvis had been drafted in June.

"I bet he won't go Airborne," said McBride.

Motz continued his complaint. "The people around here have to put up with too many military assholes. Why make it worse?"

"You callin' me an asshole?" challenged McBride and twisted to stare at Motz.

"He didn't stutter," said Breslin. "Anyone who waves a bottle out the window is a stone asshole." Breslin enjoyed fueling the fire between Motz and McBride. There was something about McBride Breslin did not like. It may have been McBride's cocky attitude and ready tongue that often beat Breslin to the punch line.

McBride slapped the dashboard and leaned toward the back seat. "Tommy, stop the car. Right here. I'm gonna take care of these leg motherfuckers."

Patterson shouted, "Sit down, Horsecollar, you're blockin' the road!"

"I ain't sittin'. I'm an ex-machine gunner and the baddest paratroop that ever wore a pair of Wings. I ain't takin'..."

McBride's voice was drowned out by a chorus of jeers about his Wings. He sat back, laughing.

When there was relative calm and Banuelous did lower the radio, Motz pointed out, "You fuckin' draftees are all alike. Piss and moan about the Army then after a couple of beers start talkin' about your Wings. You're no different than the Lifers who go on and on about World War Two. When you're old farts, you'll talk about the great days in the Eighty-Deuce. I'll tell you straight up, all draftees are scum. The last to do somethin' for their country. Forced to do somethin'. Everyone of you should be shipped out to a route step, non-jumpin' post like Fort fuckin' Dix."

Breslin volunteered. "Ship me, Colonel Steele."

Banuelous thought Motz sounded like General MacArthur.

"He's a leg. If I'm anyone, it's Jumpin' Jim Gavin."

"Hey, jump on this, Jumpin' Jim," said McBride, "I may be a draftee, but I'm still the best soldier in Headquarters and Headquarters Company—bar none."

"Where do we go? Where do we go?" shouted Mangiameli as they roared into a major intersection.

"Seven-Oh-One," called out Breslin then asked, "How in the hell do you make it to Ohio every weekend?"

"It's Detroit, Jim, and my hard-on points the way." Mangiameli jammed the gear into second to slow down then swerved, taking a wide left turn, shifting with his right hand and swinging the wheel with the suicide knob.

Patterson asked Breslin for a cigarette. "When was the last time you bought some?"

"I left them in my footlocker."

Breslin took a sip of beer and said, "Fucking Willie springs for a pack of smokes once a month then leaves them in his footlocker so they'll last another month. Fuck you. Buy some at the next stop."

"Go fuck yourself."

The Buick swayed for 100 yards, straightened, and moved on down 701, with Jim Eanes and the Shenandoah Valley Boys serenading the acres of scrub pine with "Your Old Standby."

The first few hours of Myrtle Beach were spent in the Bucket, the downtown bar where the college kids gathered every night after a day on the beach. Along with their first round of beers, Banuelous nearly started a brawl with Red, the day bartender and evening bouncer. Red did not like being called 'Chief' and Banuelous did not like being quietly threatened by Red. Quick thinking by Breslin and McBride turned the situation around; they simply told Banuelous if he fought he would be on his own. Red's large frame and boxer's countenance made a strong impression and, for once, Banuelous listened to his buddies and his fragile right hand.

Patterson left the bar on his own and wandered onto the beach, stripping off his Bermuda shorts and T-shirt, kicking loose his flip-flops, as he jogged toward the surf, his bathing suit sweat-soaked from the hot car ride. He fell face down into the first wave, deliciously discovering how he'd taken the ocean for granted until now. At home, he always knew where he was because he knew where the ocean was. At Bragg, he had no reference points except the wide Carolina sky and low rolling boondocks. He stayed underwater as long as he could, feeling his body cleansed from the oppressive heat of the supply room, KP, the sweating in dress khakis at the parades, and the heat reflecting off the dark asphalt when they rigged heavy drop in the motor pool waiting for a war to start. He felt free again. Almost.

Eventually, all except Breslin got together on the beach. They ran in and out of the surf, tossed the football McBride had brought along, fell asleep in the sun, ate hot dogs from one of the numerous food stands along Myrtle Beach's honky-tonk boardwalk, tried and failed to strike up conversations with small groups of girls, and returned to the Bucket at sunset.

Breslin had not moved from his seat at the bar. "All the sunshine I want is right here," he declared holding up a fresh tall boy Budweiser.

Now there was a band. The three-man group played piano, trumpet, sax, tambourine, and drums. All loud. Their repertoire was popular hits of the day like "Splish Splash" and "All Shook Up" as well as "Anchors Away," "The U.S. Air Force,"—also known as "Wild Blue Yonder"—"The Caissons Go Rolling Along," "The Marine's Hymn," and "Dixie." At some point in the evening, those were the only songs played, and the respective military men sang along while others booed their attempts.

After many "Dixies," the final "Dixie" of the evening arrived. It reminded Motz of a Confederate burial service at Antietam. Everyone stood up, most with too much to drink, and solemnly sang their hearts out, particularly those from the South.

The Bucket shut its doors at midnight. The men of Headquarters Company found themselves on the sidewalk in the humid summer night without a place to stay.

"I should've gone to Detroit, Jim," complained Mangaimeli. "I'd be with Judy right now."

"If the line wasn't too long," reminded Banuelous.

Mangiameli, filled with beer, stood up for his girlfriend. "You say that shit all the time, Tony. I'll kick your ass one of these days."

"What's wrong with right now?" Banuelous and Mangiameli stood face to face.

A Myrtle Beach police cruiser pulled up and shined the spotlight on the small group. "Everything OK here, fellas?"

"Yes, sir," replied Breslin. "Say, you know a cheap motel around here?"

"We've got some cells still half full, but it's early yet."

"No thanks," said Motz.

"One thing, boys, don't be sleepin' on the beach. We'll pick y'all up and book y'all and your unit won't like that. See y'all." The cruiser quietly moved along the street.

"What in the hell do we do, Jim?" worried Mangiameli.

McBride had the answer. They'd chip in for a motel room. Two guys in the car get the room then come back and pick up the rest of them. Between the car and the room there'd be plenty of space. And that's what they did after four attempts at finding a place with vacancies. The Ocean View Inn had no ocean view as it was three blocks off the main drag, but if you stood in the middle of the street you could see a sliver of water at the horizon.

They woke up feeling sunburned and like they'd been rolled in sand. After arguing about who showered first—Mangiameli won because he had the car keys—they found a Waffle House. The cheap hot food cheered them up and they joked about the grits. Motz pointed out the food wasn't as good as Sgt. Potter's, but close.

Breslin sat on the boardwalk waiting for the Bucket to open while the others headed for more beach time. They spent a long day in and out of the ocean, acquiring more sunburn and actually talking to three girls from High Point, North Carolina, who did not think servicemen were jerks; their brothers and fathers had been in the military. They even shared the girls' blanket and treated them to Dairy Queens.

Motz forgave them for not being Airborne.

Just after sunset, they picked up Breslin and started back. The Buick sped north along the narrow South Carolina blacktop, its headlights illuminating the tall pines on the long curves. Patterson, next to Mangiameli, enjoyed the discomfort of the dried salt water on his skin and light-headedness from the beers they sipped along the way. He coached himself to be ready to grab the wheel the moment the Buick left the road. Next to him, still riding shotgun, McBride rested his head on the open window frame.

Warm wind rushed into the car offering little relief from the humid night. In the back, Motz slept with his long legs tucked against the front seat. Banuelous and Breslin, directly behind Patterson and McBride, talked in low whispers.

"What the fuck you guys doin'?" Mangiameli turned with his question.

Patterson warned him again to keep his eyes on the road. "Willie, lend us your lighter and roll up the windows."

McBride mumbled and leaned his head back as Patterson reached across him to roll up the passenger side window.

Mangiameli complained it was too hot with the windows up. "Then get a car with air-conditioning," demanded Banuelous.

Patterson dug out his '04 lighter and passed it over his head without taking his eyes off the road. He silently urged the car along, wanting to get back for a shower and his military cot. Sleeping on the mattress on the floor last night between Mangiameli and Banuelous had not been fun.

Breslin leaned over the front seat. "Try this." He passed over a roll-your-own cigarette and dropped the lighter into Patterson's lap. Patterson looked at Breslin.

"Try it."

"What is it?"

"Horseshit rolled in paper," said Banuelous.

Patterson took a small drag.

McBride stirred. "What in the hell stinks?"

"Mary Jane, *ese*," explained Banuelous.

Patterson jerked the cigarette away from his lips as if it was poison. A reefer. In his hand!

"Take another drag," coached Breslin, "this time hold it deep in your throat as long as you can." Breslin spoke like he'd been smoking marijuana for years; Banuelous had just taught him how.

"You sure?" Patterson was not in a hurry to become a drug-crazed maniac.

"It's just tea, *ese*. Go ahead."

Patterson followed along, held the smoke and waited for the fireworks. All he did was cough until he had tears in his eyes.

"See," said Banuelous, "it's nothin'. Mac?"

"Fuck you. I heard that shit eats up your brain."

Mangiameli's hand came off the wheel. "My turn."

Patterson hesitated to pass over the smoke. "Come on, Jim, I'm doin' all the work here," he argued.

Reluctantly, he handed over the cigarette and said, "You crash you'll never see Judy again."

"This is nothin', Jim, you should drive to Detroit with me some weekend. I can kill a case of beer."

Mangiameli took a long drag and passed the smoke over his shoulder to Banuelous. "Come on, Mac," urged Banuelous.

"Is that really a reefer?"

"It ain't a Lucky Strike, *ese.*"

"Where'd you get it?"

"Couple of deuces in the company sell a little," said Mangiameli.

"I'm scared of it," admitted McBride.

"I don't believe it," said Breslin. "The best ex-machine gunner in the Eighty-fucking-Deuce is scared of a little Mary Jane."

"I need a good cigar. That shit's for Mexican pimps and niggers in purple suits."

Banuelous warned McBride about Mexican pimps; they might cut him a new asshole.

The four smoked the cigarette until it was too small to hold. Breslin flipped it out the window. Everyone stayed quiet for a long time except for Johnny Cash who could hear "the train a-comin'/ rollin' round the bend/ And he ain't seen sunshine/ since he don't know when/ He's stuck in Folsom Prison/ and time keeps draggin' on..."

When the song ended, Patterson asked, "You know, gettin' out will be just like gettin' out of prison. What're you guys gonna do when you get out?" No one said anything.

Breslin rummaged in the beer carton and produced the last two warm beers. He opened them without spraying a drop and passed them around then offered his thoughts.

"I'd like to just keep going tonight. Stay on the road like Dean Moriarty in *On The Road*. Be always drivin' someplace."

"I can dig it," said Patterson who had no idea who Dean Moriarty was.

Mangiameli knew exactly what he would do. During Christmas leave, he planned to marry Judy and bring her back to Bragg. After he got out, her old man would sponsor him into the autoworker's union. "Those cats make some big bucks. He's got a boat and trailer and he takes off every weekend to fish."

Patterson knew his city maintenance job waited, but he didn't want it anymore. "I'd like to do somethin' different. I saw a movie once about sponge fishin' in the Florida Keys. It was called *Twelve Mile Reef*..."

"A twelve-mile reefer could blow your brains out," interrupted Banuelous. Everyone laughed.

"...and the cat had a boat and he wore cool leather shit on his wrists," continued Patterson with his eyes closed as he recalled the aqua green waters in the movie. "Have a boat and go to warm places."

"You'll never catch my Mexican ass in a lettuce field again," vowed Banuelous who rarely ever spoke of his past.

"Let me have that lighter again, Willie."

"You got another one, Jim?" Mangiameli turned around to claim the first smoke hadn't bothered him at all. Everyone agreed. Banuelous thought it was bad weed.

Breslin lit the cigarette, took a drag, and passed it to Banuelous. "What were you sayin', Willie?"

"I can't remember. All's I know it would be cool to have a boat and move around cool warm places like Florida."

Banuelous projected a career in armed robbery for him. "Easy coin."

Breslin admitted he really wasn't sure what he wanted to do, keeping his secret about the priesthood to himself, and added he could always go back to college.

"College sucks," said Patterson, recalling the stuck-up girls in Downbeach who went off to Glassboro and Trenton

State to become teachers. Some of them went to Ivy League schools, too. All he had wanted after high school graduation was a T-Bird. If there hadn't been a draft to face, he'd have it by now.

Breslin said, "I know that. A cat named Billy Faulkner once said education, at best, makes a man unfit for work." He leaned forward to take his turn on the smoke. "You got to remember a man needs routine. A perspective to know where he came from and where he's goin'. College can do that. It won't make you a lot of money, but it gives a perspective."

"You know how I cry about per...perceptives," said Banuelous and his pals made fun of his inability to talk straight. "Up yours. I ain't high, assholes."

Motz stirred and twisted his cramped legs. Breslin blew a cloud of smoke in his face. Motz smiled. "He's hooked," said Breslin.

"You fuckers are gonna end up puttin' needles in your arms," warned McBride.

"Hey, go back to dreamin' about machine guns," joked Banuelous.

That was funny for everyone, but McBride. He rolled down the window. "Fuck you, guys."

Patterson asked Mangiameli if he was OK to drive.

"How many times do I have to tell you, Jim. This ain't nothin'. Dreamin' about machine guns! That's good." They all laughed again. Motz shifted as if waking up.

Breslin pointed out being squished next to Motz was like being next to an over grown spider. That was funny too.

Breslin and Banuelous leaned against the front seat to make it easier to share the cigarette. The four of them took turns smoking and didn't realize they were transfixed by the white line dashes in the middle of the road. Patterson, softly aloud, imagined the road speeding beneath the car and they were standing still. The others agreed.

The humid air spilling through the open windows gave the impression they were going faster than they were. The

Buick's bald tires roared along the rough macadam, rushing the six soldiers back to Bragg.

Patterson reached across Mangiameli and flicked the stub out the window. He turned up the radio.

"...the international scene. W-E-S-C, your country double station, the broadcasting company of the Carolinas will continue for another fifteen minutes of uninterrupted country music for those night owls out there..." Bob Miller and the Lonesome Pine Fiddlers came on to count stars and cold prison bars for twenty-one years.

Breslin asked suddenly, "Turn down the radio."

"It's just shit-kickin' music anyway," said McBride.

"Turn it down. Listen. I swear I hear singing or music out in the woods."

"It's my generator," explained Tommy.

"I'm telling you, something's out there."

Patterson turned down the radio. The car remained silent except for the rushing wind and the humming tires. "Hear it?"

"Are you serious?" asked Patterson.

"I swear to God."

"The weed's turned all you guys' minds to mush," accused McBride.

"Anyways, what we're saying," continued Breslin with the conversation that had been forgotten, "is after we're discharged we'll be on our own. That's big time. You're not a kid anymore. Society says sink or swim. You go for it and what'd you get? Look at Jimmy Dean. Dead, like that." He tried snapping his fingers and missed several times.

"I saw the wreck," lied Banuelous who lived near Salinas where the actor had crashed.

At Mangiameli's urging, Patterson held the wheel while the driver lit a Lucky Strike. With Breslin rambling along behind him and the Buick racing into the darkness, Patterson saw himself as a man unconnected. *Rushing nowhere without a goal.* To Bragg tonight, yes, but afterwards he was free to do anything. It was a feeling of relief and joy he'd never before experienced, but didn't know how to tell anyone.

Breslin described Bragg as a giant magnet pulling them back. "Sometimes I feel we'll never break away. Schmidt did, but he'll get caught some day and have to make up the time. I don't want any bad time, I just want to get it over with. No matter what we say or do, this time next year we'll still be at Bragg. I sometimes think it'll never let us go."

The men thought about that as they watched the headlights search the night for the curving highway.

Breslin continued, "You know what I want. What I really want. Not money. Not a nice car. I want to spend summer mornings watering the sidewalks in front of a flower store on Walnut Street. Just stand there spraying down the sidewalk and smelling the start of the summer day while the rest of the world chases Moloch. 'I'll grow old, I'll grow old/ I shall wear the bottoms of my trousers rolled...'"

"Man," said Banuelous, "you know how I cry about Moloch. Two tears in a bucket and a hi-de-ho fuck it."

Mangiameli flipped his cigarette onto the road where it shredded into tiny meteors by the wind and highway. The Buick wound on toward Bragg, carrying the weary young soldiers hypnotized by the zipping white lines disappearing under the swaying Buick, and serenaded by Lester Flat and Earl Scruggs picking and strumming about a cabin in Caroline.

*Sir, the Twelfth General Order is to make
damn sure I remember the first eleven.*

Army expression to emphasis the Eleven
General Orders.

Chapter 7

Every day, with the exactness of the solar system, regimental guard mount occurred at the parking lot in front of regimental headquarters at 1600 hours. Twenty-one enlisted men from the various companies stood a detailed inspection of uniforms, gear, and weapons. The uniform was khaki in the summer and olive drab wool in the winter. Inspection was conducted by the Officer of the Day and the Sergeant of the Guard. The sharpest soldier in the formation earned Colonel's Orderly and did not walk a post that night. The next day, the orderly served in regimental headquarters, running errands for the sergeant major and commanding officer.

Colonel's Orderly was an honor. A letter of commendation went in a man's 201 personnel file. Sometimes, a three-day pass was awarded. Being selected Colonel's Orderly was called being The Man.

Preparing for a detailed inspection taught men discipline and heightened their spit and polish abilities: spotless weapon, web belt and canteen cover scrubbed clean, canteen full and no sign of rust, and poncho folded exactly over the web belt in the back. Boots highly polished and khaki uniform clean and starched. Each soldier prepared to answer questions about the M-1 rifle, to know the Eleven General Orders and the Chain of Command, and, in addition, to spout local knowledge like PX hours and parking regulations. It took time to prepare and placed a man in the position of being embarrassed in front of the platoon. If a trooper did not measure up to regimental standards he was dismissed and sent back to his company for some type of punishment.

No one looked forward to guard duty—except gung-ho types who vied for The Man.

Some of the men of Headquarters Company drew guard duty on Labor Day weekend. They weren't happy. The every-day soldier looked at regular guard duty as another military pain-in-the-ass and an assignment on a long holiday weekend it became a monumental blockade to a host of good times like going home, hitting Myrtle Beach, or just spending an extra night away from Bragg. The good news was Sergeant First Class Richard Wisnewski, their company operations sergeant, was the Sergeant of the Guard and Second Lieutenant Seymour Margolin would serve as the Officer of the Day. The headquarters troopers knew who would be scrutinizing them.

McBride convinced Patterson, Mangiameli, and Banuelous to carry him from the squad bay to the formation in front of the company to keep his starched khaki trousers stiff. He planned on being The Man. Pfc. Motz immediately called foul for getting help. He assumed he would be The Man again as he usually was. Wisnewski conducted his own, informal inspection prior to marching them to headquarters; he didn't want his charges singled out for sloppiness, gigged for missing buttons, loose threads, stained collar brass, and lackluster boots. The only person he reprimanded was Banuelous. The sergeant took off Banuelous' helmet liner and his curl dropped across his forehead.

"Closer haircut, cool cat, and meet us at regiment." Banuelous knew better than to argue.

On the march to regimental headquarters, Wisnewski allowed the men to talk, even encouraging the competition between Motz and McBride. The men practiced their general orders and military knowledge by asking first McBride then Motz what certain general orders were and who was the Secretary of the Army and the weight of an M-

1. Motz and McBride barked their replies in crisp military fashion. As they marched up to the building, McBride declared he would run over his mother with a deuce-and-a-half to be The Man. Motz said he'd be The Man without doing that.

"You don't want it bad enough then, Pfc. Dud."

In front of headquarters, Wisnewski ordered them to halt and stand at ease with the other '04 troops waiting for guard mount. Motz and McBride, facing one another, immediately broke into the manual of arms. Left-shoulder-arms. Right-shoulder-arms. Inspection-arms. Each performed some spinning tricks and Motz did a Queen Anne salute, which requires spinning the rifle back and over the shoulder and then kneeling. "Not bad," said McBride, "you must've gone to military school, recruit."

"I'll out soldier your leg ass any day of the week and twice on Sunday."

"Who you callin' a leg, pig pen?" And it went on.

From the small Officer of the Day alcove inside the first floor of regimental headquarters, Margolin watched the troops gather in the parking lot. Knowing some of the men allowed him to relax somewhat, but he still realized he must stay on his toes. The young soldiers were quick with their weapons, executing inspection-arms, and smart with their replies to his questions. His one and only special order for the 504th area, and it was always the same, was to ensure Col. Steele's Jeep was present and accounted for in the motor pool. The requirement was to actually touch the vehicle and log in the moment.

Now it was 1555. Time for guard mount.

Margolin, wearing his best tailored set of khakis with a pistol belt around his waist and a real, unloaded .45 pistol and holster attached, walked down the stairs and started toward Sgt. 'Ski.

"Guard mount, fall in," commanded Wisnewski. Ten paces in front of the platoon of three ranks, the lieutenant met the sergeant.

Wisnewski saluted. "Guard mount present and account-ed for, sir."

Margolin returned the salute. "Prepare the men for in-spection, Sergeant."

Wisnewski saluted again. "Yes, sir." He did an about-face and ordered, "Open-ranks, march!"

The front rank took one step forward, the rear rank one step back. They held their rifles by the upper stacking swivels a millimeter off the ground along their right legs as they adjusted their ranks and returned to the position of attention, their rifle butt plates tapping the ground as they settled.

Wisnewski looked over the men then continued, "Dress-right, dress!"

In each rank, the men extended and held their left arms toward the men next to them while craning their heads hard right over their shoulders, aligning themselves on the junior NCOs who anchored the ranks.

They held that position until...

"Ready..." commanded the Sfc, "...front!"

Every man sharply dropped his arm and looked straight ahead, still at attention.

Wisnewski walked along the front rank to insure each man stood behind the man in front of him. "Cover down. Cover. Mangiameli, move left. Your other left. Cover, new man." Satisfied, Wisnewski marched to Lt. Margolin who had remained standing at attention in front of the for-mation.

He saluted. "Guard detail ready for inspection, sir."

Margolin returned the salute. "Thank you, Sergeant 'Ski. Let's go to work."

The lieutenant appreciated knowing this ceremony oc-curred at every Army post world-wide at this time of day. It was like participating in the changing of the guard at Buckingham Palace and he was the officer in charge. An officer with a pistol strapped to his side. The young lieu-tenant who had complained all through ROTC about guard mount when it was his assignment at summer camp now found himself enjoying its ceremony—a feeling he would never share with his old ROTC buddies growing soft in civilized NATO countries. Margolin welcomed the opportunity to go face to face with real soldiers. There was a rhythm to the ceremony. Right-face. Left-face. Inspection-arms. Take the weapon. Spin it up to catch the light in the barrel. Return the weapon. Order-arms. Step back. Right-face. Left-face again and again. The men were clean in their starched khakis, precise in their manual of arms, firm in their recitation of the Eleven General Orders, and polished in their drill.

Uncle Ziggy could go to hell. Lt. Margolin was an Airborne officer and liking it more every day. And the pistol on his side felt powerful even if it was unloaded and he hadn't fired one since ROTC summer camp.

Margolin and Wisnewski did not stop at every man. It was a spot check. Some men did the minimum to prepare. Some like McBride and Motz did the maximum. The lieutenant only gave a detailed inspection to those he thought wanted to be The Man or a soldier whose appearance was not up to '04 standards. When he stood in front of a man, it was easy to tell if he wanted the honor. The lieutenant used a number system to rate a man. One for the best. Ten for the worst. At the conclusion of each individual inspection, he whispered the number to Wisnewski who wrote it on the clipboard next to the man's name. No one in the front rank received a numerical designation, even though he stopped for long moment in front of a few troopers and asked for specific general orders.

The two men walked behind the first rank inspecting boot heels and haircuts. Neither the lieutenant or the sergeant noticed Motz and McBride in the second rank watching the inspection without moving their heads.

They began along the second rank. When they reached McBride, as the lieutenant did a left-face, the PFC.'s M-1 snapped up, his hand slapping the upper stock, the bolt jammed back, the weapon was ready. A perfect inspection-arms. McBride stared Margolin straight in the face. The lieutenant saw himself reflected in the man's low-riding helmet liner and the polished brass on his collars. His Wings had been polished so often they were worn down. Beneath his Wings was the expert marksman badge with attachments like miniature ladder steps showing he was also an expert in the machine gun, .45 pistol, rocket launcher, M-1 Carbine, Browning Automatic Rifle, and grenades. His gig line—the front buttons of his khaki shirt that ran through the center of the spotless web belt to align along the seam of his fly—was as straight as a ruler.

Here was a man who wanted to be Colonel's Orderly. The lieutenant wasn't too familiar with the relative newcomer.

"What's your sixth general order, PFC.?"

"Sir, my sixth general order is to receive, obey, and pass on to the sentinel who relieves me..." A snickering ran through the ranks.

"At ease," commanded the slightly grinning Wisnewski.

McBride's command voice sounded like he was shouting at the lieutenant.

Margolin accepted the defiance in McBride's attitude. Six months ago he would have been intimidated. McBride was acting like the smartest kid in class who snapped his fingers to get the teacher's attention. He got it.

Margolin slowly raised his hand to take the weapon. Intentionally slowly. McBride dropped the weapon and snapped his hands back as if to avoid a guillotine and never missed a word. "...the orders from the commanding officer, officer of the day, and officers and non-commissioned officers of the guard only, Sir!"

Margolin caught the expected quick drop, swung the shoulder stock in the air and looked through the barrel. "Immaculate."

"Affirmative, sir."

Margolin brought down the weapon to port arms and held it in front of McBride to take back. McBride stayed at a stiff exaggerated attention.

"PFC.?"

"Sir, you have to hand it back like I gave it to you."

"Good." Margolin spun the weapon into the correct position, making sure to slap the wooden stock for effect. He and other junior officers practiced often with a weighted sawed-off 2 x 4 in front of full-length mirror at the BOQ.

McBride pulled back the M-1 like a greedy child taking a toy, expertly thumbed the receiver, snapping shut the bolt. McBride brought the weapon to order-arms with precise practiced movements.

The lieutenant stepped back did a right-face then left-face to stand before the next man. He whispered to Wisnewski, "Two." while telling himself he did not want McBride to be The Man because of his arrogance.

During Patterson's inspection, the Pfc. mixed up his general orders, reciting the easy third one for the more difficult fifth. Mangiameli, as usual, could not stand still during his turn.

The lieutenant and sergeant reached the last man in the second rank; it was Pfc. Motz.

Motz took guard mount seriously, and the lieutenant knew it. He had chosen him as Colonel's Orderly the last two times they pulled guard mount together. Margolin enjoyed Motz's enthusiasm for all things military and suppressed the thought he would have made a great Hitler Youth. Motz executed a flawless, rhythmic inspection-arms.

"Pfc. Motz, what is your chain-of-command?" The lieutenant realized he had discovered the roadblock for McBride.

"Sir! The chain-of-command is Platoon Sergeant Wisnew..."

"From the top down, Pfc." He didn't want to seem too lenient.

"Yes, Sir." Motz did not sound off like McBride, but responded in firm, realistic tones. "President Eisenhower is Commander-in-Chief. The Secretary of the Defense is McElroy. The Secretary of..."

Margolin grabbed for Motz's M-1. The tall soldier, just as quickly, dropped it. Margolin caught it and turned it muzzle down, flicked open the butt plate and looked for dirt.

"...the Army is Wilbur Bruckner. General Maxwell Taylor is Chief of Staff. The Continental Army commander..."

"That's enough, Pfc." Margolin kept the rifle in his hands at reverse port arms and looked over Motz. He was spotless. Polished. Starched. Boots glistened like burnished coal. The first sergeant gave him guff every day and all Motz wanted was a transfer to a rifle company. He should be The Man. He offered Motz the weapon and the tall Pfc. snatched it away.

Margolin stepped back, made a right face, and walked behind the second rank with Wisnewski a step behind. Over his shoulder he whispered to 'Ski, "One."

They moved quickly along the third rank, stopping for close looks at only a few men. Banuelous was one of them. Sgt. 'Ski lifted off his helmet liner to check his haircut. The officer and sergeant smiled at the fresh crew cut. Banuelous did not.

The two leaders moved to the front of the formation and faced one another. Margolin said, "All squared away, Sergeant 'Ski, as usual."

"Yes, sir."

"We'll take Motz for Colonel's Orderly and McBride as his alternate."

"Yes, sir." Wisnewski saluted and Margolin returned it, did an about-face and headed back toward headquarters. With the inspection completed he wanted to write a few letters and study the Jumpmaster manual; he planned to earn the senior star on his Wings that came with completion of Jumpmaster School.

"Sir!" He turned at the bottom of the stairs.

Sergeant Wisnewski walked quickly toward him. Wisnewski informed him there had been a challenge. McBride wanted to face off with Motz.

"What's that mean, 'Ski?" This was new for the young lieutenant.

"Any man on guard mount can challenge the selection of orderly if he thinks he's better."

"What happens?"

"You re-inspect them."

The lieutenant did not appreciate the challenge; Motz deserved it on attitude alone.

"I'll make a suggestion, sir."

"I'm all ears, 'Ski."

The veteran suggested he would give them some close-order drill, then check their handkerchiefs and belt lengths.

"What's that prove?"

"Handkerchiefs have to be clean and have their laundry mark. Belt lengths can't be more than two inches past the buckle. Most troops don't ever have a handkerchief."

The young lieutenant thanked the sergeant for fixing another military problem and asked him to hurry up. "It's too damn hot to be hanging around here."

"Hotter than a fart in a furnace, sir."

"I'll remember that one, 'Ski." The two men walked back to the formation.

Except for Motz and McBride, Wisnewski dismissed the men. They headed for the shade cast along the front of regimental headquarters to watch the competition, then Wisnewski called the two soldiers to attention and commanded right-shoulder, arms. Their rifles came up, across their chests to rest on their right shoulders as if part of the same machine.

"Forward, march!" They stepped off together, away from the building and the other men. A few passers-by stopped; they understood the drama unfolding even if they did not know the participants. Men stood at headquarters windows for the show.

Wisnewski picked up the cadence. "Your left. Your left. Your left-right-left. To the rear, march! One-two-three-four, your left-right-left. To-the-rear, march. To-the-rear, march!" The marchers turned on dimes together.

"Left-flank, march! Right-flank, march! One-two-three-four. Left-right-left. Detail, halt!"

They were just about where they started. Neither had missed a step. They remained at perfect attention.

"Stand, at ease." Motz and McBride executed order-arms, bringing their weapons along their sides then re-laxed, their rifles held at an easy parade-rest leaning away from them. Each man placed his left hand in the small of his back.

"A good soldier always carries a clean handkerchief. Bring 'em out."

McBride smirked, confident he had won. He switched his muzzle to his left hand, reached into his back pocket and produced a neatly folded handkerchief with the laundry mark displayed. Motz, a little slower and not pleased at the challenge, extracted his own precisely folded handkerchief with the required laundry mark, M-9908. McBride shook his head as if to say it was impossible for Motz to have the correct handkerchief. They put away their handkerchiefs and waited.

Margolin let a sigh of relief slip out. Motz remained in the running. He wanted Motz to fix this new fellow's brashness and he knew he should not be thinking that way.

"Detail, attention," commanded Wisnewski.

The men snapped into position. Stiff. Chins out. Rifles held at the upper stacking swivels. Left hands along the left trouser seams. Heels together.

Margolin raised his hand to Wisnewski with a wait-a-minute gesture and asked, "Pfc. McBride, what's the weight of an M-1 rifle?"

"Sir, the weight of an M-1 rifle with full clip and sling is eleven and one-quarter pounds, sir." Margolin hid his disappointment and asked Motz what was the muzzle velocity of the M-1 rifle.

"Sir, the muzzle velocity of an M-1 rifle is twenty-eight hundred feet per second, sir." Margolin grinned slightly and shook his head. What or how could they...

"Sir, I better check their belt lengths."

The lieutenant waved him to go ahead; he was ready to award a tie.

Wisnewski stepped up to them, took their weapons, and directed them to loosen their belts. First, they had to undo their pistol belts that held the canteen, first-aid pack, and poncho. Each man carefully laid the pistol belt along the ground and undid their polished web belt buckles. The waiting men watching enjoyed the show.

Mangiameli wondered aloud if they were going to give them a short-arm check, the infamous penis exam for venereal disease. Patterson clumsily spun his weapon trying to learn the Queen Anne Salute as he waited. He was betting on McBride to win. Breslin voiced his opinion that McBride was too cocky, too knowledgeable to be a draftee; it was as if he was immune to the Army's wiles. "I hope he loses."

Even before McBride undid his buckle, Lieutenant Margolin knew from the man's slight snarl the belt was the regulation length. McBride actually brought out his handkerchief to cover the buckle so he would not smudge it. Motz's expression said it all; he revealed a length about two inches longer than authorized.

He gave Margolin a weak smile. "I've lost a lot of weight, sir."

As he entered headquarters, Lt. Margolin consoled himself. He had done all he could to help Motz or keep McBride from winning. The challenge was good experience.

"Lieutenant." Margolin stopped in the middle of regimental headquarters lobby. Surrounding him high on the walls were murals of the 82nd Airborne's military history. Sergeant York—a Medal of Honor winner from World War I, when no one thought about dropping men from planes—looked down on him. Drawings of infantry attacking, mass parachute drops, and tanks battled across colorful landscapes of Salerno, Sicily, and Normandy. There were large portraits of General Gavin, Colonel Ruben Tucker, and other decorated leaders. Trophy cases of awards and souvenirs lined the walls. Battle streamers hung from the many flags in the corner. The lieutenant often wandered along the artwork during guard detail after everyone went home and admired the display. Now, he looked at the stairs where Col. Steele descended like Buck Rodgers, commander-in-chief of the universe.

"Yes, sir." He did not salute; it was not required indoors.

"You're Officer of the Day, aren't you?"

"Yes, sir."

"What's your name again?"

"Margolin, sir."

"No, I mean your given name, Lieutenant. That odd..."

"Seymour, sir."

"Seymour, that's it." Steele smiled with joy hearing and saying the name. Perhaps glad such a nebbish name was not his.

Margolin did not remind Steele his nickname from Jump School was Mad Dog. He resolved in future meetings when Steele asked his name he would inject it with Mad Dog. He did want to please the colonel even if he did not like him; the man wrote his efficiency report.

"I watched guard mount, lieutenant."

Steele's bright blue eyes, somewhat shaded with thick dark eyebrows, gathered thunderclouds. No expression of a job well done would be forthcoming. The younger officer's position of attention suddenly became painful. "Yes, sir?"

"Why didn't you give every man a detailed inspection? You walked past some as if they didn't exist. Those men worked hard preparing for inspection. They take pride in their uniform and military readiness."

Margolin knew most considered guard duty another Mickey Mouse detail to be endured like KP, courtesy driver on payday, and policing up Bragg Boulevard after a weekend. He, on the other hand, enjoyed the strictness of the event. The inspections. The recitations. The handling of the weapons. It all reflected well on the regiment and the division.

Steele and he agreed to a point, but he knew only certain individuals looked forward to the inspection.

"Sir, I believe…"

"No excuse is all I want to hear, Lieutenant."

"Most of the men are from my company. They're sharp…"

"No excuse, Lieutenant."

"No excuse, sir." Margolin stared at the slight dimple in the center of Steele's magnificent chin. He concentrated on the dimple to keep his mouth shut and tried to subdue his embarrassment. Some enlisted men and lower ranking officers who worked in the building stood quietly in the background.

"If you know the men, Lieutenant," continued Steele, "all the more reason to be tougher on them. Let them know you play no favorites. Give an inch, Lieutenant, and you lose a mile." The dimple bobbed up and down with every word.

"Yes, sir."

"You're the honor graduate from your jump class. This regiment expects you to be a top-notch soldier. Do you understand?"

"Yes, sir."

"Carry on." Steele walked toward the double-door exit.

Margolin saluted his back and then wished he hadn't. He crossed to the cubbyhole OD's office and carefully closed the door. To hold his temper, he grasped the back of the chair and looked out the window toward the guard platoon marching toward the guardroom in Baker Company. *Beg-*

ging the colonel's pardon, he said to himself, *they are my men and I'll do whatever I please, goddamnit*. So shut up and move out smartly.

Steele crossed to his Triumph sports car in the parking lot.

"Why?" he asked in the little room. "Why me?" Simple. *I'm a Jew*.

Margolin did not want to believe it or think it or feel it and he did all three. He was a Jew lieutenant taking it from both sides, his first sergeant and the regimental commander. He didn't have to and he wouldn't.

Chutzpah. That would carry him as far as he let it. The word was a reminder of his people's magnificent history. Warriors. Leaders. Intellectuals. Artists. Rising above oppression. Triumphant. *Chutzpah*.

If he said it enough, it could become the magic word he needed to succeed.

Chapter 8

Sunday Fayetteville was quiet. Fall quiet as the final days of warm sunlight held off the approaching short gray days of winter. The bars were closed. Combat Alley deserted. On the last weekend of most months, the men of the division had little money remaining and stayed on post. Without the troops, Fayetteville looked like any other small town in North Carolina on a Sunday. Cars full of families visiting relatives, coming from religious services, or maybe on their way to Sunday dinners passed through.

The town could almost be called peaceful.

"Patterson!"

Patterson, smoking and leaning against a parking meter in front of the Christian Canteen, turned.

Sidney the Cook leaned out the window of his candy-apple '53 Olds coupe that rumbled with the richness of perking coffee and shouted, "Wanna get stroked and smoked?" His obscene offer shocked the late afternoon tranquility of Hay Street.

Patterson looked around. No one was staring at him. He replied, not too confidently, "Sure, man."

"Wait there." Sidney the Cook popped the clutch, caught a brief tire squeal, and zipped down the street, getting another squeak going into second.

Patterson watched the highly polished machine make a left turn on Winslow. Motz and Breslin were still in the canteen. Every end-of-the-month they stopped there for free Velveeta and tuna crustless sandwiches with Pepsis before sneaking into the Miracle Theatre. The canteen venture usually entailed a long conversation about salvation with one or more acne-covered proselytizer moving among the few freeloaders like sharks after prey.

Patterson left a little earlier to smoke and escape salvation. Now, he felt he had agreed to something he may not want.

Stroked and smoked! Everyone in the company knew Sidney the Cook was evil. He reminded Patterson of the deadly VD germ they saw in animated hygiene movies about venereal diseases that Lt. Margolin and the chaplain showed the troops. The cook and Patterson had become friendly because Patterson went into the mess hall several times a day for pitchers of coffee—pitchers he made sure he filled himself after the pissing-in-the-pot situation during his early days in the company. He could count on Sidney the Cook to have a fresh sexual adventure about girls that fucked dogs or 14-year girls on the Indian reservation near Mackall or another soldier's wife whose husband served on special duty in Korea.

Always fucking somebody or thing and always talking about it.

Sidney the Cook roared up and swung expertly into the curb. He gestured for Patterson to get in.

"I'm with two other cats," said Patterson with the hope his reluctance did not reflect in his voice.

Sidney the Cook sat high on a cushion. The front seat was all the way forward and he wore cowboy boots. He leaned over and wound down the passenger side window. "Cool, my man. The more the merrier. Where are they?"

How do you tell the most evil person you've ever known, who's asking you to be stroked and smoked, the two cats he waited for were in the Christian Canteen eating Velveeta sandwiches without crusts? Patterson hung onto the parking meter a little tighter and leaned toward the window. "So, what's the deal, man?"

"Man, like, I've got two hot-to-trot hookers waitin' three blocks from here. Screw your buddies, let's grab hat."

To his dismay, Patterson found himself interested. He could lose his virginity; however, he was also scared. Before he said another word, Sidney the Cook blew the horn and shouted, "Hey, mother-fuckers!"

Breslin and Motz came out of the canteen. Patterson played it casual. "He's got some whores lined up." Maybe his pals would turn down the idea. He'd do whatever they wanted to do, although it would be more fun to sneak in the movies like they always did on Sundays. Safer for sure.

Breslin wasted no time. "What's it gonna cost?"

"Probably three a piece."

"A piece—get it?" asked Breslin. "That's funny, Sid."

Both Motz and Patterson were quick to confess they didn't have enough money. Hearing each other's excuse sent the signal they were reluctant. Patterson was quietly glad.

Sidney the Cook wasn't going to make it easy for them. "I'll lend you the difference and buy the 'splo." Cooks were known to have money; it wasn't unusual for them to sell mess hall food to the civilian side.

"'Splo?" Breslin's interest tightened a notch.

"Lightnin'. White lightnin'. You know, corn whiskey."

Breslin opened the door and climbed into the back seat. "What the hell," he said. "We might as well look at them and get a Sunday drink for our troubles."

Motz indicated for Patterson to follow Breslin. Patterson protested. "Hey, man, I was here first. I get the coo seat."

"My legs are too long in the back."

Sidney the Cook said, "Get in the back, General, and don't say diddly-shit to these broads."

Patterson took the front seat and closed the door. "Nice car, man."

Pulling away, the Olds squealed rubber. Sidney the Cook speed-shifted into second for another tire yip. He checked the rearview mirror to ensure no Fayetteville gendarmes, as he liked to say, saw him.

Nice car, thought Willie Patterson. *Nice? Great car!*

He wanted to kick his feet with joy and pound the outside candy-apple, five-coats-of-clear-lacquer door where his arm hung in a cool style. He was riding high in a real snatch wagon, speeding down Hay Street in a dechromed '53 Olds coupe with dual exhausts and Richie Valens on the radio. He was in the cunt seat. The coo seat.

He was the big coo man. *Yeah, man, let's find those hookers.*

They pulled up and parked in the industrial end of Hay Street near Highway 301. No girls were visible. "Damn," said Sidney the Cook, "it couldn't have been no more than ten minutes."

Breslin suggested the hell with the broads just get the 'splo.

"They're the ones that know where to get the shit."

To pass the time, they smoked and listened to the radio. The Olds idled impatiently. Sidney directed Patterson to turn up the volume. When he touched the radio knob he lost the station. His efforts to retrieve the exact location were not successful. "It's all goddamn religious shit. It's Sunday," he claimed, to cover his coo-man-tuning ineptitude.

"That's my station, man," said Sidney and he pushed Patterson's hand away. With a deft touch, he found Marty Robbins dressed up in a "White Sport Coat (with a Pink Carnation)."

Patterson felt like he had crashed the plane.

Sidney the Cook asked Breslin and Motz what they were doing in the Canteen. "I used to bang this older skank up there, in the back, against the refrigerator while the jerk-offs out front were talkin' about findin' religion—there they are!"

Two Negro girls wearing inexpensive cloth coats were headed toward them. They looked like farm girls trying to dress up like city people. Neither was attractive. In fact, they looked chunky and were plain ugly.

Motz whispered in amazement, "They're spades!"

Sidney the Cook replied, "So what? It don't rub off." He cranked down his window. "Hey, sweetness!"

The girls cautiously approached the car. They both bent to look inside, their faces inches from a shocked Patterson who stared straight ahead as he lowered the window.

Sidney leaned across the seat. "Where in the hell did you go?"

"Where in the hell you been, cracker?"

"And you said they be only two," reminded the other girl.

"Two-three-four. What's the big deal?" The girls didn't reply. They stood up and had a private conversation.

Breslin leaned against the front seat to speak just past rigid Patterson. "Girls, we aren't out to take advantage of anyone. All of us don't want to...to...make personal advances, you know what I mean. But we sure would like some 'splo."

They both smiled and leaned to look in the car. "He's a gentleman," said the heavier girl named Gloria.

Sidney the Cook hit Patterson on the leg. "Let 'em in."

Patterson stepped out of the car and held the door open. The girls discussed who rode in the front and back.

In broad daylight, thought Patterson, *holding the door open in broad daylight for two spook whores*. Sunday back in Downbeach, his father would be watching football and reading the paper in a spotless living room. In the kitchen, his mother would be preparing a roast in a kitchen cleaner than Sgt. Potter's. His sister in her frilly bedroom on the phone with friends. Patterson instantly recalled sparkling bathrooms and fresh clean towels. The dull household he had desperately wanted to break away from now called him, burst into his mind like an enchanted palace to remind him of what was he doing and where was he going. *I can't be part of this.*

Gloria sat in the front. The other girl in the back.

Patterson followed them in, feeling like he volunteered for a dangerous mission. It would be so much safer to sneak into the Miracle and look at Elizabeth Taylor's tits in *Raintree County.*

The coo seat no longer felt like a throne. *More like an electric chair.*

"That's the place," Gloria pointed past Sidney the Cook's face.

The Olds swerved to a halt on the gravel road in front of a house on stilts. The house appeared pieced together with lumber, tarpaper, siding sections, and tin sheeting. It was one among many in a semi-rural area of southeast Fayetteville. All of the nearby structures sat back from the road and were jerrybuilt. The fading light hid the harshness of the buildings and lots.

Breslin volunteered to go in with the girls. With a buck from each of his pals, he followed the girls up the steep, railless, wooden stairs.

Inside, the raised house consisted of three rooms: a living room open to a kitchen and beyond, a door, for whatever was there. The living room furniture was worn: a crushed davenport and chairs that should be retired. Two small children played with homemade toys on the patchwork linoleum floor. The brightly lit kitchen with the wood-burning stove provided the gathering spot for the three adults, an older man and two women whose hefty size disguised their age.

No one had any interest in Breslin when they entered. The adults were immersed in a religious radio program. The kids followed Breslin and the girls into the kitchen area. Gloria asked for a jar of 'splo. The loud radio made it difficult for Breslin to hear even though the people spoke up. A radio preacher was claiming there was no greater employment for a Christian than to sing the songs of Zion.

Did the women ask Gloria if he was a policeman?

The preacher continued to urge his congregation to worship God with horns and string instruments because He deserved their praise.

"Amen," said the woman not involved with Gloria.

"You want a pint or a quart?" asked Gloria.

"Quart." That's what they were discussing.

"That's five dollars."

He cursed his luck not having the right amount. "Let me see a pint."

The bigger of the two big women produced a glass-preservative jar from a side cupboard. The liquid was clear. Breslin thought of nitroglycerin. A pint wasn't enough to brush his teeth; he excused himself to get more money, the preacher's booming voice following him out, demanding more than once that the listeners should turn their radios on if they wanted to hear the songs of Zion.

At the car, Motz argued with Sidney the Cook. "We're crazy to be messin' with spades. We'll get some kind of fuckin' disease or somethin'."

Sidney didn't care. Black. Blue. Red. Yellow. He was going all the way. "Airborne, man."

Patterson turned to Breslin who waited at the window, his breath showing in the first cool fall night, and said, "I smell trouble."

"Bullshit. Come on, a quarter a piece for our first and maybe only taste of white lightning."

"I'm glad to see one of you cats has some balls." Sidney the Cook handed Breslin a dollar. "Let's get crackin', motherfucker." Breslin headed back while the discussion continued in the car.

Gloria and the other girl seemed content with the sale when he paid for the corn liquor. As they started out, the older man asked Breslin if he could see the large jar. Breslin, afraid to refuse, handed it over. The man had deep-set bloodshot eyes and gray stubble on his jaw. "I wants y'all to know what y'all are gettin' here." He shook the jar hard. "Good corn bubbles real nice when y'all shakes it up."

Everyone in the room, including the children, watched the bubbles race to the top of the jar. A gospel singer talked the words to a song. "Now don't be weepin' for this pretty bit of clay/ For the little boy that lived there he done gone and run away..."

Breslin stood transfixed. The bubbles rising and rising.

Something odd was happening in the dilapidated kitchen. The room. The strong faces of the people. Their respect for the old man and the power of radio religion seemed to have made the world stop. The singer's voice sounded heavy, comfortable, a lush curtain that enwrapped the listeners, blinding them to their meager surroundings. Breslin felt the presence of God as strongly as he had ever had during the holiday masses at Saints Peter and Paul Cathedral in downtown Philadelphia or the early morning services at LaSalle's chapel. Easily, the old man could have been a priest or a traditional holy man with supernatural powers. He wanted to pay his respects, to say something, and didn't know how.

"Don't ever buy lightnin' that don't bubble, son"
Breslin took back the offered jar. "Thank you, sir."
"Where y'all from son?"
"Philly."

That seemed to make no sense to the old man. He closed his eyes and rested his head in his hands to think about it. "...He's doin' very finely/ He 'preciates your love/ But his sure 'nuf father/ Wants him in the large house up above..."

"Philadelphia, Winston," chimed in the big woman who had sold him the liquor.

Winston thought about that then advised, "Be careful with those girls, son."

"Yes, sir." He turned from the old man's suddenly accusing eyes and instantly thought, *Holy fuck—the girls might be his flesh and blood.*

The radio blared a stunning chorus and heraldic trumpets then a single, powerful God-like voice sounded, "My Lord calls me/ He calls me by the thunder/ The trumpet sounds within my soul/ I ain't got long to stay here..."

"Hush up, Winston," said an annoyed Gloria and added, "We're leavin'."

Breslin wanted to run, but forced himself to face the old man. "Winston, we're not fooling with the girls. We're just drinking."

Old Winston didn't reply; he looked like he might have a lot to say. A shift on his chair indicated Breslin and the girls were dismissed. Gloria gave Breslin a come-along look and they headed for the door.

"...Steal away, steal away, steal away to Jesus/ Steal away, steal away home/ I ain't got long to stay here..."

"Son."

Breslin looked back at Winston. "The Lord's lookin' for y'all." He turned toward the radio to avoid any reaction from Breslin.

Gloria pulled him by the hand. Her friend had the door open. As they stepped into the chill of the night, Gloria suggested, "Don't pay that old buzzard no mind. He's proud of the liquor he makes, that's all." That wasn't all.

Breslin could not rid himself of the feeling the old man had unzipped him and seen more deeply into him than even he himself could. No one else except Breslin knew the Lord called him every day.

The first timid sips roared down their throats like torched trails of gasoline. Patterson coughed so hard his eyes watered and he could not speak. For chasers, they lit cigarettes. The crowded car steamed up and filled with smoke. They had driven to a house somewhere close to the Fayetteville airport and parked. A beacon swept past them on a regular basis.

Sidney the Cook proclaimed this shit would put hair on Gloria's coos while lifting her dress and making sucking noises.

Gloria, sitting between Sidney and Patterson, tried to bum two cigarettes from Patterson. She called him honey and touched his thigh. He twitched and replied, "I ain't got none." He had bummed a Marlboro from Breslin.

"He never does," said Sidney the Cook, offering his pack of Camels. She took two and handed one over the back to her girlfriend. In a move she recalled from a movie, she held her cigarette up waiting for a light. No one moved.

"What's wrong, honey?" she asked Patterson. "You ain't never been with a colored girl before?"

Sidney laughed loudly, bent forward and lifted her dress again. "The sweet dark grotto."

Patterson's two sips of liquor had provided him a little courage. He admitted he had not been with a girl like her before, and quickly added as he pulled his '04 lighter from his jeans that he had been with a girl. "You know what I mean. I mean, I've done it," he lied and lit her cigarette.

When the 'splo passed again, Patterson took a bigger sip. It went down a little easier. Motz declared the corn whiskey tasted good. Sidney the Cook called him a lying sack of owl shit. The potent liquor helped Breslin forget old Winston; he just smiled as he watched the others maneuver. Sidney demanded to go inside and get the action started.

As they walked from the car to the dark house, a dog barked somewhere to their right. There was no walkway or lawn, just a worn patch of weeds and dirt. High brush around the place trapped wind-blown trash. Gloria unlocked a padlock and they followed her inside.

There was electricity and a kerosene heater. A single bulb shone in both rooms: a kitchen and a living and bedroom separated by a rough partition and curtain. In the small kitchen, scarred linoleum revealed where appliances had rested. Only a sink and countertop remained. Two soiled and torn chairs were in the living area along with a battered divan. Two single beds were in the bedroom.

The quiet girl turned on a Raleigh rhythm and blues station. In between songs, a vibrant-voiced Negro disc jockey who called himself Kreamy Karl talked, "...should've soothed the most wild of beasts. When Al Hibbler sings a ballad the world stops to listen, to pause, to dream, to wish the song endure forever. I promise you listeners more of Mr. Hibbler down the line. Before our next commercial presentation here at W-U-S-R, we should all pay attention to our soul singer Sarah."

My ship has sails that are made of silk.
Its decks are trimmed in gold
And of jam and spice there's a paradise in the hold.
My ship's aglow with a million pearls
And rubies fill each bin.
The sun sits high in a sapphire sky...

The song seemed oddly loud due to the silence of the strangers with different agendas suddenly in a room together. The large 'splo jar continued its rounds. Glasses were not a consideration. No one seemed to mind Gloria sipping from the same jar; if they did, nothing was said. After a few minutes, the kerosene heater warmed the room. Motz sat at one end of the couch, Patterson on the other. Breslin sat on the arm of a chair. The two girls shared a chair: Gloria on the arm and the quiet girl seated.

Sara Vaughn sailed off. Nat King Cole pronounced someone unforgettable.

Sidney the Cook prowled around the rooms. He pulled aside the partition curtain and announced the two single beds would do in a pinch. He turned to the girls and offered to show them 'his' if they would show him 'theirs.'

Gloria confidently replied, "Let's see what y'all got."

In a flash, cigarette hanging from his lips, Sidney stood at the curtain and unbuttoned his Levis. He stuck one arm down the front of his jeans and jammed it out the fly and grabbed it with his other hand as if holding a giant erection. "This good enough for you, sweet ass?"

"Y'all only dreaming, mister," said Gloria, but she and her friend did laugh.

Then he showed them the real thing. His buddies could not believe their eyes. Motz stretched to hit Patterson on the shoulder. "I'd be goddamn if I could ever do that."

Breslin said, "Sidney, you haven't let us down. You are truly the devil incarnate."

"What the fuck's wrong, man? Like, I ain't ashamed of nothin'." He spun around on his boot heels to make sure everyone got a good look then buttoned up. "Come on, girls, let's see what you got."

Gloria leaned over to whisper to her friend. She whispered something back. Gloria asked how much money they had.

"Ladies, we have the treasury of Uncle Sam at our disposal," said Breslin.

The quiet girl finally spoke. "That man keeps jivin' us."

"He likes you," said Sidney the Cook. "What's your name?"

"May."

"Like in springtime?" asked Breslin.

May shyly smiled yes. Gloria opened her coat to show off her figure. "Five dollars a piece."

"A piece," mouthed Breslin to Motz and Patterson with a wink. They missed the old joke.

"A piece," replied Sidney the Cook loudly. "You mean five bucks for all of us."

"Each, cracker."

"Sweetness, I know you ain't got no pot of gold up there." Sidney reached for her. She backed off, pushing his hand away. "That's for me to know and you to find out."

Gloria nodded to May and they went behind the curtain.

Sidney the Cook rallied his pals. "We'll get it for three each."

Breslin passed the jug to the cook and admitted, "Count me out, Sid. I'm playin' it safe."

Motz and Patterson agreed with Breslin. Sidney the Cook became indignant. "I thought you cats wanted to get laid?"

Patterson thought only one thing: *Spooks*. Their experience scared him; he'd fall through and out the other side. He'd get a disease. His reluctance embarrassed him. He wanted to be cool. A coo man. But not here. Not now.

"Fuck you candy-asses. I'm goin'." Sidney the Cook stood up and went to the curtain. On the way, he stripped off his Levi Strauss jacket and unbuttoned his long-sleeve shirt. "Number one's ready, ladies. You best be workin' on these jag-offs out here."

Gloria met him at the curtain in a white bra and pink panties; her full breasts strained against her bra.

"See," Sidney turned to the others, "she wants it too." He handed his wallet to Breslin, but not before pulling out a rubber. He tossed his shirt on the chair where Breslin sat, then faced his buddies and flexed, arms up, veins popping in his wiry forearms. His neck strained against the high T-shirt and his chest stretched across the cloth; he looked poised for the kill.

"Goddamn arms like hams," he announced and pulled the curtain behind him.

Gloria went to the couch and sat between Motz and Patterson, leaning back and touching their shoulders. Without the winter coat and in spite of her weight, she had curves. Her dark nipples and her pubic hairs were visible through her bra and panties. The sensuality of her comfortable body enticed the two young virgins.

From behind the curtain, Sidney the Cook shouted, "Son-of-a-bitch!"

Gloria stretched for Motz's crotch. "She's gonna screw that boy to his death." She rubbed. "Would y'all like that?"

Patterson looked across at Motz's frozen straight-ahead stare as Gloria reached and stroked him. Breslin offered sips to everyone.

Gloria said, "Come here, boy."

Breslin leaned over to hand the jar to Patterson. "I'm saving mine 'til I'm married."

Gloria waited for Patterson to sip, then, using both hands like treading water, she simultaneously massaged both their pricks. "Y'all know I give weddin' night lessons." She took Motz's hand to her breast. "Feel me." He did, awkwardly, like he was reaching under the couch for something he lost while pressing himself against her hand. "That's it, honey. Y'all gettin' the rhythm."

From behind the partition, the bed banged against the wall. Sidney cried, "Son-of-a-bitch!" again.

After Patterson took his sip, he looked across Gloria and asked Motz, "What'd you think?"

Pfc. Harry Patton Motz's eyes were closed; he was too occupied to reply.

Gloria turned from Motz and leaned over Patterson's privates to blow her hot breath on his erection. He said, "Jesus, Harry, we could die tomorrow. You know what I mean." He extended the jar to Motz.

Sidney drove the bed harder and harder and cursed, "Son-of-a-bitch! Son-of-a-bitch!"

Motz, with a firm jaw countenance acquired from practice in the latrine mirror, looked at his pals and admitted, "I'm ready for anything." And drank.

Gloria came up. "I'd love to do y'all both at the same time, but that gets mixed up. Who's goin' first?"

"You might need a traffic cop," suggested Breslin as he came across the room to take the 'splo from Motz.

Sidney the Cook emitted a long forced groan from behind the curtain.

Gloria stood up and took a quick sip, then pulled Breslin close, grabbing his ass and wiggling against him, saying, "Come on; y'all the only gentleman here."

"Yeah," said Patterson, "come on, Scott."

Breslin, now drunk, smiled calmly as if he was watching a game from left field in Shibe Park stated, "Not tonight, *Gloria in Excelsis.*"

Sidney leaped from behind the curtain in only jockey shorts and cowboy boots. He semi-squatted in the middle of the room like a small ape. In his hands were his Levis and T-shirt. His face and torso flushed. "You cats gonna jump in or back out?" On his right shoulder, a panther tattoo snarled at the world. Complimenting this work of art was an enlarged replica of paratrooper Wings with "U.S. Paratrooper" written under it on his left shoulder. He kicked off his cowboy boots to put on the dungarees and T-shirt.

Motz, on unsteady legs stood up. "I'm goin' all the way. Airborne, Daddy-O."

Patterson reminded, "We ain't got enough money, Sid."

"You'll owe me," settled the question. Sidney the Cook looked at Gloria. "Five for three, OK?"

Gloria never agreed and pulled Patterson up from the couch. "We're comin' in, May." She pushed Motz through the curtain and towed Patterson behind her. Patterson let his cigarette dangle from his lips like Sidney the Cook.

Sidney buttoned his Levis and smugly commented, "Sloppy seconds beats nothin'. Give me some of that juice." Breslin passed him the jug.

Behind the curtain, May lay in the single bed with a bedspread pulled over her. "You take the long one, May. I want this cherry cracker," directed Gloria.

Patterson watched Motz stand over May. Neither man knew what to do. Gloria sat on the bed and lifted her buttocks to sweep off her panties. "Get 'em off, sugar."

Motz thought she meant him. The tall man undid his jeans and slid them to his ankles. He stood pale in the half-lit room in his baggy GI-issue shorts. May pulled back the spread to offer him a place. He almost fell in the bed. Patterson resolved to follow through. He stubbed out his cigarette on the linoleum floor and pulled down his dungarees. There was nothing to show her.

Embarrassed, he quickly sat on the bed and wondered what he was doing. He could hear May telling Motz to put on a rubber. *A rubber—he needed one. Where did he...*

Gloria pulled Patterson backwards and felt his prick or what little there was. "Y'all need some help, sugar," and before he could protest, her mouth was on him, the wet heat immediately curing his flaccidity. *Maybe she'll keep it up*, he silently hoped.

She didn't. At the first moment of solidity, she laid back and commanded, "Get on 'fore that goes south, sugar."

"Damn. Damn. Double goddamn," whined Motz from the next bed. "Where'd it go?" May said something and it sounded like they were bouncing on the bed.

Gloria did not give Patterson a chance. She expertly tucked him inside and the surprise warm sweetness made him almost shout "Son-of-a-bitch" like Sidney the Cook.

He clung to her shoulders, afraid to move, afraid to fall out. His erection remained indecisive. Gloria shifted left and right, pulled his buttocks, and whispered, "Shoot in me, sugar. Shoot in me!" Within seconds, the indecisive member made a hard decision.

Another Gloria wiggle and with no hesitation he clutched her shoulders, pressed his face against her neck, held back a drool, and surrendered a single quiet convulsion. It was over.

There was nothing left of him down there. It was as if her vagina had severed him, melting his tool with its extreme heat. The brimming pot had been stirred by a little spoon. Somewhere in the middle of his body, a warm puddle and memories of summer thunderstorms and walking in gutters running with steaming rain surfaced.

"I gotta piss," he said and cursed himself for not wearing a rubber.

"I'll show you," she replied and pulled the soiled top sheet from the bed, wiped herself, then wrapped it around her body. Her bare feet padded on the worn plywood floor. "Come on, sugar."

Like an obedient pet, Patterson pulled up his shorts and Levis and followed her. He glanced at Motz and saw long white legs spread on the bed. Astride, May encouraged him to push up. He arched his back like London Bridge. "Push up, I'm tellin y'all. It's almost in." Motz grunted.

Sidney the Cook lay on the couch. "...so I raced the cat and blew the snot outta my transmission." At Gloria's appearance, he jumped to his feet, his T-shirt sleeves rolled high to show off tattoos and muscle. Breslin, across the room in the most comfortable chair, held the 'splo and looked half-asleep, definitely drunk.

"How was it, man?" asked Sidney the Cook.

Patterson's "It was great" did not disguise his weak smile.

Breslin held out the jar. "Take a slug, Willie."

"Man, I will." He took a large sip and didn't even cough. He really wanted to wash himself with the strong brew.

Sidney pulled at Gloria's sheet. "Come on, sweetness. You and me, we'll put on a show."

Gloria snapped away, showing a bit of her body, and said, "Keep your cracker hands off me. Besides, that boy done me in."

Patterson loved her lie. He nodded toward the curtain. "Harry's tryin' real hard in there."

Gloria headed for the door. "Come on, sugar."

"I got your 'sugar' right here." Sidney the Cook grabbed himself.

Gloria opened the door. "Y'all just think you do." She held the door for Patterson, then let it slam shut.

Patterson couldn't see a thing, but the cool air felt like a breeze off the winter ocean. His eyes adjusted as he followed the sheet-covered form, walking quickly to keep up then nearly stumbling over her as she squatted in front of him. "Whoa," he said and knew he was drunk.

There was a sudden sound of water running. *Oh man, she's pissing.*

He took a few steps away and pissed against the house. He held back a fart until she did. They laughed. Patterson liked her.

Coming back in, they heard Sidney threatening, "You best come out by the time I count five or I'll come in and fuck both of you!" The cook laughed. He had dressed and walked up and down in front of the curtain.

Gloria went to him and held out her hand.

"Whadda you want, baby?"

"Fifteen dollars."

He reached for the sheet. "Let me see it again."

She pulled back the corner he had grabbed. "That'll cost you two more."

Sidney the Cook reached into his jeans and pulled out a ten spot. "Let me see it." He held the bill up in her face. Gloria unwrapped herself into a spin then spun back into the sheet. On the way, she grabbed the ten-dollar bill.

Sidney the Cook confessed, "I took the wrong one."

Breslin called loudly at the curtain. "Colonel, we're leaving."

"We ain't got no more cash money," announced Sidney.

Gloria tightened the sheet around her like a sarong. Her hands were free. "Y'all owe me five more." Patterson would have given it to her if he had it.

"You only did two of us," said Sidney and pushed Breslin through the curtain. "Here we come ready or not!" May and Motz were head to feet, each lying back on their elbows. May pulled the sheet over herself. Motz, drunk, lay there, spread-eagled, some baby fat still visible. "I could've done it if I was a corporal."

May shouted for them to get out. "I ain't foolin' with no three of y'all!"

"Harry, get dressed. We're headed back," said Breslin. Although he was drunk, he remained more reasonable then the others. He pulled up Motz to sit on the side of the bed.

Sidney stepped close to May and started unbuttoning his fly. "You want a quick shot?"

Beslin helped Motz pick up his trousers and underwear, shoes and socks. He pushed him into the front room. Tall, skinny Motz was naked from the waist down. Breslin shook his head and said, "That son-of-a-bitch is going again."

"The hell he is!" Gloria pushed past Patterson and Breslin.

"Harry, get your shit on."

Motz couldn't keep his balance as he tried to slip on his underdrawers. He fell back on the couch and his legs glided into the drawers. He worked on his Levis from his sitting position.

May screamed. Gloria cursed. Patterson and Breslin pulled back the curtain.

Sidney the Cook straddled May, pinning her arms with his knees. His fly undone. She bucked against his weight. Gloria pulled him from behind. Sidney the Cook was not a big man, but he was strong and resisted Gloria's efforts by holding onto the headboard. His laughter sinister.

Gloria's sheet fell away. "Get off that girl! Get your cracker ass off her!" She began slapping Sidney the Cook in the head. He turned to defend himself and took one in the face. He lunged back for her, but Breslin beat him to her. He wrapped his arms around the naked Gloria and backpedaled her into the front room.

Sidney the Cook followed. Face inflamed. His arm cocked.

Patterson reacted without thinking about what he was doing. "Wait, Sid!" He jumped against the cook, knocking him away from Breslin and Gloria. Breslin let go of Gloria, who ran to the partitioned area where May remained.

"That fuckin' spade ain't hittin' me and gettin' away with it!"

Both Gloria and May screamed on and on about crackers and money and for them to get out. Motz rose from the couch. One shoe in his hand, a sock sticking out of his pocket and shirt hanging out, and asked, "What's the big flap?"

"Come on," said Breslin, "let's get the hell out of here before someone comes."

He and Patterson herded Sidney and Motz out the door into the darkness. They stumbled over the rough ground. Patterson stayed between Sidney and the house while the cook repeated, "I wasn't gonna hit her, man. I wasn't. Just a little bit."

Motz gimped along wearing one shoe and counting cadence. "One-two-three-four. Your left-right-left." His added imitation of seasoned NCOs cadence made the words sound like, "One-hup-ree-hore. One-hup-ree-hore. Your-lift. Your-lift. Your lift-hite-lift."

At the car, Breslin and Patterson struggled to get Motz in the back seat; he wanted to keep marching and counting cadence. Breslin followed his tall pal into the back. Patterson folded back the passenger seat and jumped in as Sidney turned the key. "Who the fuck does she think she is hittin' me like that? I oughta cut her tits off."

The Olds hesitated for a moment then roared to life, sounding as anxious to leave as the young men. The first swipe of the nearby airport beacon into the dark car scared them. Everyone froze for a moment.

"Hurry up," urged Breslin, "before old Winston shows up with a shotgun." He reached to insure both doors were locked. In his mind, the broken promise to the old man expanded. They had messed with the girls, and Winston's bloodshot eyes penetrated his drunkenness like the sweeping beacon.

Sidney swung the customized coupe through a tight U-turn. The bottom scraped gravel as the headlights swept across the house, revealing the open door and scattered papers and junk in the yard. He spun wheels along the dirt road causing the car to fishtail several times. Coming off the dirt onto the macadam of the main road, Sidney momentarily lost control and veered to the opposite side of the two-lane road. A pair of headlights came right at them.

"Goddamn," whispered Sidney the Cook.

"Watch it!" shouted Patterson who visualized himself as a dead man. Dead in the candy-apple coo seat.

Motz reacted by leaning forward to see the blinding headlights. "I'll never make corporal," he predicted. Breslin leaned back and prayed it would not hurt too much. Then Sidney came alive.

"I've got this heap!" He sat forward, used the suicide knob, twisting the steering wheel through a hard right that brought the Olds back to the right lane, then twisted the knob again to over correct and keep from going off the other side of the highway.

Meanwhile, the on-coming car had veered right, going halfway off the macadam, and both cars passed within a foot or two. Everyone except Sidney turned to watch the car; it slowed to a halt. Sidney speed-shifted into third. "Sometimes," he said casually, "I get rubber goin' into third."

"Attention to Orders," read Colonel Steele in his office. "Headquarters, Department of the Army: The President of the United States has reposed special trust and confidence in the patriotism, valor, fidelity, and abilities of Second Lieutenant Seymour Margolin. In view of these qualities and your demonstrated potential for increased responsibility, you are, therefore, promoted to First Lieutenant with the date of rank of October 25, 1958."

Col. Steele held the promotion orders in one hand and offered his right hand to newly appointed First Lieutenant Seymour 'Mad Dog' Margolin. The lieutenant saluted, shook the colonel's hand and accepted the certificate.

"Do the honors, Sergeant Major."

Sergeant Major Kaley stepped up and pinned the silver bar of a first lieutenant over the sewn gold cloth bar on Margolin's fatigue collar.

A flashbulb went off. The regimental photographer might put the photo in the *Paraglide*, the division newspaper, and it might be sent to the *Los Angeles Times* with a small press release. It would look good up on the wall behind Uncle Ziggy's cash register.

Margolin replied, "Thank you, Sergeant Major."

Kaley stepped back and saluted smartly. "Dollar for the first one, sir."

Margolin returned the salute and pulled out a dollar. "Worth every penny, Sergeant Major."

"Lieutenant, you're the acting CO at Headquarters Company," said Col. Steele.

"I'm the ranking officer, but no one's ever officially confirmed me as acting commanding officer." Margolin believed Steele had intentionally avoided notifying him; it was just another way for Steele to make him feel inadequate.

"Hear that, Sergeant Major. He needs an official appointment."

"Yes, Sir. I believe that would be your privilege," replied Kaley.

"Consider it official, First Lieutenant. Look for the orders; meanwhile, you're in charge and responsible for everything that happens in the company. Can you handle it?"

Margolin didn't mention First Sergeant Billy Martin. "Yes, sir. All the way."

Steele looked out the window toward the regiment's barracks and asked, "Who's that tall lad who runs every morning even if the regiment doesn't?"

"Sir, that's our company clerk, Motz." Motz's plan to be noticed had worked. The Pfc. had confided to the lieutenant he timed his solo runs to pass regimental headquarters when Steele arrived for work.

"What's his rank?"

"PFC., Sir."

"What would you say if I directed you to make him a corporal or acting corporal today? I'll clear the paperwork."

Margolin had heard Steele liked to reach into the ranks and reward individual effort; it made him feel in touch with the troops. Like giving out medals during wartime. Before Margolin could answer, the colonel directed, "Your first assignment as company commander is to promote that young trooper."

The new first louie headed across the parking lot to the company. Each salute he received elated him more. The stigma of the gold bar, an insignia of a novice, a mark of innocence, the authority to step on the grass, and almost a symbol of virginity had vanished. *I am a first lieutenant. A veteran officer. A commanding-fucking-A-officer in charge.*

And he had made it past Steele without the man being too condescending during the surprise ceremony. Things were looking up.

Margolin walked through the open orderly room door. As always, the first sergeant sat at his desk. Motz wasn't there. Martin glanced up, caught the silver bar, and returned to his work. Margolin asked the first sergeant to come into his office.

"In a second, sir."

The officer stopped at the doorway, exhaled and without looking around said, "Now, First Sergeant." As he went to his desk, Margolin heard the swivel chair on wheels push back.

The first sergeant came in. "Sir?" He stood waiting, his voice and expression indicating that this was an imposition on his valuable time.

Margolin directed him to draw up the orders to make Motz a corporal. "By the end of the day, First Sergeant."

"I'll check in to it, sir." Those words meant it was going to be one of their usual struggles, Martin remaining militarily correct, yet letting the officer know he would not cooperate with him.

Not this time, thought Margolin. He was a first lieutenant, the company commander. "Sergeant Martin, Motz will be a corporal or acting corporal by seventeen hundred hours today."

"Yes, sir." It had been a long time since the older enlisted man had looked directly at the younger officer. "Anything else, sir?"

"Yes. As of ten minutes ago I am the commanding officer of the company."

Martin's response was muted. "That's good news, sir." He made no offer of congratulations on the promotion and stood waiting for something else.

"That'll be all." Martin went out and almost closed the door, but caught himself. Margolin would not let him do that any more.

Lieutenant Margolin, in his role as battalion hygiene officer, spent most of the day with Chaplain Byrd and Pfc. Breslin, showing the Army training film on personal hygiene to four rifle companies. Line troops liked films; it meant a break from outdoor training. After the presentation, the lieutenant made a brief pre-written Department of Army speech on cleanliness and the chaplain spoke about curbing one's lusts with strange women. "There are too many pretty, decent women at home, your girlfriends and wives, waiting for you. Ask the Lord to give you the strength to avoid the wanton women that lure you to sin."

Almost to a man the troops wondered exactly where those wantons were and how a man got in touch with them. They sure as hell weren't in Fayetteville, unless a man dug deeply like Sidney the Cook.

By 1600, the lieutenant returned to his company. He finally referred to the company as his and felt it was his. Steele had confirmed it.

"Sir," said First Sgt. Billy Martin when Margolin entered, "that deal didn't work out." The NCO could not hide his smile. "I had Motz check it out hisself in the TO & E. There's not a slot in the company and company clerks can't be hard corporals. They have to be specialists. We could make him a specialist fourth class. Y'all know, a spec-four." The first sergeant loved to display his knowledge of Army regulations.

Margolin did not lean over Martin's desk and meet him jaw to jaw. He put his temper on safety and asked, "Did Motz know why he was looking up the corporal's slot?"

"Yes, sir. He was happy as all-get-out knowin' he was bein' considered."

"Sergeant Martin, that promotion would have been a nice surprise."

"Surprise, sir?" Martin pretended to be puzzled. "Surprise? All due respect, sir. This here's the Army Airborne not some rah-rah college party."

That was the moment freshly promoted 1stLt. Seymour Margolin nearly came over the desk and put his size ten Corcoran jump boot into Martin's face. He didn't.

He didn't even call the first sergeant a meddling *schmuck*. He didn't pound his fist on Martin's desk. And he knew Martin knew he would do none of those things. And that made him angrier. The lieutenant controlled his temper again and calmly asked, "So there's not a slot open?"

"That's affirmative, sir." The emphasis on 'sir' rang of sarcasm.

"Motz knows there's no slot."

"Like I said, sir. He checked it hisself." Martin's victory smile came slowly.

"First Sergeant, you are truly…" He did not say mother-fucking cocksucker as Sgt. Wisnewski would have; his rank required equanimity. "…a *goniff* of the highest caliber."

"What's that mean?"

"Look it up, but first call Colonel Steele and tell him why you didn't make Motz a corporal."

Martin's jaw dislocated a tad. He appeared to come to attention while sitting down. "Colonel Steele?"

"He ordered the promotion."

Instinctively, Martin's hands moved to various papers on his desk; it was as through they wanted to start the paperwork before their master could guide them.

It was Margolin's turn to smile. "Can that promotion be arranged now?"

"We could carry him as 'acting' 'til such time…"

"Until such time it'll be, First Sergeant." Margolin's tone said it all, however he was not satisfied. Invoking Steele's name as a mace to threaten Martin was fun, but goddamnit, he wanted Martin to act for him.

And he'd make him do it yet.

Do something even if it's wrong.

Old military saying.

Chapter 9

"Now, baby!"
"Let's go!"
"No Hawk's getting' my ass!"
"Comin' out, Jack, like a bat outta hell!"
Louder and louder the men screamed over the roar of more than 6,000 horsepower twin Wright engines that held the C-119 aloft in the cool November night. They shouted and stamped their feet and rattled their static lines. Every man in the aircraft faced the rear open doors, leaning toward the doors, pressing against the man in front of him. The Flying Boxcar bucked slightly, gently, like a moored boat in a friendly swell.
"Unass this mother!"
"Chogie, baby!"
"Grab hat, Jim!"
Lieutenant Margolin looked at the impatient mob that represented a disciplined fighting force. The stick convulsed in anticipation as the troops pushed forward, then the men closest to the door leaned back. Back and forth the bodies pushed and leaned under the eerie red glow of the jump command light that made everything appear slower; the troops had become an infrared convulsing creature. The last men in the chalks seemed lost in the strange crimson darkness. Many of them were making their first night jump. The jump was Hollywood style, which meant no extra gear except web belt with canteen. Back pack and reserve chutes only. Easy. Fun. Like riding in a Caddy.

Sfc. Wisnewski, the jumpmaster, had given all the commands: stand-up, hook-up, check equipment, sound off for equipment check, and now ordered, "Stand in the door!"

The first two men on each side shuffled and turned. They looked into the darkness and saw only the fiery glow of the powerful engines and the lights of Friendly Fayetteville on the horizon. Behind them, the lines surged; they had to brace themselves from being pushed out.

Sgt. 'Ski pulled the Pfc. in the door back and, while hooking up his static line ahead of the lower-ranking man, said, "I'll do the honors." He then directed Margolin to take the front door position in the other stick. A second later, infrared switched to a green glow.

The sergeant and the first lieutenant were gone, followed closely by 45 other rambunctious paratroopers madly rushing the stairless exits, falling into the darkness. The plane emptied in six seconds.

Going out the door, Margolin remembered Errol Flynn in *Objective Burma* and smiled for a single moment until he gasped at the sudden yaw his body did in the blast of the blue-hot engines. The torrid gusts lifted him up, his legs riding above his head, his nostrils stinging with the exhaust. He almost went over backwards, then just as suddenly, fell forward and—seeing nothing below—he looked in the direction of the aircraft where two glowing engines disappeared into the starry universe of a clear full moon sky. A jolt rocked his crotch and shoulders as the chute deployed.

There was never a sensation of falling, just the wind playing gentle harmonies through the risers and a sense of serenity, while drifting among the other chutes under the huge moon. Below the quietly descending jumpers, Sicily Drop Zone's vastness appeared like a lake of white tranquility waiting to embrace the descending men.

To the southwest, Fayetteville glittered like a low Milky Way. It was more beautiful than any of the first time night jumpers would have ever imagined.

In a few seconds, Sicily's outline disappeared. The men could see only the headlights of trucks at the assembly point. Below 75 feet, their speed increased as they prepared to land in total darkness. With no point of reference, a jumper didn't know if he was landing backwards, forwards, or how high he was.

Relax. Legs together. Knees slightly bent. Toes pointed down. Look up and pray.

Don't lift your feet. Relax. Relax. Relax.

They hit. Two and three at a time.

One here. One there. Another over there.

Some made classic parachute landings falls. Others came in backwards and hit hard on their buttocks. In the still cool night, their chutes settled over them with silken caresses. The night jump ended without any injuries.

The young soldiers from Headquarters and Headquarters Company burst through the doors of the Enlisted Man's Club and commandeered three booths and a few tables and chairs in the far corner of the plainly furnished, cavernous basement of Chargin' Charlie Company. Lt. Seymour Margolin came in among them. First, on Wisnewski's advice, he removed the silver bar from his fatigues and kept his hat under his field jacket. He gave Sgt. 'Ski 25 bucks to keep the beer flowing, while he kept a low profile squeezed between two men in a booth with his back to the bar. The party was in celebration of his promotion. The group also celebrated the first night jump for most of them.

Col. Steele would not be happy if a first lieutenant turned up drinking in an Enlisted Man's Club; like his first name, it would be one more strike against him. The lieutenant's plan was to have two cans of beer and gracefully depart and let the men get a little wild. On the jukebox, the Big Bopper sang about a pretty face in Chantilly lace with a wiggle as she walked.

Banuelous returned from having the sergeant bartender turn up the music. He snapped his fingers and did a few quick dance steps, "I used to sing that song to every chick I met."

"You didn't sing it much, did you?"

"Hey," replied Banuelous, "you know how I cry 'bout singin', motherfucker."

"...It was darker then a miner's asshole out there..."

"...I thought I was comin' in backwards. Turned to look and, damn, hit on my fuckin' face!..."

It did not take long for the smoke, the music, the beer, and chatter to elevate Margolin into a glow of satisfaction. Those last few seconds before he hit had frightened him. No ground to see. No one around him. He could hear other men landing and cursing nearby while he rode down the final 30 feet and hit hard on his ass at 24 feet per second.

As Sergeant Wisnewski would say, "It's good for a man to sphincter-up every once in a while. Keeps him fuckin' honest." That's what being Airborne was all about.

Finally, he could say his college pals were *schmucks* for taking the easy way. Here he was, a first louie, with decent beer and good troops in a gung-ho regiment. *Not bad,* he congratulated himself, *not bad at all. It wasn't a sidewalk café in Paris, but it was a great night jump. The only thing missing was a good deli sandwich and a girl.* He had a third can of beer and remembered to pass out cigars to the men. He still disliked smoking, but was working on liking cigars like the other young officers in the BOQ.

Across from him, Sgt. 'Ski and Sidney the Cook were having a serious discussion about a mother and daughter team they may have boffed at different times. Sidney the Cook claimed he had both in one night at their Spring Lake trailer.

"Yeah," agreed Wisnewski, "that's the trailer. I had the old lady, but the kid was too young."

"My fuckstick's got no conscience, man."

Sam Cooke's magic voice crooned about some darlin' sending him.

In a little more than an hour, most of the men had stopped at the lieutenant's booth to congratulate him and wave cigars in his face. He found himself drinking another beer and realized he had lost count. As he attempted to tally up his input by counting the empties in front of him, someone asked him, "How am I doin', sir?"

Motz had taken the place of the man next to Margolin. The tall, baby-faced soldier looked down on him. Margolin noticed the corporal stripes and wondered how anyone could enjoy the military as much as his company clerk.

"I'm OK, young Corporal Motz."

"No, sir, I mean how am I doin'?"

The lieutenant poked the chevrons. "Out-fucking-standing, corporal."

Motz did a lazy salute. "Thank you, sir."

The tall youngster leaned toward Margolin as if collapsing, staring directly into his eyes. Margolin blew cigar smoke in his face to back him up. It worked.

From farther away, Motz said, "You're a damn fine officer, sir."

Margolin lifted his beer can in recognition of the compliment. Motz tapped his can against the officer's and they sipped. Beer dribbled down Motz's chin as he leaned toward Margolin. Another smoke screen halted his progress, but did not move him back.

"Did you go to OCS, sir?"

"Hell no, corporal. I'm an ROTC tiger and proud of it."

"Mad Dog Margolin."

"Roger that, young corporal."

"Whatever way you get to be an officer's the best way, ain't it, sir?"

Margolin admired Motz's single-mindedness to build an Army career. Unlike the civilian world, there was a certain orderliness in having obvious ranks. He had learned to like that. The civilian world sometimes seemed chaotic, especially lunchtime in the deli.

"Sir?" Motz leaned some more.

Margolin put his hand on the corporal's chest and gently pushed back. "Give me some smoking room here, corporal."

Patterson, Banuelous, and Breslin argued loudly about the proper way to land at night. They were interrupted by Mangiameli who declared he did the best PLFs and would demonstrate his talent by jumping off a chair onto the floor.

Everyone's drunk, thought the lieutenant, *including me*. He looked at the cans in front of him and wondered which was his. The lift test found one relatively full and he sipped, risking a cigarette butt might be inside; it was clean. He sipped again and kept his hand around it.

"...Long tall Sally has a lot on the ball/ And nobody cares if she's long and tall/ Oh, baby. Yes, baby/ Havin' me some fun tonight..."

"Sir, that raunchy midget first sergeant's a cheese-eatin', ass-kissin' squirrel fuckin' red-neck from the word go."

Motz's strong words brought him towards Margolin again. The lieutenant held him back while watching Sidney the Cook pull Mangiameli from the chair and jump up on it to announce, "I'll do the PLF 'cause I'm a rock-throwin', pussy-lickin', Airborne son-of-a-bitch!"

"It's time," said Margolin to no one and pretended he was a British officer in a pub where T.S. Eliot hung out and as Eliot or Kipling or Sfc. Webster might have said, "The men were getting out of sorts."

Sidney the Cook took the in-the-door position on the edge of the chair.

"Sir," Motz pressed against Margolin's hand, "that fucker had himself on the jump manifest tonight and he ain't jumped lately."

Sidney leaped up, pushing the chair back, and hit the linoleum floor to buckle into a side PLF. His pals raucously graded him. Mangiameli declared he was next, but Sgt. Wisnewski demanded that they shut up and quit acting like a bunch of motherfuckin' cocksucker cherry jumpers or he'd cut off the beer. Motz persisted in leaning on Margolin.

"The first pig, sir. He's got himself down on the jump manifest I carried to Personnel today. Tonight was a pay jump for him. He did the same thing on All-American, but you and I know he drove the Jeep back."

The news washed over the lieutenant's beer-soaked brain like puddle splash from a speeding car. He thought about making a note to himself, but didn't. He would check the company's manifests before he did anything. Cheating like that could quickly send a man to the barbed-wire hotel as Martin himself might say. The news spurred him to get up. Get out.

When he stood up, Motz blocked his way.

"Goddamnit, sir, halt," said Sgt. 'Ski loudly across the table, "We just got here."

"Ski, I have to drive to Main Post. This time of night those leg MPs are on us like stink on shit." Margolin had grown to love the military analogies and it felt so good to say them.

"Hell, we'll all drive you back."

Margolin laughed. "Then the whole company'd get a DR."

"Then you put us all on hard labor, sir," joked the sergeant.

More of the men noticed Margolin preparing to depart.

"...Come on, Mad Dog, it's your party..."

"...One more never hurt no one, sir..."

He waved his hand no and silently warned them about his rank by pointing to the insignia on his cap.

Elvis warned people they could do anything they wanted, but stay off of his blue suede shoes.

"Hup thousand! Two thousand! Three thousand!..." McBride had taken over the jump chair and demonstrated how to check a canopy. "...Four thousand! Five thousand! Check your canopy!" He reached his arms high over his head, cigar in mouth, and stared at the imaginary canopy. Some ashes fell on his cheek. Like the Statue of Liberty, he didn't change his pose until Wisnewski came across and kicked the chair. "You fuckin' cocksuckers take ten. Sit down and shut the hell up!"

Margolin used the moment to head for the door. Motz ran interference for him and pushed the panic bar to open the door. "Sir, I'm gonna be an officer someday. I really am."

Margolin looked up at the serious, but intoxicated young man, and replied, "You'll be damn fine one, Corporal."

Motz let go of the door and snapped to attention. As he saluted the heavy door hit him from behind, knocking him forward. Although half-bent over, he held his frozen salute.

Margolin quickly slipped past Motz and took the concrete stairs two at a time. The cool autumn evening refreshed him. Made him content. Satisfied. He was one of the men. No longer a pudgy Jewish boy from the Valley. A paratrooper. A Jewish paratrooper. A Mad Dog paratrooper with a night jump under his pistol belt.

The remaining troops were finally chased from the EM Club by the employees closing up. The few remaining headquarters men grumbled and left behind a junkyard of empty beer cans and overflowing ashtrays. Each man made sure to smuggle out a can or two under his field jacket. On the walk along deserted Grave Street toward the company, Motz attacked Baker Company's dumpster with a beer can grenade and verbal machine-gun fire aimed at Krauts, Nips, and Commies. The others sipped their beers, keeping their collars up against the night chill.

Sidney the Cook wanted to wake up Wise and Carter and buy some marijuana.

"Hey," asked Patterson, "where was Wise tonight?"

Breslin said he had asked Wise to join them, but pointed out Wise really didn't hang around anymore since he went to work in Personnel and started bunking in Carter's cadre room, one of the other few Negroes in Headquarters Company. Personnel staff always received their rank early and had the privilege of cadre rooms because they looked after the company expenses, promotions, and penalties.

McBride didn't care. "He's just a nigger."

Sidney acknowledged Carter was and he'd cut McBride a new asshole in a minute. "I've seen his knife when I buy Mary Jane."

Patterson challenged his pals; if they really felt that way about spades they should call Broomfield that name. Patterson had learned skin color misled people's thinking.

McBride asked, "So that's where you assholes get your marijuana?"

Banuelous bragged, "If my brother ain't sent some fresh stuff from California."

"We know, cool cat, everything's better in California," joked Breslin.

"Shit, those cats have a machine that rolls a big time smoke," added Sidney.

Motz, out of breath from his assault on the dumpster, ran up and announced, "Let's get tattoos!"

In an instant, Sidney and Mangiameli stripped to their T-shirts to display their works of art. Mangiameli had the name Judy on a scroll around a heart on one forearm. On the other arm, a dagger pierced a skull and this scroll read, 'Death Before Dishonor,' both tattoos acquired on his third weekend in Fayetteville. Sidney scoffed at Tommy's gallery. He showed his shoulder tattoos, one with Wings with 'US Paratrooper' underneath and on the other a dark blue, growling panther with glowing red eyes. "I got the cat to cover up some broad's name. Cool, huh?"

"We should all get Wings," suggested Breslin. "Tonight. All of us together."

"Wings!" shouted Corporal Motz. "Let's do it!"

McBride challenged. "You ain't got a hair on your ass if you don't."

In the middle of the dark empty street, they argued about who would dare to get tattooed and whose car they would go in, Mangiameli's beast or Sidney the Cook's coo wagon. They finally agreed to take Tommy's old Buick and Patterson would drive, so that if they were stopped, he would get the DR and Mangiameli would still be able to make his Detroit runs.

McBride demanded they march to the parking lot to his cadence. Without agreeing, they broke into the stockade shuffle—a form of exaggerated marching—making it hard for McBride to call cadence. On the way off-post, they stopped at the NCO Club for half a case of Country Club Malt. Going in, Motz bragged he was the only person with enough rank to make the purchase while McBride sulked in the car. McBride's sense of military entitlements was offended that Motz, a company clerk, had made corporal before him, the ex-best machine gunner in the 82nd Airborne. "I mean," McBride reminded everyone in the car, "fuckin' tall skinny jerk-off can't blow his nose without breakin' his hand."

The Buick idled in front of the two-story house just off Bragg Boulevard in the Bonnie Doone area near Bragg. The bottom floor was converted to a storefront. In the picture window, a sign in green neon advertised, "Sailor Eddie's Tattoo Parlor." No lights were on.

"I bet the Sailor lies in bed listening for tires on the gravel," said Breslin.

McBride said, "Motz, you fall in shit and come up smellin' like a rose. The fucker's closed." McBride reached across Mangiameli who sat next to Patterson and blew the horn. "I'll wake the son-of-a-bitch up so I can watch you chicken out."

A light came on. McBride swung open the door. "Let's go!"

Walking toward the shop, Motz took a final sip of a half-filled can of beer, tossed it on the ground, and stripped off his field jacket and fatigue shirt before they were inside.

Sailor waited in the two over-heated rooms; a man of average height and some middle age softness who lived contently knowing the world came to him. He wore bedroom slippers and tired dress slacks. His sleeveless singlet revealed inked patterns running over his body. It would take a cartographer to decipher what designs lived within the faded, melted blues, greens, and reds. Sailor Eddie was not a good model for his wares.

Both rooms' walls were covered with various designs that made choosing difficult. The young soldiers stared quietly as they moved slowly along the worn linoleum floor, going from wall to wall, wondering what would be on their bodies the rest of their lives. They saw their pals' panther and Jump Wings, the skull and dagger, and the scrolled heart. There were rising suns and Elmer Fudds, fruits and flowers, Mom and girls' names, cherries inscribed with 'Here's Mine, Where's Yours?' Clipper ships and playing card symbols. Jesus rising. Eagles soaring. Tweety Bird. Smoking pistols. A zoo full of animals, and more military insignia than the Pentagon parking lot.

Mangiameli showed Sailor his designs.

"That's Diamond Jim's work over on Combat Alley. Not bad. He's in Charleston now paintin' swabbies. I drove him out," stated Sailor matter-of-factly. He lit a cigarette and offered to cover up the 'Judy' with a Liberty Bell.

"Hell no!"

McBride pointed to Motz who sat shirtless, half-drunk, half asleep, in one of the few chairs in the front room and said, "He wants Wings."

"Is there a way to get them off?" asked Banuelous, perhaps thinking about his homemade pachuco symbol.

Sailor Eddie stood up, eagle wings on his flabby chest protruding from under his singlet, took off his glasses and wiped them with a tissue from the box by his needles. "If you're thinkin' about takin' it off, don't put it on. I've got a few appointments in the mornin' so let's call it a night."

"No, no," insisted McBride, moving behind Motz, "he wants Wings. He's been sayin' it all night. Right, troop?" No one agreed except Sidney the Cook and Mangiameli.

Sailor Eddie put out his cigarette and began putting away his needles. "Come back when you're all sober, boys."

"So, like, no one's gettin' tattooed?" asked Sidney the Cook.

"Candy-asses," added Tommy Mangiameli.

Breslin, who had been quietly studying the artwork, joined them with a design, a small red and blue plain parachute hardly two inches tall. "Look at this."

"It's only a goddamn dot," said McBride.

Breslin said, "That's the point. A simple parachute. No mottos. No bullshit. I say we all get it."

Sailor Eddie thought it was too small. He volunteered to enlarge and put 'US Paratrooper' under it.

Banuelous liked the small symbol. "You know how I cry, *ese*, tattoo me."

"And," added Breslin, "we get it on our asses." That woke up everyone, but Motz.

"The quiff will love it," said Sidney the Cook.

Mangiameli felt one more would not make much difference.

Patterson asked McBride if he was ready. McBride did not answer.

"Mac, are you in?" he asked again.

McBride moved toward the door. "Not me. Fuckin' needles make me faint."

"Bullshit. Come on, Mac," urged Patterson. "It'll be like a club or somethin'." He was surprised a gung-ho guy like McBride didn't want the symbol.

"His Mommie wouldn't let him," kidded Banuelous. The others urged him to join them, but McBride stayed close to the door and refused.

"And we'll do Motz too," said Breslin and undid his belt to lower his fatigue trousers. "Sailor Eddie, this will be a far, far better thing that you'll ever do. We want your finest work."

A few mornings later, Banuelous, Patterson, Breslin, and Motz stood in the chow line just after reveille. They smoked and shivered in the cold darkness. Some troopers waiting in line did pull-ups to keep warm.

"You know, I can't feel it any more," said Motz who had awoke the morning after the tattoos to discover his. At first, he worried it was the wrong thing to do, but once he learned McBride had not joined their exclusive club he gloated over his new artwork.

"That means it's infected, Jim," advised Mangiameli the tattoo expert.

Patterson lit a cigarette bummed from Banuelous with his '04 lighter, then Banuelous's smoke. He diagnosed, "All you have to do is keep it clean." Patterson would not mention he could never let his parents see the parachute.

"Thank you, doctor," said Banuelous.

A canvas-covered Jeep pulled in the driveway at the corner of the mess hall. The fading night made it easy to recognize the white stripe across the lower part of the windshield with 'Military Police' across it in thick, black letters.

"Here comes your DR from the other night, Tommy," said Motz.

"Motherfuck me, Jim, Willie was drivin'," defended Mangiameli.

"Who, me? It's your car, man. Your license number." Everyone waiting in line stared at the now silent Jeep.

The driver MP got out and walked around the front of the vehicle. The 503rd Military Police Battalion dressed like honor guard with white ladder-style boot lacing, fancy white web belts, tailored uniforms, and polished white helmet liners with big 'MP' letters on the front and the 82nd insignia and the 18th Airborne Corps dragon on the sides. And, like MPs anywhere, they were first class pricks.

The MP in the passenger's seat handed out his shotgun to the driver and climbed out.

"Man, he's gonna blast us a new asshole," kidded Banue-lous in mock horror. No one laughed. The shotgun's sudden appearance made it serious.

Whoever was under guard had to climb from the tight back seat of the Jeep with the MPs' help because his hands were cuffed. The man wore shower clogs and a set of fatigues so large he needed to hold them up with his hands. They had to pass the chow line to reach the company's entrance. One MP walked in front of the man and the one with the shotgun behind him. The trio passed under the yellow lights coming from the mess hall windows.

"Holy fuck! Schmidt!" Breslin started toward them.

"Stand back, soldier," ordered the MP in the front with a raised white-gloved hand.

"That's right," said the prisoner. "I'm a crazed killer." Schmidt gave them a big wink and smile as if he was passing with pretty girls on each arm.

He may have smiled, but he looked frozen. His hair, what little remained, was roughly shorn and there were bruises on his face. Schmidt looked smaller, shrunken, older like a prisoner of war, which, in a sense, he was.

Schmidt's friends took turns walking past the open orderly room door to catch a glimpse of their wandering pal. All they could see was Motz, tight-lipped, playing it straight at the long-carriage Remington, putting the first sergeant's directions into print. He didn't dare look up. The passers-by could not know Schmidt was shackled to a chair in the commanding officer's room.

Without taking his eyes off his beloved duty roster, which he labored over every morning, First Sgt. Billy Martin sensed hallway traffic was more than normal. However, his concern focused on getting the morning report adjusted; an AWOL, now a deserter for being gone more than 30 days, had been returned and the company was back up to snuff.

On the sixth pass, Mangiameli's turn, Martin dropped his colored pencil on his desk, took five quick strides to the hall, and—looking both ways—loudly declared, "The next son-of-a-bitch comes down this hallway that don't belong here is gonna be meetin' hisself comin' off pots and pans!"

His high voice echoed like a siren off the polished hallway floor chasing Schmidt's supporters to their various military assignments.

Half an hour later, 1stLt. Seymour Margolin arrived.

"Sir, there's a deserter in your office. MPs brought him back this a.m. Name's Schmidt. Took off like a big ass bird right after Jump School. We give hots and a cot 'til they court-martial his sorry ass and stick him on a train to Leavenworth."

Corporal Motz kept the typewriter cracking.

Margolin had not forgotten his conversation with the first sergeant when Schmidt first went missing. He knew Schmidt. A big mouth. He didn't like him then and with his new confidence he would like him less now. "Why my office? Is he dangerous?"

Martin shook his head to let the world know the first lieutenant did not understand or appreciate the ways of the Army. "The CO's supposed to talk to him. Here's the key to the handcuffs." Martin slid the key across his desk being careful not to scratch the polished mahogany surface.

"Then I will." Intentionally forgetting the key, Margolin entered his office to find Schmidt sitting behind the CO's desk, his desk, with one hand cuffed to the chair. The lieutenant shut the door behind him to keep Martin from interfering. Schmidt looked rugged in his chopped haircut and weathered face. A slightly black eye and forehead cut added to the hard image.

He looked up as if it was his office. "Anything I can do for you?"

Margolin dropped his gym bag in the corner by the coat rack and hung up his fatigue jacket and cap. *Why am I nervous?* He wasn't a captured deserter. Obviously, the man had no respect for military authority. *Play it easy*, he cautioned himself. His style. Easy.

He pulled the other oak chair in the room to the desk and turned it backwards toward Schmidt and straddled it. "Where've you been, Schmidt?"

"You're Lieutenant Margolin, aren't you?"

"Affirmative. My name tag says it."

"You sure have changed."

"So where'd you go?"

"What difference does it make? You were a chubby second louie when we went through Jump School."

"We went through Jump School?"

Schmidt took offence the lieutenant did not remember him. Margolin did, but guessed correctly that not acknowledging Schmidt would annoy the man, just as Steele annoyed him by forgetting his name.

"Seriously, you don't remember me?"

"Should I?"

"You're different. You're a...an Airborne officer. I'm impressed."

Like that, the lieutenant liked Schmidt. Flattery would get him everywhere. Running and playing handball and lifting some weights had turned baby fat into muscle. "Didn't they call you 'Hollywood'?"

"See, you do remember. I knew you would."

"Where'd you get the bruises?"

"The marks came from an asshole Lifer up at the Provost Marshall's office. I'll sue the khaki off him when I get out." Schmidt didn't want to relive his humiliation in the hands of the Provost Sergeant Major named Templeton and the puffy SP/4 who had tapped Schmidt's shins and elbows repeatedly with a nightstick while he was naked and handcuffed in the stockade holding cell. When Templeton swatted him the second time, Schmidt had fallen on the concrete floor and pissed himself. The porky pig specialist said, "We got ourselves another leaker, Sarge."

"A dishonorable discharge and stockade time doesn't bother you?" asked Margolin.

"Mox nix as we say in the Eighty-Deuce. I've got more than enough bullshit to survive any military inconvenience. I'm headed to the movies to be a star."

Too bad, thought Margolin. Schmidt could not be released to be a movie star or whatever he wanted. It would save the Army a lot of time and money. But if they did that with every unhappy draftee, men would go AWOL daily. Fear of prison and extra time to serve were great incentives to keep troops in line. Besides, the lieutenant genuinely believed a man owed his country something, particularly the USA that had taken in his grandparents from Russia and so many others from persecuted societies and allowed them the personal freedoms no one appreciated until they were taken away. A draftee's presence in the military contributed to peace. War is peace, said Orwell's doublespeak, and there was a world of difference between peace and plain quitting. Still, some men could not or would not soldier.

He asked Schmidt if he would go again.

Schmidt smiled sadly and touched his tender eye. "No, I don't think so." The provost sergeant's doorknob knuckles had proven great deterrents.

The lieutenant did not believe him. He imagined the private chained to the panic bar in the supply room or to the first sergeant's filing cabinet for months. It would be better to simply sign him out on a Bad Conduct or Dishonorable Discharge and be rid of him without any trial.

"Didn't they call you 'Mad Dog'?"

Schmidt knew how to punch the right buttons, but duty called. Margolin opened the door to the orderly room half expecting to catch Martin listening at the door. Martin, bent over his roster, looked up through his plain-framed glasses. "Sir?"

"Get someone to accompany the AWOL to draw linen. We'll bunk him in the supply room."

"That man's a deserter, sir. It's regimental traditional for deserters awaitin' court-martial to live in a pup tent between the buildings and work in the mess hall."

Margolin recalled Corporal Brookes who had endured the tent sentence until finally being dishonorably discharged. "Is that good security? Here's a man that's been gone nearly a year. I think he needs a tight rein."

"Charge-of-Quarters checks him every hour and he'll be so tired from KP he won't be able to run to the latrine."

"Personally, Sergeant Martin, I think he should be locked in the boiler room, but let's stick to tradition." Margolin would have preferred giving Schmidt a 30-day leave to be rid of him.

"Motz, front and center. Take charge of the prisoner to draw field gear."

"Yes, First Sergeant," snapped Motz then caught himself, he didn't want to seem too eager to be with Schmidt. He gingerly lifted the handcuff key off the first sergeant's desk.

"Personally, lieutenant, sir, I'd like to put the s-o-b against the dumpster and shoot him at close range." His venom intentionally loud enough to reach the prisoner who was being unlocked by Motz.

"Be my guest," said Margolin as Motz and Schmidt left the office. He returned to his desk wishing the shooting would be the other way around.

Motz and Schmidt found Patterson sorting mattress covers in the supply room. At the rear of the long shelf-lined room, Broomfield sat at Webster's desk engrossed in the Bible.

"Willie!"

"Hollywood! I can't believe you're back."

"Not for long," said Motz.

They all laughed together for a moment, then Patterson mentioned the obvious. "They got you, huh?"

"I didn't come back because I missed this place."

Motz said, "First sergeant wants him to draw some field gear. He'll be out on the lawn."

Patterson examined Schmidt's face. "You looked fucked up when you came by this mornin'."

Schmidt shrugged off his bruises and asked for a cigarette. Patterson, never known for having his own smokes, went to Webster's desk and extracted two Tareytons from the polished wooden box with the ceramic Union Jack logo. "You remember Schmidt, don't you, Broom?"

Broomfield grunted. Deserters did not interest him.

Patterson used his '04 lighter to light their cigarettes then wandered around the supply room putting Schmidt's gear together including shelter-halves, tent poles and pegs, and a sleeping bag.

Schmidt exhaled as if tasting life all over again then coughed. "My first weed in a week." He coughed again.

Patterson asked him the same question Motz had asked as they came down the stairs to the supply room. Schmidt had ignored Motz because a corporal company clerk would normally be against him. "How'd you get away and how'd you stay so long?"

Schmidt, enjoying every drag of the smoke, replied, "The night I ran out of the Canopy I caught the first bus out of Fayetteville and got off in Charleston. Two nights later, I'm in the gin mill of the best hotel in town and ran into her. DeDe was her name. Money. Pretty. We lived the high life. I'd still be gone if it wasn't for her. The SPs and a cop showed up at this southern belle's pad at four a.m. and demanded for me to prove I wasn't AWOL Jack Schmidt. She must've turned me in, because we'd been arguing about one of her girlfriends who, naturally, liked me." Schmidt shook his head at his bad luck. "You know, as we say in the Eighty-Deuce, fuck her and the horse she rode in on."

The supply phone rang. Broomfield answered, "Headquarters Company supply. Corporal Broomfield, sir." Patterson and Motz heard Broomfield say, "Yes, First Sergeant" three times very fast then hang up.

Motz predicted, "He wants us up there ASAP."

"Just you. Willie can bring up the prisoner."

"Hang on," said Schmidt. "What's the hurry? The stockade's the best part."

Motz was on his way. "The first shirt tells you to be there you best be there most skosh."

"Fuck him. What's he gonna do? Draft you and stick you in the 'Oh-Four?'" Patterson and Motz felt timid. Schmidt was right. Martin scared them. With a flick of his pen, he could keep a man in the mess hall for months.

"He's the first sergeant," justified Motz from the doorway. "He runs our lives with his roster. I don't want more company details than I already have."

"First sergeant. Last sergeant. He's a man like the rest of us."

Patterson piled Schmidt's gear on the counter. "Remember, Hollywood, he's got three up and three down and a...

"...diamond in the middle," they said in unison.

Corporal Broomfield suggested Schmidt should tell the man how he feels.

"I just might do that."

Ten minutes later, Patterson and Schmidt arrived at the orderly room. Motz wasn't there. Martin directed Schmidt into the commanding officer's room. Patterson, carrying the sleeping bag, followed him in. Schmidt dropped the laundry bag full of gear on the floor. Martin came right behind him.

"Who told y'all to put that down, Private? Patterson, stow that bag and get the hell out of here." Patterson placed the sleeping bag on the floor and, as he walked out, he could hear Martin telling Schmidt to pick up the laundry bag and hold it until told differently. He did not hear Schmidt's reply.

First Sergeant Billy Martin then directed Schmidt to keep the sleeping bag under the other arm and stand at attention behind Lt. Margolin's chair. He produced the handcuffs and hooked Schmidt's wrist to the back of the chair. "Don't put anything down until y'all are told to and don't sit down."

Martin left Schmidt standing behind the chair, hand-cuffed, laundry bag in one hand and the sleeping bag under the arm of the cuffed hand. The door to the orderly room remained open, but Martin's view was blocked. Schmidt relaxed, slouched, shifting his weight from leg to leg. He swung the laundry bag around to rest it on the chair and put the sleeping bag on the desk. If he leaned way to his left he could see Martin working diligently on something. The way he handled the colored pencils reminded Schmidt of an inspired artist.

It must be the duty roster, thought Schmidt, the form that brought fear into Patterson and Motz's lives. To everyone in the company. A fucking bookkeeper had grown men running here and there, pissing themselves, because he could rearrange their lives with a colored pencil.

Without a word and more than several hums of satisfaction, First Sgt. Billy Martin rose from his chair and moved to the door. Schmidt did not bother picking up the gear. He simply didn't care what the man said and waited for the senior NCO to chew him out. Martin, his mind still on the rosters with the smug knowledge there were no more missing men, pulled the CO's door shut, using the inside button lock to secure the door. He never glanced at Schmidt.

Alone, Schmidt thought it would be nice to just sit down. As he started to, he sensed the first sergeant had left the orderly room. Cautiously, Schmidt carried the chair and went to the door. For a moment he listened, then quietly unlocked the door and eased it open. All he saw was the colorful roster on the desk. He couldn't go far carrying the chair. Still, he wanted to do something for himself after the days of bullying he'd experienced from his captors.

Schmidt's mind raced. What was the Army expression? *Do something even if it's wrong.* He stifled his laugh to a snicker.

The phone was ringing when Martin returned from the latrine with the *Fayetteville Observer* under his arm. He answered it before sitting down. "Headquarters Company, First Battalion, Five-Oh-Fourth Airborne...wait a goddamn military minute!"

With the phone pinned to his ear by his shoulder, the short NCO stared down at this desk. "Good God in hell..." The duty roster was gone.

He hung up on whoever had called and went behind his desk to the clipboard where he kept the roster. Empty. *Of course it's empty*, he reminded himself, *I was working on it.* On the desk. Right there. Right in front of him. And it was gone.

Martin's magnified eyes darted around the room. He looked at the papers on Motz's desk. His clerk had gone over to Personnel to turn in the day's morning report; it might be there. Quickly, he sorted through Motz's in-tray. Before he finished the tray, he stopped and dug into the wastebasket. After he cleared the wastebasket, he was back to his desk, his in-basket. Next, he sorted the to-be-filed papers stacked on top of the filing cabinet then started pulling out the drawers.

The phone halted him as if he was a boxer and the round was over.

"What in the hell do you want?" It was Motz. Personnel were questioning the return of the deserter on the morning report.

"Schmidt! That's it! Motz, get your ass back here ASAP. Move! We got a A-number-one emergency!" In his haste to reach the closed door, he caught his thigh hard on the corner of his desk. The quick thick pain did not stop him. He tried the door.

It was locked. He pounded on the door. "Schmidt, y'all best unlock this here door if y'all want to live to sundown!"

Schmidt replied in his practiced sincere voice. "I can't, First Sergeant. I'm locked to the chair and holding my gear like you told me to."

Martin nodded in frustration and almost started kicking the door until he realized the key was in his desk drawer, in the colored pencil tray. On his way to the drawer, he hit his other thigh, but never stopped.

He found the key and went to the door and opened it so hard it slammed against the jam and came back to almost hit him. "Get against the wall, goddamnit!"

Schmidt was not prepared for the desperate man who charged in. Martin's eyes bulged in a scarlet face. Veins in his receding hairline pulsed like crawling creatures. Any moment he might expire or explode.

The first sergeant pulled the sleeping bag from under Schmidt's arm and kicked it across the room. Backing away, dragging the chair, Schmidt kept the laundry bag in his hand.

"I want that roster, Private Schmidt. And I want it now! Y'all hear me? Now!"

The deserter dropped the laundry bag and continued backing away from the irate first sergeant, keeping the chair between them as he moved to the corner. In his best matter-of-fact voice he said, "First Sergeant Billy Martin, I don't have the slightest idea what you're talking about." *Maybe*, hoped Schmidt, *the maniac would hit him*. It might help him during his court-martial.

Martin could not control himself. He stopped pursuing Schmidt and grabbed the laundry bag. The contents, shelter halves, pegs and poles, air mattress, boots were spilled onto the floor, then he snapped open the sleeping bag and waved it like a flag. Nothing.

He threw the unrolled bag into the corner by the coat rack.

"Soldier...what in the hell am I sayin', 'soldier'? Y'all ain't no soldier. Boy, did y'all hear anythin' goin' on in my orderly room in the last ten minutes?"

Schmidt in a timid voice claimed he never heard anything because he was concentrating on holding the two bags the first sergeant had ordered him not to put down. "I was afraid I'd drop them and you'd chew my ass again."

"Don't give me that candy-ass bullshit. Y'all better fuckin'-A-well tell me where my roster is or I'm gonna hang yore deserter ass for disobeyin' a direct order, insubordination, stealin' government property, and a personal attack on the person of a first sergeant in the United States Army. Y'all read me, asshole?"

Martin whipped open the folded shelter halves and tossed them after the sleeping bag. He kicked at the air mattress and tent pegs, scattering the pegs around the room. He picked up a boot and held it high to see inside. He threw that across the room and picked up the other one to examine.

"Sergeant Martin, I swear to God on my mother's death I don't know what you're talking about." Like an animal trainer, Schmidt had the chair between him and the first sergeant and was ready to defend himself if the man charged him.

Martin's bubble eyes raced up and down Schmidt, head to toe, his head bobbing as he pounded the boot into his open palm like a blackjack and kept repeating, "Oh yeah, it's y'all. It has to be y'all."

He raised the boot. Schmidt raised the chair.

"What in the hell's going on here?"

Lt. Margolin and Sfc. Wisnewski, fresh from their daily coffee break, stood in the doorway.

First Sgt. Billy Martin lowered the boot and accused, "Sir, this here scumbag deserter stole the duty roster."

"No," interjected Schmidt, "he's crazy. He's blaming me because he lost it."

Schmidt rattled the handcuffs against the chair back. "I've been locked in here and the door was locked."

Motz stuck his head in the door to announce he was back from Personnel.

Martin dropped the boot and pushed past Margolin and Wisnewski to shove his face in front of Motz's. "What in the hell y'all mean leavin' the orderly room unguarded while we have a deserter here?"

Motz retreated and foolishly reminded the first sergeant he had directed him to Personnel with the morning report.

The first sergeant caught himself and, in an attempt to regain control, stated to his audience while pointing to the perplexed corporal, "If I told this s-o-b once I've told him a thousand times...ten thousand times...Never. Never. NEVER leave the orderly room unguarded. Never!"

Margolin and Wisnewski continued their silent exchanges of incredulousness. Schmidt simply shook his head when anyone looked at him.

"Do y'all know what that roster means? The duty roster? How important it is? We're talkin' theft of government property. Someone's ass is goin' to the stockade."

Finally, Lt. Margolin nodded to Sgt. 'Ski and said, "Take it easy, Sergeant Martin." His voice failed to carry the conviction he wanted. It was more a tone of weariness of having to once more tolerate the Lifer instead of booting him in the ass. Martin did not seem to hear him.

"Without the roster the company, can't function. Who can do what? Who's here and who ain't? Sir," he took Margolin's arm, "we gotta do somethin' right away." Behind his spectacles his eyes watered. "Now, sir. We gotta catch the perpetrator and run his ass to Leavenworth 'fore sixteen hundred hours today."

The small group, much to Schmidt's relief, edged into the orderly room where Motz stood terrified behind his desk. Margolin stayed close to the first sergeant, ready to grab him if he went any further toward the deep end.

Martin lit up. "I got it, sir! A shakedown inspection! We'll catch the son-of-a-bitch red-handed!"

"Wait one, First Sergeant," said the lieutenant, but Martin ignored him.

"Ski, fall out the troops. Have 'em unlock their wall and footlockers and file outside. I'm personally goin' through every damn..."

"Sergeant Martin! Get your mouth outta gear and listen up!" Margolin shouted and didn't believe he did it.

Martin's mouth stopped on a dime and dropped open. Some spittle had formed on his lips. He stared at the young officer as if he knew him from someplace and didn't know why he was in the room. His orderly room.

Margolin's shout attracted troops in the hallway.

The lieutenant almost grabbed Martin's shoulders to calm him and speak softly to him when the first sergeant quickly spun to face Motz. "Get out!" demanded the crazed NCO. "Y'all on yore way to Dog Company for dereliction of duty. That's a direct order. Y'all hear me?"

The first sergeant came around the desk. Motz moved backwards toward the door. Wisnewski stepped between Martin and Motz and nodded to Motz to take off. The sergeant shut the door behind him.

The instant the door shut, Margolin and Wisnewski, without any preconceived plan, took Martin by the shoulders and directed him to sit at his desk. When they grabbed him, he went limp as if relieved of a great burden. He rubbed the empty spot on his desk and said, "More than ten years in this man's Army and nothin' like this has ever happened. The whole company's gone just like that." He slowly snapped his fingers.

Wisnewski spoke quietly. "Sergeant Martin, you can't fly off the handle on this thing. If the troops see you unglued they'll never…"

"Unglued! Me! I'm not crazy. That roster's gone, goddamnit!"

"Goddamnit, Billy Martin, listen to us!" Margolin found he liked shouting at Martin.

Ski put his hand on the NCO's shoulder and assured him they'd have a search. He and Margolin would do everything possible to find the roster, but it would be best to do it quietly. "You don't want headquarters gettin' wind of this. You see what I'm sayin'?"

"Jesus Christ on a crutch. I'll be a laughin' stock. Steele'll hang my ass off the regimental flagpole." Margolin and Wisnewski looked at one another and nodded agreement.

Martin leaned back in the chair and pressed his fingers to his temple. "He'll send me to Dog Company as a private." Tears welled in his eyes.

"That's not gonna happen, Top," assured Wisnewski.

Margolin did not express his hope it might. Instead, he offered the opinion that a search of the company would not produce the roster.

Martin came forward in his chair. "You got to have one. For the record."

The lieutenant and the sergeant first class looked at one another. "For the record," they said together.

Margolin asked Wisnewski how a search was conducted. "At the noon formation, we'll have every man go to his bunk and standby. Meanwhile, I'll get some bodies to go through the dumpster."

"The dumpster!" Martin stood up as if ready to rush out and dive in, but he didn't. He sat back down. "Good God almighty. Torn up in little pieces in the garbage."

The phone rang in Margolin's office. "I'll get it, sir," offered Schmidt, who had not missed a moment of the drama from his handcuffed chair vantage point in the CO's office. Before Margolin could respond, Schmidt had the phone in his free hand. "Headquarters Company. Five-Oh-Fourth Infantry. Deserter Schmidt, sir."

Margolin did not want to leave the room. "Take a message, Schmidt."

"Yes, sir. Yes, sir." repeated Schmidt into the phone and hung up. "Sir, Lieutenant Hanna says he can't make handball today. He'll call you next week to re-schedule."

Patterson and a new private named Christofferson searched the dumpster. "We're lucky, it's only half-full," said the new man. *An optimist*, thought Patterson as he watched the coffee grounds slide across his polished boots. He and his helper were knee-deep in old newspapers, tattered fatigues used to clean up unimaginable messes, hair pomades and empty shaving cream containers, beer and liquor bottles contrary to the no drinking allowed in the barracks rule, towels whose final glories were buffing rags, crud-stained underwear, and—just as the chow line formed by the dumpster and much to the troop's amusement—they found a brassiere.

After chow, each man's wall and footlocker stood open. Margolin, Wisnewski, and two other NCOs walked quickly through the four squad bays, ignoring the messiness of the men's storage areas as it was not an official inspection. Breslin's secreted bottle of Early Times and Mangiameli's two quarts of oil and Banuelous' knife were not discovered. A lot of girlie magazines were and ignored. The truth was no one looked in great detail, and the brief inspection ended without any success.

Immediately afterwards, the lieutenant and the sergeant found First Sgt. Billy Martin sifting debris by the dumpster with his foot as Patterson and the new man tossed the trash back inside the huge steel container.

"We're sure lucky it ain't windy, huh, First Sergeant," said Private Christofferson.

Martin looked at the mess. "Police it up," he ordered and went back inside, ignoring the lieutenant and Wisnewski. His mind wandered; with all his years of ass kissing, wheeling and dealing to move his career along—was it now lost? *My power and prestige gone? My retirement ruined? I have to find that roster.*

Chapter 10

Under the military justice system guided by the Uniform Code of Military Justice, a man is guilty until proven innocent. Soldiers in trouble for infractions less serious than murder and armed robbery are court-martialed at the regimental level. This is a Special Court-martial by three officers, and the sentences might be dishonorable discharges, stockade time, reduction in rank, or all combined. General Courts-martial adjudicate the most serious crime: a five-member panel at division level can sentence a man to death, life in Leavenworth along with the dishonorable discharge, fines, and loss of rank. Serious consequences for serious crimes. The Summary Court-martial is at the company level and administered by the commanding officer. This covers drunk driving, AWOL, petty thievery, discipline, and violations of company policy. However, most company infractions are handled by non-judicial punishment, the ubiquitous Article 15. This option allows more leeway for the presiding officer, and it keeps the perpetrator from being tainted by the formal Summary Court-martial. The Article 15 keeps problems in-house and away from regimental headquarters. For those defendants facing a court-martial, the commanding officer usually advises not to retain civilian counsel, as this will prejudice the court-martial board against the accused. Besides, the military provides counsel free of charge. These appointed defenders are usually regular line officers, lieutenants or captains, assigned legal duties as part of their daily routines. Few have any legal training. What some soldiers in trouble forget or ignore is that these assigned defenders have their own careers to nurture. It is in their interest to guide the accused to accept the board's desires instead of arguing for their defense, as the board members often write the defending officers' efficiency reports. In the end, military justice—like military intelligence and military music—is frequently an oxymoron.

"Come out of there, soldier!"

Freshly showered and shaved after a long day on pots and pans, Schmidt snuggled inside his sleeping bag and wished whoever was calling him would go away. He was not a soldier any longer. He wished that would sink in to those gung-ho idiots.

"Do you read me, soldier?"

One day scrubbing the big pots over the hot sinks wasn't too bad. However, day after day would be exhausting and that was all he had to look forward to until his court-martial. That, and NCOs giving him bullshit like the asshole outside his tent at that moment.

"Private Schmidt, fall-in, and that's a direct order from a colonel in the United States Army." A dog growled.

Steele! Schmidt twisted around in his sleeping bag and stuck his head out the tent flap into the cool fall evening. "Good evening, Colonel." Schmidt offered his winning smile. "What brings you to this neck of the woods?"

Steele's countenance tightened. "I want you outside, young man. At attention."

"If I don't come out, are you going to tell Ike and J. Edgar Hoover I'm a bad boy?"

"That's insubordination, son. It won't help you."

"Colonel, I'm trying real hard to go along with what you gentlemen have in mind for me." As he spoke, he slipped out of the sleeping bag and came out in the too-large fatigue shirt and trousers he wore as pajamas. He was barefoot. "But I keep running into the fact no one believes I've resigned. I won my Wings and resigned. I have more important things to do with my life than keep my footlocker ready for inspection by some imbecile with a stripe on his arm. With all due respect, sir, I again offer my resignation." He extended his hand and added for a touch of humor, "I've got to be about my father's business."

Strac stuck his nose into the tent.

Steele ignored his open hand and walked from side to side, inspecting Schmidt who stood rubbing his arms to suppress the evening chill. "Soldier, we all have a military obligation to our country. You don't just walk away. We're going to make you pay for your transgression."

"Colonel, I'm not a soldier. They're all upstairs shining their booties for tomorrow."

"I take a personal interest in every man who goes AWOL from the Five-Oh-Fourth."

"You must be a busy man." Schmidt did not fear the colonel swinging on him as the stockade sergeant had. An officer had to be careful. A gentleman. He stared at the slightly taller, older man, and lifted his chin to show he would not be intimidated by Steele's commanding presence.

But Steele wasn't looking at him. The man's glances were up and down his body as if trying to see Schmidt all at once.

Son-of-a-bitch! He knew the look. Remembered the colonel's odd interest in him from the run and receiving his Wings. *That was it! The look of a man wanting—desiring something. Maybe I found a way out?* Schmidt allowed the loose trousers to slip a little and the unbuttoned jacket to fall open. He rubbed his chest with one hand and held up the trousers with the other.

Steele appeared to catch himself staring and thrust out his impressive jaw and snarled, "AWOLs are a disgrace to the regiment. Why did you go, soldier?"

Schmidt continued his peek-a-boo stance and kept turning to face the colonel who moved around him. *There's nothing to lose.*

He hung his head and said softly, "Sir, I was lying about resigning. I just didn't know what to say. The truth is I got a Dear John from my girl. We were engaged to be married when I was drafted." Schmidt considered crying.

"There are channels for that sort of thing. Did you see the chaplain?"

"I had to go right away. That night."

"Where's home, son?"

He explained he was from Indiana, but now lived in Hollywood.

"Hollywood?"

"Yes, sir."

"Hollywood, California?"

"That the only one I know, sir," he replied diffidently.

"I'd be ashamed to tell anyone Hollywood was my hometown."

Better than the Pentagon, thought Schmidt, and said, "I swear to God on my Mother's death that's my hometown ..." *Be desperate.* "... and I had to leave right away because my girl did it with a producer who wants to make her a star. She's really beautiful." He paused and looked sorrowful. "I was embarrassed to have to tell someone that's why I went."

The colonel stepped closer to Schmidt, closer than an arm's length. "You were gone a long time. The report says they found you with a woman in South Carolina."

Schmidt didn't blink. "Yes, sir. I was on my way back. She was helping me. I swear to God." He raised his hand to swear and let trousers slide a little lower. "Women kinda like me."

Steele's eyes feasted on Schmidt for just an instant, then he stepped back and spread his feet and put his hands on his hips. "Are you ready to take your punishment like a trooper and start soldiering?"

"I'm afraid, Colonel. I'm afraid they're going to lean on me and not give me a chance."

"You didn't sound interested when I first came over here, Private."

Schmidt wrapped the fatigue jacket closely around himself and replied, "I know, sir. You have to understand I've been hammered around a few times since I was picked up." He touched the bruises on his forehead. "See this. I'm a good-looking guy. I don't want to get busted up every time an NCO calls my name."

"A girl did it, son?"

"Yes, sir. She shafted me but good."

"If you keep your nose clean between now and your court-martial, I can help you. Reformed AWOLs sometimes make the best soldiers."

Schmidt ran his hand from his chest to his naval several times as he expressed his gratitude for any assistance.

"There'll be some slots opening in Headquarters this year. I might need a driver. You have to produce some behavior I can vouch for."

"Yes, sir." Schmidt saluted, looking as innocent as a Norman Rockwell teenager, while his trousers slipped to his pubic area. "You won't be disappointed, sir."

Steele wheeled around and strode away.

As the colonel reached the driveway by the mess hall where his Jeep was parked, Pfc. Patterson came down the rear mess hall stairs carrying a metal pitcher of steaming coffee. He, Broomfield, and Sgt. Webster were working late to restore order in the supply room after the first sergeant's second big search. In the darkness, Patterson never noticed Steele stop and glare.

"Hold on there, soldier!" Patterson stopped at the top of the supply room stairs and turned.

The silhouette against the waiting Jeep's headlights headed towards him. A glint of light from the kitchen reflected off the man's cap insignia. *An officer*, thought Patterson.

Steele loomed in front of him. Patterson almost dropped the pitcher and felt his bladder weaken. He switched hands and saluted. "Good evening, sir."

Steele returned the salute with a brief wave of his hand. "You're out of uniform, soldier."

Patterson, holding the pitcher with one hand, unstable on the top stair, explained he was working late and his fatigue jacket and hat were in the supply room, "… just down the stairs." He had come up for coffee.

Steele looked furious in the dim light. "Your boots are unbloused."

He looked down. He had not tucked in his trousers. He rarely did when working late. Patterson started to explain.

"Your belt buckle looks like a broken tank tread, soldier."

The young Pfc. could not say one reason before he started another. Steele's pace made him struggle with his words.

"'No excuse' is all I want to hear. What's your name?"

Patterson shut up. No excuse suited him fine. "Pfc. Patterson, sir."

"You just lost that stripe, Private. Report to First Sergeant Martin in the morning."

The colonel turned so quickly that Patterson flinched and checked himself from falling with a quick step down. He almost saluted the retreating officer. He wondered what that conversation was all about, unaware of Steele's encounter with Schmidt. Steele climbed into the Jeep and it backed out the driveway. Patterson saw it simply as a reason to fuck with him.

A suddenly enlightened Patterson ran toward the driveway. "You chicken-shit motherfucker!" and threw the pitcher at the spot where the Jeep had been and wished for the courage to throw it on the colonel. He picked up the empty pitcher and went half-way down the supply stairs where he sat for a few minutes so no one would see his tears of frustration.

Why didn't I stand up to Steele? I'm his equal—even if our ranks are different. I am. I'd earned that stripe. Patterson remembered KP with ex-Corporal Brookes his first day of assignment in the company. Brookes had warned him at any time the Army can step up and crush a man to make an example. Any man. And all he had really done was work late.

By his fourth day of KP, Schmidt had convinced Sgt. Potter he had worked as a baker in a Hollywood restaurant and that the Sfc. should let him work late to assist with the baking for the next day's breakfast. Potter provided fresh pastry every morning, and in appreciation of a man interested in the culinary arts he agreed, and even allowed Schmidt to come in later in the morning. Early that evening after the NCO left, Breslin, Patterson and Motz came into the mess hall with a case of Carlings Red Cap bottles. They drank and discussed their military futures while Sidney the Cook and Schmidt worked on pastry.

Motz was like a little boy with a new toy; he was in Dog Company, the real infantry. Any day he'd be heading for the field on maneuvers. He couldn't express his gratitude enough to Schmidt as if Schmidt had sent him there personally.

Two days earlier, Pfc. Willie Patterson had received his Article 15 from Lt. Margolin who reluctantly applied the company punishment and busted him to private. Margolin promised Patterson he'd get the stripe back and did not assign a month's hard labor cleaning regimental headquarters every night as First Sgt. Martin had demanded. He wasn't sure the first sergeant was hitting on all cylinders and wanted to shield the troops as much as possible from Martin's missing roster wrath. Patterson drank faster than the others to celebrate his new status of private.

With the pastry trays loaded in the ovens, Schmidt and Sidney joined their pals. Schmidt laughed at Patterson's concern over being a private and explained his theory about Steele being a homosexual. He could hustle Steele and maybe get the colonel to re-instate him.

"That's a pretty big maybe," said Breslin.

"You're nuts," argued Patterson. "Steele's no Q-ball. He's too squared away. Too hard looking. The cat's a real soldier."

"Wait a minute," added Breslin. "If you look at the man, you see his entire life is devoted to being with men. It's logical. Maybe Hollywood's right."

"It ain't true," advised Sidney the Cook, "'cause he ain't ever come on to me."

Motz sat silently until he thought everyone else had his say. He finally stated, "I'd bet my life he's as straight as an arrow. The man's a hero of the Korean War, for Christ's sake. They named a hill after him over there."

"Who gives a rat's ass. The important thing is for me to beat the rap," said Hollywood Jack Schmidt. "If I take off, Banuelous swears he has a place for me in Fayetteville."

"Hey, I've got an idea," suggested Breslin. "We'll drive him off post as a hood ornament on Tommy's car." They laughed and opened more Carlings.

At noon chow two days later, Patterson and Breslin passed along the serving line. Schmidt was serving mashed potatoes and string beans. The deserter KP leaned over and demanded, "You guys got to get me out of here."

"What about Steele's help?" asked Breslin.

"Fuck him. I'm going. Just get me to town."

During chow, Patterson asked Breslin questions on how they would get him away from the company without getting in trouble themselves. Breslin seemed unworried, but really had no specific answers. When Patterson and Breslin turned in their trays, Schmidt was at the tray window. He whispered, "The trial's set for sixteen hundred tomorrow. I've got to go tonight. Get a car."

"Wait 'til lights out," said Breslin after looking over both shoulders as if the FBI stood a few yards away. "I'll fix it up."

Patterson peeled off to the supply room and Breslin went to their squad bay on the third floor. Instead of taking his daily 20-minute nap, he went down the hall to a cadre room.

"What's happenin'?" he asked loudly as he tapped on the door.

Wise opened the door. "No haps, man."

Wise's roommate, Spec-Four Jerome Carter, lay on his bunk with his feet high on his footlocker to keep boot polish off the blankets. He read a paperback while Ahmad Jamal's piano quietly played on a 33-rpm portable. Wise and Carter were known to have the most serious squared-away room in the building. Fellow soldiers often stopped by just before Saturday morning inspections to view its pristine orderliness. Their uniforms were precisely tailored and boots always gleaming. Any visiting VIP usually ended up in their doorway with First Sgt. Billy Martin describing how sharp his men were. Wise and Carter supplied marijuana to fellow soldiers who passed the security test.

Once inside, Breslin said, "I'm looking for Mary Jane."

Neither man was friendly with Breslin. Working in Personnel isolated them from the troops who pulled KP, guard duty, and other company details. They kept quietly to themselves and spent most weekends in Raleigh like so many of the Negroes stationed at Bragg.

"Turn around," said Carter as he rose from his bunk.

Breslin could hear him open his footlocker and imagined him pulling the tightly rolled cigarettes from a Kiwi shoe polish can or a soap dish. "What's the going rate today?" asked Breslin.

"Because you're from Philly and a PFC., I'll do you a two for one deal."

"I'm planning a long afternoon in the chapel. Give me four sticks."

"You prayin' for somethin'?" asked Carter.

"My poor dammed soul. What're you reading?"

"Cat named Burkhardt DuBois."

"Never heard of him." Breslin took pride in his literary knowledge, but often pretended ignorance. It was easy in the Army.

"You should give him a taste. Says how it's supposed to be." Wise pointed out there wasn't any cock in it.

Breslin gave Carter two bucks and stuck the cigarettes in his Chesterfield pack. "If there aren't big pictures I'm not interested. Thanks, man."

Once in the chapel, he made sure all the doors were locked. Major Byrd, the Protestant Chaplain, was in D.C. Breslin had spent the morning buffing the floor around the altar and the vestibule. His afternoon plan was pew polishing; however, Schmidt's need threw him off. He had to think about helping his pal. *High risk. Low reward. Maybe a court-martial for anyone caught helping him. The military scuttlebutt ran that a man served the same sentence as the individual he had helped.*

He took the bottle of Early Times out of the false bottom of the trash receptacle by the chapel's interior doors and sat in the next to last pew with a clipboard, plastic cup of bourbon, his sticks of Mary Jane, and regular cigarettes.

While contemplating assisting Schmidt, he'd work on his latest and only poem since arriving at Bragg last January. The title was "On Becoming A Jesuit."

> Hard shut the chapel doors where monks
> Chant mysteries around the bridegroom of
> The blackened cross. Prostate before the imminent
> Altar the novice waits (*waited*) falling stones and blindness

Breslin wasn't happy with 'waits' or 'waited' and he needed a link to the second stanza. Maybe 'as'? "As monks…"

> As Monks mysteries filled the windowless
> Chapel with beauty denied by reason. With

Guilt not heart the body listened and lips
Kissed the polished floor. Cold the stone...

Breslin changed 'cold the stone' to...

A cold touch
But his burden told him warm. He
Remained beneath the cross of black;
Helpless in fear of the trembling altar.
Pretending to pray...

How many? Two more. A trinity.

Pretending to pray.
Pretending to pray.
His hands are clasped *(his clasped hands?)*,
His lips move. But his heart is someplace beyond
The sunless chapel amid summer songs *(songs of summer?)*
Wishing for soft wind, sun, and love.

Breslin drank and smoked and scanned his efforts. The words 'helpless in fear' stood out, and he spoke them loudly to the altar. He slid forward on the pew and knelt, slouching, facing the altar and blessed himself. And prayed for the strength to help Schmidt.

Late that afternoon, Schmidt, with Broomfield as his escort, showed up in supply to draw a Class A uniform: the wool OD dress uniform of Ike jacket, trousers, poplin shirt, tie, blue shoulder infantry cord, and overseas cap. Patterson gave him lapel brass of a U.S. Army and crossed-rifles infantry insignia to make him look more squared away.

Getting the uniform confirmed what Schmidt had said. He'd go up tomorrow.

Patterson realized he and Breslin had to do something quickly. To avoid Webster and Broomfield hearing his phone conversation, Patterson went to the pay phone in the dayroom to call Breslin. No answer. It was getting dark.

He should go to the chapel.

Patterson breezed through the supply room to grab his field jacket. He told Sgt. Webster he needed to get to the PX. The supply sergeant, leaning back in his special swivel chair with his immaculate boots on the edge of the desk just inches from his afternoon ritual sherry and his ivory cigarette holder in his hand, waved Patterson along. "Walk tall, young William."

Patterson jogged along Grave Street as the regiment's lights came on. He pounded on the sturdy chapel doors, calling for Breslin. No one answered the door. The lights were out.

"I know you're in there, Scott!" He pounded again. "We best be doin' somethin' to get Schmidt movin'!" Dead quiet.

He banged on the door and called out again. Still no answer.

"Fuck you!" shouted Patterson.

Angry, he headed back to the barracks. *What can I do on my own?* He wished McBride wasn't on emergency leave; something about his mother had come up. He'd know what to do. Then he remembered Motz. The former company clerk knew his way around rules and regulations and might have thought of something since their night in the mess hall. Dog Company was just down Grave Street.

No one liked to enter Dog Company. It was the lair of First Sergeant Jim Parker who was known as 'The Bear' for his size and ferociousness. Regimental malcontents frequently went to Dog Company as a last chance before being dishonorably discharged or sent to the stockade. He handled all discipline personally in the company boiler room, where he explained to wise guys and smart-asses they were paratroopers in the U.S. Army and he was proud of being a soldier because the Army gave him his first set of new clothing and pair of boots. Back in Harlan, Kentucky, life had been hard. He didn't mind his men smashing a tall-boy Budweiser over the helmet of an MP in Fayetteville, but when they were in Dog Company, he'd warn them with his big finger jabbing them hard in the chest that they better soldier to the best of their ability or he'd beat the piss out of them. And that was a promise.

Dog Company was the top rifle company in the 504th, the 82nd Airborne, 18th Airborne Corps, First Army Command, and the U.S. Army.

Patterson found the heavy double doors chained shut. Taped inside the glass was a cardboard sign with rough crayon letters: "Company business. See supply." Chained doors usually meant the company was in the field. Patterson walked around to supply knowing Motz would be overjoyed if he was in the boonies, but a few soldiers always remained behind. Maybe, because Motz was new, he had stayed behind.

One of the supply doors was ajar.

Webster had taught Patterson to always knock or shout when entering a supply room, or else he might witness something he'd spend the rest of his life wishing he hadn't. Patterson slapped the steel door with his open palm several times.

No answer. He inched open the door and looked. "Anyone here?" The large basement room was all shadows and shelves and wire partitions with a single light bulb at the far end.

Suddenly, from the dark right side, a slouched figure appeared. "Who goes there?" asked the figure.

The outside door light showed a heavy man in baggy field trousers and a half-tucked-in fatigue shirt. Both sleeves were rolled back above thin wrists. His fatigue hat sat back on his head. On his arm were the three stripes of a buck sergeant. He carried a canteen cup. *The Bear?*

Patterson smelled whiskey and instinct urged him to run. Slowly, he tried to back out.

The sergeant stepped forward and caught the edge of the door. "What's this 'anyone here' shit? Front and center, soldier."

Patterson was too afraid to disobey; a year in the 504th did that to a soldier. Besides, the Bear might beat him up. Then it dawned on him that it couldn't be the Bear, because this man was only a buck sergeant.

Patterson stepped forward with a little more confidence. "I'm lookin' for Corporal Motz, Sarge."

"Who, goddamnit?"

"Corporal Motz," he replied loudly, "a real tall skinny dude who just came over from Headquarters."

The sergeant waved his cup as if to invite Patterson to walk with him or to simply acknowledge he understood him. "I know. The skinny gung-ho kid."

The sergeant swayed and called over his shoulder. "Hey, Warden, we got us a guest." His authoritative tone disappeared. "Come over here, Private."

"Excuse me, Sarge, I'm runnin' an errand for my first sergeant and I..."

"Who is he?" The strong voice returned.

"First Sergeant Billy Martin."

"Fuck that homesteader. Get over here and meet a real soldier."

The soldier used his chunky frame to urge Patterson toward the light where a carefully dressed officer sat at a desk. Patterson wanted to run out and didn't know how. He knew the man would be too drunk to catch him, but his fear of the system kept him moving.

"That fake corporal is out runnin' around the boonies with the rest of the dogfaces. I'd be with them, but someone's got to mind the store. Right, Warden?"

"Right." The officer looked up. He smiled with perfect teeth. His poplin uniform shirt was tailored to his solid frame. His dark brown necktie was pulled slightly loose.

Patterson thought he was looking at a recruiting poster of the perfect soldier. The hero. Short gray hair at the temples. A weathered, tan face that had seen it all. Even in the poor light his eyes were ice blue. Over the back of his chair was his chocolate brown jacket, the only medals on it were a Combat Infantryman's Badge with a Star and Master Parachutists Wings. The bars of a chief warrant officer were on the shoulders.

Two not completely empty fifths of Jack Daniels and a steel pot of melting ice cubes were on the table. The ashtray was inundated with crushed Camel butts. Spread across the table was the parts of a Browning automatic rifle.

The officer sipped from a canteen cup, then shifted the weapon's brass buffer cones in his hands like ancient coins. With a wry smile at Patterson, he asked, "Should I give him a drink, Michael?"

In spite of the situation and the officer's rank, Patterson knew he could trust the man. He sounded like someone Patterson had known all his life.

"Does a hobby horse have a wooden cock?" The sergeant stood under the light now. His nametag read 'Kennedy.' He needed a shave and a change of uniform. The sergeant swayed to stay in one place.

"With or without ice, son?"

It seemed wise to accept. "Ice, please," replied the private.

Warden snorted at the 'please' then realized, "We're out of cups, Michael."

"Use this." Sergeant Kennedy banged his on the table. "I've got a shit pot full of them back here." He dropped his fatigue hat onto the table and wandered into the dark bins.

Warden smiled as he dished cubes into the canteen cup and doused them with bourbon. "Michael's a lot of things, but he's not contagious." He handed the cup to Patterson, wiped his hands on the soiled cloth he used to clean the BAR, and began putting the metal disks into the BAR's buffer tube.

From the dark, the sergeant called out, "You know who's makin' you a drink, recruit?"

Patterson ignored the question; he was staring at the Jump Wings on the old sergeant's sweat-stained fatigue hat. There were four bronze stars on the Wings. Each star represented a combat jump. There were not many men in the world with four combat jumps. They had to be World War II. Maybe one in Korea, which veterans of the second world war dismissed. Patterson knew the battle names: Normandy. Sicily. Nijmegen. Salerno. The Bragg drop zones were named after them. *And he was just a buck sergeant!*

Men could make buck sergeant in three to four years if they kept their nose clean.

"That's Chief Warrant Officer Milt Warden. He's the first G.I. to shoot down a Zero in the big one."

"Son," said Warden, holding up his own canteen cup, "don't pay too much mind to what Michael says. He means well. Drink up."

Warden took a sip of his drink after tipping it toward Patterson. He placed the cup down and tightened the buffer cap onto the tube with the spanner end of a combination tool. His hands moved over the parts with the easy rhythm of an experienced card dealer. Quickly finishing, he wiped his hands and lit a Camel. Patterson accepted the warrant officer's silent offer of a cigarette.

"How long you been in this man's Army, son?" Warden stretched to light Patterson's cigarette after lighting his own and before Patterson pulled out his '04 lighter.

"A year, sir. A little more than a year." He sipped his drink and realized no officer had ever talked to him like a regular person. He used the cigarette to hide his grimace from the sips of bourbon.

"Still a private."

Sergeant Kennedy's voice led him back to the table. "The son-of-a-bitch took a BAR up on the roof of Schofield and shot down a Jap Zero during Pearl Harbor."

Patterson offered he had been busted.

Warden laughed knowingly. "Hey, Michael, our visitor was 'reduced in rank,' as we say."

Kennedy used his shirttail to wipe out the new canteen cup. "He did. Blasted a Jap right out of the sky. From the hip." Michael put his cup on the table and picked up the half-assembled BAR by the carrying handle. "With this baby."

"Watch it, Michael."

"We used to have leather slings." He swung the stock-less weapon around and verbally assaulted the rear of the supply room. "Blam! Blam-blam-blam! Die, motherfuckers!"

Patterson winced from the sounds. Warden seemed used to it.

Kennedy asked if Patterson had ever fired a BAR.

"No. We didn't have them in basic."

"Take it."

The thrust weapon forced Patterson to quickly put his cigarette in his mouth and grab the weapon. His shoulder dropped. He had to put down his cup and use both hands.

"Heavy, huh? That thing you can barely lift is a pee-bringin' son-of-a-bitch. We used to call them gas-operated, fully fuckin' automatic kraut killers."

"Put it on the table, son," said Warden softly. Patterson placed the weapon on the table. The warrant officer opened the bipods on the muzzle to elevate the barrel and began assembling it again.

"See what I mean, Warden. The Army ain't shit no more. The kid never fired a BAR."

Warden asked Patterson why he was demoted. He explained about coming out of the mess hall late at night with his boots unbloused.

"The Army doesn't change much," said Warden. "Someone with more rank can always make your life difficult. I knew a boxer at Schofield who died because he didn't want to box. All he wanted was to play the bugle. A hardhead like Michael here. Our old sarge here has been 'reduced in rank' five times."

"Six," corrected Kennedy.

Warden fitted the hollow stock over the actuator tube. It took several short hits with the heel of his hand to secure it. "Does the spring come next or the actuator?"

Without looking up from pouring his drink, Kennedy replied, "The spring comes after."

"Come on, son. Knock it back," encouraged Warden with a lift of his cup.

Patterson sipped and worried about getting away. He'd finish the smoke then chogie.

Kennedy sat on the extra metal folding chair by the desk. He wheezed as he sat and caught his breath before taking a hefty swig of bourbon. The light reflected off the bald spot on the back of his head. He looked like a tired old man who should be on the front porch of his own home in a small town watching his children play on his freshly cut law. He didn't look like a man who fought across Europe and earned four stars for combat jumps.

The sergeant reached across the table to push aside Warden's fingers working the gas cylinder tube. "You gotta turn it just right," he said as he felt for the correct locking alignment while looking at Patterson. "Can't do this blind-folded no more. We just tried. There." He inserted the body lock key to tighten it all.

"I can remember field strippin' these babies at night and bein' too scared to blink there were so many krauts around. It's a real talent, like bein' a surgeon or somethin'."

"Excuse me, Sergeant Michael." Warden placed the gas regulator into the cylinder body. His strong fingers turned it until it was flush against the lock. He looked at Patterson and winked. "We do this every year."

"You got to listen for the clicks to make sure the gas ports are open," cautioned Kennedy.

Warden smiled his strong smile and asked jokingly, "Is that so?"

Patterson could not help but compare the two men and be amazed at the difference. The warrant officer was older and must have served longer than the sergeant, yet he appeared to be ten years younger. Their physiques differed by 20 years. Warden had the aura of a man who had found enjoyment and humor in life, not burdens and defeats. The heavy sergeant seemed drained of joy, perhaps from too great a struggle to survive the battles. He had matured into a fumbler, a drunk, and a complete wrong number. *I'll never be like that,* vowed Patterson.

The Army could bust him a hundred times over and he'd never be like that. The whim of a colonel took away his stripe, which can happen any time to anyone; it was the system. Ex-Corporal Freddy Brookes had warned him. The regiment could destroy a man's body and spirit and squeeze his nuts until he couldn't cry out anymore. Anyone who broke the pattern fell victim to it. *It would never happen to me. Never.*

Patterson asked, "So when are the troops comin' in?"

"Who gives a shit. They left me here to mind the store."

Patterson stayed silent as Warden finished assembling the BAR. He wiped it down with the oilcloth. His touch on the metal light and smooth, lovingly. "Mox nix, Michael. It's just as important to stay behind." Warden shifted the weapon to get a better look under the spare lighting. He leaned over to gaze through the sight and adjust the elevation screw. "Listen to Parker. He's a good Joe."

Kennedy slapped the table. "Listen to him!" He stood up. "All he ever tells me is he's gonna kick my ass if he catches me drunk."

Warden's expression had not changed since Kennedy hit the table. His thumb and forefinger still held the elevation screw. "He wants you to make your twenty. It's not far off. Don't make it hard for him."

Patterson didn't understand what was going on. He put down his canteen cup and said, "Thanks, I gotta get goin'."

Kennedy turned to Patterson. Face flushed. "You ain't goin' nowhere, Private, 'til I dismiss your ass. Now get down and give me ten good Airborne pushups."

Not this time. Not now. He put out his cigarette in the jammed ashtray.

"Michael," said Warden, "lay off."

Patterson slowly backed away from the desk.

"Lay off? These kids can't soldier. At the end of W-W-Two I was a sergeant-major with more fruit salad than any bastard in this regiment. I want a pushup I should get one. Goddamnit, start those push-ups. That's a direct order."

Kennedy stepped toward the retreating Patterson. Warden stretched his long body across the desk to grab his friend's arm. Kennedy twisted away and lost his balance. He swerved toward Patterson who initially stepped aside until he realized he was the only person to keep the sergeant from falling on his face.

The young private caught the old soldier. The sergeant's dead weight nearly toppled them to the floor. "Take it easy, Sarge."

Patterson inhaled vomit and liquor smells. Dried spit had formed on the corner of the sergeant's mouth. As Patterson held him, Kennedy's eyes rolled high in their sockets. Warden came from behind and shifted Kennedy's weight off the younger soldier.

Kennedy mumbled about ten good Airborne pushups.

"Sarge," said Patterson, "I can't do pushups with you hangin' all over me."

"Good, son," said Warden as he guided his buddy back to the table. "Sit down, Michael."

A dumbfounded Kennedy stared at Patterson from across the table. He reached and rested his hand on the weapon's carrying handle. "Look, Milt, he ain't started those pushups yet."

Would he shoot me? wondered Patterson. He took a step backwards and said, "I'm startin' now, Sarge. One."

Another step back. "Two."

Warden moved behind Kennedy slumped at the table and signaled Patterson to move on.

"Three." Patterson was no longer under the glare of the bulb. No one would fuck with him now. "Four," he said from the darkness.

Warden sat next to his long time comrade. Kennedy looked closely at him. "I carried five boxes of ammo across that canal and a kraut machine gunner caught me right here." Kennedy tried to unhook his field suspenders.

"Five," called Patterson from the door.

Warden patted Kennedy on the shoulder and assured him he had seen the scars enough times. He sat down.

Kennedy rose from his metal folding chair and shaded his eyes. "Hey!"

"Six." said Patterson loudly.

The sergeant pointed his finger toward the darkness hiding Patterson. "I carried a BAR and five boxes of ammo even though I was wounded. I was a goddamn bull."

"Seven," said Patterson feeling the cool air behind the door. He gently leaned on the panic bar.

"There wasn't a kraut in the world that was gonna stop us! They tried, but we kicked ass and took names. We went all the way to Germany."

Kennedy looked down at Warden sitting beside him. He took Warden's canteen cup and drank. Warden lit a cigarette and sipped from Kennedy's cup. Patterson watched.

"We went all the way, Milt. All the way! We were lean and mean. Fuckin' devils in baggy pants. We were. We really were."

"I know you were," replied Warden in his soft voice. "Sit down. Let's work on the bourbon."

Kennedy stepped away from the table.

Patterson quietly opened the door, yet did not leave.

"I don't want a drink, Milt," exclaimed Kennedy. "I want to know what happened. What happened to us? I'd give my right ball to be gettin' ready to cross that canal again. We were alive then. Really alive!"

Kennedy lifted the BAR. He cocked the bolt in one swift motion and swung toward the invisible Patterson. "What happened, Milt? What in the hell happened?"

Patterson never heard the reply. He had the metal door between him and the pointed BAR and ran up the stairs, listening, already feeling the blast in his back. It never came.

He was back in the cool night, still needing someone to help him, and too much time had been lost. He would try one more person. Sidney the Cook might be crazy enough to help him if he wasn't out chasing someone's wife or daughter or sister or a nun.

Since their experience with the Negro girls, Patterson and Breslin spent more time with Sidney the Cook. They would stop by his two-man cadre room once or twice to drink and just hang out. He occasionally joined them for beers at the Canopy Lounge and sneaking into the movies by walking in backwards as the theatre emptied, usually bringing along wine or quarts of beer under their jackets.

Patterson found Sidney the Cook and his roommate, Speedy-Four Adam 'Archie' Archibald, on the edge of their bunks in their dirty cook whites sharing a half-empty bottle of Zinfandel like gentlemen of leisure. The room smelled of stale cigarettes and unwashed socks. Their unmade beds revealed gray instead of white sheets with patches of hair tonic on the pillowcases. Two standing ashtrays liberated from the dayroom overflowed with butts and candy wrappers. The floor looked like someone's bad skin. Cooks' rooms were rarely inspected due to the late, early, and long hours they worked.

Patterson presented the problem of Schmidt needing to get to town.

Archie interrupted to ask Patterson if he knew he was dying. The two men didn't really know each other. Archie and Sidney usually worked different shifts.

"So fuckin' die, man," encouraged Sidney the Cook.

Pale and emaciated, Archie wore GI-issue glasses with thick lenses like First Sgt. Billy Martin. He lived vicariously through Sidney the Cook's escapades and drank in the Combat Alley bars. Once in a while, he'd hitchhike to New Kensington, Pennsylvania, his hometown.

"This is great," said Patterson aloud. "I need help and you two are all fucked up."

"Great," repeated Archie. "My fuckin' hair's fallin' out and my blood's poisoned and this asshole says it's great. He a friend of yours?"

"I said, go on and die, motherfucker."

Patterson returned to his task of helping Schmidt. As he talked, Sidney changed into his fatigues and cursed himself for being drunk while taking several more swigs of wine. Patterson refused a drink.

"I got atomic poisonin' at Jackass Flats, man," continued Archie to no one. "Just like in Japan when they dropped that fuckin' A-bomb."

Sidney looked up from tying his boots, which had extra soles to make him appear taller, and asked, "What'd you wanna do?"

"What do I want to do?" asked Patterson.

"That's what I said, man."

"Youse should'a seen that blast. The ground shook hard enough to knock you outta your socks."

"Jesus, I was hopin' you'd have some ideas. All's I know we got to get him to Fayetteville and meet Banuelous at the Canopy."

Sidney stood up and announced, "You know me, man. I'm in for the whole motherfuckin' ball of wax. Damn!" He sat back down, almost falling backwards. "There's all little fuckin' dots." He stared at the ceiling light, waving away the intangible spots.

Archie laughed so hard he started coughing. His glasses fell in his lap and tears came to his eyes. "You got it too!" Archie carried a distended belly from drinking too much. His short blond hair showed bald spots. He could not have been more than 19 and like so many others in the 82nd he had the Jump Wings tattoo on his shoulder, and on his thin left forearm stood a tiny red devil with a pitchfork. 'Born To' in red letters arched over the devil's head and 'Raise Hell' rocked under its feet.

"Shut the fuck up, Archie." Sidney rose from the cot and added, "He did that 'Operation Smoky' thing last year at Camp Desert Rock in Nevada and swears it fucked him up."

"It did, man. We pulled a John Wayne and walked through the A-blast and the rays went right through us. It was like getting shot with a space gun."

"It's the fuckin' Zinfandel, asshole. Let's go, Willie."

They found Mangiameli sitting on his footlocker writing a letter to Judy. The three of them went into the latrine for privacy. There wasn't much in a squad bay of 40 men. Before the door shut, Mangiameli wanted to know what they were going to do. Patterson signaled quiet with a finger to his lips and checked the stalls. He bummed a cigarette from Mangiameli and admitted he had no idea, except Schmidt said he had to meet Banuelous in town later.

Sidney thought it too high a risk to just drive him off post. The MPs set up roadblocks when someone bugs out.

Patterson came up with the idea to drive him off post in a staff car like he was a VIP. "Anything loose in the pool, Tommy?"

"You want a five-ton wrecker or a deuce-and-a-half, we can do it."

Mangiameli asked about Breslin. "Busy. Chaplain's jerkin' his chain," replied Patterson. "You know, we could take the wrecker, hook up a car, and tow it off with Schmidt in the trunk."

"Not my fuckin' car, Willie," declared Sidney the Cook.

"No, no, not mine neither," said Mangiameli.

"You know, and all's I'm sayin, man, is if we're caught movin' his ass off-post we do stockade time too," reminded Sidney, "and I'm a short-timer compared to you cats."

Patterson asked why they should risk their asses for Schmidt. He would not do it for them.

"My man," said Sidney, "you shouldn't even think that."

Patterson looked at them. "So we're all in?"

"Airborne, motherfucker."

"Good," said a relieved Patterson. "I got an idea."

Schmidt stayed covered by the sleeping bag while watching the far corner of the barracks from inside his tent. He wore his dress winter uniform: OD Ike Jacket, wool trousers bloused in his Army issue boots. He even had on his own Jump Wings, which he had carried with him during his exodus from the regiment. The uniform was odds and ends, but it looked official, correct down to the soft overseas cap with the glider patch on the front.

Schmidt watched the barracks lights extinguish floor by floor. *A new beginning*, he thought.

The CQ runner came out of the barracks to check on him. Schmidt worried he might be moved inside.

"You there, Schmidt?" The young soldier shined his flashlight inside the small tent.

"Hollywood Jack at your service."

"You're goin' up tomorrow, ain't you?"

"Sure as hell am."

"Good luck, chief."

"Thanks."

At that moment, for an instant, Schmidt wanted to change places with the faceless, nameless private until his military obligation vanished like the nightmare it had become. The reverie ended quickly when he spotted someone waving from the far corner of the building.

Time to grab hat.

Schmidt climbed from the tent, swirled the sleeping bag around his shoulders like a cape, and strode toward the building with his shaving kit in hand.

"Come on, motherfucker," urged Patterson quietly waiting against the building. He looked like a cat burglar with his blank field jacket showing where his Pfc. stripes had been and Wings and nametags ripped off. A soft field cap pulled low over his eyes. He wasn't imitating a thief; he intentionally looked like a military prisoner.

"Willie, what's the haps, man?" Schmidt tossed the bag/cape over his shoulder.

"Let's chogie, Hollywood."

Schmidt picked up his pace to stay with Patterson. Over his shoulder, Patterson asked how much time they had before the next check. Schmidt estimated 45 minutes. They could be in town by then. Schmidt could not see Patterson was scared. He called, "Hey, man, slow down. Someone will think we're runnin' away or somethin'."

Son-of-a-bitch thinks this is funny, thought Patterson.

Ahead on the street was the supply room's three-quarter ton truck. Inside, Sidney the Cook and Mangiameli sat smoking and sipping Zinfandel. The idling engine provided some warmth. Sidney was dressed like Patterson. Mangiameli wore an Army overcoat with the 82nd patch on the shoulder over his fatigues. Sidney jumped from the cab to meet them.

Schmidt whipped the sleeping bag above his head and announced, "We're goin' in style."

"You wish. Here's the deal," explained Patterson. "You're our guard and Sid and me are prisoners. We're going to Pope Air Base to be flown to Third Army prison in Atlanta." As he explained, he draped a web belt holding a holstered .45 around Schmidt's waist.

Schmidt slapped the holster. "Man, I like this. Where in the hell you get it?"

"I got the keys to the arms room. It ain't loaded, it's for effect."

"You guys are making me nervous," said Schmidt.

"We're scared as hell," admitted Patterson. "Our asses are in a sling if we're caught."

"Where's Breslin?" No one answered.

"I mean, like, he planned this, right?"

"We can't find him," said Patterson. "He might be in town."

Schmidt laughed. "Just like him. Avoid the issue. I'm ready."

The three men climbed in the canvas-covered back of the truck and Mangiameli shifted into gear.

"Remember," called Patterson over the noise of the engine, "we're your prisoners. You're the regimental guard taking us to Pope and then Fort McPherson in Atlanta."

"No sweat," shouted Schmidt sitting by the tailgate, aiming the pistol into the night. "I know the job like the back of my hand."

"Goddamn, put away the weapon," said Patterson.

The truck picked up speed. None of the men spoke. The wind beat against the canvas top. Patterson watched Schmidt under the glow of the streetlights as they rolled along Gruber Road toward Smoke Bomb Hill. Patterson relished the fact he wasn't the one running away. He'd never have the courage and, in a way, knew it was wrong. *But that never bothered people like Schmidt.*

He stretched his pack of Luckies to Schmidt. "Hollywood?"

Schmidt nodded OK and shifted on the long wooden seat toward Patterson to light up.

From his dark huddle under Schmidt's sleeping bag, Sidney asked what he was going to do.

"The first thing I'm gonna do is hump somebody. Then, I'm gonna take off this cap." They laughed.

"Where's the wine?" asked Schmidt. "This trip calls for a celebration."

"In the cab," said Patterson. "Don't drink it. We get stopped and smell like booze someone might get serious."

"You fuckin' candy-asses."

It became quiet again. A tie-down rope began knocking against the side. It seemed colder. "If Breslin was here we'd have that wine."

"But he ain't," said Sidney, who remained worried about his short-time status.

Fast moving headlights behind the truck attracted everyone's attention. Patterson told Schmidt to sit by the tailgate and let the pistol show. Schmidt slid to the rear and Patterson and Sidney buried themselves in the sleeping bag folds, cupping their cigarettes from view.

The width of headlights indicated it was a Jeep, and as it pulled past them, they could see the white band across the bottom of the windshield with the black block letters spelling 'Military Police.' Schmidt waved.

"The word's out. Fifteen fuckin' minutes and the word's out. I knew it. Here goes my discharge." Sidney kicked off the sleeping bag and turned to look through the cab to see where the Jeep was headed.

"Somethin's wrong," said Patterson. "We should have at least forty minutes to get to town. Maybe it's not for us. Just a coincidence."

"The Pees!" shouted Tommy as the Jeep cut back in front of him. "They got us!"

Patterson shouted for him to watch the road. All of them watched the Jeep disappear around a curve, then they flipped their cigarettes onto the road.

"We can cut back," screamed Mangiameli. "Go on Yadkin!"

Patterson told him to shut up. "We're goin' the way we're goin'." If there were roadblocks, Yadkin would be covered too.

As they came around the long curve, they saw the Jeep's headlights shining across the road. Two men with MP armbands and white helmets were setting up small white sawhorses with reflectors on them. Mangiameli slowed down, still loudly wondering if they should swing a U-turn. "Motherfuck us, Jim."

Patterson reminded everyone their deal; they were prisoners. "Schmidt's our escort to Atlanta. Tommy, don't say shit. You're the driver, that's all."

"You cats better keep your story straight or you'll get a taste of this." Schmidt slapped the holster.

"Don't fuck around, Hollywood." Patterson's fear almost made him piss himself, but he held back. Resentment toward Schmidt built up. They were risking their asses for him and he's being cool. Breslin was smart to disappear.

The three-quarter ton truck slowed to a stop. One of the MPs, a young corporal from division, came to the cab. "Where're y'all goin' this time of night?" A Gulf Coast accent.

"Pope," replied Tommy.

"Y'all got a trip ticket?"

Mangiameli had footlockers full of dispatch forms needed to operate a vehicle. He had made one up and pulled it from the glove compartment for the MP. Patterson watched Mangiameli squirm as the MP held it up to the light. His partner continued putting together the sawhorses.

Patterson shut his eyes and waited for the MP to ask Schmidt for travelling orders to McPherson. He never thought of the paperwork. *They were caught.*

Schmidt jumped out of the truck.

Sidney and Patterson moved toward the tailgate with the same thought. Schmidt was running away and sticking them with the whole deal. They were fucked.

Then they heard Schmidt speak, but not in his normal voice, but a recently acquired South Carolina accent. "We got us a plane waitin', Corporal."

A civilian car pulled up behind them. The headlights bright in everyone's face.

Patterson believed the driver would be someone from the '04 and recognize them. He and Sidney watched Schmidt step away from the tailgate and stand spread-legged, his cap low on his brow. He looked as if he wanted to draw his pistol and shoot someone.

The MP asked Schmidt if he had seen anyone moving alongside the highway.

"I ain't about to take my eyes off these sons-of-bitches. Come here and look at these sorry bastards. They're goin' down to McPherson, then maybe Leavenworth."

Another car pulled up behind the waiting one. The MP handed the trip ticket back to Mangiameli and walked to the rear of the truck. Schmidt smiled and said, "Shine your light on 'em".

Flashlight and headlights made Patterson and Sidney shield their eyes. They had their collars up and soft hats pulled low. Schmidt stood behind the MP.

"Between me and y'all, Corporal, if we shot 'em right now we'd be doin' someone a favor. I hear they got 'em for rape and car stealin' up in Richmond."

The MP spoke into the back of the truck. "I hate punks." He turned to Schmidt. "You goin' all the way with them?"

"Airborne."

"McPherson's good duty."

Schmidt grinned knowingly. "No sweat, Corporal. I've been there before."

The MP stepped from behind the truck to signal his partner to let them go. As Schmidt climbed back into the truck, he could hear the MP questioning the car behind them. Mangiameli pulled away so fast, Schmidt almost fell out.

"Goddamnit, boy!" he shouted in his accent, "I'll have your ass wishin' y'all never heard of Hollywood Jack Schmidt!"

A block off Hay Street, in the alley that ran behind the Canopy, they passed around the bottle of wine. Banuelous wasn't there, but Schmidt knew his way into the back of the bar and felt they had done enough for him.

Patterson, worried, said, "You ain't got no ID. No pass. Nothin' to cover yourself."

"Willie, I've got my good looks and bullshit. In this wonderful world that's all you need."

Patterson washed down his bitterness toward Schmidt. He had to hand it to him; the man had brass balls the way he jumped out to face the MP. He would survive anything. Patterson just wished he had some of whatever Schmidt had. "Here." He gave Schmidt five bucks. With no prompting, Tommy gave him two and Sidney offered another fin.

"Once I'm set up, I swear to God I'll give it back with interest." Schmidt turned over the pistol then thanked Sidney for looking after him in the mess hall. "Tell Potter he should've let me make that blueberry cobbler."

They shook hands. "You know," said Mangiameli, "you really look like a soldier."

Schmidt cocked the cap a little lower over his eye and headed down the alley. He stopped and turned, silhouetted by the neon lights from Hay Street. "I swear to God I feel like MacArthur going back to the Philippines. See you Sky Soldiers in the movies."

He saluted and walked away.

The success of their mission and release from Schmidt made them ecstatic. They raced back to Bragg, jammed together in the cab and bouncing with the rough ride, the sleeping bag across their laps. The remaining Zinfandel added to their exhilaration. Mangiameli kept cracking Sidney the Cook in the knee with the floor shift. To avoid passing the roadblock, they took the Yadkin cut-off.

There was a roadblock at Yadkin and Reilly Roads. They all stared at the white sawhorse barriers as if the barriers were racing toward them. Sidney tucked the wine behind his feet under the sleeping bag. Patterson sat on the holster.

"What'll I say? What'll I say, Jim?" called Mangiameli as he geared down the supply truck.

Patterson said, "Same story. We just dropped off a prison...shit. We look like prisoners!"

The three were dead silent as they came almost to a stop. The MP flicked his white glove to tell them to keep going. Military vehicles going on post had no interest for them.

Mangiameli jammed it into second and goosed it.

"Tell 'em," shouted Patterson, "we ain't stoppin' for no motherfuckin' MP, Jack. And give 'em the finger." Everyone laughed.

Sidney invited them to his room after they returned the truck and weapon, he had some more wine and Archie usually kept beer on ice in his footlocker.

In the disorganized room, Archie lay back on his bunk in his boxer shorts, his cook's white trousers around his knees, one flip-flop on and a soggy empty paper cup in his hand. It appeared he started to get dressed or undressed and collapsed backwards.

A few beers were lying in the tepid water of a 16-inch steel mixing bowl. The ice had long melted.

"You know, man, I see him like that and I sometimes believe him about dyin'," said Sidney as he passed out the beers.

"If the atomic rays don't get him, the booze will," diagnosed Doctor Private Patterson as a prelude to his first swig of room temperature Carlings Red Cap.

Mangiameli asked for wine. Sidney said it was all gone. "Fuckin' Archie killed it, I bet."

Almost as if that was his cue, Archie sat up and announced, "Youse cats don't know shit from Shinola. Speedy-

Four Archie of the Five-Oh-Fourth Transportation Motor Corps..." He swung his hand with the cup toward Patterson who poured him a little beer. "...We got two-bys, four-bys, six-bys and those..."

"Shut the fuck up, cookie," demanded Sidney.

"...big motherfuckers that bend in the middle and go psssh, psssh." Archie drank then fell back, spilling the remainder on his leg.

Sadly, Mangiameli said, "That's what Uncle Sam can do to a cat."

Sidney the Cook turned up the radio, a rock-and-roll station in Raleigh playing Dakota Staton's *Summertime*, and slow danced as if holding a girl. He stopped and said, "Archie's a fuckin' asshole. He blames the Army 'cause he's away from home. Big fuckin' deal. I've been on my own since I was fuckin' sixteen. You cats can scream on me, but I don't see nothin' wrong with the Army. I like jumpin' outta airplanes and humpin' trailer park wives." He did several more dance steps then dipped. As he bent over, he shook up the beer bottle.

"Sid," said Patterson, "I don't know a whole hell of a lot, but there's more to life than bangin' broads in trailer parks." Patterson told himself he was sounding like Breslin. *Where was Scott?* Drinking without him didn't feel right. They should have found him before coming to the cook's room.

Sidney squirted some beer in his mouth, then said, "If I stayed I'd go into Sneaky Petes and be a motherfuckin' throat slitter." As he gestured with the bottle across his own throat his thumb slipped off the top and beer squirted out. "Son-of-a-bitch!" He jumped away, holding the bottle out and ended up spraying Archie. The unconscious cook didn't flinch.

Patterson and Mangiameli laughed hysterically.

Sidney the Cook shook the bottle some more and squirted Archie again. "He'll never know the difference. We could piss on him." The cook put down the bottle and started to open his fly.

Patterson stood up. "Sid, Jesus Christ on a crutch. Don't do that."

"How about we take shoe polish and paint a heavy drop on his chest?" Sidney was inventive.

"I bet neither one of you cats has shoe polish," said Mangiameli sarcastically, who would never be mistaken for Soldier of the Month himself.

Sidney pulled out a can of shaving cream from Archie's footlocker and tried to write his name across Archie's thin chest. Archie raised his head and spoke clearly. "It's in East Liberty." He turned on his side, wrapping the shaving cream in his arms as if it was a blanket. His glasses fell from his face.

Before Patterson and Mangiameli opened their fresh Red Cap Carlings, Sidney the Cook, the self-professed sex maniac of the entire 82nd Airborne Division who loved trailer park women and would fuck mud if it was warm, produced a push broom. Tipped with shaving cream.

In the blink of an eye and to the astonishment of his audience, Sidney pulled aside Archie's baggy shorts and inserted the tip into Archie's exposed rectum. The stunned soldiers watched the tip go in.

Sidney the Cook's face was satanic. "Get up, motherfucker! Get up and take it like a man!" he growled. Patterson knew someone must have heard them. It was well past lights out.

Archie rose off the bed, a mess of shaving cream, spilled beer, his trousers around his ankles revealing his sudden erection, and tried to walk. Sidney had to squat to keep the broom inserted and followed Archie to the middle of the room where he began ejaculating as he turned in circles seemingly unaware of anything.

Sidney, unable to keep up with circling Archie, pulled out the broom.

Patterson and Mangiameli bumped into one another getting to the door, but they did not run out. They watched Archie drop to his knees and crawl to Sidney's bunk and pull himself up chest high and close his eyes, his face taking on a cherubic smile.

Sidney stood at a modified parade rest with the broom. "He fuckin' loved it."

The following Tuesday night at the Main Post gym, Lt. Margolin, sitting in just his GI undershorts, reached into his gym bag for his jockstrap and PT shorts. He could not pull them out. He lifted up the bag and opened it wide. The jockstrap was twisted around some papers that had been stuffed in the bottom of the bag.

Without touching the papers, he knew what they were. "Hollywood Jack."

"What'd you say?" asked Lieutenant Hanna, his handball partner.

"Nothing," he said and laughed. "You know, I wish we played more often."

Chapter 11

The military likes to recognize acts that go beyond the norms of duty. To ensure recognition there is a form to complete: USA Form 157. Witness names. Dates. Boxes to tick off determining what medal should be issued. MOH = Medal of Honor. DSC = Distinguished Service Cross. SS = Silver Star. BS = Bronze Star. Purple Hearts (PH) are awarded to anyone wounded in action. OLC = Oak Leaf Cluster equates to a second or third BS, SS, PH. A colorful description on Form 157 can elevate a medal to a higher decoration. Silver Stars have become Medals of Honor and Bronze Stars for Valor boosted to Silver Stars. It is well known that some individuals write up their own exploits or those of their comrades, assisting one another to enhance the event. A favorite and almost required line is "…disregarding his own safety, he rushed across the fire-swept terrain…" Decorations always seem less important to those who endure the most to earn them. On occasion, promotions become part of the award.

Schmidt's sudden disappearance did not improve First Sergeant Billy Martin's disposition; it lingered in his heart and added to his inability to adjust to a new duty roster. Regimental Headquarters Personnel provided him with hard-to-read stenciled copies of previous morning reports dating back six months and a copy of the last quarter duty roster, but he didn't like piecing together all the annual leaves, three-day passes, KP, guard duty, Charge of Quarters assignments, and the myriad of the company's daily obligations. The simple everyday headcounts by rank, time-in-grade, and promotion were too difficult to bring forward from unclear copies. The old roster was Martin's anatomy of the company. The new one, on crisp virgin pages, was a black and white puzzle that Martin reluctantly and slowly tried to solve. He mixed up assignments as some men had been promoted and a few demoted; rank was important in assignments. He had sergeants on KP and new privates assigned to be Sergeants-of-the-Guard. He screwed up the Thanksgiving roster by ignoring the holiday. His beloved colored pencils now tricked him: did red mean present or absent? Green for sick call? It was so easy before, and now he had to stop and think too hard about what each color meant.

Orange indicated light duty? Maybe? It was just too complicated to figure out every day.

Due to the roster pressure, he'd forgotten to replace Cpl. Motz and those minor chores of typing and running errands and answering phones contributed to the increasingly dysfunctional orderly room. On top of his roster angst, he blamed himself for Schmidt's flight and inadvertently continued to assign Schmidt on KP as if he was still there.

Sergeant First Class Richard Wisnewski was foolish enough to point out to the first sergeant that the assignments were not accurate.

"Mind yore own goddamn business and get yore ass out of my orderly room! I run this here company. I'm the first sergeant. I'm the only man in the company with three up and three down and a diamond in the middle. Count 'em if y'all don't believe me!"

Two days later Wisnewski found himself assigned to KP. Of course, he ordered a private to cover him.

"Sir, Top's blown a gasket."

Sgt. Wisnewski sat across from Lt. Margolin. A steel pitcher of hot coffee sat on the table. Outside, a cold early December rain smacked against the mess hall windows.

The lieutenant knew exactly what Sgt. 'Ski was talking about. Margolin hadn't dared to confront Martin. He had wanted to say, 'I told you so about locking up Schmidt,' but discretion was the better part of valor. On more than one occasion in the past week, the first sergeant had wandered into Margolin's office to seek official permission for another company-wide search. Margolin would accompany him the way someone might not wake a sleepwalker.

Why is Martin asking me? He had never asked permission for anything before. Maybe because he had hollered at the NCO?

Martin never searched seriously. He listlessly opened desk drawers, checked wastebaskets, peeked under his desk blotter, and, in general, drifted around the company looking under mattress covers on the supply room shelves, peeling back squad bay bunks, and standing on a day room chair to see into the dumpster.

"I keep hoping he'll settle down," replied the lieutenant without admitting to Wisnewski he had the roster in his BOQ.

Why had he kept it? He didn't know. Just in case? In case of what?

Maybe it was like holding a voodoo object to wield power over the diminutive enlisted dictator. One sure thing: he did not want to be associated with the document.

Wisnewski claimed he could no longer talk to Martin. "Not that the asshole was ever someone to talk to. He just barks." The sergeant reminded the lieutenant they needed a good company clerk. "But I'm afraid to bring it up 'cause the son-of-a-bitch hollered at me last time I mentioned it."

They drank their coffee. Wisnewski smoked. "Sir?"

Margolin raised his eyebrows.

"Can you get him to go on leave?"

It was a good idea. "Who would fill in for him?"

"Me and Sergeant Craven from the service platoon can take up the slack. We'll get a flunky up from Personnel to keep the paper movin' 'til we get a clerk trained."

Regiment was already asking for a survey of private vehicles before Christmas. A year-end TO & E report on all office furniture and serial numbers was due to S-4, regimental supply. The monthly weapons inventory had not been done. The Community Chest and Savings Bond drive details had been lost, and company punishment reports were due at regiment. Failure to meet these obligations could affect the lieutenant's efficiency report and initiate a face-to-face with the colonel.

"Sir, I'll bet you dollars to doughnuts none of that gets done and you know he ain't gonna let anyone else do it."

Margolin thought aloud. "We can farm out a lot of work to supply and the motor pool." He saw it could work. "How can we get him to leave?"

Wisnewski shifted forward on his chair and put both hands around his mug as if warming his fingers. "You order him, sir." Wisnewski drank.

The flush in the young lieutenant's pale face rose like a red tide. He turned away from the older NCO and, watching the DRO buff the linoleum floor, asked, "Order him?"

Margolin didn't like the sound of it. It would take every ounce of his genetic *chutzpah*. No, he did not like the idea even if it was right.

"Yes, sir. Order him and tell the dumb son-of-a-bitch if he doesn't go you're gonna drag his ass up to Steele and have him order him. You're the CO, sir."

"Don't remind me, 'Ski."

In front of Steele? Never. I could never do it. My chutzpah *doesn't run that deep.* It was moments like this Margolin wished *he* was a Pfc. company clerk in Korea. He agreed to think it over.

That night he did not sleep well. The restlessness wasn't new to him. Many times he had sleepless nights inventing scenarios of himself and First Sgt. Billy Martin—actually ordering him would be different. For the first time, he would create the battle and it would not be a small one.

It's the whole ball of wax. The kit and caboodle.

Fish or cut bait. Shit or get off the pot. Put up or shut up.

It's time to command. I'm the CO. And I'm not going to shout.

What if the first sergeant takes the news so hard he shoots himself with a .45 from the arms room? What if he shoots me?

Early in the morning, he woke from a bad dream in which he parachuted in slow motion and bounced hard and slow, tumbling along the drop zone to end up at Martin's feet. Martin held out a steaming cup of coffee. Margolin smiled, glad to accept. Martin slowly tipped it toward...

Margolin fluffed his pillow and said aloud, "A girl could cure some of this." Where were they? His troops chased the barmaids. They liked enlisted men. The college girls he'd met at Charlotte's Woman's College and at North Carolina State in Raleigh did not like soldiers. A nice Jewish girl must live somewhere...Jewish? A girl. Any girl.

At 0650, a tired First Lieutenant Seymour 'Mad Dog' Margolin walked into Headquarters Company orderly room to stand in front of First Sgt. Billy Martin's polished light mahogany six-drawer desk. Martin did not look up from his struggle with the morning report.

"Sergeant Martin, I want to see you in my office."

No glance up of recognition. "Yes, sir. Soon as I..."

"Now, First Sergeant." Margolin reached and took away Martin's pencil and tossed it on the desk. "That's an order."

Margolin turned and went into his office with the same insecure feeling he experienced each time he confronted the first sergeant. *What if Martin doesn't follow me?* He kept his back to the door as he unzipped his field jacket and hung it on the four-point coat rack. He already regretted grabbing the pencil.

"Yes, sir?"

Without turning around, he told Martin to shut the door and he turned to see the first sergeant doing as he was told. *So far, so good.*

He gives the orders and the sergeant follows them. He wondered if he should speak louder; it was hard to hear himself over his rapidly beating heart.

The two soldiers faced each other across Margolin's cluttered desk. Margolin forced himself to stare directly at Martin. The first sergeant usually glared holes through people, but he avoided the company commander's look.

"I'm First Lieutenant Seymour Margolin and I'm responsible for this company."

"Yes, sir. No one says you ain't."

"I didn't ask for an opinion, First Sergeant. I stated a fact. A fact you too often choose to overlook."

"Yes, sir."

"You work for me; do you read me?"

First Sgt. Billy Martin's face reddened. There were involuntary movements in his body. "Yes, sir."

"First Sergeant Martin, I want you to take a leave. Nothing less than thirty days." Margolin took a step back as a precautionary measure.

Martin spun around in a quick about-face as if to walk out, then turned back to face the young officer. His feet shifted, unsure where the body was going. Finally, he took a step back as Margolin had done. His countenance changed from red to mauve. "I ain't gonna, sir. I gotta to find my roster."

The lieutenant resisted shouting the roster was gone. Instead, he calmly stated, "Sergeant Martin, we have a company to run. You and me. Your extra concern for the roster is screwing up the every day business of this company. You need a rest."

"A rest? What kind of bill of goods are y'all tryin' to sell yore first sergeant. I've been in this man's Army over ten years and…"

"At ease, Sergeant Martin!" Margolin did not like raising his voice just as he didn't like voices raised at him, but he had promised himself he would not stoop to that level, even though it might feel good again.

"Sir, once I find the roster we can…"

"'At ease' means shut up, First Sergeant."

Veins pumped in his receding hairline and neck. His eyeballs extended like painted eggs and his color deepened to maroon. Margolin saw a coronary rising in front of him, but he could not stop. "You either go on leave or you're going to Womack to see a head shrinker."

Martin shuddered and pulled himself together. "Beggin' the young lieutenant's pardon..." The words were forced as if the pressure in his head squeezed them out. "... it'll be a cold day in hell 'fore a lieutenant college boy can send me anywheres. Since y'all come 'round here, all y'all college boys, the Army starts talkin' 'bout wearin' Bermudee short pants like the 'Oh-Four's some fuckin' college campus. Y'all talk palsy-walsy like and flash yore college rings and discipline breaks down. The R-O-T-C can kiss my Alabama ass. Do y'all know, lieutenant, there's talk about doin' away with the Ike jacket..."

Margolin shook his head; he had asked for it, taken the risk, and here it was coming back at him head-on as he had feared. He leaned forward on the desk and hung on to keep from walking around to shout what a piss-ant Martin was and he would kick his ass all the way to Regimental Headquarters if he didn't shut up.

Suddenly—like a proverbial music-filled sunrise after a terrible dark storm—another option opened up in front of him.

"... and changin' regiments into some contraption called Battle Groups. Y'all might think it's funny callin' my ass in here..."

Softly, the lieutenant said, "Martin, shut the hell up."

"Boy, y'all can't talk to me that-a-way. I'm a senior NCO with as much prestige..."

Lt. Margolin walked slowly around the desk. Martin took a step back. Margolin came closer. Martin moved back. *He might be scared*, thought Margolin as he leaned back on his desk and crossed his arms. "With all due respect to your rank, First Sergeant Billy Martin, when was the last time you were in an airplane?"

"... as any officer wearin' a fancy college ring—what do y'all mean?"

Martin's eyes retreated to their normal size. His complexion drained to sub-normal pale and his pupils darted back and forth as if looking to escape their sockets.

"I didn't stutter, Sergeant Martin. I'm dead serious. When's the last time you jumped?"

The first sergeant didn't like being so close to the lieutenant. He walked to the door as if to leave. Margolin watched and waited.

The first sergeant faced the closed door. His usually stiff shoulders sagged. "I like to jump with the old timers. All we want are our pay jumps."

"I checked with Personnel, sarge," he bluffed, "and their records show you jumped with us on All-America. I recall you drove the Jeep back. Should I go back and check every jump the past five years? The last night jump? I've gone out the door fifteen times since Jump School and don't remember seeing you on a plane." *Motz had better be right.*

The first sergeant turned around. The spark ignited by Margolin's demand he go on leave extinguished. No visible rage. No bluster. Again, he was the haunted man who had lost his roster. Just a short, balding individual with Army-issue glasses who looked funny in a uniform. He could have been a Salvation Army soldier overcome by the world's sins.

Margolin didn't like feeling sorry for him, but he did.

"Sir, do y'all know what it's like to have the world by the short hairs?" He balled his fist for emphasis.

"Not really," Margolin replied except he, finally, now had him that way.

"That's how I have this company. The battalion. The regiment. Right here." His fist tightened up. "Even after I got scared jumpin' I still had 'em here. A first sergeant is a man to be reckoned with. No way in hell I'd give it up." Margolin nodded in understanding.

"No one's ever questioned me jumpin' or not. No one. Now y'all do."

"It's against Army regs to collect jump pay without jumping." The lieutenant delighted using 'regs'. "In fact, it's actually a crime."

From nowhere, Martin asked, "Did y'all steal my roster?"

"No, Top, I wouldn't do that to you."

"The key to my kingdom. Not a goddamn thing's gone right since I had to make a new one. Nothing fits. Names. Ranks. Duties. The orderly room's comin' apart and y'all catch me fibbin' about jumpin'."

Martin moved close to Margolin. The sergeant's eyes were moist. Margolin actually considered putting his arm on the older man's shoulder, but didn't.

"Y'all know, I once moved the furniture around in my daughter's playhouse just to show her a different setup and she bawled like a baby. Well, she was—maybe five or six. I held her in my arms and we put it back just the way she wanted. But she still wasn't happy, we couldn't get it exactly like she had it. Does that make sense to y'all? Y'all are a college boy?"

"Top—can I call you 'Top'?" He already had. *Why ask now?*

"Call me anythin', but don't call me late for chow." The first sergeant tried to smile.

So did Margolin. "Top, that's a nice story and I understand. The truth is everything changes. Go on leave. Let the company fall back into place without you looking for a roster every other hour. Step back. Relax."

"Y'all really mean get the hell out of the way."

"No, not...yes. That's what I mean." He walked back to his chair behind the desk. It felt better to say it straight.

"If I don't go y'all will blow the whistle on the jumpin' business. That'll ruin my career."

Margolin sat down. "Top, I'm not here to ruin any careers. You can simply stop putting your name on the manifests—or you jump."

The humbled man let out a sigh of relief and came to attention. "Sir, with your permission I'll start that leave now."

"Permission granted, First Sergeant."

Martin saluted and did an about-face. He took his field jacket and cap off the orderly room coat rack and was gone. *Almost like a bat out of hell*, thought the lieutenant. He felt a numbness with an inkling that the first sergeant had conned him somehow. *Maybe by not turning him in, he had? Too...*

The phone rang.

He grabbed it, happy for the distraction. "Headquarters and Headquarters Company. Five-Oh-Four. Lieutenant Margolin speaking."

It was Captain LaMar from Personnel. He wanted to know why the morning report was late again.

"Sir, we're working on that as I speak. I'll have a man up there ASAP."

He hung up and stood up, feeling like he escaped from being run over by speeding car or had defeated the schoolyard bully. Neither of which he'd ever experienced, but he felt good. Wonderful. Actually, he felt so god-damned good he laughed and wanted to laugh forever.

"I did it! Son-of-a-bitch, I did it!"

Margolin stepped into the hallway and stopped the first man passing. "Find me Sergeant 'Ski. No matter where he is, find him and tell him to get here on the double."

"Yes, sir."

Yes, sir! That's the way it's supposed to be. He caught himself from throwing up his arms in exaltation. "Yes, sir!" he called to the empty orderly room.

His orderly room.

The Moonlight Gambler, Spec/4 Nicky Lazor, stood between Banuelous and Patterson's steel cots. He was waiting for Banuelous to get dressed. As usual, they were on their way to romance the Fayetteville barmaids. Lazor, not a 504th soldier, had long hair combed into a ducktail and a forehead curl that women liked to hang onto when he licked their clit.

So he said.

Patterson wondered what a clit was, but didn't ask.

Banuelous came from the latrine with a towel wrapped around his waist and dropped his shower kit into his open footlocker. "You updatin' Willie on the facts of life?" He took out a stick of Old Spice and touched up various body areas including his behind.

"Cat's got to grow some hair. He'd look OK with somethin' on top."

"Impossible around this fuckin' place," said Banuelous as he slipped into brightly colored, non-military boxer shorts.

Again, Patterson asked what he could say to a barmaid to make her interested, and again, they told him he had to ignore them. It didn't make sense to Patterson. "If I don't talk to them, they won't know I'm ignorin' them."

Banuelous said, "You ignore them, but you gotta sit there for a while and you gotta go in when a joint ain't crowded." He took his trousers off a hanger and dressed.

"And you gotta look like a civilian, not a doofuss GI in a sweatshirt," added Lazor who produced a handkerchief from the breast pocket of his three-quarter-length jacket and patted his forehead.

Banuelous and Lazor usually wore cool pegged gabardine trousers and solid colored shirts buttoned to the neck. They had heavy ID bracelets and pinky rings and wore thin gold chains displaying St. Christopher medals and their girlfriends' rings. Their shoes were pointy-toed. Banuelous often wore a pork-pie hat to hide his close-cropped hair.

Patterson examined the clothes in Banuelous' wall locker. There was far less room for uniforms than in Patterson's wall locker, which held few civilian clothes—and more uniforms. "I like this," he said.

"Cat picks my best shirt. French cuffs and white on white," pointed out Banuelous, "and you ain't ever wearin' it, Jim." He slipped into his black three-quarter-length car coat.

"Quit jackin' around," said Lazor, "I wanna bang this broad before Alice gets off work."

Banuelous studied himself in his small wall locker mirror. He practiced a sneer. "Like I tell you, Willie, you go in, dressed nice, put some money on the bar and hang around. They'll come to you like fish to bait."

"Not with that fuckin' shaven head, *ese*. Like, let me tell you this too, change your name."

"My name? Whadda you mean?"

"Chicks ain't gonna listen to some cat calls himself Willie. It sounds like a chump kid or a janitor who picks up the trash. Be cool. Bill's cool. William. Even Will, but not Willie. Dig? Come on, Tony. She's waitin'."

Patterson watched them depart the stark squad bay, Old Spice wafting behind them. Two cool cats heading for Fayetteville and any girl they wanted. Pvt. Willie Patterson watched, again left behind to shine his boots and sleep on the small bunk. Private Willie, the supply clerk and jerk. An un-cool, un-hip meatbeater.

On Saturday morning two weeks before Christmas leaves started, Lt. Margolin came into supply carrying a manila folder. Patterson was alone. Broomfield and Webster were gone for the weekend. Earlier that morning, during the inspection in ranks, the officer had told Patterson to meet him in the supply room at 1200 hours.

"Willie," said Margolin, placing the folder on Sgt. Webster's luxuriously polished wide mahogany desk, thanks to

Patterson's elbow grease, "I've got a top secret mission for you."

Top secret, thought Patterson. *That can't be good. Thanks, but no thanks.* But what choice did he really have? Maybe it wouldn't take too long. "Sir?"

"I'm trusting you to keep this between us." Margolin liked Patterson because they had bumped into each other at night school on Main Post. The lieutenant was enrolled in a college credit business course and the private had signed up for high school English in case he decided to go to college after the service. Patterson lasted three weeks. Too many details like guard and KP and maneuvers made it difficult for an enlisted man to plan ahead. Margolin had remained; attending class made him feel like a civilian and there was always a chance a nice girl would show up.

"What's up, sir?"

"If you pull this off, I'll have your stripe back before you go home for Christmas." Patterson wanted the stripe; it provided a barrier between him and the stockade. *What will it cost me?*

"If word of this gets out, your buddy Schmidt might end up in Leavenworth someday." *Uh oh. Anything connected to Schmidt means trouble.*

The lieutenant extended his hand. "Let's shake on it. Rank aside. Man to man." Patterson held out his hand as if reaching for something that might bite him. Margolin flipped open the folder. Inside were four sheets of legal-sized paper filled horizontally with tiny squares, numbers, and names, all in a variety of colors. "This is Martin's missing roster. You're going to sneak them into the first sergeant's station wagon."

"Like hell...No, sir!"

Margolin raised his hand in a calming gesture. "I know. Relax."

"Why me, sir?"

"I trust you."

"Where'd you get it, sir?"

"Schmidt stuffed it in my gym bag the day he came back from AWOL."

"You've had it all this time."

"Affirmative, but I didn't know it until a week later. It's taken me a while to come up with a solution. All you do is slip the folder onto his seat when the car's empty. It'll help him with his problem. If I did it and he saw me, he might have a heart attack or try to blame me for stealing it."

"What'd he ever do for me except threaten me with the stockade?"

Margolin understood all that. He swore as an officer and a gentleman he'd stick up for him if he was caught and, no matter what, he'd have his stripe back faster than a bee's bite stings.

"Sir?"

"Never mind. Here's the plan."

Breslin faced the non-denominational altar as he worked the buffer backwards and along the center aisle of the chapel. The carpet was rolled up against the base of the altar. Strung along the dark wooden rafters were boughs of pine and a Nativity crèche took up the right front alcove. Religious Christmas carols played quietly. Breslin worked alone, humming along with the music and sipping sacramental wine, while effortlessly handling the buffer as most men in the 82nd learned to do—polishing was a way of life, be it floors, shoes, trucks, weapons, or collar brass and belt buckles.

Spit and polish every day.

The early winter darkness outside, the carols, and the spotlighted crèche made the world warmer. The regimental week had ended. Men were in their barracks or on their way home. The officer and NCO clubs crowded. No more marching, training, commanding until Monday.

It was Breslin's favorite time of the day. He felt satisfied; the chapel would be ready for the holidays.

"How about a fuckin' beer!"

Breslin turned so rapidly the buffer spun free and cracked against a pew. The handle, spinning loose, smacked against several pews until he grabbed it.

Patterson and Sidney the Cook stood in the doorway with a case of PX Carlings. Breslin waved them away, adjusted the buffer, and continued.

"Pull the fuckin' plug, Sid." Sidney the Cook's cleated boots sounded like a mason's hammer on the linoleum as he marched up the aisle to the socket.

"Quit fuckin' around, Willie," said Breslin. The machine died.

"Great Scott," said Patterson, "me and Sid were havin' a few coldies in the supply room and we got to thinkin' about you..."

"What a jerk-off dud you are," interjected Sidney. Breslin deftly curled up the cord over his elbow.

"... and we decided we ain't lettin' you drift off into some kind of reefer smokin' altar boy. Like, I mean, we're bunkies ain't we?" Breslin had been avoiding his pals since failing to help Schmidt get away.

Everyone watched the cord snake its way toward Breslin. Sidney belched.

"Sid, this is the house of the Lord. God's squad bay, you dumb fuck," admonished Patterson.

Breslin finally cracked a smile. "OK. Bust me open one of those." He hung the cord over the handle.

They sat in three separate pews, smoking and drinking. After the second round, Patterson brought up the secret mission of delivering the roster to First Sgt. Billy Martin, once they had enough beer-courage to do it.

Breslin said, "You're asking for help after I let you down with Hollywood?"

Sidney considered that water over the dam. Patterson agreed and added, "I mean, if you had shown up I wouldn't have had to do it and you'd get all the credit. We did pull it off, didn't we, Sid?" They re-hashed their adventure getting Schmidt off post and then what happened with Archie when they got back. Breslin didn't believe the Archie story.

"Like Hollywood always said, we swear to God on our mothers' deaths. Ask Tommy if you want too, but don't ask Archie. He still don't know," suggested Patterson.

On their way to Main Post, Breslin played beermaster from the back seat of Sidney the Cook's Olds. Drinking did not affect Sidney's driving; he handled his candy-apple jewel with the steadiness of a hearse chauffeur. Patterson kept the manila folder next to him in the front seat. He had wiped it clean with a blitz cloth usually used to shine brass and wore his issued wool gloves to prevent fingerprints.

Patterson confirmed he and Breslin were still going to hitchhike home on Christmas Eve.

"I wasn't sure you still wanted to go," admitted Breslin, "but I'm in if you are."

"Sid's gonna give us a ride to the highway."

They had Martin's address, but couldn't find it on the tree-lined curving streets of enlisted housing in Anzio Acres. It was Martin's station wagon in the driveway that attracted their attention, then Sidney noticed that each house had a wooden sign indicating the name and rank of the occupants. It was the first sergeant's house for sure.

The lights were on. No one was out on the cold and dark street. The streetlights were too far apart to provide good illumination. Some of the houses had Christmas lights. Patterson suggested they should wait until later when everyone was asleep. Sidney and Breslin turned him down; they wanted to get it over with and get back to barracks to drink. Besides, driving around Main Post was always risky for 82nd troopers; they were considered scum by the 18th Airborne Corps staff officers and Third Army desk commandos on Main Post.

"Ain't we drunk enough now?" asked Patterson.

"Who's drunk, man," challenged Sidney the Cook. "A few beers don't bother me." To prove his point, he speed shifted into second and burnt rubber.

"Not here, Sid, you asshole. Someone will call the Pees."

They cruised past the first sergeant's house again. The Olds pipes rumbled with a rich baritone.

The plan was to drop Patterson at the far end of the block. He would walk to Martin's, move up the driveway, silently slip the roster into the wagon and keep walking. They'd pick him up at the corner. Sidney suddenly worried his car might be recognized.

"Sid," asked Breslin, "how could they tell this from Tommy's heap?" Breslin was getting back to his old sarcastic self.

"Your ass is suckin' wind, man."

Patterson got out. He wore his Army overcoat and his fatigue hat tilted low on his brow. One more drag on his Lucky, then he stepped on the butt, deliberately crushing it into the ground. In the '04 a cigarette butt never touched the ground; it was field-stripped. With the folder under his arm, he headed up the street with enough beer in him to subdue the adrenaline.

The Olds stayed beside him the first ten yards, then moved slowly up the dark street. The few Christmas lights reflected off the polished car. Patterson watched it pull away and felt alone. *A man on a mission.* As he came around the long curve, he read the various occupants' signs. Every house seemed to be a first sergeant's. *Dangerous territory for a private. No man's land for any enlisted person under a buck sergeant.*

Ahead, the green and white station wagon waited. He tried to identify the make. Maybe a Ford? As he approached, his mind sorted through potential pitfalls: Martin would see him coming? Going? Trying to open the wagon door? He'd hide under the car? A guard dog would get him?

At the house, he could not see inside past the curtains.

Here goes nothing. He murmured, "... with complete disregard for his own safety, the young private carried on to win back his stripe."

Staying low, he approached the driver's side, keeping the station wagon between him and the porch. The door was locked. He moved around the front to the passenger door. Open.

Quietly, he pressed in the door button and, keeping the door's weight off its hinges, cracked it open and slipped the folder onto the floor. He eased the door closed, but before it went all the way, First Sgt. Billy Martin's front door opened.

Light leaped over the porch like a net. Someone said, "... bowling ball."

Patterson scooted low around the front of the vehicle and hid by the driver's door. He thought he recognized the first sergeant's voice. By dropping to all fours, he could look under the car to the porch steps. A pair of loafers and civilian trousers were taking quick short steps toward the car.

The only man who walks like that is First Sergeant Billy Martin.

Patterson waited to see which direction the feet went. Toward the front. The private scuttled to the back. Martin unlocked his door and climbed in. Patterson, crouched against the back bumper, felt the wagon shift. The car started. Patterson took exhaust in the gut and face.

The front door opened again. "Daddy, don't forget ice cream!"

Patterson stifled a cough and squatted lower. The car didn't move.

"Mom said, don't forget the ice cream! Strawberry!" A muffled reply came from inside the station wagon and the young girl went inside. Patterson stayed low by the taillights. To sense the car's motion, he kept his fingers on the bumper like a blind man reading Braille.

The wagon shifted as the first sergeant put it in reverse.

In a mini-second, the station wagon backed quickly along the driveway. Patterson attempted to run alongside in a duck walk. As he and the vehicle entered the street, Martin cut the wheel to the left to align a departure to the right. Patterson went to his knees. His fatigue hat came off. Martin shifted gears. Patterson rolled toward the shadows of the curb. With his head tucked into the crook of his arm, he heard the rear tire crush the plastic liner in his cap.

First Sergeant Billy Martin drove away.

Patterson rose quickly, scooped up the hat, and headed for Sidney the Cook's Olds, which framed him in its approaching headlights.

He checked the squashed cap; his Jump Wings were bent.

Chapter 12

Long before the creation of interstate concrete arteries, America's major highways were often just two- and four-lane asphalt ribbons that reflected certain personalities. Perhaps the most famous is Route 66, Chicago to L.A. Trans-continental Highway One runs from Atlantic City to San Francisco and also traverses the scenic California coast from top to bottom or bottom to top depending on a traveler's direction. On the East Coast, Highway 301 in the '50s was the major North/South automobile trail—the route to warm weather for winter escapees. It ran from industrial Delaware; avoided Washington, D.C.; through Richmond and Emporia, Virginia; Rocky Mount, Dunn, and Fayetteville, North Carolina; Orangeburg, South Carolina; Jessup, Georgia; Jacksonville and terminated at St. Petersburg, Florida, also known as God's Waiting Room. Long stretches of 301 were deserted except for occasional small motels. Brand name hotels were limited to major metropolitan areas. Speed traps and traffic lights were part of the roadside ambience. In the '50s there weren't any fast food stops, but there were Stuckey Pecan cafes, Bob's Big Boys and other colorful eateries reflecting the culture of their locales. On most Friday nights or holiday weekends, many of the cars on the curves of 301 were carrying servicemen northbound. Overloaded machines racing through the night. Sailors from Jacksonville and Key West. Air Force men leaving Homestead, Florida, and Marines out of Camp Lejune and Cherry Point. Soldiers from Forts Jackson, Lee, and Bragg. All speeding to spend a brief weekend at home away from regimentation and mess hall food.

So, until the introduction of air travel and interstate highways, 301 was the fastest way home.

Christmas Eve was well underway by the time Sidney the Cook dropped off Breslin, Patterson, and their self-appointed guide Specialist Fourth Class Adam Archibald on Highway 301 just outside Fayetteville. Before stepping into the cold night, they shared swigs from their pints of Old Rocking Chair purchased minutes before from the State Liquor store on Hay Street. The three soldiers wore their wool-lined Army overcoats over their OD wool winter dress uniforms, scarves, and gloves. Each man's jump boots were highly polished and each carried an AWOL bag with shaving gear, clean underwear, cartons of cigarettes, and Christmas presents from the PX. They kept the Old Rocking Chair in their overcoat pockets for easy access.

The winter night on the highway promised to be long and cold.

Within a few minutes, other soldiers in groups of two and three showed up at the same busy intersection. Some headed south. Others north, the same direction as Patterson and his pals.

"Let's hump to the next light," said Archie, the hitchhiking expert and ranking man. He started without looking at his comrades. "We could freeze out here waitin' for a ride."

They headed along the highway toward the next light two long blocks away. Archie attempted to count cadence. They told him to shut up.

Breslin said, "And don't be given us all that radiation dying bullshit all night."

Archie, a few steps in front of them, looked back, turned and walked backwards, replied. "All's I'm sayin', man, is this trip could be my last. Now, watch an expert. You gotta hitchhike with style."

Archie adjusted his cap to an exaggerated angle over one eye and put out his hand as traffic from the intersection raced towards them. Archie was not wearing his usual thick Army issue glasses. "You make people see you ain't no scuff-booted recruit. You gotta be Airborne."

An outside set of headlights coming at them cut across the two cars in the inside lanes and swept past the soldiers with the horn blaring. It was a new 1958 Suburban Plymouth Station Wagon. The car slowed to a halt 100 yards down the highway.

"Son-of-a-bitch!" shouted a surprised Archie. "That's us!" He took off his hat and ran toward the convulsing turn signal. Patterson and Breslin did the same. Archie climbed into the front seat. Breslin and Patterson scrambled into the back.

The driver made no response to their expressions of gratitude. He stared into the rearview mirror waiting for a chance to pull into traffic. "The way the traffic's running you'd think something special was going on. Hell, its only Christmas Eve," he said and released the clutch to join the flow of vehicles. After several seconds of going through gears and traffic adjustments, the man settled back and lit a cigarette with the car lighter. The soldiers lit up too.

The man drove at a steady fast pace, effortlessly passing other cars. "You boys are gonna have to earn your keep. How about mixing us up a drink?" he said to Archie and patted the cardboard carton next to him that held cups and cans of Seven-Up.

"You mean," asked Archie, "the bar's open?"

Breslin leaned forward on the seat. "We'd be glad to assist."

The driver pulled a quart of Old Granddad from under the front seat and handed it to Archie. "You know, I start mixing this stuff myself and this and that and the next thing I know I got cigarette ashes in my lap, the cup spills, and I'm running up the median strip with a state trooper bouncing along behind me. And I'm speaking from experience."

Archie distributed the cups then opened the Seven-Up with the driver's church key from the glove compartment and poured everyone half a cup of soda. He added healthy shots of bourbon.

"Here's to your futures, gentlemen." The driver toasted them.

Patterson embarrassed himself by omitting a loud 'phwee' after his sip.

The three soldiers unbuttoned their overcoats and Ike jackets. Quiet Christmas music played on the radio. The car was warm. They had been up since 0500 and could easily fall asleep. Patterson loosened the laces of his stiff new boots. Out of courtesy and sensing the man wanted to talk, Breslin said, "Cold night, huh?"

"Let me tell you about a cold night on Christmas Eve, Nineteen-hundred and forty-three. No, goddammit, it was forty-four."

Patterson and Breslin reached over the front seat for a re-fill. Archie already had his.

The driver explained he was a shower point truck driver with the VII Corps Headquarters, a part of the First Army, pushing through Belgium. "We were going like a bat out of hell across the countryside when we ran into the big German Christmas counterattack. It was their last one of the war."

He and his fellow drivers and clerks were rear-echelon types. "I hadn't fired a rifle since basic training at Bliss in Texas." They were ordered onto trucks and shipped to a place called Bastogne and attached to the 101st Airborne to help stop the krauts. "That's why I stopped for you fellows and not the others at the light. I recognized the glider patch caps. I knew you were paratroopers."

"Whadda I tell youse," interjected Archie as he sipped. "Just before you stopped I told them you gotta look Airborne."

The driver stopped his story to point out they were passing through Smithfield, the home of Ava Gardner. "A fine frame of female. Here's to you, Ava." He drank and seemed to think about her for a moment then continued, "I wasn't a paratrooper, but those thirty this or that frozen days I spent with Charlie Company of the Five-Oh-Second were enough to leave me with hard memories. I've never seen braver men."

Archie gave the seatback steady pats of agreement.

"They went out every night looking for krauts trying to infiltrate our lines. Lines. Shit, you didn't know where anybody was. Everything was covered in snow and fog. For a while we thought we might go hand-to-hand with tooth-brushes, but we held the bastards."

The driver's memories quieted him for several minutes. "I remember we didn't show mercy on prisoners. I don't approve of killing unarmed men, but both sides did it."

Archie the cook, who never touched weapons except spatulas and long-handled ladles, admitted he would have no problem killing someone. "'Specially if they was tryin' to kill me."

"To make a long story short," the driver finally said, "I can't help not remembering those guys every Christmas. They kept me alive." He drank to them and held out his cup for Archie to refill.

"Easy on the Seven-Up this time." They passed the highway marker that read: Rocky Mount—10 Miles. "That's it for me, boys. Christmas Eve in Rocky Mount. Got to see a pulp man in the morning."

Patterson, knowing his family waited for him, asked, "Wouldn't you rather be home with your family?" Breslin jabbed his thigh. "I mean, if you have one?" Breslin rolled his eyes.

The driver said he was divorced. His wife hated him and was making his kids hate him. "Just because she caught me giving her girlfriend a quick bang in our car outside this gin mill where I always hung around. We were hitting it pretty good and this and that. Next thing I know, my old lady's got my ankles and pulling me off."

He never went home. "Funniest goddamn thing is her and this girl are best of buddies now."

He volunteered to drive them to the other side of Rocky Mount and had his drink re-filled. Breslin and Archie joined him. Patterson passed; the liquor wasn't sitting well. Breslin thanked him for the extra effort.

"Hell, it's Christmas Eve," the driver replied, then continued. "You know, back then, living on the edge. Eating when you could. Not knowing if you would be alive by the end of the day. Nothing's really counted since then. Just being alive was so good. I ate it up. You boys are lucky. You don't have a war to worry about."

Buttoned up against the cold, they climbed out of the station wagon. The driver pulled away, made a squealing U-turn, blew the horn and disappeared down the empty highway. It was dead cold quiet in every direction from the intersection.

"This ain't gonna be an easy row to hoe," declared Patterson.

"You ain't said shit," replied Archie and offered his bottle to his companions. Patterson refused. Breslin did not.

Headlights appeared in the distance. Archie ran to the intersecting street and shouted, "We'll jump on the light signal and it'll have to stop. Come on, Breslin, we need the weight."

Breslin and Archie stood poised over the rubber covering that protected the remote signal switch for cars entering from the side road. They jumped together. They could hear the overhead signal click to amber.

The approaching car drifted toward the center of the road to avoid stopping too close to the soldiers hitchhiking under the streetlight. It stopped about ten yards short, the headlights blinding the three soldiers.

Feeling his liquor, Patterson decided to get close. He shaded his eyes and walked into the glare. Behind the lights, he discovered a shiny black 1953 Jaguar convertible with chrome wire wheels. The traffic signal colors reflected off the spokes making the wheels look like jewels of a mythological chariot. A beautiful young woman with long blonde hair sat at the wheel, staring straight ahead and smoking. Her Great Dane pressed its snout against the slightly opened passenger side window.

Patterson hoped the dog could not charge out as he stepped closer. "Hey," he said and thumbed in the direction she was headed. She looked him up and down for a moment and slowly shook her head no.

Patterson thought she might be crying. There was moisture on her cheeks. It was hard to tell looking past the dog. He moved closer. The entire car became green as the light changed.

She used the hand holding the cigarette to shift into first.

"What's wrong?" called Patterson.

The Jaguar inched forward. Again, she shook her head no. Her tongue wet her lips and she turned away. The Jaguar roared voluptuously away from the intersection. It had New York plates.

"You guys see her?" shouted Patterson.

"Does a cat have an ass?" replied Archie.

"Someday, man. Someday," vowed the restored Pfc. Patterson.

Breslin reminded, "You have to watch broads with big dogs. I dated a couple in Bryn Mawr. They were weird. Loved to talk. Rich babes. You just listen a lot, then fuck 'em. They liked that too."

In less than five minutes, but what seemed longer, another car appeared in the distance.

Breslin and Archie, taking credit for his scientific approach to stopping cars, manned their station while Patterson stood under the streetlight with his thumb out. They had to jump twice; Archie had stumbled on the first try.

The car slowed. A Fleetline Chevy with a Negro couple in the front.

Archie threatened, "I ain't ridin' with no boogies."

Breslin turned to keep his back to the car and said, "Can it, cookie."

"Oh, what're you gonna do? Kick my ass?"

The couple talked as they waited, bathed in the red glow. The young lady rolled down the window halfway. "We're going as far as Emporia."

Breslin stepped up to the rear door. "That'll help, ma'am."

Patterson stood amazed that a colored couple would pick them up. He would never give three coons a lift.

The driver reached behind his wife to unlock the rear door. Climbing into the back, they noticed the driver's blue Air Force jacket draped across the rear shelf. On the sleeve were the upside down Air Force stripes of a sergeant. His bus driver type hat sat on the jacket.

"It's too cold to be standing out there," commented the sergeant as they drove away. He was big across the shoulders. The young woman turned to them. She was beautiful in the light and shadows. "We guessed y'all must be tryin' to get home same as us."

Instantly, Breslin imagined he was talking to a dark angel. There was a mystical quality about her, or maybe just the headlights from approaching cars gave her an air of mystery. "You're right, ma'am." She was the most beautiful woman he had seen in a long time.

"I'm Sergeant Joe Jefferson from Emporia. This is my wife, Marie."

The three paratroopers mumbled introductions. To Breslin's surprise, Archie asked the civilized question of how was the Air Force was treating him.

"Mighty fine. Y'all know. Three hots and a cot." They laughed at the familiar phrase.

Patterson almost had his cigarette lit when Breslin asked if they could smoke. It was OK with the sergeant as

long as they cracked the window. The three men lit cigarettes. Archie slipped his pint out. Breslin elbowed him.
Archie gave him a silent finger, but he didn't drink. They
settled in for the ride.

"How far did you say you were going?" asked Breslin.

"Emporia," responded Sgt. Jefferson. "'Bout a hundred
miles up ahead."

Breslin wanted to talk to his dark angel. From his corner
seat, he appreciated her strong profile and the luster of her
skin. Her presence warmed him. Under the highway and
dashboard lights, she became his ebony goddess. The
queen of dark highways and dark nights.

After a long period of silence and finished cigarettes,
Patterson offered to drive.

Jefferson thanked him, but declined the offer. "We
were in Florida this morning. We're pushing through to get
home tonight. Marie's ready to have a baby."

"Congratulations," said Breslin. "Looking for a boy or
girl?"

They wanted a boy. If they timed it right, he could be
born in the same house where the sergeant was born and
his father before him. The minister who baptized him would
baptize the new baby.

"Good luck," added Breslin.

Gradually, the rear seat grew colder. The chill penetrated their legs and lower backs. Finally, Archie unscrewed the
pint and took a quick sip. Breslin reached across Patterson
and punched his thigh.

Archie whispered, "Who died and left you in charge?"

"Cold back there, ain't it," said the sergeant and apologized the heater didn't reach the back seat.

"It beats the highway," said Patterson and saw his
breath. Sitting in one place, between his pals and unable to
even stretch his legs, made the cold more penetrating.
Across the front seat, the glow of the dashboard looked like
a crackling fire and he was stuck outside in a blizzard. He
mentally undressed the girl in the Jaguar, imagined her in

her panties and bra like the magazine ads in the Christian Canteen, and held himself under the overcoat. At least his hands were warm.

And he had to piss. Bad.

In her soft voice, the girl asked if they were churchgoers.

Archie offered, "Breslin is. He's the chaplain's assistant." His tone indicated the disgrace of it all.

"I've been hanging around churches all my life," Breslin admitted. He explained he went to the same church his parents were married in. His older brothers were deacons there and his sister belonged to the Rosary Sodality. Every Sunday, the entire family attended nine o'clock mass. Cousins. Nieces and nephews. "We're a regular convention of Irish Catholics."

Breslin didn't mention he believed his bad luck with girls had to do with the Virgin Mary and mortal sin. It was a subject he avoided after failing with a few of the girls from Bryn Mawr who readily offered themselves. In his heart, he again wondered if there was a connection and drifted into a half-sleep remembering his childhood love and his family's adoration for the Virgin Mary. His religious professor described their excessive veneration of her as Mariolatry.

None of the three soldiers knew they were falling asleep. They were too cold.

Slowly, each heard a voice singing in their dreams. A voice beautiful enough to awaken them and warm their blood. A woman's voice.

They realized it was Mrs. Jefferson quietly singing on her own, unaware anyone was listening. Maybe singing for her unborn child. The tone was soft and carried an invisible strength like an albatross' wings silently gripping the wide-open sky.

The three young soldiers listened. Mesmerized.

"Fall on your knees/ Oh, hear the angel voices..." she sang. "O night divine/ O night when Christ was born/ O night divine/ O night/ O night divine…" The words trailed off.

When she stopped, something disappeared from the Chevy; it seemed barren and colder than ever. Breslin asked her to sing again.

Startled, she turned to face the window with her hand up as if to hide. "I…I forgot we had company."

Sergeant Jefferson laughed and patted her knee. "I keep telling y'all, y'all can sing."

"She sure can," added Breslin and he cracked the window to smoke. As the three rustled to adjust their positions, Archie took another quick sip.

On the outskirts of Emporia, the paratroopers climbed stiffly from the Chevy. Breslin asked them to pray for him. The couple wished them well and drove down a side street. Breslin stared after the car carrying away his dark beauty.

"Let's hump," said Archie, "my blood's cold enough to make red fuckin' rope."

"Wait, goddamnit," called Patterson. "I've gotta piss so bad I can taste it."

By a steel-shuttered auto parts building, they pissed against the wall, steaming up the night, then half-marched along 301 through the run-down section of Emporia taking swigs off Breslin's bottle. Archie tried to count cadence, but his companions shut him up again. Patterson kept his laces loose and cursed himself for wearing new boots. He knew better.

A young soldier in civilian clothes picked them up after they had walked hard for what seemed like an hour as cars sped by. His car was a four-door, '57 Chevy Bel-Air with small rear wheel skirts and Virginia tags. When they opened the door, the warmth smothered them like a summer wind.

"Damn," praised Breslin as they climbed in. "You could grill cheese in here."

"Are y'all Airborne?" asked the driver.

"Hope to shit in your mess kit we are," replied Archie.

The driver volunteered he was stationed at Fort Lee and in the Quartermaster Corps. Patterson asked what his Military Occupation Speciality was.

"Just a cook."

"A cook," said Archie sarcastically, "I ain't ridin' with no leg cook."

The driver looked across at Archie, worried. Breslin leaned across the front seat. "Get out then, Cookie," said Breslin forcefully. "He's a cook too. The biggest fucking dud in the Eighty-Deuce."

Archie defended himself by pointing out he was a cook, but he was not a leg cook.

"Forgive our friend's manners," Breslin explained to the man behind the wheel, "he doesn't have any. By leg he means soldiers who are too smart to jump from planes."

"I know," said the driver. "Riggers school is on Lee. Those guys are big hell raisers."

Riggers, according to Archie, were not worth the powder to blow them to hell. "Jesus, Archie. Take it easy," said Patterson.

Archie turned in the front seat to face his highway companions. The warmth had softened his features. They saw he was drunk. Drunker than they were. "Well, how come you ain't one then?" Patterson waved him off.

Archie turned to the driver and held out his pint. "Is the bar open?"

Not only did the driver acknowledge Archie's request, in a gesture of goodwill he pointed out there was a case of PX beer on the back shelf. "Three-point-two stuff."

Breslin had already noticed the Carlings Red Cap logo. He pulled open the cardboard folded top. "You want one?" he asked the driver.

"Do people in hell want ice water? There's a church key in the carton somewhere."

"Good man," said Breslin who already had the opener in hand. He cracked open two bottles and passed one over the driver's shoulder and the other to Patterson. "You're a gentleman and a scholar."

"And a leg."

"Fuck off, Archie."

Breslin opened two more bottles and passed one to Archie and kept one himself. With the bottles in hand they relaxed, lit cigarettes, opened their overcoats, and unbuttoned their Ike jackets. Archie drank Old Rocking Chair and chased it with swigs of beer. After several drinks, Archie related the popular company jump story about Specialist Dean Reininger. "Spec-Four Dean talked a lot," explained Archie. "The man talked all day accordin' to his bunkies in the commo 'toon and talked all night in his sleep. He was from Poth, Texas, wherever in the hell that is, and had this high accent." Archie raised his voice in a bad imitation. "He never said nothin' important, just ran at the mouth like music you hear in supermarkets all day long. Sometimes NCOs gave him a direct order to shut up," added Archie, jabbing the air for emphasis with the pint bottle in one hand and beer in the other.

Archie set the scene about jumping into Fort Polk, Louisiana, from Camp Mackall, an often used marshalling area near Bragg. It was Operation Sagebrush. "All the time we're chutin' up Dean's mouth runs on and on. He believed he was jumpin' for the hometown folks 'cause Texas was right next to Louisiana. The plane ride was long and rough and he kept talkin' while most of us got sick. I swear as I went out the door I could hear him right behind me yappin' on and on." The storyteller paused to take several alternate sips of beer and bourbon.

Archie could not see Breslin and Patterson making jerk-off signs about him and the story. He had never jumped with Dean. The story was a company legend, a myth, based on a long ago event. Everyone passing through Headquarters Company heard it more than once.

Archie's voice grew louder. "When Dean jumped behind me, he landed right on top of my chute." Breslin groaned. The driver smiled.

"That's the God's honest truth, so help me God. What in the hell do youse cats know? When Sagebrush happened youse still thought a T-Ten was a shoe size." He leaned toward the driver, bottles in hand and continued. "There was ten thousand jumpers in the sky at once. See what I'm sayin'." The driver took a sip of beer and nodded.

"I looks up and all I can see are feet walkin' 'cross my canopy. The cat walked off me, fell past me and I saw his face as close as I'm seein' you, you know what I mean. Like a rock he went by. His eyes were as big as that fuckin' speed-ometer."

The falling Dean, continued Archie, landed on another open chute and walked off that one to fall on another one. When he walked off that one he fell about 40 feet and hit the ground like a bag of shit. "The son-of-a-bitch's chute never opened and after that neither did his mouth. The fear of the Hawk was in him to stay." Archie sat back with the pint between his legs, beer in hand, and lit a cigarette.

"What's the Hawk?" asked the driver.

Archie leaned toward the driver. The illumination from the dash created shadows across his face as he exhaled smoke and said, "That's the unknown waitin' in the sky that'll bring death and destruction to any son-of-a-bitch crazy enough to unass an airplane. Every jumper fears the Hawk."

"Well said," praised Breslin. "Who taught you that?"

Patterson offered the driver another beer. He turned it down and confessed, "I was going to go Airborne."

There was dead silence for a moment until Patterson spoke. "You ain't missin' nothin' except spit-shine and chicken-shit."

The intoxicated Airborne cook wasn't letting the driver take a pass. "Everyone you meet was always goin' to go Airborne. Why in the hell didn't you?"

The driver looked straight ahead and recalled. "I wrote to my folks during basic at Jackson and told them I was thinking about it. My Daddy called and asked me not to. He said if I got killed, it would kill my mother."

"Your daddy," scoffed Archie, mimicking the young man's voice.

Breslin pointed his bottle across the seat. "Archie, you keep fucking around I'm gonna stick this up your ass." Breslin didn't realize the irony of his remark until Patterson nearly spit out his mouthful of beer to suppress his laugh.

Archie twisted in the front seat to face his companions. His head weaved back and forth as he balanced himself. "You and what fuckin' Army, chaplain's assistant?"

"Just lay off, Pancake Jockey. You don't know when someone's doin' you a favor."

"Who's doin' who a favor? I'm a paratroop ridin' in this leg's car."

"You don't know the difference between a spatula and an entrenching tool, Cookie."

Archie braced himself against the dash. The driver leaned against his door trying to keep as much space as possible between himself and his odd passenger.

"Come on, you guys," asked Patterson without much conviction.

"I was goin' to go Airborne," repeated Archie in a whiny voice. "What kinda talk's that? There's two kinds of people in this sorry-ass world. Paratroopers and them that wish they was."

Breslin rested his beer against the door and leaned across the seat to grab Archie's overcoat lapels and pull him towards the back. Archie, off balance, spilled some beer on the seat. Breslin held him face to face. "Dudes like him are too smart to go Airborne, because there're too many phonies like you, Cookie. Now, you say one more word, I'm gonna bite off your fuckin' nose."

"Like, you ain't..." Breslin bit Archie's nose. Not hard, but a bite.

"Goddamnit!" Patterson came up to shoulder away Breslin. "Quit fuckin' around."

Archie felt his nose. "You could've bitten it off." He whined like a child being unjustly punished. Sure, his nose was all right. He pulled himself across the seat and swung a roundhouse right that missed Breslin by a mile and hit Patterson in the ear as he leaned forward to stop Archie. Breslin backed himself in the corner and lifted his boots. "Come on, motherfucker! I'll kick your face in."

"Youse cocksuckers!" shouted Archie sitting back. "I'm a dyin' man."

A blowing car horn silenced them. It was the Bel-Air's horn. "I'm turning here," the driver said timidly.

The three men stared at the driver. He looked frightened. How long had he been blowing the horn?

Passing traffic reminded them they were on a highway. Slowly, they gathered their gloves, scarves, bags, caps, and opened the doors. Without a word, they climbed into the cold night.

"Merry Christmas, leg!" shouted Archie to the departing car.

They were barely a quarter-mile from the junctions of Highway 17 and US 1 in Fredericksburg, Maryland. It was well illuminated by powerful overhead yellow lights. Seventeen was Archie's point to cut across Virginia, where he'd pick up US 40 toward Pittsburgh. Due to their arguing, Patterson and Breslin had no idea they missed the 301 cut-off 20 miles behind.

"I ain't hangin' with youse assholes," griped a sullen Archie. Overcoat unbuttoned and cap on backwards so the glider patch faced the rear, he lurched toward the intersection lights. Several times he stumbled. His AWOL bag kept banging against his leg. Patterson and Breslin stayed close behind him to keep him from wandering onto the highway. Even though it was late Christmas Eve, there was a lot of traffic. Mostly trucks.

A trio of gigantic semis sat with their taillights blinking like pinball machines to make the turn onto 17. The traffic signal flicked from red to green. The trucks shifted, wheezed and ground gears as they turned. A few late travelers in cars dared to maneuver among the behemoths. The surrealistic yellow lighting distorted the colors of the machines and the night.

Archie started across, then stopped in the first lane of the highway. "Didn't anyone ever tell youse when you meet a leg you gotta let him know a leg ain't worth the powder to blow him to hell?"

Breslin nodded, "Sure, Archie. Watch out for those big motherfuckers that bend in the middle."

"Fuck youse."

"Your hat's on backwards," called Patterson.

From the middle of the highway, Archie called back, "When you're Airborne, you wear it anyways you fuckin' want!"

He picked up an exaggerated marching stride. "Gotta go!" he chanted. "Gotta be! Airborne!" And kept the cadence going as the lights changed and trucks and cars halted. Archie disappeared behind them. Horns sounded. "Get the hell out of here!" shouted someone.

"He'll never make Pittsburgh alive," predicted Breslin.

"Hey, like he's dyin' anyway," reminded Patterson.

When the traffic cleared, there stood Archie on US 17. Overcoat blowing in the wake of the trailer trucks. Cap still backwards. He waved at cars swinging onto the highway. Breslin and Patterson watched a car loaded with Marines from Quantico stop.

"Jarheads!" they heard the cook shout and he climbed into the car.

"Like I said," repeated Breslin. "He'll never make Pittsburgh alive."

It did not take long for their next ride.

A four-door maroon Mercedes pulled out of traffic and stopped. Both young men were impressed with the idea of riding in a fancy car. The driver waved them into the front seat even though it was a tight fit. He explained it was warmer. They tossed their AWOL bags into the back and climbed in.

The driver wore a suit and tie. His face reflected an outdoor life. He introduced himself as Dave and advised them they had missed the 301 cut-off, but they were lucky, he explained, there was more traffic on US 1. A lot of people went to Washington for the holiday.

Both soldiers silently thanked God for another nice warm car and asked if it was OK to smoke.

Patterson unlaced his boots and one at a time brought out a foot to massage it for warmth and relief from the new boots. The Mercedes heater was wonderful; it was like standing beside a coal furnace with an open grate. He ignored the conversation Breslin and the driver were having, flicked his cigarette out the push-button window, snuggled against the passenger door with his overcoat over him like a blanket, and slowly drifted into a deep, warm, Old Rocking Chair sleep. Sometime soon he'd be back in his own bed...

"Get out! Goddamnit! Get out!"

Patterson woke up half falling out of the car with Breslin pushing him. His leg was asleep and before he could even stand up straight Breslin had their AWOL bags and the Mercedes zipped away.

Patterson finally caught his balance and realized he had only one unlaced boot on. "Scott! You asshole! My fuckin' boot's in the car!" His leg woke up quickly.

Breslin turned around. "Asshole? While you were catching zzzzs, the son-of-a-bitch made a move on me. He was a fucking queer cruising the highways looking for action. Asking me about girls in Fayetteville and did we want to stay with him tonight."

"That guy? Bullshit."

"Sure. Like I wanted to jump out of the car right here because it's fun."

They were at the intersection of 14ᵗʰ Street and Independence Avenue. It was deserted except for a few passing cars. Without agreeing, they started walking. Patterson hobbled in his one boot then stopped. "Goddamn, Scott, if the MPs see I'm out of uniform, I'll never make it home."

Breslin looked around as if they could go hide somewhere. He suggested they keep walking to stay warm and if any MPs show up Patterson would stand behind him. "We have no choice, pal. Besides, we're lost."

At that moment, car headlights headed right for them, blinding them. MPs? Was someone trying to run them over?

The car stopped; it was the maroon Mercedes. The electric window came down. Dave looked across the seat. The car moved alongside the walking soldiers.

"I'm sorry," said Dave, "let me make it up to you boys. I know what it's like to be away from home. I used to be a Marine."

Patterson hollered, "Give me back my boot!"

Dave didn't seem to understand the question. Patterson grabbed the door handle. "My boot's on the floor, motherfucker."

Dave looked down and saw the boot. He stretched and picked it up. "I might keep it for a souvenir." He stopped the car. Patterson tried to reach past the window. Dave pulled back the boot.

"Come on, man. Give it to me."

Breslin stepped up to the window. "Look, you hand over that boot now, or I'm finding a cop and pressing charges against your faggot ass. You read me?"

The car speeded up. A second later the boot flew onto the street. The Mercedes vanished behind its white exhaust.

Patterson sat on the curb to lace up both boots. To their left, across a vast illuminated lawn, they could see the Washington Monument and farther up the White House Christmas tree. On their right were unending silhouettes of imposing government buildings.

"I wonder," said Breslin, "if Ike knows his two best paratroopers are standing out in the cold and don't know which way to go."

"Ike ain't home," replied Patterson ready to continue their journey. "You can bet your ass he's off playin' golf somewhere warm."

"Archie would call him a leg. Let's work on my Rocking Chair."

Breslin produced his pint. They sipped, lit cigarettes, buttoned and belted themselves against the cold and walked along the street, backs to the sparse traffic, with their thumbs out. They talked about going in on a car together when they got back to Bragg. Sgt. Webster would finance it. Breslin wanted a step-down Hudson like the cats drove in *On the Road*. It had to have a blast furnace heater and a luggage rack on top.

"What in the hell's wrong with a T-Bird?" Patterson hadn't forgotten his pre-draft automobile desire.

"As Sidney the Cook would say, 'luggage racks drive quiff crazy'," said Breslin. The men laughed and shared sips.

"You know, you think about that queer and you gotta feel for him." Breslin walked with his AWOL bag looped high on his arm so he could keep both hands in his pockets when he wasn't drinking. "I mean, put it in perspective; its fucking Christmas Eve and he's out hustling hitchhikers. That's tragic, man."

Squealing tires turned the soldiers' heads. A bright yellow Henry J with Florida tags screeched to a halt halfway through the wide intersection they were crossing. The window came down. Four sailors were squeezed inside. Breslin and Patterson expected wisecracks.

"You cats wanna pay for the bridge tolls?"

Breslin stepped closer. "What's that?"

"We're headed across the Bay Bridge to the Jersey Turnpike. You cats can ride if you pay the tolls."

The paratroopers looked at one another. Anything was better than being cold and stuck in the city. They climbed in. Before they settled in what little space the rear seat afforded, the Henry J zipped away, flying across the empty Washington streets, seeming to take every turn on two wheels. The man in the front passenger seat volunteered they were from Jacksonville and this was their fifth weekend in a row going home. Any day now they were headed back to sea. He had a heavy New York accent and added, "Gonna hit the Big Apple and get Mama's home cookin' and Angie's home pussy." The man sported an un-military ducktail haircut.

"Dago pussy's like fuckin' a meatball hoagie," muttered the man next to Breslin who seemed grumpy from lack of sleep. The other sailor, asleep, crammed in the corner, oblivious to the speed, the new passengers, the cramped conditions, and the pending New York weekend.

"I-tie lovin's the best," said the man in front and snapped his fingers as if he'd forgotten something. He produced a gallon jug of cheap wine from the floor and sipped. "Top drawer, as they say on Fifth Avenue."

"Does wine come with the tolls?" asked Breslin who was never shy when it came to drink.

"We'll sell you a sip," said the man.

The grumpy sailor said, "Christ Almighty, Frankie, give him a swig."

"One each," ordered Frankie as he passed the jug to Breslin. When Patterson sat up to drink, he intentionally looked at the speedometer. Pushing 50 through the city. They occasionally slowed, but never stopped for red lights.

Frankie continued about what a great time he would have in New York. Each event accompanied by a finger snap and his head bobbing to an internal rhythm. Sex. Food. Drink. Cars. Parties. Movies. Nightclubs. And always, Angie.

"You guys on leave?" asked Patterson for a distraction from the speed.

"Liberty," he said, "Maybe our last weekend." He was going to be busy, thought Patterson.

"I like sea duty, though." Frankie went on. "I save bread and live clean. I do fifty pushups a day and brush my teeth every four hours." He leaned toward Breslin and peeled up his top lip. "You ever seen choppers as good as these?"

"Frankie, if you weren't in your sailor suit, I'd swear you were Tony Curtis."

"Hey, this cat's all right. Have some more wine." The half-filled jug came over the seat again. Neither Breslin nor Patterson declined.

Patterson asked if the driver always drove that way. "Nah, sometimes he drives fast." Frankie laughed and reached over to shut off the headlights. The driver calmly put them back on.

"You cats ever play blindfold the driver?" He placed his palms in front of the driver's eyes.

Grumpy in the back complained, "Quit fuckin' around, Frankie. That's why we missed the Three-Oh-One turn off. Every trip you're an asshole."

"Don't worry, you guys," assured Frankie. "Louie's a hell of a wheelman."

Patterson moaned quietly to himself and settled back in the cramped space between Breslin and a sleeping sailor. He wasn't cold and he couldn't complain about speed; it would ruin the paratrooper image. He closed his eyes and monitored the humming tires while waiting for the inevitable vicious crash. *A crack-up so swift and thorough it would be painless.*

The Henry J hit 70 miles per hour, banking along the sweeping curves of Hwy 50 leading to the Bay Bridge. The car sounded and felt like any moment it would either disintegrate or break the sound barrier.

"Fog," said Louie. His first word.

"Gettin' near the bay," responded Frankie.

Patterson opened his eyes and edged up to see patches of fog. The element had no effect on Louie's heavy foot. Brilliant lights appeared ahead.

The Henry J nosed forward as Louie pumped the brakes. They rolled into the tollbooth area. Breslin paid the $3.50 toll and took two bucks from Patterson.

"Drive carefully and Merry..." The toll collector's words vanished as the Henry J scooted into the thickening fog that looked like a solid wall. Louie turned on the wipers and seemed unperturbed as he rolled down the window to look out.

Frankie passed around the wine to celebrate reaching the bridge. They needed it to ward off the sudden slap of rushing cold air.

A huge façade of white, yellow, and red lights rose in front of them as if to devour them, then passed within inches. The Henry J yawed then adhered to the concrete again.

Patterson realized he had shouted, "Look out!"

"Trailer truck," said Louie as if he was saying good morning and rolled up the window.

Patterson looked at Breslin with a 'what-should-we-do' gesture. His pal lifted his hands in helplessness. A split second later, like a blinking steel tidal wave, another truck appeared. The Henry J gave not an inch and charged its way through the swirling wake.

The next giant truck added its air horn to the moment. Squashed in the back, Patterson actually flinched. Frankie thought the horn was terrific and passed the wine. Before Breslin finished his extended sip, the fog was gone.

"Like that," Frankie snapped his fingers. "You OK, Louie?"

"Lucky." Frankie offered a Chesterfield. Patterson hurriedly brought out his Luckies and extended one over Louie's shoulder.

"Light it."

Patterson pulled back the smoke, lit it with his '04 lighter, and then passed it to Louie. For some reason, he now felt confident they would make it. Frankie was right; Louie was a hell of a wheelman.

The Henry J dropped them on the overpass of the Black Horse Pike. West was Philadelphia. East led to Atlantic City and Downbeach. They followed a worn path down the embankment and had to scale a half-bent chain link fence. By the overpass, they shared Breslin's remains of Old Rocking Chair and smoked.

Breslin brought up the night he hadn't helped them when Schmidt went AWOL. "It's been bugging me, man. I should've been there."

"Hey, man, we put that to bed the other night when we pulled you out of the chapel." Patterson assured him it was forgotten. Besides, he reminded Breslin, Schmidt wouldn't have done the same for him. "You came with us to put back the roster. It all comes out in the wash."

Breslin wanted to confess. "I learned something when I didn't help you guys. I found out I could be too scared to do something, so I just wiped myself out on booze and Mary Jane."

Breslin made a big deal out of finishing his pint then threw it hard against the concrete overpass. It didn't break. Patterson brought out his bottle and offered Breslin another drink. He accepted and said, "From my perspective, I let Hollywood down. I won't do that again, and I learned you never cop out."

"Man," replied Patterson, "the next thing I know you'll be swearin' off drinkin' drinkin' liquor." He tossed his cigarette and stuck the bottle in his overcoat pocket. "It's too cold to be hangin' around. Gotta go. Gotta…"

"Gotta be…"

"Airborne," they said in unison.

Breslin headed underneath the overpass. "See you in the war," he hollered.

A New Jersey state trooper gave Patterson his first lift. He had little to say except he'd once been a Marine on an aircraft carrier. Patterson relayed the adventure with the sailors. "That sounds like a bunch of swabbies," he said.

The dashboard clock read 1240. With a gruff apology for not taking him all the way to Downbeach, he dropped Patterson at an empty rural intersection with only a single streetlight.

To keep warm, Patterson drilled himself, calling cadence, marching in squares of 50 steps each, always keeping under the light in case a car came. He sipped after every ten squares were completed. For a moment, he recalled the girl in the Jaguar at the red light in Rocky Mount; it seemed a long time ago. *Will I ever have a girl like that?*

A big panel truck loaded with Christmas Day *Philadelphia Inquirers* stopped. The cigar-smoking driver, a squat man bundled in a lumber jacket, informed him he had been at Normandy—Day Two—on Utah Beach with the 4th Infantry Division. It wasn't pretty, but it wasn't as bad as Omaha. The rest of the war was easy for him, meaning he wasn't as scared. He drove a deuce-and-a-half for engineers across France and Belgium. "Engineers always figured out ways to stay warm."

Across the bridge into Atlantic City, the truck went left. Patterson climbed out to go toward Downbeach. He estimated he was three miles from home and started walking to his own slow cadence in the street. "Lift your head and hold it high/ Pfc. Patterson's passin' by..." He was glad the stripe had come through before going home. "... Sound off/ One-two/ Sound off/ Three-four/ Break it on down/ One-two-three-four/ One-two/ Three-four!"

A car approached from behind. He turned to face the car and put out his thumb. His breath fumed in the headlights as he hummed, "If I die on the Russia front/ Box me up with a Russian cunt/ Tell my Mama I done my...Headley!"

The '50 Ford station wagon with ersatz wood trim had passed so slowly Patterson had recognized the passenger.

The wagon stopped. Patterson opened the door and pushed into the front seat. Forget being polite, be warm.

They all knew one another from high school and greeted each other as if old friends, but they weren't. The car's occupants dressed like the college guys they were. Ivy League button-down shirts and crew style sweaters. Parkas lay across the back seat. They were part of the jock *cum* class officer *laude* social whirl of Patterson's class. He had never taken college prep courses.

"Someone said you were in the Army," said Garry the driver.

"Paratroopers, man, not the Army. It's different."

"What'd you mean?" asked Headley, the young man in the middle.

Patterson struggled to extract his pint of Rocking Chair from his overcoat pocket. "We jump from planes. The rest of the Army don't. Want a drink?"

They refused. Patterson forced himself to take a large swallow, suppressed his gag and lit a cigarette. He told them about hitchhiking up from Bragg.

"Bragg?"

"Fort Bragg. Home of the Airborne. You never heard of it?" They were in college. Rutgers and Glassboro.

"Well, college dudes drink all the time, I heard." He extended the bottle again. Each man had a small sip. "The draft's gonna get your asses sooner or later," cautioned Patterson and took another sip followed with lip smacking, spurious satisfaction.

Headley was giving some thought to ROTC.

"If you do, go Airborne. There ain't nothin' like it." And in a moment he was telling the story about Spec-Four Dean Reininger's jump. This time Specialist Reininger walked across Patterson's chute on All-America last year. While relating the story, he blew smoke toward his acquaintances and took quick sips from the pint. He noticed Garry elbow Headley as if to say, humor him. Telling the story made him feel warm and wonderful like a world-weary Airborne prince if there was such a thing.

"Did you jump often?" asked Garry.

"Nah. Maybe twice a week at the most," he lied. Most regular paratroopers jumped every two or three months. "I would've stayed at Bragg, but its dead for the holidays. You should see the women there. More quiff than you can shake a stick at. I've got me a honey with a Jaguar and a big dog."

Headley reassured Patterson there were plenty of girls at school. "We all meet at house mixers." Patterson didn't know what a house mixer was. They explained it was when fraternities and sororities got together.

"Man, you cats are livin'. I bet there's wall-to-wall pussy to be had." Patterson would be as crude as possible. "My bunkie, the Moonlight Gambler, we call him that, a cool cat from Calumet, has a broad with a tattoo. His name on her arm."

"A real tattoo?"

"Fuckin'-A. Just like the chute I have on my ass." Both young men were surprised he had a tattoo.

"Everyone's got one, don't they?" Patterson swore to himself only one more sip. He might be sick.

Headley asked what was it really like to jump. Patterson smiled. He didn't have to lie. "It's like...like man...somethin' you can't talk about." Try and stop him. "One minute you're hooked up, jammed against everybody squeezed into a Cee-One Nineteen screamin' you want out. The green light pops and you're hotfootin' it out the door. Through the engine blast. Going ass over teacups. The next thing you're hangin' all sweet and pretty. There's nothin' below you except a DZ two thousand feet down. It's so quiet the wind plays songs in the risers."

Patterson moved his cupped hand diagonally across the dashboard to show the drifting chute. "You come down and land soft as a flower in the wind. I love it. I swear to God I love it." He chanced another sip then added, "It's better than gettin' laid."

Garry wanted to know what a DZ was. "Man, you cats don't learn too much in college. It's the fuckin' ground. The drop zone."

Are they wincing at my language? He hoped so. "Right here's good." They had just passed his street. He kept the door open a moment longer than necessary to offer them another sip. They declined. "Remember one thing while you're sittin' around college ..."

They waited. Their faces revealed they wanted him to shut up and shut the door.

"... there's two kinds of people in this world. Paratroopers—and them that wish they were." He swung the door shut.

The station wagon pulled away. Patterson walked across the main street to his street with a drunken smile on his face. They would enjoy telling their friends about how Willie Patterson had become a gung-ho Army jerk-off. He had given them enough rope to hang him. Patterson laughed aloud. "Fuckin' college assholes. They don't know shit from Shinola." He was a lean mean paratrooper. A whiskey-drinking, cigarette-smoking badass who said, shit, piss, and fuck. He stood full-field inspections and un-assed C-119s. No college kid did that.

The house was dark. It had to be past 0200. Now that he had arrived, the sense of urgency vanished. Even the cold seemed diminished. Time for a drink and a smoke. Once inside, he couldn't do that. He sat on one of the porch chairs, pulled the overcoat collar up high, adjusted his scarf and cap, and lit a cigarette. The bottle rested on the wrought iron table next to him and the AWOL bag was by the door as he snuggled deeper into his Army overcoat. It was worth its weight in gold, a lesson learned on many nights of guard duty. He'd vowed to take it with him when he was discharged. He toasted with the pint. "To the lord and lady of the manor."

Just as he raised the bottle, the porch light came on and his mother opened the front door. In her winter bathrobe, she stared at him from behind the storm door. "Willie?"

He toasted his mother. "Merry fuckin' Christmas, Mom!"

He drank and took a long drag on his cigarette, wondering why his mother looked so startled.

Chapter 13

Sergeant First Class Potter worked his cooks late on Christmas Eve and brought in the morning shift earlier to ensure that everything was prepared for the big noon Christmas Day dinner. Every Christmas, the mess sergeant took it upon himself to provide the troops more than the basic military Christmas menu prescribed in Department of Defense mess manuals. They soldiered hard in the regiment, and the men deserved a meal with all the trimmings, including holiday décor in the mess hall. A few extra rations of meat and chicken to the right civilian employee at the Main Post PX warehouse and the company had the biggest Christmas tree in the division, a tree decorated in balls and lights of blue and gold, the regiment's colors. There were no kiddy candy canes, tinsel, or angel's hair; this was a military tree and various enlisted rank insignia were hooked on the branches as well as miniature tanks, planes, howitzers, and parachutes. No officer brass allowed. Along the walls there were holly and pine clusters from the Bragg boondocks. A two-foot high papier-mâché Santa Claus stood on top of the milk machine. Large green wreaths with electric red candles in their centers hung in the elongated mess hall windows facing the street.

The serving line steam trays were packed with mashed potatoes, yams, creamed onions and peas, and Sergeant

Potter's special stuffing. The cooks worked right behind the lines, cutting fresh slices of turkey and ham. Fruit cups and cranberry sauce were available along with two kinds of pie: pumpkin and mince. Small vats of whipped cream sat on the side. In a box next to the milk machine, dry ice kept individual ice cream cups frozen, and on the other side of the machine were the mess sergeant's special Christmas cookies baked in the shapes of parachutes and airplanes. All diners were encouraged to help themselves to as much as they wanted, but always heed the overhead sign, 'Take what you want, but eat what you take.'

No alcohol was served the troops. However, in Potter's small office there were bottles of bourbon and scotch for visitors, and the KPs secretly dipped into the big jugs of wine kept in the walk-in reefer.

Bing Crosby, Perry Como, Nat King Cole, Gene Autry, Eddy Arnold and others serenaded with carols from the small 45-rpm player supplied by the mess sergeant and handled by the DRO.

"At ease!" shouted the charge of quarters, the NCO assigned to look out for the company and execute the headcount during off-duty hours. In the doorway, Col. Steele and Major Byrd, the Chaplain, stood next to the CQ. Everyone and everything came to a halt. Silence except for steam tables hissing and Perry Como singing about being naughty or nice because Santa Claus was coming to town.

"As you were," commanded Steele.

Talk resurfaced like a wide splash of water. Chairs scraped. Trays clanged on the serving line. Eddy Arnold's song about Christmas in Old Shantytown replaced Perry Como.

The mess sergeant came out to meet the officers. They wore their three-quarter length chocolate brown jackets with Sam Browne belts and their twill pinks were bloused in their spit-shined boots. On the left breast of the colonel's jacket rode a pyramid of medals topped by the Combat Infantryman's Badge, the most valued of Army decorations.

Under the rows of medals was his Master Jump Wings with a bronze star signifying a combat jump. The patch of the 187th Regimental Combat Team, the unit he served with during the Korean War, showed on his right shoulder. On both men's left shoulders were the 82nd Airborne Division patch, double white As on red and blue backgrounds.

The colonel tapped his leg with his overseas cap as his formidable chin bobbed approvingly of the mess hall's appearance.

"Merry Christmas, sir."

"Looks outstanding, Sergeant," said the colonel.

Chaplain Byrd nodded and said, "The men appreciate your effort."

"Thank you, sir." Potter ushered the two officers to the rear of the mess hall in the section reserved for NCOs and officers. Several NCOs already dining stood up and greeted the men and wished them a Merry Christmas. The officers reciprocated.

"Hark the Herald Angels Sing" played.

"I'm glad you have some religious records, Sergeant," noted the Chaplain.

"Wouldn't be-be-be Christmas with-without 'em, si-si-sir. I'll ge-get the D-D-RO to bring your pl-pl-trays."

"That won't be necessary, Sergeant. We'll go through the line ourselves," said the colonel. The officers left their caps on the table and headed for the serving line.

The chaplain asked the mess sergeant to turn off the record player for a moment so he could share a prayer with the troops. The cooking veteran signaled the CQ to turn off the record player by slicing his neck with his fingers as he followed the officers to the line. Without music, the general chatter sounded louder.

"Listen up!" ordered Potter. The chaplain stood at the beginning of the serving line and waited for quiet.

"I said, li-li-listen up!"

Most of the talk died. The KPs held up their serving utensils. Men waited in the serving line. Some, holding their trays almost ready to sit down, stayed standing.

"Thank you, Sergeant," said the chaplain, "and Merry Christmas and Happy New Year to all of you today. I want all of us to take a moment and bow our heads to express our thanks for being lucky enough to be in the Eighty-Second Airborne on this Christmas Day. I always like to think our good Lord would have been a paratrooper. In a sense, he started the world's greatest army. Bow your heads now and each in your own way give thanks and accept this holiday blessing."

Sidney the Cook, wearing cook's white trousers, a T-shirt and apron, smoked as he leaned against the metal railing on the back stairs of the mess hall. The long morning and too much wine had wearied him. He planned to work until 1300 and then go to an off-post party given by some of the girls who worked at Bonnie Doone Cleaners. In the trunk of his Olds were two pies and half a turkey he planned to contribute. It was his way to catch the eye of the chunky, older Italian woman with the near moustache whose sergeant husband, an Air Force radar expert, was serving a six-month tour on Kwajalein Atoll. Sidney's plan involved getting his cook's whites washed and starched and a piece of ass on a regular basis at no charge for either event.

A dirty, tan, four-door Ford squealed into the driveway, stopping so quickly the car bounded forward and back with suppressed energy.

Sidney thought he recognized the car, but continued his contemplation of his next 19 days in the Army. *Will I really re-enlist for Sneaky Pete's, the 77th Special Forces Group? I'd get a bonus and...*

A capless buck sergeant in fatigues charged out of the car with a .45 Army issue pistol in his hand. He made no effort to hide it. And he headed for the mess hall stairs.

Sure, Sidney knew the car. *Motherfucker! It's her car! And that must be Carole Lou's husband!*

The cook's mind and body petrified into a low tide that beached all boats and fish. He was dead.

Sidney had met her at the Main Post car wash. She had remarked on the candy-apple color of the Olds and they took a ride. The next thing Sidney knew he was fucking her every Thursday on the far side of Fayetteville near the Veterans Hospital. Great daytime car seat fucking. Her three kids were in school, and her Lifer husband served as an MP on Main Post.

Sidney took a long drag. Maybe his last. He took the cigarette from his lips and started to raise his hands in surrender, when the enraged sergeant demanded to know where was that son-of-a-bitch Sidney the Cook.

The cook's throat constricted to the point he had trouble breathing. His almost gesture of surrender became a convulsive hand motion toward the mess hall screen door as the thought came to him as spontaneously as the piss running down his leg into his left boot.

The cat doesn't know me.

The sergeant pulled open the door, and waving the pistol like an usher escorting a theatre patron, demanded for the real Sidney the Cook to show him the motherfucker.

Sidney could not talk. He stepped into the mess hall and the sergeant pushed past him ready to shoot up the place.

Bing Crosby was deep into "The Little Drummer Boy": "rump a pum/ I played my drum for him/Pa rump a pum pum/ I played my best for him/ Pa rump a pum..."

The cook's mind rolled like the big city presses in the old movies pumping out headlines. 'Extra! Extra! Cook Survives Mess Hall Slaughter! Read all about it!' He managed to point toward the back of the mess hall and squeak out, "The asshole was back there just a minute ago."

Carole Lou's husband strode to the serving line and fired the pistol into the ceiling.

Dead silence. Except Der Bingle finishing "Drummer Boy." Someone laughed and stopped.

In a frozen montage of disbelief, the troops, goggle-eyed and slack-jawed, stared across the serving line at a man with a pistol.

"Sidney the Cook!" shouted the sergeant.

Finally, the troops realized the man might be danger-ous. They hit the floor faster than rocks through thin ice. And "Drummer Boy" played again.

Lt. Margolin hurried along the battalion street from the parking lot. He was running late for the Christmas meal and knew if he wasn't there, someone like Steele would show up and wonder why he had not dined with the troops.

Hurrying towards him, in just his cook's whites and T-shirt, was Sidney the Cook. Margolin raised his hands as if to stop the cook. "Specialist, what's the rush?"

The cook had no time for pleasantries. His words came out as he ran past. "There's a crazy son-of-a-bitch shootin' up the mess hall!" and he zigzagged toward the parking lot, dodging imaginary bullets, where he'd find his beloved candy-apple Olds with a bullet hole through the front window, driver's side.

The lieutenant wasn't sure what he heard. *Someone's shooting up the mess hall? Shooting a weapon in a mess hall? Headquarters mess hall?* He stopped and asked himself if he wanted to keep going. He had no choice—this is what he got for not going home for *Hannukkah.*

Headquarters Company was the last building on the street. He jogged slowly towards it. The outside looked normal enough except for the tan car without a 504th sticker and the driver's door open in the mess hall driveway. Quietly, he went up the rear stairs and eased open the door just in time to hear the second shot. The round went into the automatic toaster where it rattled for a moment like a shaken can of nails.

"Where is he? Which one of you sons-of-bitches is Sid-ney the Cook?"

The crazed sergeant took a few steps past the serving line, his eyes searching the room where every man lay in the floor. They hid their faces in fear that he might mistake them for the horny cook. No one lying on the floor, including Mangiameli who was on KP, was going to volunteer anything. Mangiameli worried he might be shot and miss going on leave in six days to see Judy. She said she had a Christmas surprise for him. He couldn't wait.

Margolin knew they needed help. He eased the screen door closed and ran to the orderly room to alert the MPs.

Sergeant First Class Potter, hands over his head, rose slowly from behind the low partition that separated the NCO section from the rest of the mess hall. It was the second shot that spurred him on. No one was going to shoot up his mess hall.

"Easy," whispered Col. Steele who came up alongside him. "Don't move too fast."

"No sweat, sir," replied Potter and he called out, "Sarge, what're you doin?" The drummer boy asked Jesus if he could play for him.

"Get down for God's sake!" hissed Chaplain Byrd from the prone position. He had happened to look up when he heard Steele's caution about moving too fast. He decided to recite the Lord's Prayer to take his mind off the situation.

"I'm gonna kill that cook!" admitted the sergeant although his point had already been well made.

Potter stepped through the partition opening for the NCO section and said, "I'm Sergeant First Class Potter and I'm the mess sergeant." The tranquility of his voice amazed him. "I don't think you'll find Sid here." Potter assumed the cook was lying among the others on the floor and wasn't about to volunteer his presence.

Steele followed Potter through the entrance. Together, with a table's width between them, they moved slowly toward the serving line where the MP stood waiting for Sidney to appear.

"Sergeant, I don't know what kind of beef you got with Sid. For sure it's a big one. But shootin' up my mess hall and innocent men ain't gonna help you." Potter's throat yearned for the bourbon sitting on his desk.

Steele added, "He's right, Sergeant. All these troops are innocent men."

"You know him?" He pointed the pistol at Potter. "Point him out or I'll shoot you."

"Hold on there, Sergeant!" called Steele in his best parade ground voice; its resonance caused most of the men to look up. "I'm Colonel Steele, the regimental commander. You're about to do something you'll spend the rest of your life regretting. Think about that, Sergeant." It was a command.

"I ain't got no life now."

"What in the hell you sayin'?" reasoned Potter. He lowered his hands to aid his argument. "We all got somethin' no matter how bad it seems."

Men on the floor inched toward the main door where the charge of quarters sat frozen at the small headcount table. He dared not try to shut off "Drummer Boy."

Meanwhile, Margolin finally reached the Provost Marshall and explained the situation. He knew he had to go back to the mess hall and didn't want to. He was afraid. After several deep breaths, he hurried outside to the rear door and again peeked.

"... rump a pum pum/ I'll play my song for you/ A rump a pum pum/ A rump a pum pum/ On my drum..."

Steele's voice dropped in volume when he asked the MP to listen very carefully. "I'm going to give you a direct order to put the weapon on the floor in front of you. If you do that I'll testify at your court-martial that you cooperated..."

"If I don't?" The sergeant posed in the correct position to fire the .45. Legs spread. Arms forward. Aiming down the barrel. Left hand bracing his firing hand. Potter believed the man was aiming at Steele and Steele thought the target was Potter.

"Duck!" called out the chaplain from behind the partition.

The sergeant fired.

Later, the chaplain would swear he heard the bullet sail past him to smack into the World War II Army-In-Action picture hanging on the rear wall depicting the crossing of the bridge at Remagen before it fell to the floor.

"I want that fuckin' cook! Where in the hell are you, you chicken-shit son-of-a-bitch!" He swung the pistol back and forth over the heads of the frightened men.

Margolin entered the kitchen and stayed as flat as possible against the wall.

Potter silently hoped Sidney would not move. He couldn't see him anywhere. He did notice Margolin come in the back door. "Sarge, you and me are NCOs in this man's Army. We've been fucked over more times than a Georgia mule..." Potter and Steele were just ten yards away. A hard to miss distance. "... and we know what hurts. You and me, we've seen it all. Dear Johns. Loose women. Rotten..."

"I should kill her! She's the one I should kill! The fuckin' whore!" He whirled around as if looking for his errant spouse.

Margolin, caught in the open between the doorway to the pantry and the horizontal pot and pan rack where he planned to duck, froze.

The sergeant never stopped, but swung back to face Potter and Steele as if Margolin did not exist.

"Sergeant!" shouted Steele when the man turned, then lowered his voice to say, "We're trying to help you here. Listen to reason."

"Put down the weapon," said Potter, "and I'll make us a cup of joe. Your career's on the line here. No woman's worth that. No woman's worth the pain..."

The MP started to cry, but he kept the pistol pointed at them.

Margolin looked for a weapon. The only thing handy was a rolling pin. When he picked it up he asked himself why he hadn't gone to the arms room and taken out a pistol and rounded up some men to arm as well? *Jesus, am I an asshole.* He really wished he'd run down the street with Sidney.

"Sarge, women ain't all bad," said Potter. "They make mistakes too. We all do."

He and Steele were close now. Hardly more than five yards away. Margolin, holding the rolling pin, came low across the tiled floor fearing the man would spin around again. KP Mangiameli had low crawled away from the crazed Sergeant to the point he was under the steam table and his ass felt like it was burning.

The drummer boy insisted he wanted to play his drum, "...a rump a pum pum..." A lot of the men on the floor repeated the words of the song to distract them from the situation.

The MP sergeant wasn't listening. "I can't live with her no more after this. A man can't. Jesus Christ, what're you supposed to do?" He raised the pistol toward the ceiling with one hand.

No one in the mess hall moved.

"...a rump a pum pum..."

The desperate man lowered the weapon and placed the barrel against his temple.

"No!" screamed Potter. He lunged at the sergeant and knocked him off balance.

The pistol fired into the papier-mâché Santa Claus on top of the milk machine. The figure exploded into confetti. Potter held the pistol arm high and wide. Lt. Margolin dropped the rolling pin and joined Steele in holding the man's arms. They fell to the floor in a heap with Potter keeping the weapon pointed away from the men toward a sidewall.

In an instant, the CQ threw open the double doors. The troops scattered onto the outside lawn.

KP Mangaimeli crept out from under the steam table with a burnt ass, but he wasn't telling anyone—he was going home in six days now that he was still alive.

Potter and Steele moved the now-passive sergeant into Potter's office where the cook took a hefty slug of bourbon and offered one to the sergeant who accepted and Steele who refused. "You know, sa-sarge," said Potter, "I've had th-th-that Santa Cl—Cl...for more 'an te-te-ten years."

The saddened MP sheepishly replied, "I'm sorry, Sarge."

Margolin stood in the doorway holding the rolling pin he had dropped. He waved off the drink and asked if the man was all right.

Potter pushed past Margolin, "Excuse me, sir." He shouted, "DRO, sh...shut off that fu...fu...fuckin' record player! Cooks, get the god...god...damn chow line movin'!"

Everyone heard the sound of the MP's siren approaching.

Steele looked at Margolin with the rolling pin. "The man isn't all right and neither would you be if you suffered what he did. I was wondering what you planned to do with that rolling pin, Lieutenant," said Steele, amused.

Margolin looked at the pin. "I can't say I knew what I was planning either, sir, but I wasn't going to make a pie."

"Who called the MPs?" he asked moments before they charged through the back door.

"That's the first thing I did, sir."

"Smart thinking, Margolin. Next time come prepared with more than a rolling pin."

How about a fully loaded, water-cooled .30 caliber machine gun to shoot you in the ass, sir?

Patterson and Breslin returned to Bragg separately. Breslin had taken the Atlantic Coast Line train from North Philadelphia station to Fayetteville and Patterson hitchhiked. They didn't meet up until reveille on the 31st. Each had unpleasant stories about their short leaves. Breslin's family bothered him about the priesthood and his college pals made fun of him being in the service. "I want to call the draft board and find out why their asses aren't in basic training at Fort Jackson."

Patterson's parents wouldn't let him smoke in the house and watched him like hawks while repeatedly reminding him he had arrived home drunk and cursed in front of his mother. They wanted him home at 6:00 p.m. for dinner and borrowing the car required a serious lecture from his father. The topper was his tattoo. He showed his sister to impress her. She thought it was too small and told her mother who told his father. They lined up for a viewing. His mother gasped and left the room. "At least," his father said, "it's not on display in public." *Wait until I have Wings on my shoulder. That will really get them.* Patterson found himself wishing he was back at Bragg to be around his own kind—cool guys like Breslin and Banuelous.

They drew their gear from supply and set up their wall and footlocker displays while sipping from Breslin's bottle of wine. Men going on New Year's leave were packing while those on Christmas leave were returning. Everyone was talking about Sidney the Cook and the shooting. No one knew where the cook was hiding.

And the major rumor was that First Sgt. Billy Martin would be back after New Year's.

One good thing happened to Patterson on the way back, besides being stuck in a warm gas station during a brief snowstorm in Dover, Delaware. Two young guys had picked him up outside of Wilson, North Carolina and dropped him at the Fayetteville bus station. They worked ten-day trips on fishing boats out of Key West and had gone home to Virginia Beach for Christmas. The money was good. Beer cold. Weather hot. And plenty of tourist snatch who liked guys who worked on boats in Key West. Patterson believed he should try that once he was out of the service.

Breslin knew he was headed back to college.

They half finished their standard uniform and gear displays for wall and footlockers and then borrowed Mangiameli's car after paying him two bucks and promising to be back by 1400. Tommy was going on leave at 1700. For the next two hours, they cruised the used car lots of Bragg Boulevard looking for a step-down Hudson like Dean Moriarty drove in *On the Road*. The generous Sfc. Webster loaned them the down payment at a special only-for-them low interest rate. There were no Hudsons of any kind. Breslin knew that was a good sign; people hung onto them. They switched to the town lots at the far end of Hay Street and there it was, between a Ford Crestliner and a four-door '50 Kaiser, a shiny black 1950 Plymouth Business Coupe, the kind with the large hump-backed trunk, and a bonus factory-installed chrome luggage rack running the length of the roof.

It wasn't a Hudson, but it had the luggage rack.

"She handles like a dream," promised the salesman, an off-duty leg sergeant from a Main Post files record company.

The test drive took them past the Turf Club. Breslin stopped and blew the horn to see how many barmaids would look out. "None. That's what I thought. Sold," he said to the salesman. They drove away owing Sergeant George $200 dollars and the car lot $26.00 a month for the next nine months.

Mangiameli was throwing stones in the enlisted man's parking lot when Breslin arrived in his Buick. Patterson wasn't far behind him. They were just two beers late from their transportation celebration at the Seven Dwarfs. As Breslin drove up, Tommy ran alongside the car. "Where in the hell you been?" he shouted and pulled at the driver's side door. He wasn't wearing his fatigue cap, and soldiers never walked around the regimental area without a fatigue cap.

Breslin stopped and Tommy roughly opened the door. "Get the fuck out!"

"We stopped to have a couple of brews at the Dwarfs. Wait'll you see the car we bought."

"Who gives a fuck." Uncharacteristically, Mangiameli pulled Breslin by the arm to hurry him out of the driver's seat.

"OK, man. Take it easy." Breslin now realized Mangiameli was crying and wrapped him in a bear hug. "What the hell's wrong, Tommy?"

Mangiameli pushed him away. "Let me go!"

Breslin reacted with, "OK." And stepped back.

Mangiameli walked away, turned and came back. "Are the keys in it?"

"You know they are." Tommy wiped his eyes on his sleeve and moved past Breslin to sit in the driver's seat.

"Tommy, don't be a man with a paper asshole. What's wrong?"

Mangiameli turned away from Breslin and answered that Judy had just called him and told him not to come home for New Year's.

There was a long silence until Breslin said, "So you're going anyway?"

Before Mangiameli answered the obvious, the '50 hump-backed Plymouth pulled up with Patterson grinning behind the wheel. He blew the horn and shouted, "Wait 'til you feel the heater in this mother! We got a real coo wagon!"

Breslin stood between the two cars. "Willie, Judy called and told him not to come home."

Patterson ran his hands over the steering wheel several times as if not wanting to let go, then shut off the engine. "Is he goin' anyway?"

"Wouldn't you?"

"I'm goin'," said Mangiameli.

"I don't know what I'd do," replied Patterson.

Mangiameli started the car. Breslin asked him if he was going now. This minute.

"Fuck yeah, Jim."

Did he have his leave papers? Was he going in fatigues? "I don't give a shit. They ain't givin' 'em out 'til seventeen hundred. I can be in West Virginia by then."

"And you can be in jail by then, too, if you just take off," said Breslin.

Patterson said that Lt. Margolin owed him a favor. He and Mangiameli would talk to him and try to get the papers early. Mangiameli could change and pack and chogie like a normal person.

"I can't talk to nobody. I'll start cryin' like baby." He lit a cigarette and tapped his hand on the steering wheel.

"Give us the keys to your footlocker and we'll get your shit and bring it here. You got a present for Judy in there?"

"Yeah."

"See, asshole. Stop and think before you run off."

"I need someone to go to my gas stash with me." Patterson and Breslin and the entire world knew of Mangiameli's hidden stash of five-gallon GI gas cans in the boondocks. No one ever wanted to know where it was or wanted to help him. Getting caught with stolen gas meant hard time in Leavenworth.

Breslin and Patterson looked at one another. Breslin said, "You talk to the lieutenant and get his shit. I'll go to the boonies with him." Patterson was glad Breslin volunteered. He knew he would not have gone. They agreed to meet in 45 minutes at the parking lot.

On the way out Longstreet Road, Breslin got the details from Mangiameli on what happened. Judy had called him in the dispatch office and told him not to come home. She had a date. "Like she said it ten fuckin' times, 'I have a date'. I mean, we were talkin' 'bout getting married while I was home." Mangiameli threatened to kill whoever it was, and he had a good idea who to target.

Breslin worried about Mangiameli's always-erratic driving as he gestured with his hands and kept turning towards him as he talked. Breslin suggested he should stay with him and Patterson. They'd take their new car and hit all the bars in Fayetteville. They'd find women just like Banuelous and the Moonlight Gambler.

As they swung onto the hard gravel surface of Chicken Road, the Buick momentarily skidded.

"What broad's gonna look at this face? You know the joke; I'm the cat who couldn't get laid in a women's prison with a fistful of pardons." He drove faster.

Breslin asked how far they had to go. "Ahead," replied Mangiameli and stuck his arm out the window to pound on the roof. "What in the fuck she's gotta go and do that for?" Breslin took one of Tommy's Luckies from the pack on the plastic tray on the dashboard and lit it. "We had somethin' special. I mean, you know, we've been together since we was sixteen."

Breslin leaned toward his heartsick pal. "Maybe it's something else, Tommy. Maybe her family's putting pressure on her to get out more."

Mangiameli slammed on the brakes. Breslin had to hold himself from hitting the dashboard. Without looking, Mangiameli threw the Buick into reverse and backed straight up. Slowly, still in reverse, he pulled off the gravel road, backing up along a two-lane trail using the suicide knob to expertly maneuver among the tall pines and holly trees. The trail curved and dipped in several directions. When he stopped, he was tired from the effort. They could not see the road. He lit a cigarette. "It's smart to wait a few minutes to see if the Pees followed us."

Breslin remembered being afraid of bad time if he helped Schmidt escape. *This could end up being worse.* He opened the door and the fresh smell of woods from the unseasonable warm weather wafted in.

December, and it was like spring. "I'm goin' home, Scott. Nothin's stoppin' me."

Breslin stepped out of the car, stretched, then ground his smoke into the trail. "If I was in love, I might do the same. Go home. You'll feel better. Besides, you got leave coming."

Mangiameli sat back in the seat and took a long drag. "It's a great day for a jump, huh?"

"Only a Hollywood one. No extra gear."

"Yeah," agreed Mangiameli and got out. He carefully buried his cigarette in the rough trail and walked about ten yards into the brush where he pulled apart dead branches and a blanket of leaves to reveal a carefully dug hole covered with planks and a shelter half. In the hole were six five-gallon gas cans with the screw-on tops and a case-and-a-half of motor oil. Two 12-volt batteries—still in their shipping cases—were there, along with a muffler wrapped in a rough piece of canvas. "Tommy, you could start your own trucking company."

"Help me load it up. Those batteries get me fifteen bucks apiece at home."

Except for the muffler and the full case of oil, they hefted the stolen property into the Buick's trunk. All Breslin thought about were his fingerprints were now on the loot. It took two slams of the trunk to catch.

"Tommy, when you're home, don't do nothing crazy. Be cool like Hollywood Jack would be and come on back and do your time."

Mangiameli looked away. "I don't know what's gonna happen."

"Just don't be an asshole is all..." They both heard the engine at the same time. It wasn't passing, the noise headed toward them.

"Pees!"

Mangiameli squatted behind his car and looked through the winter brush and evergreens toward Chicken Road, which led back to Longstreet Road.

Breslin wondered if he should escape through the boonies. He had no idea where he was. Mangiameli waved Breslin over and said, "I can't run. My tags are on the car. You take off."

Breslin hesitated, then low crawled away from the Buick. The vehicle stopped and started on the dirt trail; it sounded like a Jeep.

Mangiameli slipped into his cache and pulled boards and canvas over himself then stuck his head out like a tank commander to keep track of the approaching vehicle. About ten yards from the Buick, Breslin hid behind a tree and watched. A Jeep growled along the trail. At a bend about 40 yards away, it stopped.

Breslin asked himself if he should he run all the way home like the scared little boy he was. *If I start running, someone might hear and see me. By lying here and covering myself with leaves, maybe Mangiameli will get caught and they won't look for anyone else.*

Patterson went to the orderly room and signed himself and Breslin out on three-day passes. The new orderly room clerk, Pfc. James Lee Hunter, formerly of Weapons Platoon and now in Headquarters Platoon, stood up from his desk and looked at the passbook. He wanted to know where Breslin was.

"You've been a company clerk all of three weeks and you're sounding like the first shirt. Remember I knew you before you got your Wings," replied Patterson. Hunter and several other new men's presence in their squad bay tainted the area with a Southern aura neither Patterson or Beslin liked. Their accents reminded them of First Sgt. Billy Martin and 'nigger' was a frequent word. Their music twanged and discussions on stock-car racing made Patterson and Breslin roll their eyes.

"The lieutenant says every swingin' one has to sign out personally." They also applied seriousness to regulations not usually seen in draftees.

"I'm looking for the lieutenant," said Patterson. "Where is he?"

"Not 'til Breslin comes in and signs."

The door to the CO's office was open. Patterson smirked at Hunter and stuck his head in. "Sir, you got a minute?" Since Patterson returned the rosters and had his stripe back, he considered the lieutenant more like a friend than a commanding officer.

Margolin put aside the personal letter he held and gestured Patterson in. Patterson looked back at Hunter smugly. "Keep up the typin', Jimmy Lee Bobby Boy."

Hunter clutched at the keys on his belt. "It's 'James' to y'all."

Patterson closed the door. "It's kinda private, sir." He stepped up to Margolin's desk, which was covered with several Army manuals, notepaper, and sections of the Sunday *Los Angles Times*. He saluted.

Margolin returned the salute with a relaxed wave of the hand. "At ease, troop. What's on your mind?" Patterson explained about Mangiameli's phone call and his desire to take off immediately.

"We're cutting everyone loose at seventeen-hundred."

"Sir," Patterson wished Breslin stood beside him, he talked a smoother line. "He pulled KP on the Christmas Day shooting, and, you know Tommy, he's itchin' to get goin' to fix his situation. He can barely sit still."

Margolin laughed slightly. "That's nothing new."

The lieutenant liked Patterson and even his buddy Breslin. They were decent enough soldiers and didn't cause problems. It was typical of them to stick up for a pal. He remembered the first sergeant trying to intimidate them when Schmidt had gone AWOL. That was almost a year ago. Margolin also knew Mangiameli was headed for trouble due to missing material from the motor pool, but he couldn't say anything. Stealing was stealing, GI material or not. Why not let him go home one more time? Go early?

The lieutenant stood up and went to the door. He opened it and directed Hunter to get Mangiameli's leave form ready ASAP.

"Anything else, *Pfc.* Patterson?"

Patterson grinned. His stripe was an ongoing joke with the two men. He snapped to attention and saluted. "Yes, sir. Happy New Year, sir."

"Cut the bullshit." He thumbed Patterson out of the office.

Margolin knew he was too easy on the troops, but someone had to look after them. The first sergeant sure as hell never did, and most of the regiment's company commanders lived in a dream world of their almighty power over 130 men. He wished he could tell Patterson to warn Mangiameli, but it was too late. He returned to his mother's letter. One came every month with life instructions and the reminder that none of her friends understood why he remained a paratrooper. Why didn't he transfer to Fort MacArthur in the Los Angeles area? Uncle Ziggy knew a politician who knew a congressman who might help him make the move. He'd at least sleep in a decent bed at night and eat decent food. How can a place called a mess hall make a decent meal? And on and on and on. His father wrote quick words of encouragement in the margins.

It was a relief to be on his own.

The woods were warm and quiet except for a breeze that played in the upper branches of the tall pines.

"Scott." Breslin heard the strong whisper and looked around the base of the tree to see Mangiameli slide out of his hole and low crawl toward the car. He stopped and gestured with both arms for Breslin to join him.

"Yes, sir!" Breslin heard the words distinctly. An officer had found them.

Mangiameli twisted around, looked, twisted back again. He sat halfway up and his waved his arms as if juggling invisible balls. His wide-open eyes frozen in shock.

"Yes, sir!"

Someone else's voice followed. It wasn't clear. Then a struggling sound then, "Again, Corporal!"

"Yes, sir!"

Breslin remembered a moment from basic training in Fort Jackson when several men ganged up on a problem trainee. A little fat kid who refused to take a shower. It was night, and he heard them outside the barracks pushing, then punching the kid. Breslin had laid in his bunk listening, angry at himself for not intervening—and then there was Schmidt.

Maybe this time I can help someone. He crawled as quietly as he could toward Mangiameli. Would they have to act to keep someone from getting hurt? What if it was murder?

Mangiameli wiggled and waved him to hurry. Breslin crawled close to Mangiameli and then lifted his head.

Mangiameli whispered, "It's fuckin' Colonel Steele!"

Through the thick dead winter underbrush, Breslin saw the black Jeep parked on the same road they were on, but only half the distance off Chicken Road. Because of the bends and dips in the trail they were not seen, but the Jeep was no more than 30 or 40 yards away, and Steele leaned against the Jeep with his fatigues down around his ankles. His tall Negro driver's trousers were down too, and he was locked tight against the senior officer's pale ass.

"Harder, corporal!"

"Yes, sir!"

The colonel reached back to pull the driver closer. The corporal responded by gyrating and lifting. "I'm comin', sir!"

"Come on," groaned Steele. "Give your best shot! That's it! That's good!" The spent corporal bent forward over the colonel. Both men slumped against the Jeep. Breathless.

Mangiameli and Breslin watched; the immensity of their vision blanked their minds like condemned men seeing the gallows the first time or pedestrians frozen in the path of a runaway car. A noise behind startled them. Caught.

Holy fuck, it's Strac! The dog wagged his tail. He seemed to be grinning, leaning forward on his paws ready to play or get a reaction from his discovery.

Breslin shifted onto his back and quietly asked, "Don't bark, Strac. Good dog." Slowly he began to cover himself with leaves. Mangiameli did the same.

Strac sniffed at the dirt by the enlisted men's feet and began pawing.

"Good doggie," encouraged Breslin. "Keep busy." Strac seemed to understand. He turned around, away from them, and began to dig, pushing the leaves and dirt between his legs onto Mangiameli and Breslin. The two soldiers rolled over and covered themselves with their field jackets as the debris rained down on them. There wasn't anything they could do. They just wanted it to be over.

Voices were muffled. One of the men laughed. There was no sense of hurry. Would they be seen now? What could happen? Trade the secret for the gas theft?

"Strac!" The dog stopped his digging and looked at his new playmates.

"Strac!" The Jeep kicked over.

"Come on, soldier!" called Steele. "Good dog." They heard the Jeep shift into gear, turn, and slowly grind its way to the main road.

Finally, Breslin and Mangiameli dared to raise their heads. Sand and twigs sifted down their backs. They could hear the Jeep pick up speed. Both rose at the same time, hastily brushing off leaves and dirt as they jumped into the old Buick. Tommy drove too fast. When he goosed the Buick coming off the trail, they slid across Chicken Road. About a mile down the road, moving in the opposite direction of the Jeep, Breslin lit them cigarettes. Neither man had much to say.

Just before they reached the built up area of Bragg, coming back the long way off Yadkin Road, Mangiameli said, "Scott, I wanna go home. I don't ever wanna do that dirt road stuff."

Breslin reminded his pal he was stealing gas, which meant Leavenworth, and if he goes AWOL at home he'd end up in the stockade where that could happen. "The one thing you gotta do, Tommy, is come back. No matter what happens at home, come back on time." They were quiet again.

Breslin internally juggling what he saw and what he knew of Col. Steele. The perfect soldier. Hero. He guessed Mangiameli might be thinking the same thing.

"Tommy?"

"Huh?"

"Don't ever tell Motz what we saw."

"I ain't sayin' shit, Jim. I still don't believe it."

"How come everyone seems to have something to do tonight except you and me and the other assholes haunting the bars?" asked Breslin as he and Patterson stepped out of the Seven Dwarfs into the cold wind that had kicked up at sundown on New Year's Eve.

Their New Year's resolution was to have one beer in every bar in town. They parked the Plymouth at the far end of Hay Street and walked from bar to bar. There wasn't much else to do. The other GIs on the street were as bored and restless as they were. Movies and stores were closed. The streets were mostly empty of people and cars as if a plague had swept through. Even the bars were half-empty and the jukebox holiday tunes sounded insincere. The barmaids were more surly than usual. They hung around the service areas showing one another Christmas jewelry, smoking, and talking about where they were going that night.

It was time to start on the few bars on the south side of Hay Street. The two soldiers hustled across the street into the half-empty Turf Club and sat at the bar.

"Tommy should've stayed with us," said Breslin after a few sips. The beers weren't going down easily on the depressing night.

Patterson disagreed; he wanted to go home and he did. "You got to give him credit for that."

"What're you some kind of J.C. Penney philosopher?"

Patterson forced down the remainder of his tall boy, burped, and said, "Steele."

Both soldiers could not absorb what had happened. At first, Patterson would not believe their story. Steele had been Patterson's hero until the man busted him for nothing. They recalled Hollywood Jack had sensed something about Steele. Still, Steele appeared to be the perfect soldier.

"Unfuckin' believable!"

"Yeah, Steele," replied Breslin. "Let's head back to the Canopy."

"We were there twenty minutes ago. Half-hour tops."

"Nothing going on here."

"Nothin' there."

"We can ask Margie if she's seen Hollywood." They liked to do that to get her pissed-off reaction.

Outside the Turf Club, Patterson shouted into the pressing wind that he wanted his beloved Army overcoat. They passed the Christian Canteen; it was closed as was Pagano's, the most popular restaurant on Hay Street. The lobby of the Liberty Hotel, the last wooden structure on Hay Street, was deserted. Breslin commented that it would be a great whorehouse, which is what the town needed more than parking lots or schools. "A real whorehouse like I hear they have in Hamburg and Amsterdam. I'd go in and get whipped or something."

They laughed and had just about entered the Canopy when they heard, "Hey, *ese*, what's the haps?" Their heads had been buried in their jackets so they hadn't noticed the Moonlight Gambler's white Cadillac parked a few spaces up from the Canopy.

Banuelous looked out the rear side window. "No haps," replied Patterson. He and Breslin walked to the car and leaned over to see who was inside.

Banuelous slumped in the back seat with two babes next to him. He wore a rust-colored suit with rounded lapels and a thin brown tie tied in a barely visible knot under the flare of his Mister B collar. The neon of the Canopy's sign reflected off the hair pomade he used to make his short hair seem longer. The girls wore gowns billowed by crinolines with their coats draped over their shoulders; they looked like they were going to a high school prom.

Patterson asked, "Where's Nicky?"

"Pickin' up his bitch. Hop in, assholes, and taste some tequila."

Without realizing it, Patterson had his chance to show Banuelous how cool he could be. After all, he had boffed a spade chick and had a tattoo. Inside, he leaned over the front seat and pointed at the girls. "There's two of you. One more is comin'. So who's left over?" Patterson stared at the blonde with a poodle cut next to the street window. She was pretty in a hard way. *She might be trying to look like Marilyn Monroe*, he thought. She smiled, but didn't say anything.

Banuelous offered a quart bottle of clear alcohol. "Tequila, *ese*. It makes it stand up all night."

Breslin was quick to grab it. "Looks like 'splo."

He sipped, chased the sip with another, and passed the bottle to the blonde while suddenly saying as he wiped his lips, "'What lips my lips have kissed and where and why/ I have forgotten...'"

"Son-of-a-bitch," screeched the other girl who was plainer than the blonde and heavily made up. Patterson and

Breslin recognized her from the Seven Dwarfs. "He's talkin' poetry!"

"You know how I cry about fuckin' poetry," snarled Banuelous.

The girl deferred to Banuelous. "I mean, it sounded like it."

Banuelous told Breslin to say it again. "I need another drink. I can't say it without a drink."

"What about me?" asked Patterson and he held out his hand for the bottle from the blonde. She passed it to him and held his eyes for a moment. Patterson gave her a small toast and took a sip. He had to take a deep breath to keep from coughing.

The bottle went to Breslin. "Ready?" Breslin looked at the girls.

"Fuckin' chaplain's assistant," said Banuelous, who might have a touch of jealously, not that he'd ever admit it.

Breslin took a strong sip, wiped his mouth on his jacket sleeve, and sat back against the steering wheel and recited. "'What lips my lips have kissed and where and why/ I have forgotten...'" Banuelous reached over the seat and pulled the bottle away from Breslin. "'... and the rain if full of ghosts tonight that tap and...tap and?...tap and sigh/ Upon the glass and listen for reply/ My heart stirs...' No wait. Give me a sip."

Banuelous handed back the bottle. "Cats are bleedin' me dry."

Breslin sipped and held onto the bottle. "I need it. It's a prop. '... Upon the glass and listen for reply/ My heart stirs...' Hold on. Aaah. '... And in my heart there stirs a quiet pain for...'" Breslin stared at the blonde. "'... unremembered lads that not again/ Will turn to me at midnight with a cry.'"

Silence.

"There's a line here about a lonely tree. A winter tree. I can't remember. '... I cannot say what loves have come and gone...' I'm getting it. Amazing. '... Thus in the winter stands the lonely tree/ I can not say what loves have come and gone/ I only know that summer sang in me/ A little while and in me sings no more.'"

Silence. The blonde thought it was pretty.

"*Ese*, you got more bullshit than a wetback with a fin and pool cue."

Patterson knelt against the front seat and leaned towards the blonde. "Who are you?"

"Terri." She smiled.

"I'm Bill Patterson." He extended his hand and gently shook just her fingers.

"Sheeet," chuckled Banuelous. "'Bill'. Fuckin' Willie."

The other girl told Banuelous his friends were cute. Banuelous claimed he didn't even know them. "These cats comin' in here and blowin' smoke." He laughed and took the bottle from Breslin, sipped and passed it around.

"I'm Claire," said the other girl. She looked older than Banuelous.

"And she's with me, dudes." Banuelous put his arm around her and pulled her close.

"Sweetie, don't mess my hair."

Patterson asked Terri to come with them. They had a car. "A fuckin' Business Coupe," said Banuelous. When they had told Banuelous of their purchase, he had refused to walk to the EM parking lot to look at it. Without seeing it, he had declared he wouldn't even drive it to a funeral.

Terri smiled. The invitation flattered her. Patterson and Breslin felt a moment of hope.

Nicky Lazor, the Moonlight Gambler, opened the door. Breslin had to move over.

"Motherfucker." Nicky sat half in and out of the car. "She can't get off 'til fuckin' midnight." He stared at Breslin and Patterson. "Whadda you assholes want? Besides the tequila." He stuck out his hand for the bottle and wiggled his fingers in an impatient 'give me' gesture to Patterson.

Patterson handed it over. Lazor took a hefty swig. Like Banuelous, Lazor wore a blue suit and a thin light blue tie with an acorn knot. "You cats got your Army issue low-quarters on?" he asked and looked at Breslin's feet.

Banuelous cracked up. He had to take out his handkerchief to wipe his mouth. "Like, these cats are tryin' to move on our broads. You should hear them talkin' shit. Willie's 'Bill' now, you know."

"Fuck, he can have 'em. I'm tired of hangin' around." He started the car.

"Where are you goin'?" asked Patterson.

"I'm gonna run the heater. Do you mind, Daddy-O?"

"Tell him the poem," suggested Claire.

"I don't tell guys poems."

Moonlight Gambler played a nervous melody on the steering wheel with his heavy ID bracelet. "The fuckin' dance will be over by the time we get there."

Claire said, "We should go. Alice knew what time we're supposed to go. She had plenty of time to ask."

The bottle made the rounds. Lazor lit a Pall Mall and got out of the car. "Come on, Scott. We're gonna split."

Patterson leaned farther over the seat toward Terri. "I like you." She reacted with a soft smile, a little girl beneath an adult disguise.

"Don't like her too much, cat," warned Lazor. "Johnny Starr from Seven-Eighty-Second Maintenance is her old man, and he can bench press a Jeep and carries heat."

Patterson opened the door and asked. "Is he goin' to be there tonight?"

She smiled again. Patterson's alcoholic reasoning indicated she liked him. "He's working," she replied. Patterson held out his hand. "Stay with me."

Lazor did a quick tap dance on the sidewalk by the open door to stay warm. "Hey, cats. How's about haulin' ass."

Terri leaned forward and put her hand into Patterson's then looked at him and shook her head no. The crackling of the crinoline stirred Patterson's loins. Her slow denial reminded Patterson of the girl in the Jaguar on the Highway 301.

"Happy New Year," he wished her and added, "I could've fallen in love." He let go of her hand and shut the door.

Breslin moved past Lazor and said, "Willie's on the move. Lock up your daughters."

"Listen to these squares," said Lazor slipping into the driver's seat. "Tony and me knew these jag-offs when they didn't know shit from Shinola." He shut the door and put the Caddy in reverse. The heavy car swung back, the tires turned, gears shifted, the Moonlight Gambler floored it. Breslin and Patterson watched them drive away.

Inside the Canopy, Breslin and Patterson spotted unhappy Alice pouting at the service area. She smoked quickly as if to hurry along the minutes. Margie worked the bar and gave them a rare hello.

"Two tall Buds."

Breslin asked if she had seen Schmidt. "If and when I do, he's gonna get one of these where the sun don't shine." The bottles thudded on the bar. She slapped their money off the bar. "Tell him I said that when you see him."

"We ain't seen him," said Patterson.

"Yeah. And people in hell don't see hot coals." Margie walked away.

There were a few patrons with party hats and noise-makers. A box of them was available in a front booth. Every other song on the jukebox was Lombardo's "Auld Lang Syne." By their second tall boy, the young men realized how gloomy they were. The tequila hadn't helped.

"It's a sad fucking night," said Breslin. "In the Army. In Fayetteville. We should've gone somewhere."

"I wish I was in Key West workin' the fishin' boats like those guys who gave me a ride," replied Patterson.

"Not a bad idea, Willie."

"Bill."

"Bill."

"It'll be warm all the time. Tourist broads to latch on to. I could go for it."

Breslin saw Key West as the end of the line, literally. "You know what I mean?" Patterson didn't. He saw it as an adventure.

"I wish I could just walk away from the family obligations. It ain't that easy."

"I can't wait to *not* go home. The hell with my old man and his ass kissin' job. They drove me nuts when I was home."

Breslin suggested they should head back to the barracks instead of backtracking to the bars they already visited. It was too depressing. Margie sold them a six-pack of Schlitz and over-charged them two bucks as she wasn't allowed to sell off premises. They grabbed two party hats and went to the car. Patterson drove. Every radio station did frantic time checks, as it was almost midnight.

"Slow down, Willie. Let's not be on Bragg for the New Year."

"Bill. My name's Bill."

"Sorry, man. I keep forgetting."

"We get out this year. Nine and change."

"Nine fucking months." Breslin opened two more beers with the church key. "I wish we were in some clerical company at Fort Dix with no Saturday inspections."

"So, you don't like the Key West idea," said Patterson. "What're you gonna do when you get out?"

Breslin felt he would never leave Bragg. "But if I do, like I said, I want to water sidewalks in front of flower shops on warm summer mornings. Spraying the sidewalk and sweeping up. Maybe I'll own a bookstore. I don't really know."

"Like I said, I ain't goin' home. I got some money saved and..."

"You sure do you cheap prick."

"... Jersey's too cold in the winter. I'm gonna go to the Keys. Collect unemployment 'til it runs out and then work on a boat and wear leather shit on my wrists like the guy in *Beneath Twelve-Mile Reef.*"

"Gilbert Roland."

"Who's that?"

"The guy in the reef movie who wore leather shit. And you know, Bill, that sounds like a cool idea." He took a long sip of beer.

The excited WFNC disc jockey informed the world it was officially the New Year. 1959. Guy Lombardo confirmed it with "Auld Lang Syne." Breslin continued over the song. "We'd work the boats. Drink beer. And just generally fuck around. Maybe collect the GI Bill without studying too hard. I could dig that."

The song wept on. "I go home to Downbeach, I either go to college or work for the city. Big fuckin' deal. Either way, my old man'll be on my case," pointed out Patterson. "I'd rather be in the Keys. I know it doesn't get cold there. Wait one, are you serious?"

"Fucking-A-well-told, Jim."

"Seriously?"

"Does a bear shit in the woods? Yeah."

They toasted each other with their beers and drank to their marvelous idea. Patterson thought they should round up more guys to go with them.

"Who? The first shirt?"

"I don't know," replied Patterson. "McBride maybe. Tommy."

"Fuck McBride, but, you know, we should drag Tommy with us. Keep him from hurting himself."

"He's got more time left than us. A whole year."

"He could meet us later. It would give him an option over Detroit. Put it in perspective for him."

"I hope the crazy bastard's all right." Each man took a moment to think about Mangiameli. In the silence, a special announcement came over the radio.

"... Year's exodus of Cuban dignitaries continues in the early morning hours of the New Year. Havana has been declared an open city, although the leader of the popular revolution has yet to be heard from. Three years ago in Oriente Province Fidel Castro started his..."

"Man," responded Breslin, "that cat Castro took over Cuba. That's a hell of a way to start a New Year."

Loud banging and shouting echoed from the hall into the squad bay. It sounded like a fight. All the troops woke up. It was early and still dark on New Year's Day. Someone turned on the squad bay's harsh lights. Breslin and Patterson joined the others at the squad bay doors looking down the hall.

Two husky men in civilian clothes and two MPs from 18th Airborne Corps along with First Sgt. Billy Martin were crowded at the entrance to the cadre room Wise and Carter shared. They were pounding on the door and threatened to break it in. The door opened.

The men rushed inside, shouting for the occupants to raise their hands and keep them raised. Then Wise and Carter were in the hall, naked, and spread-eagled against the wall while their room was torn apart.

Men in their skivvies came up from the second floor to complain about the noise. It was a holiday, for Christ's sake. Go back to sleep.

"What the fuck's happenin'?"

"Who're those cats?"

"Pees and FBI, I bet."

They stayed to watch. Breslin nudged Patterson and pantomimed smoking a cigarette.

Patterson wiped imaginary sweat from his brow. Thank God, he stuck to Luckies. Having marijuana was automatic dishonorable discharge and time in Leavenworth. Wise had about the same time left as Patterson and Breslin. The two suspects were pushed back into their room.

Pfc. James Lee Hunter said, "I bet they have those nigger boys for bein' dope fiends." Another man said it was more likely rape of a white girl. Both, offered another man.

"Martin's mother," said Patterson and did not add his silent, *I hope.*

"That ain't funny," said Pfc. James Lee Hunter. "He's your first sergeant."

"And a white man," said someone else.

Patterson and Breslin looked at one another and sensed again how they had become a minority in their own squad bay. More young soldiers from the south kept showing up and playing their music and talking their way. There was a coldness or lack of camaraderie Patterson and Breslin had not felt since their first days in the company as new guys.

One of the MPs started down the hall. A sergeant lifer. Behind him came Wise, handcuffed to one of the civilians. Carter followed handcuffed to the other civilian. Both men wore their field jackets, fatigues and low quarter shoes. The other MP and First Sgt. Billy Martin followed.

There were tears on Wise's cheeks as he passed. Carter's face showed only fury. He lunged at the men gathered in the squad bay door. "You cheese-eatin' motherfuckers! I'm gonna get all of you!" He spit. The spray caught Hunter.

The prisoners went down the stairs.

Patterson believed Carter had looked right at him as if he had ratted him out.

Martin, his first day back, stopped at the squad bay and told the men to break it up. "Get back in your bunks." He turned and called down the hall in the other direction. "The show's over. Y'all best be gettin' sack time!"

The red-faced Martin followed the slow-moving men into the squad bay. "Some of y'all know me and some of y'all newer men don't. I'm First Sergeant Billy Martin and I run this here organization and don't think for one Alabama minute I don't. See these stripes. Three up. Three down. A diamond in the middle. If y'all can't read 'em, count 'em. I'm in the saddle again. Y'all don't scratch yore ass without me knowin' it. I can make yore life hell if I have the notion to no matter what that college boy Jew lieutenant tells you."

Martin looked directly at Breslin and Patterson and then walked the length of the squad bay. The men stood in their skivvies by their bunks.

"Those two coloreds have been making reefer cigarettes in this barracks. U.S. government property. My barracks! Y'all can bet yore sweet ass they're gonna wish they never heard of 'merrywanna' and so will anyone who's ever bought some from them. This company went to hell in a hand basket since I've been gone. I'm gonna shape y'all up even if that means sendin' every swingin' dick to Dog Company."

On his way back to the door, he stopped in front of Breslin and Patterson. "Yore friend would be in handcuffs with those nigras if he was alive." They didn't know who he meant. Breslin asked for clarification, omitting Martin's rank.

"First Sergeant. Y'all address me as such. Y'all hear me?" he asked the squad bay.

Only Hunter replied, "Yes, First Sergeant."

"Only one alert individual in here. Y'all hear me?"

"Yes, First Sergeant," they chorused.

He turned back to Patterson and Breslin. "Y'all must think we're pretty damn dumb 'round here. We know about the gas in the boonies. The minute he came back from leave he was goin' straight to the barbed-wire hotel..."

"Sarge, you said..." interrupted Breslin.

"First Sergeant! I'm your First Sergeant, Pfc. Breslin, and if y'all continue to forget I will ensure y'all have extra duty the rest of yore days in Headquarters Company."

"First Sergeant, what did you mean about 'if my friend was alive'?"

"Y'all don't know, do y'all. He went and got hisself killed up in Ohio."

Patterson asked, "Mangiameli?"

"There ain't no one else in this here company with a spaghetti name like that. The CQ's report's on my desk.

Ohio state police called early this a.m. Tore up his car and hisself."

Breslin sat on his footlocker. "Holy fuck." Patterson went mute. He looked around at the staring faces.

Martin took a step closer to Breslin. "I'm not done talkin' to y'all. Stand up and listen like a soldier."

Breslin's eyes glazed over. The muscles in his neck tightened. Patterson poised to jump him when he went for the first sergeant. Breslin looked up, "You just told me Tommy's dead."

"I sure as hell did; now on yore feet."

Breslin's head rolled from side to side then slowly he raised himself to face the shorter man. "Sure, First Sergeant. Three up and three down."

"Y'all knew he kept gas in the boonies. Government gas and other motor pool paraphernalia. There's no doubt in my mind y'all could lead the MPs there this minute. Y'all and yore buddy here should go to jail for just knowin' that and not tellin' anyone. Mangiameli's lucky he died. He'd be facin' five in Leavenworth." Martin headed for the door then stopped. "Let that be a lesson to y'all. Don't touch Uncle Sam's property and never, never bring a reefer cigarette into my company. Any man who does, I will personally deliver his ass to the Third Army prison in Atlanta."

Martin turned and walked his quick walk to the door. Over his shoulder he called, "Patterson, collect the gas thief's gear and turn it into supply ASAP."

Martin was gone. Everyone relaxed.

Patterson sat on his footlocker and held his head in his hands. Lt. Margolin had been wrong; returning the rosters did not help the first sergeant. He was worse than ever.

"Happy New Year," said one of the newer men.

Breslin, his face still tight with anger, looked down the squad bay at Pfc. James Lee Hunter. "There's your first sergeant at his best, Jimmy Lee Bobby Boy."

The words were a threat Hunter avoided answering.

First Lieutenant Seymour 'Mad Dog' Margolin

Chapter 14

Officers' clubs vary according to state or country locations. For example, an Army officers' club in Hawaii might reflect Polynesian culture with fake palms and tiki carvings. In Japan, there might be pictures of Mt. Fuji and the female staff would wear traditional geisha garb. Teutonic décor of medieval armor and indigenous beers can be found in German clubs. However, no matter how hard they try, in the end they all look like Hilton hotel lobbies with their low divans and cushioned chairs scattered among low dark wood coffee tables. Soft carpeting. A discreet bar off to the side. Quiet, background music of harmless pop standards.

A certain decorum pervades these clubs. Rank maintains its privilege even more so when fueled with firewater. Young officers often find their attractive wives being groped by their senior leaders. There are male-only nights when one is allowed to let down one's hair—but not too much—a man is always being observed. The exceptions are obnoxious senior officers who might do the lamp-shade-on-the-head-and-pinch-the-ass-of-every-woman-in-the-joint routine, and everyone agrees it's just old general so-and-so or colonel what's-his-name; they're funny that way. The people who keep these clubs functioning are enlisted personnel.

On Fort Bragg, there were two officers' clubs: a newer one in the 82nd Division area and traditional one in the Main Post area, home of the 18th Airborne Corps Headquarters which oversaw all that went on at Bragg and further afield in the world-wide military scheme. The division club, modern and spartan by comparison to the other club, catered to young, go-getter lieutenants and captains who wanted World War III to start immediately so that they could win their medals and line up with their heroes from Airborne military history, like Colonel Ruben Tucker, Jumping Jim Gavin, Westy, and Max Taylor. When they graduated from Jump School, they had prop blasts, parties which amounted to guzzling alcohol and behaving like fraternity adolescents until they were lifeless. The club on Main Post was old-style like the entire area; it was tradition like Bradley and Eisenhower and MacArthur. A gentlemen's purview. Formal dress uniform was frequently required. The brick, three-story barracks dated from before World War II. Trees dated further back. There was a parade ground behind headquarters. If there were still polo ponies, they would be grazing there during the daily flag raising and lowering ceremonies. Part of the daily military ambience was The Retreat cannon firing at 1700.

Most of the clerks and jerks, enlisted and officers, on Main Post were not jumpers. They were the unpardonable—the unforgivable—legs. Which explains the behavioral and décor difference between the 82nd O Club and the Main Post O Club.

And when a man wants to return to civilization for social interaction, he does not go to the 82nd Airborne Division Officers' Club to exchange alcohol lies and jump stories. He treats himself to the sedate boredom of the Main Post Officers' Club or more officially the Fort Bragg Officers' Open Mess.

And besides—and more importantly—there were women there. Sometimes.

First Sergeant Billy Martin heard First Lieutenant Seymour Margolin's every utterance loud and clear after his return to the company on New Year's Day. The senior NCO even feigned being pleasant to the young officer; however, Margolin quickly realized that returning the rosters had been a mistake. The first sergeant still treated the troops harshly and indifferently, filling slots and ticking off duties without compassion, but, at least, accurately again.

The first sergeant did make a jump in January. A pay jump. That's all the NCO ever intended to make. Pay jumps.

Margolin and Martin did not discuss past non-jumping.

The first sergeant was canny enough to realize the lieutenant would never report him unless strongly provoked. First Sgt. Billy Martin wasn't about to do that; he wanted *his* lieutenant to be content and knew the lieutenant did not have enough experience to manage 150 men. The officer depended on Martin like a politician depends on his aides, so the first sergeant grasped the company reins and recreated his Headquarters and Headquarters dictatorship.

However, Lt. Margolin wasn't content. Even though he felt he had somewhat tamed the senior sergeant, he understood that under the surface, the man was danger-ous. For example, if Martin knew there was going to be an arrest New Year's Day by the CID, he kept it to himself and claimed it was a coincidence that he was in the orderly room getting ready for the next working day—his suppos-edly first day back—when the MPs arrived. It could be true. They had discussed unofficially and non-specifically ways to apprehend Mangiameli when he returned from leave, but the lieutenant never knew about any marijuana smoking.

The real truth was the lieutenant's victory over Martin had proven temporary, and he remained frustrated trying to become involved in company business. *Why worry about it?* He could turn in the career NCO anytime he wanted to for making paper pay jumps, but he wanted more. Some-thing to make him feel he was really in charge. Make him feel like the honor graduate again and not someone who signed whatever the first sergeant put in front of him.

On his way back from his short March leave, he realized he had become Lt. Stewart without the tennis. And his leave had been a successful disaster.

He gained weight from his mother's cooking and Uncle Ziggy's sandwiches. The two easy lays left over from college had become nice Jewish brides. When he phoned one of the girls, the mother remembered him as a nice boy and advised him he should think about settling down and getting a real job. He couldn't go around flying airplanes his whole life. He didn't bother to correct her.

After ten days, he returned to Bragg heavier. And hornier.

Bragg in late March was not the Mardi Gras or the Riviera or spring break in Florida. It was routine: reveille, inspections, reports, police up, dress right and cover down, officer of the day, the week, the month, First Sgt. Billy Martin, and every 40 days or so, an electrifying parachute jump.

Margolin found himself leaving the company early on Friday the way Lt. Stewart used to do. He just wanted to escape the jabber between the first sergeant and the company clerk. To top off his frustration, the new OCS second lieutenant named Yeager was from West Virginia and laughed at Martin's cornpone jokes. The first sergeant's southern empire was, once again, firmly ensconced.

Go play handball. Go to the O club. Be gone the rest of the afternoon. Make a sandwich. He had finally found almost acceptable ingredients for a good sandwich at the Winn-Dixie in the Haymont section of Fayetteville, which he kept in the small fridge in his BOQ. He had ten months left and his one goal was to find a woman which might cure his Bragg blues.

Women? Enlisted men banged everything on and off post. He had tried night school a second time to find a woman and found only homework. Even the weather wasn't cooperating; March seemed comprised of endless, cold, wet days that challenged any concept of spring.

On this particular gloomy and wet Friday afternoon, he went to the Main Post Officers' Club where he understood there were a lot of civilian females, although he rarely saw them. The problem with the club, as he had learned on past forays, was that there were too many higher ranking officers who believed their rank gave them first shot at stray women or lower ranking men's dates.

One positive thing about Lt. Margolin was his persistence. Maybe even his eternal optimism. A perfect example being his desire to cure First Sgt. Billy Martin's sadistic insensitivity.

Margolin had arrived too early and drank too much. Now, he sat at the bar with the other dozen males and watched in the mirror as two leg captains swooped around the only female.

One woman with about 15 guys. Not good odds.

He rattled the ice in his empty scotch glass and surveyed the club that seemed more like a large corporate boardroom. The kind of place no one ever raised his voice. The interior was dark oak and leather chairs and there wasn't a jukebox, just innocuous FM radio background music. Large wall pictures in sepia depicted old Fort Bragg when horse carriages were still used to pull cannons, and soldiers wore wide-brimmed campaign hats. He wore his fatigues, which never went over well on Main Post where most of the officers were not jumpers and wore more formal pinks and three-quarter length brown jackets and old-fashioned Sam Browne belts. They were the bureaucrats who ran the Army and ordered people like him to jump from airplanes.

The enlisted bartender brought a fresh scotch before he could refuse.

Quit looking around, he coached himself. He knew women didn't like hungry guys. What he really wanted more than anything was to lie in his BOQ bed in his GI undershorts while a halfway decent looking girl showered after furious lovemaking. Like those few times at the fraternity house when everyone was away.

It didn't have to be a Jewish girl. Any *shiksa*. Not even decent-looking. A fat WAC or his favorite image: a skinny pizza waitress with a pencil in her hair. Any port in a storm. To get a girl in that room meant he had to do what he was doing. Prowl. *God, my scotch is gone already.*

"Let me have a beer this time," he told the bartender. "A Country Club."

The bartender apologized. They only had Budweiser and Heineken.

Can I make that decision without Martin's help? He looked around as if expecting the first sergeant to direct him on what to drink, and saw a WAC officer standing in the doorway.

"Oops." He turned back to the bartender. "Heineken will do."

From his stool, he could not tell what she looked like; the gray light of the door glass silhouetted her. However, the uniform fit snugly. She looked around then came in.

Lt. Margolin did a quick headcount. Twenty-one to two.

Trying not to be too obvious with his leer, he followed her progress from the entrance then picked her up in the mirror. *Will she come to the bar? Who is she looking for?* His heart and body English pulled her towards him. There were several empty seats right next to him. Maybe...

She took a table. Alone. A lady doesn't sit alone at the bar swilling drinks like he was.

His beer arrived. He pretended to be interested in the label while keeping the new arrival under mirror surveillance. Not bad looking. *Wasn't she there last time I was here? Some leg colonel had her cornered?* That was a good opening line. He estimated, at this moment, there were at least ten males ready to pounce.

An enlisted waiter approached and took her order. *He's probably going to put the make on her too.* Strike Hold, chaps, as Sergeant Webster might say.

Stand up. Margolin belched quietly. *Hook up.* He slid off the stool. *Shuffle to the door. My first combat jump.* And he landed at her table and hadn't closed his eyes. "Good afternoon, Captain."

He was ready for a higher-ranking officer's inspection, ma'am. Starched, faded, tailored fatigues. Infantry blue scarf ironed and carefully tucked beneath his collar. His Corcoran boots shined as well as he was ever able; spit shining was an art form he would never master.

She paused in her smoking, exhaled, waved the smoke away, and looked up. "Hello." Absolutely no trace of friendliness.

"May I sit down?"

She responded with momentarily deliberation, then an ambivalent hand gesture to a chair on the opposite side of the low coffee table. A sensitive man would have taken it as a motion of dismissal. Margolin's alcohol courage ignored the gesture. He sat down and scooped some peanuts from the dish.

"What unit you with, Captain?" She wore the caducei on her lapels. Her black plastic nametag read 'Melby' in white letters.

"Womack." The large military hospital on post.

"Nurse?"

She nodded and crossed her legs while glancing toward the door. The rustle of her stockings startled Margolin as if someone had slapped him across the back. He coughed on a peanut and prayed she'd cross her legs every chance she had. He suppressed another cough and continued the impressive conversation. "How long you been at Bragg?"

"Two years and five months."

"That's longer than I've been here." *She has to be four years older than me. At least.* "I've seen you before. Do you show up here every Friday?"

"I'm here sometimes," she replied with a slow disinterested look around the room.

"You don't like me."

"I don't know you."

"My name tag reads 'Margolin,' but I'm really Mad Dog of the Five-Oh-Four."

"Please spare me a heroic jump story."

"I don't have any except for the time..." He stopped to catch her reaction. A smile? "Tell me a hospital story."

"I started at six this morning."

"That's a long story. You smiled."

"You remind me of someone."

If she says her brother or best friend I'll throw peanuts at her. Girls wanted to be his friend; he wanted to seduce them. He pinched his chin and said, "Kirk Douglas? A lot of people tell me I look like him or Fats Domino."

Her shoulders seemed to unlock. Her mouth softened. "Lieutenant, I...just..."

The waiter appeared. He ordered two more drinks. A beer for him and whatever the lady was having.

"Gin and tonic. Thank you. Lieutenant, let me be candid. I don't like paratroopers. Officers. NCOs. Privates. They bore me. They run up and down Longstreet Road shouting about being men. I'm sure most of them fail, Lieutenant Mad Dog."

"Is that knowledge gained from personal experience?"

Her mouth sealed. She looked around the room again. Who would rescue her? She waved to someone behind him. The leg colonel?

"You know, you're right. I'm one of those people." His candor stopped her swivel for help. "Would you know how I might have my first sergeant committed?"

She laughed, more of a release from her pretended haughtiness. "I've never heard that before."

"What's your name besides 'Melby' or should I say 'handle' as in Tex..."

"Captain Melby." She stayed focused across his shoulder on the main entrance.

"Should I say 'peach'?"

"You just did."

"Sorry." He vetoed lighting the cigar in his breast pocket. "If you think you dislike paratroopers, I have to put up with them seven days a week. I have to be Mad Dog."

She stubbed out her cigarette in the ashtray and sipped her drink. "I don't envy you."

Margolin shifted his chair to enable him to lean farther across the table. Lifting his glass in an unpretentious toast he said, "You're the prettiest captain I've ever seen."

"Thank you." Her crossed leg subtly kicked with impatience.

He barely sipped, and as he started to put down the glass he froze; coming across the room, almost marching, was Col. Jack Steele. The lieutenant watched most everyone in the room attend the colonel's crossing as if he was Charlton Heston at the Red Sea. He also noticed a few more women in civilian clothes had arrived.

"Are you all right?" asked Captain Melby.

"I need a complete physical immediately."

She shook her head in disapproval. "I thought paratroopers took themselves seriously. No frivolity. Killers from the sky."

"Don't stare, but the paratrooper I dislike the most and who you just described has commandeered the bar." She nodded as if agreeing and then peeked.

Steele joined several higher-ranking officers at the bar. Like Steele, they wore the dark brown jackets with Sam Browne belts and pink trousers. On their left shoulders were the distinctive blue and white dragon patches of XVIII Airborne Corps. All of them wore Wings.

"He's a handsome man."

"He's my nemesis and writes my fitness report. The reason I came here is because I thought he didn't."

"How is your fitness report?"

"I'd rather forget about it. Are you eating tonight?"

"Later. I have a date."

"He's lucky." Margolin took a long swallow. *Struck out again.* "When you don't have a date and you're not working from dawn to dusk, what do you do?"

She had no ready answer. "Sometimes…" She thought some more. "Sometimes, I drive up to D.C. to visit friends. I know some people at Walter Reed."

"I'm glad to hear that. I thought you were going to say you spent your free time laying out your uniforms and practicing inspections." Melby actually laughed.

I wonder how her GI-issued panties looked. Plain white? OD? A GI garter belt? Can a lieutenant fu…intercourse with a captain? I'll charm her bra off. Urbane, witty, Mad Dog. And he was drunk.

"Mad Dog, you're silly, did you know that?"

He almost said, no, just Jewish. "In this serious Airborne business you need a sense of humor."

Among the growing after-work crowd, Lt. Margolin sensed he and the captain were enjoying themselves, but he understood someone would appear, a higher-ranking officer with a drink in his hand, and snootily escort her away. He didn't care. The lieutenant planned to stick around, hang in, leech, suck-up, until the moment she departed.

"Melba…" He caught his slip of the tongue. She nodded it was all right. "Captain Melby, may I ask you a serious question instead of kidding?"

She smiled as if a joke was imminent.

"I'd love…" He paused to drink. The beer kept tasting better. "… I'd love for you to say…I mean I want you to leave with me right now. We'll go any place you want between here and the Pentagon for dinner. Any place. But no mess halls."

She crossed her legs for the umpteenth time. Margolin hadn't missed one. She appeared to consider his offer. On a hunch, Margolin continued, "Look, it's none of my business, but whoever you're meeting seems to be late."

"He always is."

A flicker of sadness touched her eyes and mouth. "You'd find Mad Dog Margolin as punctual as a Swiss train if you were waiting for me."

"Mad Dog, you're not really one, are you?"

"A mad dog?"

"Yes."

"In real life, a puppy." He stopped himself. Don't get sloppy. *Chutzpah*, Mad Dog.

The captain lit a cigarette. "I'm going to say this and I'm not sure why."

He raised both hands in a cautionary manner. She didn't have to tell him anything. *A confession?* It could lead to the brother syndrome, which he didn't want.

Captain Melby looked him in the eye and confessed she was involved with a colonel in finance. A former patient. No names, he would not know the man. Every Friday they met at the club, if he wasn't there by 1730 it meant he couldn't get away. Away from his wife and family, she added sadly.

Both she and Margolin looked at their watches. Eighteen-ten. Margolin got a kick out of her using military time so casually.

"It irritates me," she said and it showed in her voice. "I get angry at myself. I drink too much and I'm tired of waiting for him."

The waiter brought the fresh drinks. She finished her present gin and tonic, set the glass down hard, and said, "There. I told you. No one knows but you, the colonel, and me. And you're a paratrooper, so I know I'll make it a point to never see you again."

Margolin recalled he was a tall, silver-haired man. "I've seen you together." She agreed.

He stood up and stamped his boots to adjust the trouser blouse over his boots. "Wait five more minutes and then come with me. I'll be right back."

"Why did you do that?"

"What?"

"Stamp your feet."

"All paratroopers do that. Fix the blouse. It's one of our childish habits. Don't disappear, Captain, and that's a direct order."

She toasted him with her fresh drink and smiled. God, she was gorgeous.

Margolin worked his way around the jetties of people along the bar. The sensation of a carpet under his boots made him realize he rarely walked on a carpet. In the entire division there weren't any carpets. *An alcoholic enlightenment! Going off to the head...latrine...the men's room...bathroom...accepting the risk she will be surrounded by higher-ranking officers on my return.* At the urinal, he needed to touch the wall to keep his balance, so he knew he was drunk and knew he was happy.

He had spoken to a real live female who was waiting for him at that moment. It was as good as watching Uncle Ziggy slice Swiss cheese without looking at the spinning blade. He laughed at the comparison and himself.

"What outfit you with, son?"

Margolin hadn't realized someone else had entered. He looked to his left. At the second urinal down, stood Col. Steele, staring straight ahead, relieving himself.

Fucking Colonel Steele. Fuck him.

"How are you, Colonel?"

The taller officer turned toward Margolin. "Never better...ahh...What's your name again?"

"Margolin, sir. First Lieutenant Seymour Mad Dog Margolin, commanding officer of Headquarters Company, 'Oh-Four."

The lieutenant emphasized 'Seymour' knowing Steele didn't appreciate it. From nowhere, except maybe his deep subconscious, Lt. Margolin heard himself ask, "Colonel, how come you never remember my name?" *Did I say that? I did. Goddamn.*

Margolin finished and carefully buttoned his fly—wanting no wet spots on his walk back to the beautiful captain, who might still be there.

The colonel continued his watery task and replied, "Lieutenant, I don't think that's any consequence of yours."

From the sink, Margolin looked in the mirror at Steele and said, "Begging the Colonel's pardon, but it's a big consequence to me." It must be the closeness of the latrine that made him feel confident. And the alcohol. "I think a good leader should respect the names of his men, no matter if they're Finklestein or Clark Bar."

The colonel shook his member hard enough to make Margolin think of a Louisville Slugger and said, "What first lieutenants think and what colonels do are worlds apart."

A cold swallow stuck in Margolin's throat. It was as if his voice was blocked off. Dammed up. His mind shrunk while his desire to make the colonel always remember him swelled. He actually wanted to scream, but no sound came.

Steele zipped up and came toward the sink. "That's enough for tonight, Lieutenant."

He was being dismissed, like the cloth hand towel the colonel lifted off the stack over the sinks, used to wipe his hands, and tossed into the bin.

"Sir?" At last, a voice. "I want to ask you one question, Colonel Steele."

"You've been dismissed, Lieutenant."

Margolin no longer knew who was talking; it was all emotion. "Like hell I am."

That turned the colonel directly to the lieutenant, his cold blue eyes chilled the younger officer. *Like fucking Moses to a tee.*

"You're out of line, Lieutenant and, I believe, drunk."

Margolin stepped between the colonel and the door. He wasn't Seymour any more, he was Mad Dog and he didn't know it. *Chutzpah* out of control. "What happens, Colonel, if I ask you to take off your shiny bird and you give me this shit?"

Without any suggestion of hesitation, the colonel reached to his right shoulder insignia and worked off the bird. In the silence, Margolin almost apologized, but held himself back. He had crossed the Red Sea, but he suspected the man would never fight him.

"I'll tell you something, Lieutenant, I've been keeping my eye on you for a long time. You're in charge of a mess hall that was shot up. An AWOL escaped. Duty roster stolen…"

Margolin's only come back. "This is my fault?"

"You're responsible. On New Year's Day the CID found two men selling those funny cigarettes and a man you allowed to go on leave early ended up dead in an auto accident."

The lieutenant knew Steele was crazy; his assignment of blame proved it. *Dumping Mangiameli's death on me is going too far.* "Have you ever been in love, Colonel?"

Steele held one bird in his hand. He started unpinning the other. "That has nothing to do with the U.S. Army."

Margolin raised his voice. "That's everything!" Someone entered. Heard Margolin. Exited. Both officers heard the door open and shut.

"That boy on leave was in love. One of your men. He had to get home."

Steele's volume increased. "That's no excuse, Lieutenant."

"No excuse. No excuse. The command school's answer for everything. For Christ's sake, Colonel, cut loose once in a while. Feel something! You had a kid busted for having his trousers unbloused. A soldier who idolized you."

"I'm justice in the Five-Oh-Four and don't you ever forget it. A word to the wise is sufficient." Steele showed both silver eagle emblems to Margolin and said, "They're off and I'm leaving if this is all you have to say or do."

Margolin dared not grab him. He stepped back from the door and said, "You're a first class prick! A first class prejudiced…"

Steele punched Lt. Margolin square on the jaw, knocking him against the partition that shielded the door. Margolin went to his knees and spun toward the urinals. Without a word, the colonel walked out.

"It didn't even hurt," boasted Margolin on his knees by the pissoirs to the empty latrine. Because he was unsteady on his feet, he had ridden with the punch like a veteran boxer. As he stood up, he was surprised. He wasn't afraid.

"Goddamn him," he said to no one. "If colonels swing, so can I."

Still unsure of what he wanted to do, he pulled open the heavy men's room door. Steele was there, a few feet in front of him, replacing his eagle insignia. Mad Dog, without a thought, leaped onto Steele's back.

Steele fell forward, but caught himself and allowed Margolin's momentum to carry him over the colonel's head.

His legs cracked against a solid oak chair. "Shit!" he hollered.

A collective gasp arose from the club's patrons as they shifted like dominos, falling away from the end of the bar where Margolin had tumbled. A woman emitted a small scream.

"Break it up!" ordered someone is a strong voice.

"...that's an order..."

"...let them go..."

Steele had two hands on Margolin's fatigue shirt. The lieutenant imagined the colonel was helping him up. "Let me go!" he shouted. He wanted no mercy from Moses. "Let me go and I'll kick your ass!" Mad Dog wasn't to be trifled with.

Steele pulled him almost to his feet as Margolin threw a wild roundhouse right that caught Steele in his left eye. Steele took the punch with a twist of his head and cocked his fist. "You asked for this, Lieutenant."

Margolin attempted to duck, but Steele had aligned him up just right and the lieutenant moved too slowly. Steele's hard fist struck his temple like a pounded railroad spike. Margolin felt himself going down. To stay on his feet, to fight for the moment, he shouted, "Seymour! Call me Seymour!"

Steele dragged him in a half circle before hitting him again, this time on the cheek and nose. Margolin tasted warm blood. *Bleeding—my mother wouldn't like that.*

He grabbed the colonel's Sam Browne belt and pulled him close and threw his arms around the bigger man's shoulders, driving him backwards across the room. The colonel could not connect with any punches, because the lieutenant's head stayed tucked against Steele's side and shoulder.

Margolin snarled and gasped between clenched teeth, "I'm Seymour!"

"...Here they come..."

"...I thought the Eighty-Second boys only did this sort of thing at prop blasts..."

"...someone call the MPs..."

Steele tried to push against the lieutenant's assault; however, his feet failed to catch any leverage. The grappling men bounced against tables, spilling drinks and peanuts, and chasing spectators like a wild tire off a racing car. A couch topped Steele over backwards and out of the lieutenant's grasp.

They stared at one another from opposite sides of the couch.

Blood ran from Margolin's nose into his immaculate scarf and fatigue shirt. His face carried welts from Steele's blows.

"Colonel Steele!" called someone in the crowd.

The colonel waved off whoever wanted his attention. He eyed Margolin with his one good eye. The other had swollen nearly shut. Along his right trouser leg were dark bloodstains from Margolin. The colonel sucked in deep breaths. His face glowed through several shades of red.

The lieutenant spoke with a strained voice. "I'm Lieutenant Seymour Margolin, the Mad Dog." As if to prove his claim forever, he took a step on the couch and leaped toward his superior officer. Steele stepped back then came forward, his long right hand catching Margolin's chin in mid-air, and then he braced both feet and caught the lieutenant with a glancing left and right on his shoulder and temple as he went down. The blows sank Margolin against the overturned couch.

Steele rubbed his knuckles as if wiping something off. With a slight smile, he said, "That's what happens when you ask a colonel who boxed at the Point to take off his rank."

Half-a-dozen men came between the two combatants. Staff and guests set up the furniture. A rotund colonel in dress uniform with a drink in his hand stood in front of Steele demanding to know why there had been a brawl. Colonels, the uppity tone indicated, did not brawl. At least not publicly.

Steele surveyed the man and his Adjutant General collar insignia and replied casually, "A discipline problem." He touched his sore eye. "Don't blame the Lieutenant. I take full responsibility." He looked at his fingers as if they would reveal something about his eye. One of his officer club pals handed him a scotch on the rocks.

Captain Melby stepped past the small group of men and announced, "I'm a nurse." She had a towel with ice in it. In a professional manner, she knelt by the lieutenant and tilted back his head to start the repair job. He winced when she pinched his nose. The small cut on his cheek came from Steele's West Point ring. She iced the cut then wiped the drying blood off his chin and lips.

Finally, Margolin exhaled as if he had been holding his breath and boosted himself up on his elbows. He ran his tongue around the inside of his mouth where something was sore. *Goddamn, Melby is taking care of me!* It hurt to smile.

She bent close to him and whispered, "Mad Dog, you were wonderful. Hungry?"

"Captain, I have a sudden craving for peaches." He moved too quickly and had to sit back down. She kept her hand on his shoulder and advised him to go slowly.

Another officer assisted her in getting the lieutenant to his feet. "Just one second, Lieutenant." Steele's voice grabbed Margolin like a vice.

Steele leaned against the bar with 18th Airborne Corps cronies on each side of him. The lieutenant knew the moment with Melby had been too good. He would be stripped of any dignity he had left. Suddenly, he felt hung over. *That Anglo-Saxon bastard is going to court-martial me.* "Yes, sir."

Steele crossed the short distance between them. Margolin saw the swollen eye and bloodied uniform; all was not in vain. The man would remember him now. *Maybe I should go for the good eye. One last swing before the Army bounces me out on my ass.*

"You prefer Seymour or Sy?" Steele's rare smile broke free, his hand extended.

"Sy will do fine, sir." They shook.

"Sy it shall be then, and remind me if I forget. Good job, Mad Dog."

Margolin squeezed harder and looked Steele in the eye. "All the way, sir."

When they walked out into the wet March night, Captain Melby held his arm as if they'd been lovers for months. Through his clotted nose, he could smell spring. A damp spring. The warm days were fast coming.

And if he wasn't the baddest motherfucker who ever came down the pike, then God never gigged Gabriel for a rusty horn. "You know," he turned to Melby, "I really am Mad Dog Margolin." She hugged his arm and shook her head at his bravado. He couldn't stop—it felt so good.

"When the going gets tough. The tough get going. Fuck you, Uncle Ziggy and the rye bread you rode in on."

Melby asked, "Uncle Ziggy?"

"No one important."

Chapter 15

On the first of every month, a flood of green flows across Bragg into Fayetteville and the surrounding communities. It's payday, cash directly from the government into the hands of the men who defend it. And, being military, there is a ceremony.

Enlisted men, in mandatory uniform of the day, form a line in rank order into the dayroom. The executive officer sits at a card table or desk with pay envelopes arranged in rank order. Standing beside him is the Charge of Quarters; both wear a .45 pistol.

A soldier strides up to the desk, comes to attention and salutes. "Pfc. So-And-So reporting for pay, sir!"

The salute is returned, the trooper gets a quick once-over on his appearance, then the officer counts out cash from the man's pay envelope. The Pfc. signs for his money, thanks the officer, salutes, and executes a right-face and heads toward the exit and unknown adventures.

On post, payday activities vary. After the mandatory donations to the Red Cross or the United Way or whatever the regiment's cause of the month is, a Pfc. can take his $100 base pay and $55 jump pay and join the immediate unauthorized card games in selected cadre rooms. Gambling is prohibited, but gambling first sergeants have been known to restrict all fellow gamblers on paydays. Company loan sharks wait outside dayrooms for their accounts to appear with fresh greenbacks and, when necessary, extract their payments with coercion. They even wait outside the dayrooms of other companies. A few conscientious soldiers head for the post office and send money orders home or already have some pay put away in Soldiers' Savings. Young soldiers with families head right to the PX for the major grocery buy of the month.

Off-post is different. The life of a military town is resuscitated on the first of every month like a nearly drowned man sucking fresh oxygen.

The bars fill up. Restaurants are crowded. Movie lines grow longer. Military stores and tattoo parlors stay open later for the intoxicated customers. Men finally have enough money to get their fatigues out of the cleaners, fill their gas tanks, purchase cool rims for their cars, claim their watches and jewelry from pawn shops, and chow down away from a mess hall.

In some circles, this payday phenomenon is known as, 'The Eagle Shits.'

Patterson and Breslin found a parking spot near the wine store on Russell Street. They pooled some dollars and bought six bottles of New York State pink Catawba, which they carefully wrapped in a supply-room blanket and placed in the large trunk. One bottle was kept for walking around. Their planned excursion to Greensboro was abandoned after their first sips of wine while sitting in the car with the windows down on the warm April afternoon. Too long a drive and no place to sleep. They'd rather drink.

With the bottle under Patterson's jacket, they went to the Turf Club. Before they could find a waitress or a spot at the bar, Patterson suggested they head for the Canopy to catch up with Banuelous. He hadn't been around the barracks lately, because one of his girlfriends insisted he stay all night every night. His tightly made, unrumpled bunk in the squad bay looked like a memorial to an unknown soldier. With the influx of Southerners, they missed their tough guy buddy who wouldn't hesitate to tell the crackers to shut off their shit-kickin' music. As they entered the Canopy, a very drunk young man, with cigarette pack twisted in the short sleeve of his tight-fitting T-shirt, intentionally bumped into Breslin. They ignored him and sailed among the trays of tall-boy Budweisers looking like the masts of clipper ships skippered by waitresses cruising through a sea of GI bodies.

Behind them, someone punched the drunken kid. His payday wish fulfilled, the bouncer rushed him through the crowd out the door.

"There's more assholes out today than Carter has liver pills," said Breslin. They leaned against the rear sidewall waiting for a bar or booth opening.

"Tommy would've made a fortune today with bus fares."

Breslin sneaked a sip of wine. "You know what would be cool. We could drive dudes back and forth for free. Give them slugs of wine and tell them they're on the Tommy Mangiameli...The Pfc. Tommy Mangiameli Memorial Ride."

Patterson sipped and acknowledged Tommy sure loved driving guys off post on paydays.

There was no sign of Banuelous, and the crowd was rough. They looked at one another and both said, "Terri?" And they were out the door, choosing to walk to the Carousel on Combat Alley.

Since meeting her on New Year's, they had made repeated stops at the Carousel just to say hello and hope her dangerous boyfriend wasn't around. She seemed to enjoy their company and they kept their appearances fun and friendly.

Combat Alley held up its raw reputation every payday. Today wasn't any different. Patterson and Breslin's experience along the street kept them from reacting to the surface chaos of young soldiers in civvies with fresh haircuts looking for ways to prove their manhood after weeks of training for Jump School. The two soldiers headed past the bus station toward the Carousel. Troops were already waiting to board the Vomit Comet ride back to post. A private's salary did not last long in Fayetteville. Three young men whose freshly shaven heads advertised new jumpers went out of their way to bump into them. Patterson and Breslin just kept walking. "Must be fuckin' legs," said one of the men. Since Breslin and Patterson did not fight, they couldn't be paratroopers.

"The only way to take this place on payday is to be as drunk as everyone else or smoke some of Wise's cigarettes," said Breslin.

Wise and Carter had been court-martialled in February: three years in Leavenworth and dishonorable discharges. Patterson had not forgotten the hate on Carter's face as they were escorted past by the MPs, and neither man had dared to search for a new source of marijuana.

They walked through the open doors of the Carousel into the traffic jam of bodies. Men stood two deep at the bar. By sheer luck, the moment they came through the door, five guys in a booth rose to leave. Patterson and Breslin slid right in.

Their waitress, an unattractive heavy girl, took their order for tall boys with glasses—the glasses for the hidden wine, of course, not the beer. They smoked and tried to catch Terri's eye as she maneuvered her way through the crowd on the other side of the bar. When the waitress returned, Patterson, in his best Hollywood Jack imitation, asked her if she wanted to go for a ride in his '56 T-Bird. "It's right outside."

"My old man would kill me six ways to Sunday," she replied and expertly swept their money off the table and departed.

Breslin thought Patterson was crazy. "The broad's got terminal thunder thighs. She should be driving an eighteen-wheeler, not serving us poor damn souls in hell."

Patterson explained a kind word does a lot of good. "She'll think someone actually wants her. What do you call it? Perspective. You taught me that. All these dudes give her shit. She'll remember us." They were so caught up in hiding their wine bottle they never noticed Terri approach. She was just there.

"From out of nowhere," said Breslin.

"How you doin'?" asked Patterson. Terri raised her eyebrows and shook her head; it couldn't be much worse.

"Seen Banuelous?" asked Patterson as he patted his brow with his handkerchief, a smooth Moonlight Gambler trait he'd copied. She shook her head no.

"Join us for dinner?" asked Breslin.

"What're y'all havin'?"

"Red wine. Nothing but red wine." He revealed the bottle by his side. It was a standard joke between the three of them.

To their surprise, she replied, "I get off at six."

Patterson instantly asked, "What about Starr?"

She leaned over their table and said, "What he don't know won't hurt him. He's on CQ runner."

Breslin spread his hands on the table, looked at her, and said, "Well, the chauffeur will be outside when you get off work."

"Y'all wait down the street by the Cadillac Lounge. Johnny's got too many friends around here." They agreed. Terri slipped into the crowd and told the heavy girl to bring them two more beers.

"My kind of girl," said Breslin. "She turns on my lights." Patterson swore Terri liked Breslin. Liked his poetry.

"No, man, its your cool handkerchief she digs."

"You're a fuckin' poet-schmoet."

"I'll undress her with words and wrap her in poesy."

"Fuck that. Roll her over and do it doggie style."

"That's class, Bill Patterson. Did you learn that from Colonel Steele?"

"Spec-Four Evil, Sid the Cook. He says chicks love it." And they went on and on until they finished another beer and the bottle of wine.

Happily drunk, they left the bar and now absorbed the rhythms of Combat Alley. The April dusk was warm and humid. No angry GIs looking for trouble bumped into them. The bikers at the Gillespie Street Drive-In were cool as they spun around on the drive-in gravel and the stores' neon glowed with enticing colors. Music emanating from the various bars' jukeboxes had them singing along. Payday wasn't so bad after all.

To kill some time, they walked back to Hay Street and stopped in the military store where Patterson had bought his '04 lighter on their first pass to town more than a year ago. He bought a pack of Luckies and a Trojan three-pack from the sales girl, acting as if he bought rubbers all the time.

"What're you gonna do with those?" asked Breslin.

"You never know. I'm overdue for somethin'." Patterson smiled at the clerk. She ignored him.

"Man, I didn't know I was hanging out with such a coo man."

"It could happen." Patterson led Breslin to the rear of the store and showed him the jacket Motz had wanted to buy that first night in town. They took turns putting it on and looking in the mirror at the huge Wings and slogan:

> When I Die I'll Go To Heaven
> Because I Served My Time In Hell.
> 82nd Airborne Division
> Fort Bragg, N.C.

The sales girl did not appreciate their raucous laughter and asked them to leave.

Outside, Breslin's afterthought was they should buy one. "We are 'perrytroopers,' aren't we? I can wear it when I'm serving soup at the Franciscan mission in downtown Philly. The old winos will love it."

"What in the hell are you talkin' about?" They reached their car and and tapped into a fresh bottle of wine, sitting with the windows open. The sunset seemed determined to last as long as possible after the cold and gray March.

"You're out of your gourd, man. We're goin' to Key West and wear leather shit on our wrists. Fishin' for a livin'."

"Bill, what the fuck do you know about boats?"

"Same thing you know about soup kitchens."

"You stopped thinking realistically. You know I talked about being a priest or a brother."

"Fishin's real. Jesus, serving soup to winos? That's more KP. You want some soup? I'll give you some." Patterson climbed out and leaned against the rear fender and pissed in the gutter. Passers-by ignored him as well as they could.

Breslin didn't join him, but pointed out they should go to the Turf Club so he could use the facilities like a normal person, a gentleman.

Inured by the wine, they dodged their way through the jarring Turf Club crowd to the men's room. Patterson, pursuing his point of Breslin's insanity of serving soup, followed him into the men's room. Vomit covered the floor. A man in civvies pounded on a closed stall door and shouted for someone named Gilmore to open up. Behind the door, the suffering Gilmore moaned and mumbled, "Leave me be."

"I mean, Bill, you hardly know where Key West is," said Breslin over his shoulder.

"I didn't know nothin' about jumpin' outta planes, but I did that." Patterson eyes searched the graffiti on the wall above Breslin's head. The most interesting line, heavily penciled across the wall, was, "Piss hard. It's a long way to the 503rd MPs drinking fountain." He continued, "I learned jumpin' and pots and pans and full-field inspections. I can spit-shine a fuckin' chocolate bar. I'm goin', motherfucker, and you are too. Fuck a bunch of realities and perspectives and winos."

They walked out leaving the drunken man still pounding on the stall door.

Terri walked down from the Cadillac and joined them in the car. She appreciated the wine and relaxed. With the door open, they smoked, listened to jazz from Raleigh, and made small talk about payday assholes until Breslin suggested Chinese food.

"We can take it to my place," offered Terri as she took another Marlboro from the pack in her little drawstring purse. "You trust us?" asked Patterson as he spun the wheel on his '04 lighter for her.

She gave them a tough look. "I trust Johnny to keep trouble out of my life."

Breslin and Patterson looked and nodded in silent agreement. No trouble from them. The long day of drinking made them too weary to fear or fight Starr.

Neither one of the two young soldiers made anything out of Terri producing a two-year old boy from the apartment below hers. They were in the kitchen dishing out chow mein, rice, and egg foo yung when Terri introduced him, "His name's Christian." Her blue eyes suddenly a mother's eyes, her countenance full of pride.

Christian looked nonchalant. The food had his attention.

"What a handle," commented Breslin who tossed back the remainder of his wine and pulled his kitchen chair close to Christian. Leaning over the boy, he said in his best British accent, "I say, old chap, did anyone ever say to you, 'I'll see you hung from the highest yardarm in the British Navy'?" A slight shake of the head no.

Between changing her work clothes, fussing over Christian, and digging through her stack of long-playing 33s, she gave little time to her guests. Once the records started, a Ray Price ballad, she joined them. She wore a pale blue robe pulled high around her neck. Patterson found cold cans of Schlitz in the refrigerator and they switched to beer; it tasted better with the Chinese food. Christian ended up on Terri's lap for his meal. Breslin gave him sips of beer and blew smoke rings for him.

They talked about their home towns. Terri came from Richmond. A friend of hers had followed a guy to Fayetteville and invited her down because of the good tips working the bars. She'd been there more than four years. The Cadillac wasn't her favorite place to work. She had worked at the Canopy, but Margie didn't like her. "She couldn't take the competition," Terri explained in an uncharacteristic catty manner. She was waiting for a job on post. The PX paid great and it was a government job.

"Why don't you come to Key West with us?" asked Breslin. He may have been inspired to ask by seeing Terri's robe slip open at various places as she adjusted Christian on her lap.

Patterson laughed. "Now he's fu...now he's goin' to Key West. An hour ago he was goin' to the soup line."

"Sometimes," said Terri unsmiling, "I'd like to go anywhere. Just get away from this place. The bars."

Without attracting Christian's attention, Breslin asked if Johnny was his father. "No, but Johnny's good to him. His real daddy was a California pretty boy. All suntanned up. He was the lifeguard at the officer's pool and chased their wives. Y'all know how that is."

Patterson wondered if the chasing bothered her. "G-D right it did. And more than once I told him, too." She took a short hard drag on her cigarette as if getting ready to tell him again. "He'd just laugh and grab me and the next thing I know we're making love. It was like he had a spell over me."

"He got out," she replied to Patterson's query where he was now. "Like that, up and gone. I ain't seen or heard since. He don't even know about this one." She ruffled Christian's long hair.

Patterson said to Breslin, "Just like McBride. Never came back off leave."

"Good riddance, man. The cat annoyed me."

Terri stood up with Christian in her arms. "Time for bed, sweetheart."

Christian shook his head no and said, "No."

"One last jigger of grog, Mr. Christian?" Breslin offered him a sip. "Ration's running low, matey."

While Terri fixed up Christian's bed on the living room couch, Breslin confessed to Patterson he was drunk as hell as he filled their beer glasses with more wine. The record player shut off. They could hear Terri saying prayers with Christian.

"You know, I really like her."

"So do I," agreed Breslin. "Look at her when she smiles. There's something there."

"What a bum fuckin' deal to be stuck…"

"Stuck where, mister?" Terri closed the door behind her as she came from the living room. Patterson wanted to take back his words. "Stuck here?" She turned on the radio sitting over the sink. "Stuck with a kid? Y'all know what; it's a tuff life if you don't weaken…"

And the three of them said, "… but who wants to be strong." They laughed.

Breslin brought more beers from the fridge. He had punched holes in the cans before Terri remembered the beer belonged to Johnny. "Shit. He'll think I drank it all." She pouted and sat down hard on a chair. Patterson offered to go for a case.

"Would you?" She genuinely needed help with the problem.

"If you give me a kiss." Terri broke into a rare sweet grin. Usually, she maintained a stoic exterior to protect her in the bars. Once her softness and loveliness showed, it became obvious.

"When you smile like that, Terri, we can see your soul," said Breslin.

"I hope it ain't all black," she joked and stood up and walked over to Patterson. Her robe came open without her noticing. Patterson slipped his hands beneath her robe and kissed her. His hands cupped her ass. In the ashtray, her cigarette burned an undisturbed sliver of smoke into the humid air.

Lloyd Price intruded rudely from the radio with "Stagger Lee."

"Hear, hear!" Breslin spoke loudly. "My cup is dry, innkeeper, and watch your hands." The couple separated and gazed at one another with the intensity of those to be shot at dawn.

Breslin complained, "Christ on a crutch, he's only going to the store." Terri closed her robe and moved quickly to sit with her cigarette and beer.

Patterson hitched up his crotch and took a few long strides across the kitchen. He stopped at the door. "Keep an eye on her for me, will you?"

"Both eyes. And bring up a bottle of wine and get some smokes. You spring for them, you cheap bastard." They heard the Plymouth turn over and sat in silence.

She finished her cigarette with a strong final drag and stubbed it out. "Place is a mess," she said and moved around the kitchen discarding the paper plates and leftovers. Her robe seemed unable to remain closed. Breslin offered to help.

"Y'all sit still. It's too hot for both of us movin' around in here." She filled a large plastic bowl with hot water and soap flakes for glasses and silverware. Breslin sat, awkwardly nursing his beer and smoking, but he couldn't help glancing at Terri's firm body in bra and panties. Finally, he said, "Remember that poem on New Year's?"

"I thought that was so beautiful. I was even gonna look it up in the library, but didn't know who wrote it or nothin'. Did y'all write it?"

"Nope, I wish I did. A lady did. Edna St. Vincent Millay."

"I remember there's words about lonely trees and lips kissing. Now that I think about it, it sounds like a woman. A woman would know those things. I'd love to hear all of it."

"That's pretty good appreciation. I'm glad you didn't forget."

"No. No, I thought it was beautiful. I guess you're a person who feels a lot."

"Not really. I'm just a draftee killing time at Bragg." He asked for a pencil and piece of paper so he could write it out for her. A brief search produced a pencil stub from the silverware drawer, and the only useable paper was the side of a brown grocery bag.

"First things first," said Breslin after he took a sip of beer, "The lady's name." He wrote lengthwise on the bag. "It's called a sonnet, and it's the first line that gives it its title." Terri stood over Breslin, smoking and watching him write.

Breslin talked as he slowly laid out the words. "A girl from Bryn Mawr and I memorized this one spring afternoon in Fairmont Park on the upper Schuylkill. We thought we were in love. Did you ever hear about the girls from Bryn Mawr? 'Whose desserts were as tight as jars/ Instead of just flopping/ They loved to be topping/ And the boys lined up from afar.'" He gave Terri a wise guy look. She pushed his shoulder and smiled.

"I was rich then. Rich in ignorance that everything worked according to some rules. It took about a month to get the setting right. Her old man and old lady took off for the weekend. The *theatre* in New York. I brought some wine. Good stuff. We put Brubeck on the console. You know Tommy Eliot? He's the cat that called April the cruelest month. This is April, ain't it?"

Breslin didn't look up to Terri's silence. He wrote and talked. "That was a cruel April." He stopped as if deciding. "Right in her bedroom we made it on the bed. Then everywhere we could afterwards. But I got tired of the trolley rides and stopped going over there. To Bryn Mawr."

He wrote quickly. "Terri, no lie, you're nicer than she was. Ten thousand times nicer." Breslin looked at his work. Surprised he remembered so much. "'… thus in the winter stands the lonely tree'… that's what you wanted, isn't it? You're inspiring me like some sort of southern Madonna." His scrawl grew larger as he hurried to finish. "Here you go."

He looked up. She stood close by his side, the firm stalk of her body blocking his vision. Light blonde down swept up from her panties. Her nipples firm in the half bra. She sipped from her beer then licked her lips. "Read it to me. Read it to me like you did that night."

Breslin stared a long moment. There was stillness in his eyes, in his whole countenance, that could have been adoration. His lips moved slowly like a priest cherishing a favorite incantation. The words came from memory: "'What lips my lips have kissed and where and why/ I have forgotten and what arms have lain/ Under my head till morning…'"

He turned away from Terri to sip his beer and didn't look back at her. He concentrated on the penciled words across the rough paper bag. "This ain't a hundred percent, but it's close enough for government work. 'But the rain is full of ghosts tonight who tap and sign/ Upon the glass and listen for reply…'" Slowly, in rhythm to his words, Terri gently rubbed his neck and shoulders. '… but in my heart there stirs a quiet pain/ For unremembered lads who not again will/ Turn to me at midnight with a cry…'"

"That's so beautiful." Her warm stomach pressed against his shoulder, her scent penetrated his mind and filled him with a unique experience like a slow beautiful dream he wanted to last forever.

"'Thus in the winter stands the lonely tree/ And birds have vanished one by one/ Yet knows its boughs more silent than before…' He looked up at Teri and recited from memory. '… I can not say what loves have come and gone/ I only know that summer sang in me/ A little while, that in me sings no more.'"

Terri pulled Breslin tight against her pelvis. He leaned to kiss her through her panties. She lifted herself to feel his lips on her soft flesh. Like a hungry snake, his tongue searched and licked. From behind, he pulled her thighs apart, his fingers slipping inside her panties to feel her wetness. He wanted to reach far inside her with his tongue.

She pushed his head back. "Fuck me." A request. No, a plea.

Breslin rose and wrapped his arms around her. Their mouths combined. She reached to touch him and found softness. Her suddenly motionless hand made him lean back. He waited for her mockery. Terri pulled him close and whispered in his ear, "What's wrong?"

"Terri, I'm the lonely tree. The girl in Bryn Mawr never worked. It's a lie. Make it hard. For once, make it hard." His request almost a prayer.

She didn't hesitate; she devoured his prick through his jeans as her hands fought the buttons. Breslin balanced himself against the sink and silently prayed to the Blessed Virgin to finally give him the strength or whatever he needed to succeed with a woman.

Desire subdued his plea as she lavished herself on him. To his amazement, a rock-solid erection appeared.

Terri came up to him and turned him so she could half-sit against the sink. She placed him inside and clung to his neck. He grabbed her buttocks, feeling her juice run into his fingers. He felt no weight, only her motion, as they worked against one another. With gentle words, she asked for the poem.

Breslin repeated the lines, forgetting, retracing, hurrying, slowing, stalling.

"Faster," she pleaded, "say it faster."

His words rushed to keep time with her frenzy. Her body became his. He bent her backwards, forcing her down as if trying to push her through the sink. She clung to his neck tight enough to hurt.

Breslin lost himself. "*Ave Maria. Gratia plena et benedictus fructus ventris tui...*"

Her wet body urged him on, strained for him to feed her every ounce of semen as if her heart was parched. He did. His joy a series of spasms.

They held each other in their fierce embrace until Breslin relaxed and spoke, his words punctured by his heavy breathing. "The sky turned pale," he said, "and I saw the midnight sun. It was Terri. You."

She rubbed against him. Her tongue delicately touching an ear, his lips, his neck.

"I want to tell you this. I want you to hold me tight when I say it. Like this. Put your lips to my ear like mine to yours." She obeyed and her hand caressed his crew cut.

"Tonight, when I looked up at you I saw the same woman I saw every morning, morning after morning, in the college chapel. She has her own alcove and I used to kneel there for long minutes, maybe longer, praying for her to help me the way I prayed to you just then. Somehow, she never did. Up on the pedestal she stood like an unsolvable mystery, a barrier, a mother superior between me and all the girls I knew. I prayed. Goddamn, I prayed to make it work..."

Terri stared into his eyes looking for the sign of a joke. All she saw was glistening joy.

"...to feel the wonder of being in a woman. It never worked until tonight." He gently kissed her on the lips. "Thank you. In your own way, you are the statue who made my wish come true. You're a real Madonna."

Terri edged back. "Y'all like your poem. Beautiful."

Breslin stepped away and nearly tripped over his Levis and shorts around his ankles. She caught him. They laughed and slowly extracted themselves. Terri boosted herself onto the edge of the sink and picked her panties off her foot. She slipped off the sink, clasped the panties in her hand, closed her robe and announced, "I'll be right back."

Breslin did not adjust his Levis. He leaned over the sink, resting on his elbows, to absorb the wonderful feeling of exhaustion. "Guardian Angel, thank you." With that, he pulled up his Levis and went to the refrigerator for a beer.

A few minutes later, Patterson clambered up the wooden stairs with beer and a bottle of wine. He passed Christian sleeping on the couch and found Breslin seated at the kitchen table in his T-shirt. On the radio, Tony Bennett vowed to not cry anymore.

Patterson stocked the refrigerator with beer while describing the street atmosphere. "I mean, I'm fucked up, but I ain't nearly as bad as some of the cats I just seen. Combat Alley looks like fuckin' D-Day. Cops. Pees. Sirens. All kinds of crazy shit goin' on." He dropped three decks of cigarettes on the table.

Terri, her wet hair in a towel and her robe closed, came in. She opened a pack of Marlboros.

"I had to sit and watch eight assholes...guys...try to unhook two cars stuck together before I could get out of my parkin' spot at the Red, White, and Blue." He opened three cans of cold beer with the church key and passed them around.

Breslin took a long, long swallow and said, "I hope to tell you I'm drunk. I belong out on the street, dancing on car roofs. Posterity should record I never felt better in my life."

"I love the way y'all talk," said Terri. She put her hand on Breslin's.

Patterson didn't miss her look or touch as he lit a Lucky. So what? *So what if something happened between them? No one owned her. Not even Johnny Starr.* Maybe that's why he suggested they get a tattoo.

Breslin stood up. "Willie...Bill. That's a hell of a idea."

Ten minutes later, they were on their way in the Plymouth coupe. Breslin in the cramped backseat and Terri with Christian on her lap in the front. On the way, Breslin kept singing love ballads and inserting Terri's name like "Terri by Starlight" instead of 'Stella' and 'Terri' instead of "Laura." And again they invited Terri to join them in Key West.

Arriving at Sailor Eddie's, the inexplicable happened. On a payday night, Sailor Eddie's was closed. No matter how hard Breslin knocked no light came on. "I want those fucking Wings, Eddie! Open up you son-of-a-bitch!" Breslin seemed obsessed.

Patterson called him to leave. "No, man. I want those Wings! Tonight! Now!"

Patterson took his arm and tried to lead him away. Breslin pulled away and pinned Patterson against the coupe. "Let me go, you fucker! You don't understand!"

Terri interceded. She used Christian as an excuse for them to go home.

Breslin sat in the back mumbling he wanted Wings; it was the perfect night to get them. By the time they reached Terri's, Breslin slept heavily in the rear seat among empty beer cans. Terri wanted to wake him, but Patterson stopped her. He carried Christian up the stairs to the couch and, without any talking, they went to the bedroom where they bumped into one another in the darkness and fell on the bed. There was little tenderness. Their clothes quickly disappeared. Terri went at Patterson, showing him the way, using her body to take as much of him as she could. The alcohol gave him confidence and he didn't hold back. There was time to feel every moment and he learned how it really was, not with a smoke in a shack.

That was his last thought until a ringing phone woke him up. He was in bed with Terri and Christian.

"Hello." Terri's pleasant voice contrasted with his headache and body offal. Terri told someone...Johnny Starr, guessed Patterson...she'd make him breakfast. Time to chogie.

Patterson walked out with the sheet around him to find Breslin in the kitchen with a beer and cigarette. He lifted the can. "Breakfast of champions."

Patterson took the offered can and forced down the cold liquid. "My head's gonna be worse if we're here when Starr arrives. I'm getting dressed A-SAP."

Terri, in her robe, entered and was all business. "Y'all take every beer can from here that ain't his." She emptied ashtrays in the paper bag carrying Breslin's copy of Millay's sonnet. Terri scrubbed the table and counter as they carried out the trash. Her sense of panic still hadn't subsided as they were leaving.

Breslin, in the doorway, said, "If he's a problem, Terri, tell Banuelous and we'll back you up."

"And the Key West offer still stands," added Patterson.

Christian stood on the outside landing and watched them drive away.

Sunday morning neared noon.

They were half-drunk, stretched out on the warm grass by the small creek in downtown Cross Creek Park, drinking wine from paper cups and discussing their futures.

Breslin asked why stop at Key West. Why not go farther? Virgin Islands. Cuba?

"There's no place called that," challenged Patterson.

"Willie, the Virgin Islands are..."

"Bill."

"... in the Caribbean. St. Thomas. Supposed to be a really cool place."

Patterson wasn't ready to give up on Key West. He stared at the blue sky and flipped away his smoke. "We'll stick to Key West first and reconnoiter the other shit."

The paper cups had become soggy. They crunched them up and tossed them into the bushes. The bottle went back and forth. "Hey, before we go anywhere I want you to know something," said Breslin.

Patterson chuckled at his pal's sudden seriousness. "Like what?"

"I know you dig Terri and all..."

"You fucked her." Patterson tried to make shapes of the overhead clouds. He heard Breslin sit up. "How'd you know?"

Patterson sat up and pulled the bottle out of Breslin's hand. "I may be a dumb fuckin' cat who don't know about the Virgin Islands and never been to college, but I know you fucked her last night, you fuckin' Jap bastard."

Breslin saw Patterson's smile. Paused. "You know what you don't know?"

"What's that?"

"That's the first time I got laid."

"And a pig's ass ain't pork." Patterson rolled to his side and took a fresh cigarette out of the pack on the grass. He slid the '04 lighter from his jeans and looked at Breslin as he lit up. "You're grim, man. You must be serious."

"It's not like I never had a chance before. It just never worked before. She made it happen. Maybe it never worked because of religion or my *cojones* not operating up to specs. I don't know, but it worked last night with the lights on and the radio going. Like, I didn't know if I should laugh or cry I felt so good. So fucking happy, Jim, as our pal Tommy would say. You know, it was even better than my first communion."

"You fooled me with all your jive talk. I thought you were above it."

"Don't bust balls."

Patterson sipped and passed the bottle back. "It was really my first time too. With a white girl. That shit with Sidney and the spooks was bad. I get the creeps thinkin' about it sometimes."

"She's a smooth lady. We're lucky."

Breslin literally poured some wine into his mouth and said, "Bill, she made a miracle happen. It was a miracle. That's why I wanted the tattoo. I wanted to remember it forever and, you know, you have to give her credit."

"For what?" Patterson held the bottle.

"She's got impeccable taste. She banged both of us."

He toasted the bottle and sipped. "Fuckin'-A-well told, Jim."

Breslin stretched out on the grass and opened his shirt to the sun. "And you know what else?"

"What?"

"We need a case of cold soldiers, a bottle of Catawba, and Terri—and do it all over again."

Patterson took a quick sip and laid down, placing the bottle between them. He smoked and said, "This time you go for the beer."

"I hear you, Jim. And next time we get the Wings."

Patterson felt drowsy in the warm afternoon. Overhead, the small puffy white clouds looked pasted in the blue sky. Breslin repeated, "Next time we get Wings."

"I'm hip, Jim," whispered Patterson now spread-eagled in the sun. "Key West," he said to no one.

Chapter 16

The spring pay jump flight wasn't supposed to be rough.

A scorching day created air pockets, which lifted and dropped the droning machines navigating their way through the sky's invisible currents. What made the flight even worse were the Air National Guard crews flying to build up their flight pay. They lacked the experience of formation flying like the regular crews, so instead of a quick beeline to the DZ after an hour aloft, the formation stayed airborne another two hours, flying beyond Nag's Head on the coast and then banking for the run to Bragg's Drop Zone Normandy.

In every aircraft there was always a first man, sometimes a veteran, to get sick. Once one man started, the others—infected by the sounds and smells—followed. By the time they passed the coastline on the outbound leg, half the jumpers were vomiting and the other half waited to join them in the rocking and dropping Flying Coffins. And the ride never smoothed out.

"Get ready!"

Almost simultaneously in each aircraft, the jumpmasters extended out their arms, palms up, to alert those in the rear of the chalks who could not hear. In each aircraft, four chalks of men, two sticks on each side, held up their static line fasteners and looked at the jumpmasters while trying to adjust into a position from which they could rise.

Slowly, the jumpmasters raised their extended arms to command, "Stand up!"

Because it was both a Hollywood jump and a pay jump, the planes were jammed. Men struggled up from their pull-down canvas seats. Sudden air pockets sent them bumping forward and back into one another. Burp bags dropped, the contents flooding across metallic decks. Some men continued throwing up, spewing on the deck and splattering those around them.

"Hook up!" ordered the jumpmasters with a high hooking motion of their arms. The static line fasteners clipped onto the anchor line cables. Finally, the jumpers had support.

The command came: "Sound off for equipment check!" Many men on the planes, bouncing with the planes' motions, waved off the equipment check. Everyone just wanted to get out the door.

"Twenty-three OK!" shouted the last man in the first stick and slapped the buttocks of the man in front of him. The sounds of a number, an OK, and butt slaps ran from forward to aft in every plane.

Red command lights glowed in aft door panels. The troops began the ritual tugging on the static line cables as they rode the bucking aircraft, shouting they wanted out. Now. The vocal demands nearly drowned out the powerful engines.

"Stand in the door!" The first two men in every stick swung into door positions. Behind them, the impatient chalks squeezed forward. Some men slipped on the messy decks, fell and quickly stood up, worried they'd be trampled if the green lights came on. The jumpmasters swayed with the aircrafts' motion, staring at the red lights, making sure the men in the doors watched the lights, too.

Red. Red. Red. Waiting. Red. Red. Red.

Crew chiefs, wearing headsets to communicate with the cockpits, stuck the thumbs-up signal simultaneously with the green light igniting. "Go!" shouted the jumpmasters.

And like bubbles rising from a popped champagne magnum, the men surged out, static lines cracking whip-like in the heavy blast.

In the headquarters plane, Patterson and Breslin were the last two men in the opposite chalks and allowed some space to open in front of them as they slowly shuffled toward the doors. "Now," called Patterson, and they did a clumsy race to the doors. Lt. Margolin, the assistant jumpmaster, saw them running towards him. He gave them a sharp MP type across-the-chest hand salute that indicated, 'move on smartly.' They didn't hesitate; both went out with tight body positions. Gone.

In seven seconds, the aircraft emptied except for pilots in the cockpits, jumpmasters, and the Air Force crew chiefs.

Below, and miles behind them, 600 parachutes opened like green blossoms carrying their human seeds to earth. The paratroopers landed almost in the order they left the planes. The lack of ground breeze allowed many of the veteran jumpers to make standing landings. Once on the ground, each jumper undid his harness and rolled up the chute from the apex down, folded it, and stuffed it into the kit bag that was always carried behind the chest quick-release button. Reserve chutes were hooked to the kit bag handles. Men then shouldered their burdens and humped across the hot sandy soil of Normandy to the assembly point where trucks and spectators waited. The troops gathered in small groups, sitting on their bags, smoking, thirsty if they hadn't filled their canteens, rehashing the jump, particularly the rough conditions in the aircraft. No one was sick now.

Inside the Flying Boxcar, acting jumpmaster Lt. Margolin and Shellum, the Air Force sergeant crew chief, hauled in static lines at separate doors. At the end of each line, the chute deployment bag—a light piece of canvas that protected the packed chute—flapped in the engine blast. The bags and lines usually tangled up making it difficult to pull them all at once.

At the last minute, the lieutenant had switched with Wisnewski to act as assistant jumpmaster. He was working on earning his senior jump wings and needed in-flight time. Except for so many men being airsick, the jump had gone well. He especially enjoyed First Sgt. Billy Martin's queasy condition. Margolin had most of the lines from his chalk retrieved when Shellum tapped him on the shoulder and hollered over the engine noise, "I need some help, sir!"

The crew chief gestured the lines were too heavy for him to pull in himself. Together, they grasped about eight lines and began the tug of war against the powerful thrust of the engines. After straining a moment, the crew chief tapped Margolin and shouted he thought the bags might be stuck on the tail. He'd take a look. The lieutenant held him by his web belt as he leaned out the door. Like the lieutenant, he wore a B-12 chute. The blast blew up his collar and pulled his shirt out from his waist. He did not look long.

The sergeant pushed himself back into the plane hard enough to almost knock over Margolin. He fought to keep his balance while looking at Margolin with eyes that had seen horror. "Someone's out there! Hung up!" He pulled away from the lieutenant and reached for his headset.

Margolin dropped on the sticky deck and inched his head and shoulders out the door, his ears stunned by the engines roar, and the hot exhaust on his face and arm felt like a series of blows. Behind the plane, entangled in a swirling pack of deployment bags, was a body. A man. Someone.

Margolin stared, frozen in disbelief, but knew it was real. He blocked out the noise and wind and willed the man to be alive. *Did I see an arm move?* He did.

The man attempted to reach over his head to the static line. "He's alive!" Margolin rolled back into the plane. "He's alive!" He stood up to stare in the face of the pilot—a captain wearing sunglasses and a unit baseball cap.

The captain, cap in hand, checked out the man while the crew chief held his belt. The pilot's sunglasses were too tight to be blown off. 400 hundred yards to port, a fellow C-119 dropped toward them for a visual. The captain pushed himself back inside.

Margolin told him they would pull the man back in. Working together they could. "Just slow down the plane."

The captain's hand extended toward Margolin in a halting gesture. "Lieutenant, this is my aircraft. I'll give the orders."

The officer's nametag on his gray flight suit read, 'Leeds.' The cool aviator sunglasses hid his eyes. "Yes, sir. Let's just pull him in."

The captain put on his hat and took the crew chief's headset. He instructed the co-pilot to reduce power to just above stall speed and shut down the port engine. "We have an emergency situation here. Continue doing squares within five miles of the DZ at two thousand feet. Contact Pope and Cherry Point and advise of our holding pattern, location, and sit-rep." The captain hung up the headset and went forward to dig out a B-12 chute from a storage locker.

The crew chief and Margolin continued pulling in individual deployment bags from both doors. They managed to clear all except the one which held the trapped body. When the captain joined them, they realized there was not enough room for all three men to work in the door. Only two men could pull, then the third joined once they had enough line to share. None of the men were exceptionally strong. They braced themselves in various positions around the door and fuselage and struggled against the slipstream, which remained powerful even though the engine had been shut down. Their combined effort brought a few feet of the 15-foot, half-inch nylon static line into the cabin.

They paused; each took a new grip while the others held on to the little gain they'd made.

"We can do it," coached Lieutenant Margolin as his gut tightened. Slowly, they dragged in more line, about five feet of the 15-foot line. They were exhausted.

The co-pilot jockeyed the aircraft through the thermals trying to keep an even keel. Since they were no longer in a formation, the flight smoothed out somewhat. Just past the South Carolina border, the C-119 on one engine gently banked and turned back toward the drop zone.

At the assembly point, the humid spring morning broke into a verbal squall of officers and NCOs descending on the men lounging against their kit bags. The troops were ordered into chalk formations immediately—if not sooner. Two three-quarter-ton trucks headed across Normandy to chase down stragglers.

There were gripes: "What's up their ass?" "Hurry up and wait." "Can't even stack a few zzzzzs." "They got their head up their ass."

Sgt. Wisnewski walked up and back along Patterson's stick with a manifest in his hand making sure people were in the correct place. "I want every man with his gear, not his buddy's, not off smokin' or pissin' somewhere. You ain't there when I come by you'll be explainin' it to First Sergeant Billy Martin when we get back to the company." The first sergeant had already returned to the company in a Jeep he had waiting.

The 50-man-plus sticks created 12 lines and a few leftovers. It was confusing there were so many non-coms counting and re-counting and shouting orders. Sgt. 'Ski started with the first man in Patterson's stick and asked each man to sound off. He reached Patterson and called out, "Twenty-three."

"Hup, sergeant." replied Patterson.

He repeated the process on the other chalk, starting with 'one.' When he called out 23, no one answered. He looked up and said, "Fertig?"

"Here, Sarge." Pfc. Fertig stood in the twenty slot.

"What in the hell you doin' standin' there? You too fuckin' dumb to count..."

"We switched. I went..."

"'You went', your dud ass. I told you stick order. No nothin' about switchin'. Get over here." 'Ski pointed to the 23rd spot, the end of the stick. Fertig dragged his kit bag to the end of the stick.

"Who'd you switch with?" asked Wisnewski.

"What's-his-name."

"Breslin," offered Patterson to assist the situation.

"He asked me, Sarge," offered Fertig quickly to avoid any blame.

'Ski looked at his manifest and looked up. "Breslin! Number twenty! Where the fuck are you?"

Banuelous said, "Probably waitin' for a ride on the DZ." Patterson and Banuelous laughed, both imagining Breslin sitting on his kit bag dreaming about cold beer and waiting for a ride to avoid the long hike.

Wisnewski looked at Banuelous like he wanted to say something, but he went to the small group of NCOs and junior officers waiting for results. Word came to make another headcount.

The men shifted around their kit bags. No one could go anywhere. They smoked in place and watched the energy of the NCOs. The count went quickly, except for the port stick of Patterson's plane. Sfc. Wisnewski and the new officer in the company, Second Lieutenant Yeager, went from the first man to the last, making sure each man was in his appropriate spot.

Again, there was no answer when 20 was called. They nodded to one another and finished their count.

Wisnewski looked at Patterson. "You see him on the plane, Willie?"

"He switched with Fertig to go out last with me. I went out the starboard side. He went out the other door."

"It's got to be him, sir," said Wisnewski.

Patterson said, "Him? What? Whadda you mean?" The two ranking soldiers walked away without answering Patterson.

He looked at Banuelous. "What the fuck's goin' on?"

"Beats me, Willie."

"Somethin's fucked up with Scott."

The order came to turn in their gear. An uneasy stillness and unusual efficiency made the turn-in go quickly as if the men were participating in a numbing ritual and not celebrating their successful jump.

Col. Steele appeared among the men, his boots and uniform dusty from the jump. Next to him were Sgt. Wisnewski and Lt. Yeager. They approached Patterson and Banuelous. Wisnewski said, "Here's Patterson, sir." Patterson came to a casual attention and started to salute.

"At ease, son. This man Breslin is a friend of yours?"

"Yes, sir."

"You're certain he was on the plane and jumped?"

"Yes, sir."

Steele looked around at the men watching. He put his hand on Patterson's shoulder. "We'll do the best we can to get him down, son." Steele and the others walked away.

Get him down? What in the fuck..."Jesus, he's hung up!" All Banuelous said was son-of-a-bitch and hitched his trousers.

Broomfield came up and told Patterson and Banuelous to ride back in the three-quarter-ton with him and Webster. The other men loaded in deuce-and-a-halves. A moment before the truck engines started someone hollered, "Here they come!" Every head turned toward the sky.

At the far end of Normandy, the C-119 appeared at 2,000 feet, barely visible at first, then growing larger, larger, until everyone saw the minute figure dangling in the slipstream.

"... that's all she wrote, Jim..."

"... Goddamn..."

"... Poor bastard ain't got a snowball's..."

"Hells bells," diagnosed company clerk Pfc. James Lee Hunter, "all they got to do is pull him in."

The body of the hanging man was not four feet from the door when they let go. The release was not intentional; the combined weight and drag of the man and a sudden pitch of the plane yanked the line from their hands. The captain let go first. Then the chief. Margolin couldn't hold on by himself. He let go or would have been pulled from the plane.

The lieutenant lay on the deck, head out the door, looking back at the man. The ache in his body had turned into a numbing weariness. His hands were rubbed raw. He pressed his face against cool steel and boosted himself up. There was no time to waste.

Without a word, the captain had gone forward.

"Where'd he go?" asked the lieutenant.

"Get the co-pilot. He's bigger."

Margolin thought they should have done that on the first try. If Wisnewski was there, he might have thought of that. Thought of something. "Do something even if it's wrong" was one of 'Ski's expressions. Margolin knew it was his turn to do something. He dropped to the deck and looked at the body. "We're gonna get your ass, soldier. We gonna get it or die trying." He wanted the words to pierce the man's mind like darts of assurance. He noticed the man's helmet had blown off.

The co-pilot joined them. He had no chute on. He wasn't much bigger than the captain, but beefier. He knelt by the door and shouted to Margolin, "I'm supposed to tell you it's Breslin!"

"Son-of-a-bitch." Margolin banged his palms on the deck and stood up. He gripped the metal frame of the door to keep from storming around the cabin and cursing. He pushed off and said, "Let's roll."

Again, they worked the nylon line down from the static line cable and took up positions at the door. They agreed they'd pull on three and hold on three. Margolin envied the Air Force men's gloves.

"One. Two. Three. Pull!"

"One. Two. Three. Hold it!"

They braced themselves and each took a moment to switch his grip. The slipstream didn't wane. Only the starboard engine operated, but the plane needed to maintain a specific speed to stay aloft which kept the slipstream strong.

"One. Two. Three. Pull!"

Margolin silently asked Breslin to stay alive.

The familiar jolt on Breslin's crotch and shoulders meant his chute had opened. He arched himself up to check the canopy, expecting to see the sweet, wide green nylon blocking out the sun. It wasn't there and he wasn't hanging softly in the risers.

He saw the twin tails overhead and the engines roar had not faded. He spun in the noxious blast, going in all directions at once. The pressure on his shoulders felt tight enough to stop his circulation. His static line was caught under the chute's harness at the shoulder. It would never deploy without taking off the harness. His reserve was attached to the harness, so he couldn't slip out of one chute and use the other. He'd simply fall.

He was stuck. Helpless.

In an effort to free himself he squirmed, kicked, and pulled at the harness, but nothing happened except the deployment bags from the other lines slapped him again and again, like some medieval punishment. He dangled, every ounce of energy drained from his struggle against the harness, eyes and nose stinging from the powerful exhausts of the Pratt and Whitney engines. He realized that by not moving, he had stabilized into a swaying motion as if floating on his back in the air. Riding and rocking in one position allowed him to evaluate what had happened. He kept his eyes shut to avoid the vicious exhaust and gained a little control by spreading out his arms and legs. Slowly, he went over his body part by part. He could not feel his feet or hands and was growing colder by the second. *Am I being pulled in? Am I just dreaming?*

More of the tail came into view. He was close enough to see the headless rivets and metal patches as the tail section widened. He was being pulled in.

Make it happen, God. Take me back inside. He'd do anything if God got him back in the plane. He would. He promised. He promised again. God can stop this. *Save me.*

A sudden sensation of falling and the harness straps pulling tighter emphasized he had fallen away. The wind ripped off his steel pot, cutting his nose, and the violent spinning started again. Slowly, using what little strength he had, he worked his arms and legs away from his body to regain the bizarre floating position.

"I'm cold." His words lost in the rushing wind.

"I'm cold," he cried out, trying to shout over the engine's roar.

He reached over his head to pull himself up the static line. His arm barely moved above his shoulder. He realized his body was quitting, his limbs cold and unfeeling. Only his mind worked as his body hung like a lure battered in a rushing mountain stream.

When he closed his eyes, Sister Xavier was telling him to say the Rosary. She stood right above him in her Dominican habit just like in seventh grade. He and his pals—Lombardi, Hogan, and Fitzsimmons—had been cruel to her kindness, and she had had a nervous breakdown. Now, here she was again, being kind. In times of trouble say a Rosary, Mr. Breslin.

Her wire-rim glasses reflected the classroom ceiling lights. She waited. When he opened his eyes, she vanished. "Sure, Sister." He laughed. He was too smart to pray. "I'm cold. Pull me up. Pull me back inside."

He shut his eyes. *Sure, Sister.*

"I believe in God, the Father almighty, Creator of heaven and earth, and in Jesus Christ, his only Son, our Lord, who was conceived by the..."

Her presence warmed him. Breslin kept his eyes closed; it helped shut out the engine's scream and stinging exhaust. *Recite the prayers*, he coached himself. *Pray like hell.* When he finished the Apostle's Creed, he silently said the Lord's Prayer and three Hail Marys. *Glory be to the Father, the Son, and the Holy Ghost. As it was in the beginning, is now and ever shall be, world without end, Amen.*

There was no question which of the Mysteries of the Rosary he'd recite. The Joyful ones. He didn't remind the Virgin Mary of his spiritual collateral of college chapel prayers and early morning Communions. He prayed, his fear rushing the internal words.

The Annunciation. *Our Father who art in heaven, hallowed be thy name. Thy kingdom come, Thy will be done on earth as it is in...*

Sometime among the Joyful Mysteries, he imagined himself being lifted again. His back felt like a strongman was kneeling on it while bending his arms and legs behind him.

He opened his eyes. The plane was close. So close. *Closer, Mary! Please, closer.*

So much nearer than last time. Near enough he might bang off the fuselage. *All the way, man. Pull me all the way in.* He didn't know if he was shouting or just imagining the demand.

He hung there. Swaying back and forth. He forced up his arm, surprised it moved. He twisted to look at the door and his body suddenly shifted and he turned face down. The ground below appeared motionless. By tilting back his head, he could see the door. Just a few yards away.

He screamed, "Pull! Pull your nuts off!" He dropped.

The 15-foot line caught him, but the harness no longer hurt. He was numb. Still on his stomach, he looked up and caught Lt. Margolin's stare as the officer laid with his head out the door. He realized the officer's helplessness. "Do it, sir! Please, do it! Don't give up!"

Margolin vanished from the doorway. That was it. He was buying the farm.

He shut his eyes and rolled over in his bunk to find Terri next to him, an enchantress, telling him her lips were like a warm and ruby chalice, as warm as a summer night. Her words passionate. What lips her lips have kissed and where and...

Wait, Terri. You're mixing the poem with the song. Beautiful Terri in her blue robe, hot against the sink. My midnight sun. My Virgin Mary.

The part he could never remember. *The winter tree. Thus in the winter stands the lonely tree...*

Margolin and the two Air Force men could no longer raise the body as close as the one time it came so close. Each attempt became unsuccessful faster. Margolin knew he had little strength left, and the others must have less. After they dropped him the fifth time, Margolin went to the cockpit and suggested flying low over one of Bragg's lakes and cutting him loose. "Set it up on the radio. Have men waiting."

The captain tapped the fuel gauge on his panel; it appeared to be on empty. "Fifteen or twenty minutes tops. Ten to fifteen airborne."

"We could try it."

"Going low like that then pulling out would eat up what little fuel we have. These crates don't maneuver like that. Too many trees."

"Goddamnit, try it! I'll go with him." Margolin pulled a Mae West from behind the co-pilot's seat. "I'll keep him up until someone gets us."

The pilot acted indecisively as if he might actually try it, then shook his head to himself and said, "Lieutenant, your concern is understood, but he's one man. I've got a U.S. government aircraft and five lives in my hands. This ship can't skim a lake, climb out, and make it to Pope."

The lieutenant did not follow his instinct to pull the captain from the seat and fly it himself. If he could have, he would have. Frustration clenched his body and mind. "What in the hell's the plan then?" The captain stared at the compass heading. "Sir, what's happening?"

The captain's jaw line tightened. "We're headed for Pope."

"With him hanging back there?"

"Get aft, lieutenant, and strap yourself in. We're landing on foam."

Margolin saw disaster, but held himself to a few calm words. A plea. "Sir, try the lake. Come in higher. Give that kid a shot."

The captain took off his sunglasses and faced Margolin who stood on the ladder between the two cockpit seats. "I want to give him a shot. I want to save him as much as you do. But planes don't fly without fuel, lieutenant. We'll be lucky to make Pope. Now strap in and let's get down."

Defeated. Margolin climbed down and walked toward the two Air Force men who lay on the deck. He checked with the co-pilot who confirmed what the captain had said.

The crew chief interrupted to advise the co-pilot he was needed forward.

Margolin paced the metal deck. He could not change the fuel situation or fly the plane. Wisnewski would have...an idea sprang up like a vision and it wasn't the lake. He asked the crew chief for his knife.

"What for?"

"I'm going to climb down the static line, tie a general-purpose strap around both of us, cut us loose, and pop the chute."

"You're fuckin' nuts, Lieutenant."

"Just give me the knife and don't tell Smilin' Jack up there."

The sergeant handed over his knife. "I got to tell him."

"Tell him after I start down. Tell him to take us up to five thousand feet, because we're gonna try one more time to pull him in."

Margolin took a GP strap from the canvas supply bag stowed in the gearbox in the cone-shaped tail section and furiously cut into the tough nylon. He produced a manageable line of seven feet. He wove the line through the B-12 harness across his chest. All he needed to do was take the strap's loose ends and wrap them around Breslin, tie them off, and cut the static line.

He stowed the knife in his boot. The crew chief offered his gloves. The comfort of the gloves made him believe it could be done. He sat in the doorway, legs out. The chief lifted the static line across his shoulder and squatted next to him. "One more time, sir; don't go."

"We got to give it our best shot, Sarge."

The young crewman shook his head and laid his hand on Margolin's shoulder for a moment. "Good luck."

Margolin wrapped his legs around the line and reached high to bring the line tight to his chest. With the crew chief holding his shoulders, he eased off the slight metal door edge.

The wind tore at him like a howling mob. He swung under the line. The slipstream demanded for him to let go and the B-12 felt like an anchor. It took all his strength to keep his legs around the line and hugged to his chest. He moved one hand down. Then the other. He moved his legs in unison. That took him a few feet from the plane. He moved one hand again. The other. He tried his legs and the wind pulled them off the line. For a second, he hung like a pennant in a breeze then fell away, somersaulting through the empty sky.

"D-ring." His voiced sounded loud in the suddenly quiet sky.

As he tumbled, he grasped the ring. For a moment he could not get his fingers in the handle; the gloves made it difficult. He panicked and forced his hand in and pulled hard. The folds of the chute rushed by him as he tumbled.

Wham. The opening jolt stopped him cold. His momentum carried his legs high above his head, then they swung down as he bobbed in the sky. He stared up at the canopy, then down. He wasn't more than 50 feet off the ground and headed for trees. He didn't care.

The soft tops of the pine trees broke his landing and caught the canopy. As he fell, he bounced hard against the thicker lower branches and ended up suspended about eight feet off the ground. He ignored the bruises and simply allowed himself to hang and wished he had thought of the lake sooner.

"It could've worked," he said aloud. "The lake could've worked."

The continuing radio broadcast over WFNC drew several hundred spectators to the Pope Air Force Base area. Air Police kept them outside the perimeter so they parked along the dirt roads near the runway approach area. In every company in the division, men crowded into day rooms listening to the broadcast. Without asking permission, Patterson took the three-quarter-ton supply truck. He didn't want any company or anyone to know where he went. By swinging through the back roads to the marshalling area, Patterson avoided Pope's front gate.

The marshalling area appeared deserted at first; however, when he pulled around the issuing shed to the briefing area, he saw the 82nd Division riggers in their red baseball caps lined along a raised embankment that paralleled the runway. Far down the runway, he saw the blinking lights of fire trucks headed in his direction. That must be where they would land.

He decided not to drive along the runway. Instead, he parked and started running along the asphalt apron toward the trucks. When he reached the first group of riggers he asked, "Seen the plane yet?"

"Nope," answered one of the men, his red baseball style cap with rigger wings and a radically curved bill almost hiding his eyes in true rigger cool. Patterson kept running.

The rigger nudged his buddy and they watched Patterson head away from them.

"Hey! You can't go out there!" It was the strong voice of an NCO.

Patterson ignored the challenge. He realized the fire trucks were spreading foam just as they did for emergency landings. The trucks turned around.

Two riggers chased after Patterson. Patterson guessed the plane had to touch down at the beginning of the runway and head toward him. He thought he was in the right place to be as close as possible. He stopped and looked for the aircraft.

The two riggers caught up Patterson. One of them said, "Hey, man. You best come back with us."

Patterson looked at them.. "Not yet. I've got a plane to meet." Patterson's expression signaled the two men not to push the issue.

They stood facing one another until they heard the engine. The sound was in the opposition direction from where Patterson had figured the plane would land. They turned to face east and watched the C-119 grow larger as it neared the runway. In the distance, it looked like a bird of prey with talons extended.

Then the plane dropped lower. Patterson realized it was going to land far past him where they were still spraying foam. *Damn, I should've kept the truck*. He ran. Ran hard. Taking long strides. The riggers watched the plane.

Patterson heard the plane catching up with him. He ran harder, pushing himself, his legs and his lungs, convincing himself it made no difference how much it hurt. The engine noise seemed to be inside his head. Pistons cracking. Props grasping the air. Still running, he looked over his shoulder. The plane passed him like he was a statue.

A single figure lay in the doorway. Drifting behind was a body oscillating in the wind. Breslin. Arms and legs spread.

Patterson stopped and stared, gasping, "He ain't got no pot on."

The aircraft left him far behind and blew great hunks of foam into swirling patterns of the prop blast. The reversing of the engine sent more foam into the air without any patterns and the plane was lost in the flying muck

"Holy fuck, Scott," Patterson gasped out the words he had been avoiding. "I should've checked your gear. I should've."

During the final downwind leg, at the last bank to start the approach somewhere under 1,000 feet, Breslin regained consciousness and heard himself saying the words of the Mass. His voice drowned out the engine's racket. The sky, trees on the horizon, the tail were all visible, but he saw

himself inside the dark morning chapel at LaSalle. *Dominus vobiscum. Et cum spiritu to. Oremus.*

Mass in the warm winter chapel had been wonderful. Quiet. Simple. He always felt like singing the Latin. When he was younger, before college, he had dreamed of someday singing the High Mass the way he watched it performed every Christmas and Easter. The smell of incense made the ceremonies exotic. He smelled it now, deep in his mind. He kept his eyes closed to appreciate the rich red and white vestments.

Kyrie eleison. Christe eleison. Kyrie eleison.

Christe eleison. Kyrie eleison. Christe eleison.

The words were beautiful. He should have paid better attention to his Latin lessons. *Corpus tuum, Domie, quod sumpsi, et Sanguis, quem potavi, adhaereat visceribus meis. Miserere mei...He who lives and reigns forever and ever, amen. The Lamb of God who takes away the sins of...*

The words changed. New words intruded. Strange and dominating. Unfamiliar. Words no longer his.

The Mass disappeared. The ceremony gone. The emptiness filled with a single powerful voice. "...*My Lord, He calls me/ He calls me by the thunder/ The trumpet...*"

Breslin knew the words. They were red and black like jagged cracks in a blood red atmosphere. He recalled the words and knew someone was coming for him. He became the congregation in the spotless chapel. Floor buffed to a dark warm glow. The pews waxed. And he knelt in prayer enthralled with the voice of the gospel radio preacher.

"*... sounds within my soul/ I ain't got long to stay here...*"

The crew chief cut the body loose as soon as the landing gear touched down and the engines reversed. The moment he sliced the line, the body disappeared into the foam at more than 90 miles an hour. Men from the rescue vehicles waded into the foam, lifting their legs high and moving as quickly as they could, searching. A man raised his hand and waved. The ambulance, the Air Force runway Jeep with the checked yellow flags, and a rescue truck plowed through the soft covering that hid their wheels toward the raised hand while men on foot forced their way through the foam to the spot. Then everyone stopped.

Some men turned away.

Chapter 17

Every Saturday morning after uniform and rifle inspection in ranks, there is a wall and footlocker inspection. If a man fails any of the inspections he is restricted to the barracks for the remainder of the day, and if he fails to a greater degree, he pulls KP for the rest of the day. This is known as motivation.

A footlocker is the enlisted man's personal security locker in a squad bay of 30 to 40 soldiers. It has a single rugged hasp that locks with either a key or combination lock purchased at the PX. The bottom depths of the locker are a man's refuge for personal items: letters from home, photos of girlfriends and family, money, valuables like cuff links and watches, civilian clothing, cigarettes, girlie magazines, cans of Brasso and contraband items like liquor, pilfered cans of motor pool oil, brass knuckles, knives, and maybe, a pistol.

Usually, what the inspecting team sees is the two-compartment top shelf lifted against the locker lid and the first six inches of the bottom where winter and summer underwear is aligned by pinning it on measured cardboard cutouts. Each top shelf compartment has a small barber's towel tightly stretched across the surface and thumb tacked in each corner. In the left hand section, there is a deodorant can, a soap dish with wrapped soap bar inside, cheap aftershave, razor with blades, comb, toothbrush with unused toothpaste, and a handkerchief with the correct laundry mark. The right side holds six pairs of rolled field socks, a pristine can of Kiwi black shoe polish, a shoe brush, a small sewing kit, and the paperback *Those Devils In Baggy Pants* by Ross Carter. There are also two highly polished collar brass insignia: U.S. Army and the crossed rifles of the infantry.

All laid out in a specific formation: centered and aligned.

With the exception of the shoe brush, none of the items are ever used. It is all show and to prevent a soldier from having an excuse for not shining his boots, not washing, needing a shave, not having clean socks, missing a button, and so on.

To keep everything clean and in place, a trooper simply covers the top tray with a towel and drops his smokes, lighter, watch, wallet, change, dog tags, shaving kit, and other daily junk onto the towel. For inspections he simply lifts out the towel and stashes it in the laundry bag tied on the end of his bunk. With a few quick adjustments, the footlocker is ready for inspection.

And then there's the wall locker...

Lieutenant Margolin gave up handball after Breslin died. He replaced exercise with cigarettes and drinking with the other junior officers at the 82nd Airborne Division Officers' Club. They often started early on Wednesday afternoons. Sometimes Thursdays. Always there for the Friday Happy Hour when the prices of beer dipped to a quarter and scotch and water cost 40 cents.

Capt. Melby questioned his sudden interest in hanging around with the boys, as she called them.

Margolin knew and didn't know. He had become one of them. Accepted. Liked. A hero among them for the Soldier's Medal he received for his futile effort to save Breslin.

He had accompanied the coffin home to Narberth, Pennsylvania on a C-130 and paid his respects to Breslin's parents and family. He did not attend the funeral nor did any other Airborne soldiers. It was kept as a simple family affair. The medal came out of the blue. A phone call from the Regimental Sergeant Major notified him and advised, "Colonel Steele put you in for special recognition." He smiled at the news and how he and Steele had become friendly since their O club battle. Sometimes Steele even called him Mad Dog. The ceremony was performed at Regimental Headquarters two weeks after the accident. Too short a notice to invite his parents. Thank God.

His mother would have been hysterical learning he had climbed out of the plane.

Margolin knew he really wasn't one of the boys, because he could not put Breslin's death to rest by simply acknowledging it was something that happened to paratroopers. In the club, he saw pleasure in the faces of the men, because the publicized notoriety of Breslin's death made their act of jumping braver, more hazardous, perhaps glamorous. They seemed to reward themselves with Breslin's death, and—including Margolin—they subconsciously knew their activity said, "Look at us. We have the balls to face death."

Feeling that way did not make Lt. Margolin proud, but he did feel something. A feeling he admitted to Capt. Melby as they lay in her bed in the Medical Officer's housing.

"I have to confess getting that medal for trying to save Breslin justified every decent and fair act I have beaten myself up about for not being tougher. It makes me as good as any man. A person willing to sacrifice..."

Melby shushed him with a finger on his lips. "Sy, the more I know you the more I see what a good man you are. A decent person. You never needed a medal to prove that."

He sipped some beer from the pilsner glass on the night table. "I think I did."

They had made love in the dark bedroom. Since the first night at the Officers' Club they had been together often. There were no attachments between them, except they liked each other's company and listened to one another. He helped the captain avoid her married lover.

"Sy, it was just an accident. Don't make more out of it."

"By trying to save him, I did make more out of it. And you know..."

"Here we go. You worry about it."

"No. No. Listen, I've been thinking about this for a long time, even before the accident. It might be the most worthwhile thing a man can do." He sipped and lit a cigarette.

Melby elbowed him. "Lieutenant, I'm ordering you to tell me what in the hell you're talking about."

He smiled and reached. "Like you order me to pull off your panties."

She slapped his hand. "In your wildest dreams. Tell me what you're talking about."

"I'm staying in."

"Staying?"

"Staying in the Army."

"The Army. The paratroopers?" She covered herself with the sheet and boosted herself up on her elbow, staring in his face, searching for the joke. "You're not kidding." He shook his head no. "Sy, you don't belong in the military. You're too...you're pulling my leg."

He reached and rubbed her thigh and moved his hand to her center. "Your lovely leg and I'm not."

He explained his logic for staying in. He wasn't gung-ho or a rules and regulations type. He would stay in to protect the troops from the system. Keep the Breslins and the other enlisted men safe and sane from the Steeles and the Martins. Instead of demoting a man—like he had done to Patterson—now he would stand up for the man. He could be a military lawyer. The Judge Advocate Corps needed men like him, individuals from infantry regiments who understood the troops. He enjoyed being an officer, being lean and mean, regardless of the few extra pounds he recently gained. It was better than his family's plan of being a coleslaw advocate for his Uncle Ziggy. As an officer, he looked at himself as a benevolent dictator.

"Sy, I thought you were crazy when you went after the colonel. Now I know you are. Mad Dog Margolin, the enlisted man's savior. The Airborne Messiah." Melby laughed and kissed his cheek.

"It gets funnier, Connie. Before anything, I'm going to Ranger school."

She pulled away. "Oh, no. Don't do that." She held his hand to her mouth and softly kissed his fingers. "I know your intentions are good, but don't do it. You're forgetting the Army's a machine designed to kill. You can be a military lawyer and a military anything, but at some point in your career you may be in so deep you'll have to kill. Don't do it."

He pulled her closer and said, "Did I ever tell you what a *schmuck* is? I have an uncle in the Valley in Los Angeles…"

Patterson returned from his leave early. He really hadn't wanted to go on leave, but Margolin and Sfc. Webster suggested it, so he could get away from the grimness of Breslin's death. After packing up Breslin's personal gear, he was glad to get away. Still, all the time at home he moped around, wishing he and Breslin were still planning a Key West adventure. The icy silence between him and his parents grew as they slowly realized he could not be dictated to. He had grown up and talked differently and drank too much. His failure to check Breslin's static line outweighed anything his parents berated him about. Breslin hadn't checked it either. They were still half drunk from the weekend with Terri. How could his parents understand what happened?

They warned him he was headed for trouble; his city job might not be waiting for him when he returned which wasn't long now. Five months and change.

"Do you think I'm going to spend the rest of my life in the city yard?" he asked.

What was wrong with that? It was secure and he could retire early.

"But I'll never wear leather shit on my wrists."

His parents looked at one another. What had happened to their son?

He didn't drive the coupe around his hometown. He preferred walking to the bars and then coming home on the boardwalk where he could smell the night ocean and imagine life in Key West.

There wasn't anyone at home he could relate to. It was almost a relief to return to Bragg so he could face his final months in the service.

Patterson kept close to the company the first few weeks back. He drank beer in the supply room at night with Webster and other NCOs who told stories about WWII and Korea. Webster advised him he wasn't at fault in not checking his buddy's static line. Others missed it too. "Young William, you weren't even in Mr. Breslin's chalk. Don't carry a weight like that. It can become rather burdensome."

To avoid the atmosphere in the squad bay, he slept on a mattress on the supply room floor and used the squad bay just to clean up and change uniforms.

Finally, after payday, Patterson drove to town and went by Terri's place. The Pontiac parked outside with a Bragg enlisted sticker on the bumper had to be Starr's. The car was as good as a locked door. He chose to visit the Canopy; then, fortified by three tall boys, he went to the Carousel. Terri wasn't working. "She's off," said one of the girls. He didn't leave a message.

The following weekend he went by again. The car was there and she wasn't working. He felt uncomfortable going on his own. Breslin should be with him. But he wasn't. Goddamn, son-of-a-bitch, he wasn't.

His turns at KP and guard duty came with the usual punctuality. The assignments didn't bother him; he was just killing time and dulling the pain of not catching the static line trapped under Breslin's shoulder harness. Each day and night, like the invisible momentum of a deep riptide, carried him closer to his September discharge date.

"…y'all must be lost, boy…"

Patterson had gone to the squad bay for a pack of Luckies and to brush his teeth after noon chow. When he walked in he heard the words, their tone sounded like trouble.

"…I sure hope y'all didn't come through the front door…"

Patterson continued toward his bunk. He'd get his toothbrush and mind his own business. After all, he was nearly a short timer.

"Don't push me!" A frightened voice.

Patterson stopped at his footlocker. What the hell…even if Breslin wasn't there, he had to check it out. Yellow-winged butterflies exploded in his stomach as he walked toward the group of men near the end of the squad bay.

In their midst was a short, soft-looking, sweaty young Negro whose unfaded nametag on new fatigues read 'Fairley.' No Wings and no jump boots. A real new guy with his eyes popping out of his head. His pristine duffel bag lay on a bottom empty bunk.

"Push y'all. Y'all must've slipped, boy," said Sonny Williamson, a tall lean Pfc.

"What's happenin'?" asked Patterson. Like a well-rehearsed chorus line, every man looked at him.

"None of your goddamn Yankee business," challenged Williamson with his long finger from his long arm aimed at Patterson like a lance.

Patterson's knees were not sturdy. "You OK?" he asked the new man, ignoring the obvious. Fairley explained that the first sergeant told him to take any empty bunk in the squad bay.

Pfc. James Lee Hunter stepped up next to Williamson and said to Patterson, "Your head's gonna look like a stomped cantaloupe if y'all don't move out smartly."

Patterson swung his arms back and forth and his leg shifted in preparation for the rush. He tried to gaze calmly at his antagonists, but he only managed to look at two of them, neither Williamson or Hunter. "You guys should let him alone, that's all I'm sayin'." He walked away feeling weaker than if he had stayed.

"Best thing y'all ever did, Yankee trash!" called Williamson.

Patterson stopped. Turned. "Let him alone! Let him be. Look at you. Four to one."

Williamson walked toward Patterson. "Y'all don't hear too good do you, Yankee."

Patterson knew Williamson from many trips on supply room errands in a two-and-a-half-ton truck. "I didn't know we were enemies, Sonny."

"Fuck him, Sonny Boy," said one of the others, a man named Clarke who had replaced Mangiameli in the motor pool dispatch shack. Oddly enough, he had Mangiameli's complexion.

Patterson stepped beyond Williamson's long reach. "You cats are wrong. All wrong."

Hunter, the first sergeant's favorite, said, "That's the way the cookie crumbles, Patterson."

Where it came from he didn't know. It might have been Hunter's high voice and accent that sounded so much like the first sergeant's. Maybe it was the frustration of not having Breslin to give him perspective, but he slipped past Williamson and attacked Hunter, swinging like a wild man, driving Hunter into a crouch. Patterson's punches fell on his shoulders and head. "Let him alone you fuckin' cracker! Let him alone!"

It took only a moment for Williamson to grab Patterson from behind and pull him off Hunter.

A red-faced Pfc. James Lee Hunter rose to the demands of his pals to let Patterson have it. Patterson, trapped in Williamson's bear hug, twisted and weaved as well as he could to avoid Hunter's punches. He took a fist to the side of his head and one in the mouth. Hunter said, "Coon lover."

Before Hunter threw another punch, Patterson and Williamson were pushed across the squad bay. Standing in front of the breathless Pfc. James Lee Hunter was Corporal Marcus Broomfield, one hand holding his fatigue shirt over his shoulder.

"Did y'all say somethin' 'bout a coon, PFC.?" Williamson released Patterson as if he had burnt his hands.

Patterson's mouth hurt, but he didn't care. He was just glad to see Broomfield. There was dead silence as everyone waited for Broomfield to destroy Hunter.

The corporal stepped up and pushed Hunter backwards, then took three steps to Williamson and pushed him backwards, hitting him hard in the chest, into an upper bunk. "What about coons? Hit me. Both of you. Two on one. That's how y'all like it."

Hunter, hoping his status as company clerk carried leverage, tried, "Hey, Broom. We were just kiddin' around."

"So am I." He shoved Hunter again and pulled Williamson away from the bunk and pushed him next to Hunter. "See, I'm smilin'. And it's *Corporal* Broomfield." Patterson finally appreciated military protocol.

Broomfield turned to the new man, Fairley. "They hit you?"

Fairley was still scared—he saw himself as the source of trouble and had no inkling who Broomfield was and how long he'd be around. He claimed they hadn't hit him; he just wanted to find a bunk.

"You take anyone you want, recruit. Hunter, which one's yours?"

"Hey, Broom, come on. We were just doin' some new guy harassment." Hunter's tone invited Broomfield to let him alone.

"Corporal Broomfield. And what were y'all doin' to Patterson?"

No answer. Broomfield asked again where Hunter bunked.

"I got a room down the hall."

Broomfield wasn't fazed. "Too far. Williamson, where's your bunk?" Williamson pointed to the upper, two bunks over. He was glad to sacrifice it instead of his body.

Broomfield walked over and pulled off the bedding. "You two. Where're your racks?"

Clarke and the other man showed him. The corporal pulled their bedding off also. He turned to Fairley. "Recruit, take any one you want. Isn't that right, troop?" Everyone agreed.

"See," acknowledged Broomfield, "southern hospitality."

Fairley preferred to stay where he had placed his duffel bag originally. Broomfield put his hand on his shoulder and invited him to the supply room for sheets and blankets. "Willie and me are always there," he assured him. "Count on it." He looked at the silent four men. "Now, let's talk about Patterson."

"That's my beef, Broom. Let me worry about it." Patterson loved brute power and regreted he had none.

Broomfield went to Williamson and stood inches from the taller man's chin. He stood on his toes to get closer as if to bite him. "Willie P's my friend. No one messes with my friends. If they do they better be ready for me. If any of you white trash ever give that new man or Patterson any crap y'all best be movin' to Alaska, 'cause you know I'll be comin' 'long side your head. You dig, moatengator?" Broomfield said moatengator slowly.

Williamson nodded in agreement, as did everyone else.

"I can't hear you."

"Yes."

"Yes, what?"

"Yes, Corporal Broomfield."

Finally, Broomfield smiled and stepped back from Williamson. "Boy, y'all ain't got a hair on your backside, do you?

Two against one. Four against one." He scoffed and turned to Hunter. "I want y'all go tell your good old daddy, the first shirt, the coon from the supply made y'all eat dirt. I want to hear y'all did that so I can break your sissy typin' fingers one at a time." He put his fist under Hunter's nose. "Tell him, Hunter. Tell him and start runnin' for your life."

Broomfield shifted his fatigue shirt to his other shoulder and walked out. At the door he looked back and spat, "Crackers."

Patterson didn't leave with the corporal. He forgot about brushing his teeth and rummaged for nothing in his footlocker to pass a few moments. It was his way to be brave because he hadn't been tough enough to take on all of them. For a few moments, he couldn't even focus on why he was looking in his footlocker. He listened to the silence as the men re-made their bunks and reveled in joy that Broomfield had not hurt them. He took out his Luckies, nervously lit one, and said loudly, "Fairley, come on down to supply and I'll get you some linen."

He walked out with Fairley, wishing Breslin had been there. And Banuelous. It would've been duke city. They would've cleaned house. It felt so good to hit Hunter he'd like to do it again.

A few weeks later, Patterson missed the regular Saturday morning inspection to run an errand for Sgt. Webster. He had to go to regimental headquarters—S-4 supply—and turn in two sets of binoculars. The beautiful June morning made the task even more pleasant. On the way, he high-balled the officers headed toward their companies for inspection. Each salute accompanied with an enthusiastic, "Good morning, sir."

In the back of headquarters, there was a group of 12 men laying out full-field inspections. This was punishment for DRs; actions like on-post traffic tickets, a few days AWOL, missing formations, or just generally fucking up. It was called Hard Labor. The same men would police up the parking lot and clean regimental headquarters every night, even on weekends. It was the way the regiment took care of its own transgressors.

Patterson knew a few of them. One asked him how much time he had left.

"Two and change. I'm shorter than a midget tyin' his shoes."

"Short shit," replied a man called Grzanich whose fatigue shirt showed the shadows of where his Pfc. stripes had been. "If I had that much time left, I'd let a five-ton wrecker run over me." Grzanich was a motor pool mechanic. "Thirty-eight and a wake-up left in this tuff fucker."

"And hard labor for every one of them," joked the man setting up equipment with him. The sergeant in charge told them to quit grab-assing and do their job.

"Duty calls," said Patterson and he headed down the ramp to the cool basement interior of regimental supply.

At the counter, old Sergeant Kennedy from Dog Company argued with a tall, pasty looking Pfc. named Pearson who was the supply clerk. The sergeant wanted to use one of the 1524 supply forms visible on Pearson's desk to type up a request. Pearson wasn't interested; the form should be filled out before he came to regimental supply.

Patterson recalled Kennedy from the night he was looking for Motz and the few times he had seen him around the regiment. He and Sgt. Webster were mates, as Webster liked to say. It was the first time he'd seen the veteran in dress khakis. The rumpled shirt and baggy trousers did not look neat on his pear-shaped body. However, the decorations on his chest stood out like neon lights: his Combat Infantryman's Badge carried a star signifying two wars. His Master Jump Wings had four bronze stars for four combat jumps. His Purple Heart had two clusters for being wounded three times. The Bronze Star carried two 'V' for Valor attachments. And many more medals he did not recognize. On his right shoulder was the 82nd Airborne Division patch, the unit he served with in WWII. There were not many men left in the division who could wear that insignia on the right shoulder.

"Hey, come on, Pearson. Help old sarge out. Save me a trip."

"'Hey', yourself, Sarge. If we let everybody fix their fucked up paperwork, we'd never have a place to sit down." Pearson threw back his narrow shoulders as he spoke.

Kennedy asked for Sergeant Curray, the regimental supply sergeant.

"It's his rule, man. He'll say the same thing."

Kennedy gathered himself. "I wanna talk to him." Kennedy noticed Patterson watching and he seemed almost apologetic for taking up time.

"Man," declared Pearson as he moved toward Curray's office, "you guys can be a royal pain-in-the-ass." Pearson's khakis, like Patterson's, were tailored to his skinny body and his boots glistened. The many keys on his belt jingled.

Patterson knew Pearson thought of himself as a sharp soldier, not a petty asshole who took advantage of a petty job to fuck over people. Did the job make the person a jerk-off, or was the person just an asshole anyway?

Patterson quietly said to Kennedy, "He's one of the world's worst shitheads, Sarge." He knew the sergeant would not remember the night in Dog Company's supply room.

Kennedy managed a weak smile. His leg moved nervously as he waited, leaning on the counter. "The regiment's full of kids like that. I'd love to get his ass in Dog Company."

"He'd last about five minutes," agreed Patterson then offered, "Shoot over to Headquarters Company. Webster's there."

"Hell, if I did that I might as well go all the way home."

Home? Dog Company is home to him—the barracks. Damn, that's sad.

Kennedy's nervous hands produced a pack of Camels. Patterson quickly dug out his '04 lighter and lit the cigarette. He refused Kennedy's offer of one.

Sergeant First Class Curray came out. He smoked a huge cigar. Curray was a light-skinned Negro who spoke in a high voice. There were no decorations on his stiff khaki shirt except his Wings. "What can I do you out of?" he asked Kennedy, using his favorite phrase.

"This here Spec-Four of yours tells me I have to go back to the company and re-do the supply request."

The cigar came slowly out of his mouth. "He told you right, Sarge." Pearson stood behind Curray. His smirk hard to hide. *Twins of a different color*, thought Patterson.

"Does that make sense to you, Sarge?" Kennedy's face became redder.

"If you make that walk enough times, you'll make sure it's right when you get here. It's for your own good, Sergeant." Curray said, emphasizing his rank.

Kennedy wanted to say more, but didn't. With the Camel in his mouth, he nodded and crumpled up the incorrect 1524s. On his way out, he threw them in the trash container by the door.

Patterson watched him trudge slowly up the ramp in the sunlight. There was a dark sweat stain across his lower back.

"He keeps acting that way I'll keep his ass out of here permanently." He nodded towards Patterson.

"*Was ist los*, young Private First Class? Looking for a job?"

The job topic was a running joke with Patterson and Curray. Patterson's canned response was that he couldn't handle the responsibility of a big-time supply room. He did not mention he'd never want to work with ass-kissers like Pearson. "Turning these in for salvage, Sarge," he said, putting the binoculars on the counter. Pearson reached for them.

Patterson placed his hands on them. "My daddy Webster says they're for your eyes only."

Curray replied, "The man always says that. He thinks he's running a plantation in Jamaica. Go ahead, Pearson."

Pearson opened up the cases and pulled out the glasses. "All the serial numbers have been eradicated, Sarge," pointed out the clerk.

Eradicated? What in the hell does that mean? Patterson knew, but wondered why the cat didn't just say there ain't no numbers. Big word dude. Hell, he knew big words too: elephant, Grand Canyon, Empire State Building, other stuff, too. He had eradicated the numbers with Webster's special acid, then painted on serial numbers provided by Webster.

"They're on the side," said Curray casually. "Sign for them."

"I don't know, Sarge," said Pearson as he signed for the glasses and pushed the receipts to Patterson.

Patterson looked at the tall clerk and said, "Pearson, you know that man who just walked out of here has four combat jumps from World War Two and a canteen cup full of medals. You should treat him better. Respect his experience."

Sergeant Curray grinned. "Private First Class Patterson, this is the pay-as-you-go Army. The new Army. We can't be carrying deadwood from yesterday. Right, Pearson?"

Of course, Pearson agreed and added, "Those medals and a quarter wouldn't get him a record on a jukebox."

Patterson sat his cunt cap low on his forehead. "Pearson, you and me are just passin' through Curray's Army. You best be thinkin' how you're gonna make it in the world. You'll have your ass kicked five ways to Sunday without an NCO to cover for you."

Pearson had the binoculars in his hands. He turned and headed for the wire cage storage area. "You'll never kick it, Pfc."

"You know where my bunk is. Anytime."

"Wheeee," joked Curray. "You're turning hard core on us, Patterson."

Patterson stopped at the door. "There's more wise-ass PFC.s and Speedy-Fours in this regiment than there are second lieutenants. See you, Sarge."

Feeling pretty good, he headed up the ramp on the balls of his feet. Patterson wished he could give Curray the same static as Pearson and hoped his words would make Curray consider Kennedy's record the next time something came up. He hated the rules and regs men he ran into. They always come out of the blue to make someone's life just a little more difficult. They should all be locked in a room and have a loud speaker play parking regulations day and night until they vowed to reform.

On his way toward the PX to kill some more time, he saw Kennedy coming out of the Ardennes Street door. The shape of the brown paper bag outlined a six-pack.

"I can't say I blame you, Sarge." Patterson words under his breath were as soft as the summer morning.

Chapter 18

They jumped on the 4th of July. They shouldn't have, but they did. It went like this.

All the other division's regiments had the holiday weekend off, but because only the best was needed for the guests of honor—Army Chief of Staff Maxwell Taylor and the Vice President of the United States, Richard Nixon—corps and division wanted a combat demonstration. The order came from the commanding officer of 18th Airborne Corps to the commanding officer of the 82nd Airborne Division to the commanding officer of the 504th Airborne Infantry Regiment. The event consisted of the troops jumping, then assembling and forming multiple skirmish lines that moved north to south down the length of Sicily Drop Zone. The men would leave their chutes stuffed in their kit bags and double-time toward the reviewing stand at port arms, and from 100 yards out, drop in the prone position and fire blank ammo toward the guests. Get up, charge, and drop again. There would be wave after wave of advancing paratroopers.

Maxwell would remember the 504th. He was, after all, an Airborne man. As Sfc. Anderson, the Headquarters Company supply sergeant, proudly said, "Completely an 'Oh-Four show, chaps."

The flights in the C-130 Hercules were short and rough. The last lifts to take off were still climbing out as the jumpmasters started jump commands. Within 10 minutes from the last wheels-up, the 25 droning troop carriers formed in lifts of six and made their approach over Sicily. As the planes neared the North end of the DZ, a fast-moving afternoon thunderstorm from Pamlico Sound—near Cape Hatteras on the Outer Banks—arrived over Bragg. The sudden storm and aircraft formation mixed without warning. Hot and cold air made the sky a cauldron of invisible torrents and cascades that swept through the unsettled aircraft.

And it started raining.

Just seconds prior to the first lift going out the door, a ground-to-air conversation took place: Major General Busby, standing by the Command and Control Jeep, spoke to the regimental commander, Col. Steele, in the lead aircraft. The colonel advised that the gusting winds might be too strong to safely jump. The general, just off to the right of the official reviewing stand, indicated that it was wet and windy there, but asked if the men were prepared to jump anyway. Both officers knew Maxwell Taylor, a veteran of combat jumps in World War II with the 101st Screaming Eagles, would not want a little weather to keep paratroopers from their mission. In the Army, the mission must always be accomplished.

"Yes, sir," replied Steele. "One hundred and ten percent ready, sir. Over."

The colonel was his kind of trooper, thought Busby and added, "We brought these people down from Washington for the show. Our mission is to jump. Over." There was a silence except for the wind rushing through the general's mike.

In the aircraft, crew chiefs poked fingers at the jumpmasters and pointed out the door at the stormy conditions.

"By the time they hit the ground the rain will stop," the general assured himself, "We better go, or we'll have egg on our face. Over."

"Airborne, sir. Roger, it's a go. Over."

"Good luck. Over and out."

When the storm began rocking the planes, Patterson—holding onto the static line cable while jammed among the shouting anxious men—shut his eyes and tried to ride with the motion. He didn't want the jump. He hadn't jumped since Breslin died, but he needed a pay jump. The fun was gone. This was serious. He had Banuelous check his static line twice to ensure it was clear of his shoulder harness.

Lt. Margolin stood in the door, looking ahead into the wind-driven rain. He saw the chutes of the first lifts flick open, while far to his right the red smoke of the Pathfinders on the ground blew horizontally across the DZ.

Red smoke meant a cancelled jump. *Why are we going?*

The aircraft were not really over the DZ; they were aligned nearly half a mile to the east, so the jumpers would be blown over to the DZ. Margolin stopped thinking about where they'd land and why the red smoke and should they jump. He concentrated on his door position. It was hard to stay on his feet or even remain inside the bucking plane.

From the corner of his eye, he stared at the red jump light. Surely, someone would cancel the jump even though a few lifts had already dropped.

Wisnewski's extended thumbs-up came over the lieutenant's shoulder. They were going.

Margolin shouted over the C-130's four engines about red smoke. Wisnewski nodded his head yes, but they were going anyway, according to the crew chief with the headset.

They both witnessed the light flash green. Margolin did not hesitate. He dropped out the door and the stick of adrenaline-filled shouting troopers followed close on his heels. Wisnewski couldn't believe how quickly the aircraft emptied. As jumpmaster, he stayed behind.

Against the standard peacetime rule of not jumping in winds above 15 knots and rain—which damaged chutes— the regiment dropped. They jumped as traces of lightning stung among the dark clouds on the advancing storm's perimeter. And every man knew they shouldn't have gone as their wind-swept chutes carried them at rapidly descending angles. It was almost as if they could hear a howling of furious pleasure across the turbulent Fourth of July sky.

It was The Hawk waiting, with spread wings and sharpened talons.

Patterson pushed against the man in front of him while being shoved from behind. Going out the door, he felt he was piggybacking and being ridden at the same time. The prop blast blew apart the closely-packed jumpers. Patterson rolled sideways, saw the ground swing over his head then he was jerked upright as his chute popped.

Immediately he found himself standing on an open canopy. *Holy fuck! Walk.*

He tried giant steps toward the edge of the other man's chute, but the clumsy pack and weapon tripped him. He landed face-first into the nylon bubble and crawled frantically to the edge, terrified his chute would collapse before he could apply his weight to it. A shift in the wind dumped him off and his half-collapsed canopy blossomed to pop him upright.

Two men swung past and bounced off his riser lines, then the sky grew less crowded as he descended quickly across the sky. The wind carried most of the jumpers back to the DZ, skimming them over treetops to land on the wet soil. On Patterson's first chance to get a good look at the drop zone, all he saw were men being dragged across the ground, their wind-filled chutes towing their bodies, leaving dry furrows behind them. Some men landed short of the DZ in trees. There would be no charging and firing at the assembly point.

For the first time since jump school 15 months earlier, Patterson rehearsed aloud how to recover from wind drag.

"... PLF. On your back. Reach over your head. Pull the riser to pull yourself up..." He hadn't forgotten. *Goddamnit! I'm too short to be making these kinds of jumps.*

At 50 feet, he estimated that he might clear the wall of trees heading toward him at high speed. He barely missed the trees and pulled down hard on the right risers to brake his near-parallel descent. The wind was too strong.

"Here it comes!" he called out to himself and heard men beneath him shouting for assistance.

Wham! Instantly, he was pulled up and bounced on his back. It knocked the wind out of him. He plowed along the ground on his empty chute harness as wet coarse sand filled his fatigue shirt and trousers. He caught his breath and pulled the left riser with both hands. He swung around and planted his feet.

The chute lifted him ten feet off the ground and dropped him. He twisted to take the fall on his shoulder. His left arm and rifle were caught high in the risers. He hit and it was as if someone twisted his arm up over his head. He shouted in pain. Loose suspension lines stung his neck and face. He rolled onto his reserve chute and knapsack, kept his head down like a running back going into the line, and dragged along.

His helmet ripped off. His shelterhalf pulled off his knapsack. And the rifle was gone. Every bump against his shoulder felt like a dagger thrust.

Finally, someone seized the apex of the chute and pulled it into the wind. "Get up and help someone," demanded his benefactor. *Like hell.*

He lay on the ground, wondering how bad his shoulder was and how he would get out of his gear. Cautiously, he rolled slowly over to let the rain cool his face. With his good hand he unhooked the reserve chute. He couldn't feel the suspension line burns on his face and neck. He kept his mouth open and allowed the rain to wash out the grit as he fumbled to punch the quick-release button that unlocked the parachute harness and knapsack.

"You OK, Willie?" Lt. Margolin looked down at him. The lieutenant was covered with mud as if he just waded through the Okefenokee Swamp. When he saw Patterson's reaction, he knelt down.

"You're not OK."

"You look like hell, sir."

"I feel like hell. How can I help you?"

"Help me up so I can light a smoke, sir." Margolin extended his hand to Patterson's outstretched one and stood up, pulling Patterson to his knees. The Pfc. winced. "Damn, that hurts."

"Here, let me," said Margolin as he unbuttoned the flap on Patterson's fatique pocket and took out the crushed and soiled Luckies pack. He found the best one of the bunch and gave it to Patterson who jammed it in his mouth and fumbled with one hand for his lighter.

The lieutenant leaned over the injured PFC., providing some shelter from the light rain. Patterson managed to light the cigarette. He exhaled, coughed, and said, "Sir, I'm fucked up. My shoulder's killin' me. I don't want to move."

Margolin stood up and looked around. "Wait here. I'll find a medic."

"Where am I gonna go?" Patterson leaned over his cigarette to keep it dry and looked up. The darkest edge of the storm had moved on, and gray clouds raced away in the empty sky. Groups of ragged-looking men passed. Patterson continued to decline help. He stayed on his knees and listened to the comments.

"… the whole regiment's fucked up, Jim…"

"…all time SNAFU. Situation normal, all fu…"

"…Forty-mile-an-hour wind…"

A deuce-and-a-half, roaring in snatches like the MGM lion, worked its way along the edge of the DZ. Patterson watched Lt. Margolin wave it over and point to him. He waited as the heavy truck ground its way toward him, windshield wipers working in spurts with the engine. There was a man on each running board and standing in back, holding onto the raised wooden sides, was a cluster of bedraggled and helmetless men. Steele and Sergeant Major Kaley were on the running boards.

"What's wrong, trooper?" called Steele as he jogged toward him.

"My fuckin' shoulder," replied Patterson who saw the worry in Steele's eyes.

"Another malinger, sir. We'll shoot his ass at dawn," joked Kaley. He bent over and put Patterson's good arm around his neck. "Ready, troop?"

The sergeant major half carried Patterson to the truck where other injured waited. Most of the men had been burned with suspension lines. Four men lay on the truck bed with leg injuries. Discarded backpacks, web belts, helmets, and weapons were piled behind the cab. One man huddled in the corner wrapped in a parachute even though it was warm.

The deuce-and-a-half wound its way slowly toward the assembly point, passing Lt. Margolin on the way. Patterson leaned over the wooden rail and called, "You need a steam cleanin', Lieutenant!" The officer waved to Patterson and gave him a thumbs-up.

By the time they reached the assembly point, the wind had died. Sunshine blazed through the dissipating clouds. A beautiful day. A perfect Fourth of July holiday for fireworks and barbecues and family fun. At the assembly point, the sun reflected off the elongated puddles in the bleacher seats. All the VIPs were gone.

On the ground, in front of the reviewing stand, three bodies were wrapped in white reserve chutes. A tired NCO medic sat smoking a cigarette on the bottom row.

Patterson stared. *Holy fuck, they're dead.*

No one in the truck said a word as it crawled past then picked up speed, but everyone watched the three white shrouds grow smaller and carried the unasked question in their minds: who were they—it could have been anyone of them. The truck rolled onto the macadam and sped up, dipping down the road, and Sicily disappeared.

Gradually, as the truck moved onto Longstreet Road and headed toward the hospital, Patterson felt so good at being alive he wanted to explode with firecracker joy. The

Hawk had tried, but he had made it. Being free, white, and 21 wasn't so bad. In fact, it was a goddamn pure-ass ball.

The article in *Life* about the jump circulated through the wards of Womack Army Hospital as well as in numerous publications throughout the country. "It's all part of a paratrooper's job," said the division commanding officer Major General Harold 'Howl' Busby, looking ruggedly splendid in his chin strap close-up. He and his staff jumped the next day to prove the disastrous jump was a fluke. The article did mention the sudden wind and rain, but did not elaborate on who made the decision to jump. The injured in the wards were proud to have been a part of the fiasco.

Someone called it the 'Nixon jump.' The article gave the impression that paratroopers dropped no matter what. It failed to mention the 15 to 20 knot wind rule for training jumps. Patterson's initial delight at being alive and suffering only a separated shoulder gave way to anger and incredulity. They weren't heroes. The troops had been fucked to please some big shots from Washington. *How do the dead men feel*? asked Patterson.

Sgt. Webster and Cpl. Broomfield brought Patterson cigarettes and assured him his job was secure. Lt. Margolin showed up the afternoon of the second day with a pretty nurse next to him. He didn't introduce her, and explained he came to give Patterson the good news.

Patterson asked, "Are the rosters missin' again?"

The lieutenant laughed. "Willie, you don't trust your lieutenant worth a damn do you?"

"All due respect, sir, not this much." He used his good hand to pinch his thumb and forefinger together.

"The good news is that Webster and I are putting you in for Speedy-Four." This was the rank used instead of corporal: specialist fourth-class. It wasn't considered an NCO rank, as the specialist had no direct supervisory authority. For example, cooks were specialists, while a mess steward was an NCO. The system allowed promotions—and pay raises—without creating too many NCOs.

Patterson boosted himself up on the bed with the hanging bar. "Sir, come here. I don't want the lady captain to hear me." Margolin came around from the foot of the bed.

Patterson leaned toward him and whispered, "Take the Speedy-Four and stick it up Steele's ass." He didn't mention he knew what else had been up there. "Nothin' personal, you understand. Just a matter of professional pride in being a Pfc."

"We're going to do it anyway."

"The less I have to do with rank, the happier I'll be. And maybe safer." He tapped his shoulder. "Someone with a lot of rank didn't call off the jump. I don't ever want to be one of those people."

"Willie, we're paratroopers. When the going gets tough, the tough get screwed."

"Roger that, sir."

The lieutenant almost started to make excuses for the jump until he remembered his own thoughts as he saw the red smoke blowing across the DZ while the men jumped from the lead planes. The lieutenant grabbed the bar over Patterson's bed and looked at Melby then the injured soldier. "Willie, I'm going on…"

"Bill."

"Bill. I'm going on an extended leave. I won't be there when you get back."

"Gettin' married, sir?" asked Patterson with raised eyebrows hinting of marital pleasures.

"At ease, Pfc. What I'm trying to tell your wise ass is that when you get back to the company, keep your mouth shut and follow the program. Be STRAC. I won't be there to bail your ass out and neither will 'Ski. The first shirt will be on a rampage with us gone."

"Where's 'Ski goin'?"

"He's gone. Yesterday. Sneaky Petes."

It now dawned on Patterson why Margolin wanted him to have the promotion. Another rank would be a barrier between him and the stockade if the first sergeant rode him hard. He said, "Thanks for the warning, sir. I mean it. You've always been straight with the troops." He used his good arm to pull himself up and sit on the side of the bed.

He and Margolin shook hands. "Take care of yourself, Wil...Bill."

Captain Melby had moved down the ward. Margolin started toward her. "Sir," called Patterson, "do me a favor. You owe me for the rosters. I'm a hell of a Pfc. Don't ruin me with rank."

Patterson saluted from his sitting position. Margolin returned the salute with his own abbreviated wave.

"One more thing, sir. Don't drink coffee from mess hall pitchers anymore." The lieutenant didn't seem to understand, but waved again and walked away.

After chow on Monday evening, a Spec/5 walked through the ward looking for injured men from the 504. Half the ward raised their hands and someone asked what he was doing. The Spec/5 said Col. Steele was visiting, and a moment later the colonel and Sgt. Maj. Kaley appeared in the doorway. A Pfc. photographer was with them.

The Spec/5 hurried to greet them. After a few words among themselves, the Spec/5 pointed out who was from the regiment and led the small group from bed to bed. As always, the lean sergeant major stood a stride behind the colonel and carried his swagger stick tucked under his arm. If Steele turned too fast he'd knock the man over. At each bed, the colonel spoke to the occupant and a picture was taken.

"I ain't shakin' his hand," said the man next to Patterson, a Pfc. named Franklin whose knee ligaments had been torn apart. The man claimed he ran the 100 in ten seconds flat before he was hurt. Franklin was one of those guys from California who had done and seen everything. The rest of the country needed to catch up.

"You don't have a hair on your ass if you shake his hand," challenged Patterson.

"You with me?"

"No, you said it. Now do it. I ain't no hero," said Patterson.

Patterson watched Steele work the ward and felt a sense of calm. Whatever the colonel did, the Pfc. did not care anymore. The Army could take his stripe, put him on hard labor, even put him in the stockade, but he knew his time was up. He knew he could not be harassed by the system anymore. He felt he could see deep into the hearts of Lifers who never stepped out of their uniforms because of the security offered and the fear they'd be mistaken for something as mundane as a movie usher.

And if he wanted to, he could scare Steele shitless with one anonymous midnight phone call to the man's home. He'd never do it.

"Evenin', son."

Franklin lowered the Batman comic book he was pretending to read and sat more upright. "Yes, sir." said Franklin.

"Recovering all right?"

"Yes, sir. I'm boss."

Steele stepped closer to Franklin. "We're proud of the sacrifices you men made."

"Thank you, sir." They shook hands. The flashbulb popped.

Steele said good-bye to Franklin and turned to Patterson. "Evenin', son."

Patterson sat upright. "How are you, Colonel Steele?"

"Why..." The directness caught him. "... never better. Do I know you?"

"Yes, sir. We met on the stairs of Headquarters Company one night. You admired my uniform." Steele passed over the subject and told Patterson he looked fit. "My shoulder's fucked up, Colonel."

Sgt. Maj. Kaley leaned forward just past the colonel and wiggled his swagger stick as a signal for Patterson to watch his language. Kaley nodded his head to show he understood manly language, but the colonel would not.

Patterson overheard the Spec/5 at Franklin's bed explaining the photo would be sent to his hometown newspaper. Franklin nearly tore the ligaments in his elbow reaching to sign the press release.

"How's the chow, son?"

Patterson grinned. All the man knew were stock questions. He wasn't human. All rules and regulations. How's the chow? Mail call OK? See the chaplain. Fall in. Shape up or ship out. Jump in the wind because the big shots are here.

"I miss Sergeant Potter's great fried chicken."

The sergeant major gave Patterson a big wink of approval. That's how to talk to the colonel.

"Is this goin' to be in our hometown paper, sir?"

"Would you like that, son?"

"Yes, sir, on one condition." The sergeant major cocked his head. Steele asked what.

"I'd like the story to read we shouldn't have jumped because of the wind and rain."

Kaley stepped up next to Steele. "That's no way to talk to a ranking officer."

The words, a surprise even to him, felt delicious as if he'd be waiting two years to say something, anything to someone who outranked him. "What about the dead men, Sergeant Major? How do they talk to the colonel?" Patterson maintained his calm exterior. He was invincible—the avenger for the dead.

Steele touched the sergeant major's arm as a sign to not interfere. The colonel moved to the side of the bed. Patterson adjusted himself as if to meet him head-on.

"Son, the wind was too strong. Your youthful idealism can't accept that. But in life men sometimes face situations where everything isn't apple pie and roses. You just did. You and all the men in this ward and the other wards. You're a better man for your experience. You wouldn't believe me now, but you will as you get older." The swagger stick tapped impatiently against the sergeant major's leg.

"Yes, sir," agreed Patterson, "I only hope they court-martial the son-of-a-bitch who decided to jump."

"That's enough," ordered Kaley. The swagger stick banged on the bed frame. "No picture here." The photographer and Spec/5 stepped back from the bed as if its occupant was contagious.

Steele stared silently at Patterson with his steadiest frozen glare. Patterson met him eye to eye. "I think I remember you now," said Steele.

"I sincerely hope so, sir." Patterson recalled the boots sticking out from under the white canopies to keep from averting his eyes.

"You'll be all right, son. Good luck," said Steele. He backed off a few steps and headed across the ward. The sergeant major remained to write down Patterson's name from the bed chart.

"Kick ass and take names, huh, Sarge?"

"Barracks lawyer, wise guy, huh?" Kaley smiled with the certainty he knew how to handle upstart privates first class. He followed the colonel to the next bed.

Motherfuckers, thought Patterson. Three dudes dead and they go around sending home pictures like the regiment was on a picnic. Someone's ass should be headed for jail or at least a fucking DR. He had been busted for having his trousers out of his boots. Patterson accepted the fact he lacked the courage to shout his feelings across the ward.

"Your ass is gonna be in a sling," predicted Franklin in a whisper. "He didn't have to come here. He's a boss dude."

"Tell me how boss he is when you do the hundred in ten flat again."

Three days later Patterson was released from Womack. He spent the morning clearing the different medical departments and found himself facing a butterball Spec/5 WAC in personnel. For a moment Patterson imagined he might have to bang her to get cleared. Too bad Terri had set such a high standard for him. He wasn't about to hit on a girl who reminded him of a can of tuna fish. He played cute with her and she signed him off.

With his sling as his badge of courage, he cruised down the corridor to the cafeteria. After a good cheeseburger, fries, and a Pepsi, he asked himself, *Why hurry to get back to the company and First Sergeant Billy Martin?* He decided to hang around, and stretched out on an empty bunk in the ward. In a few moments he fell into a deep sleep, one of those unconscious naps that pin a person down no matter how hard one tries to wake up.

When he did wake up, he was startled to find himself in the hospital. He had dreamed he was in South Carolina getting ready for All-American. Breslin was alive and they were talking about Key West. He collected his shaving kit and medical records, reluctantly accepting the fact he had to return to the company, and walked out of the ward. At least Martin would be gone for the day by the time he made it back. Maybe his light duty status for a month could keep him from any tough assignments like KP.

Patterson sat on a bench under the hospital entrance canopy, smoking and wondering how to get back to the division when a shiny, dark blue '56 Corvette sped up the circular drive and came to an abrupt halt in the restricted parking area by the main doors.

Two people climbed out of the car. The driver was a WAC major and the civilian passenger looked familiar to

Patterson...*Jesus Christ on a crutch. Is that Hollywood Jack Schmidt? Wearing shades and tooling around in a 'Vette?*

Patterson stood up and intercepted the couple. "Hollywood?"

The man behind the sunglasses had long hair and his collar turned up. He gave no indication he was the person the Pfc. was calling. He did hold the major's hand to stay by his side.

"Hollywood. That is you!" The man's face relaxed.

"Willie!" Schmidt gently slapped his good shoulder. "You look like a million bucks. Major Broadhurst, this is Willie Patterson. A friend of mine from the Eighty-Deuce."

With a cigarette in one hand and the other arm in a sling, he clumsily almost saluted, then stopped.

Broadhurst said hello and excused herself. "You want to talk buddy-buddy stuff. I'll see you in a few minutes. Don't let the MPs give me a ticket."

"Miss me," said Schmidt.

"Nice to meet you, Willie. I didn't know Jack had such nice-looking friends." The major walked into the hospital with an athletic stride. She wore no wedding ring and looked older. He hadn't said a word to her.

"What's the haps, man?"

"I'm short. Two and some change. I got fucked up on the Nixon jump, but I'm gonna make it."

"Well, Willie," Schmidt adjusted his collar and took off his sunglasses as if getting ready to make a speech, "being a civilian isn't half bad. I'm getting used to it."

"You can't be."

"Two weeks ago."

"Man, you're AWOL. I mean you have good and bad time to do. Fuckin' Martin's still lookin' for you." Patterson's fear of the system forced him to believe all men were subject to it. Or all should be.

Schmidt looked around as if spies were lurking behind the canopy supports. "There's some things better left unsaid. I'm as legit as any soldier who ever got an honorable."

"You lucky fuck. You always were." Suddenly, Patterson resented his semi-hero. He recalled Schmidt's lighted-heartedness the night he risked the stockade to help him go AWOL. "How'd you do it?"

He nodded toward the revolving doors into the hospital. "She helped me." He grinned. It was hard for Patterson to hide his feelings. He felt cheated. "Willie, I've always been captain of my fate. Every man should be. I met her playing golf on the officers' course. A retired colonel and I were talking business...and she passed by..."

"You're fuckin' her?"

"Willie, civilians don't talk like that. I took golf lessons from her. I didn't even know she was military. Next thing I know..." His fist made a pumping motion.

Schmidt continued his story about telling her who he really was, an AWOL and on his way to fame and fortune in Hollywood, and it made no difference. She and her doctor buddies who disliked the military system wired him out with a medical discharge. "I'm supposed to have been hurt on a jump."

"Three cats just were. They died."

"Tough darts."

The major came out. "Jackie, we better hurry."

"We'd give you a lift, but it's a little tight and we're in a rush."

Patterson walked them to the car. "You could stop in and see the first shirt. He'd go apeshit."

At the 'Vette, Schmidt extended his hand. "You're different, Willie. I can't put my finger on it, but something's different."

"I'm Bill now and I got through this tuff fucker."

"You know, I swear to God the Army's been good for me. Like Scott always said, it gives you a perspective. I learned to appreciate the common man. He has hopes and dreams, too."

The mention of Breslin opened Patterson's mind up to his failure to check his buddy's static line. He'd almost forgotten it because of his own brush with disaster—but it was back.

He wanted to tell Schmidt, but the man wouldn't be interested. Schmidt took Patterson's sudden change in demeanor as resentment about his comment on the common man.

"Not you, fucker. I mean the man in the street. The legs of the world. You might have been, but...that's it. That's what's different! You've touched greatness and it's rubbed off." Schmidt's handsome face laughed with genuine pleasure. "You've known me."

The bastard. Nothing bothered him. Nothing. Maybe because he's a phony bastard and he just doesn't let it bother him. He'd sell his mother to get an advantage and he'd be the first to admit it. He'd laugh at Patterson for worrying about Breslin. "You're still full of shit, Hollywood."

From behind the wheel, the major leaned over and called, "Jackie."

"I gotta run. Gotta go. Gotta be a civilian." Schmidt worked his arms in quick little pumps as if running.

"I'm hip," replied Patterson. The man would never be down because he knew what he wanted and had the balls to go after it no matter what anyone else thought.

Schmidt ducked into the low-slung car and slid the window down.

"Hollywood, one more time. Give me a 'swear to God on your mother's death'." The car moved slowly. Patterson walked beside it.

"Willie," Schmidt raised his right hand, "I swear to God on my mother's death and may God strike me dead if everything I ever said to you wasn't..." The car picked up speed. "... the gospel truth," he shouted and laughed. The Corvette zipped away.

Heartless fucker.

A Spec-Four leg in a Third Army Jeep gave him a ride to Main Post. On the way, he silently resented Schmidt for not doing his full time. For not being caught. For avoiding all the bullshit he and the others from the platoon had endured. For being gutsy enough to go AWOL. And he berated himself for not telling Schmidt how he resented Schmidt's good fortune and about Breslin's static line.

He hopped out and walked along McComb toward Longstreet Road, the main thoroughfare between the division and Main Post. Just as he lit a cigarette, a cannon fired. The signal for *Retreat*.

He had heard it more than once while on the ward. Every day at 1700, the cannon in front of 18th Airborne Corps Headquarters, just a block behind him, was fired by a guard detail and the flag lowered. The military day had ended. He watched two men scramble back into one of the older brick barracks to avoid standing the ceremony.

Cars stopped. The military occupants climbed out and stood at parade rest. Bragg was silent. Even the quarreling birds seemed to respect the cannon. However, the sprinklers on the 18th Airborne Corps lawns continued to swirl, their drops reflected in the late afternoon sun like golden coins being tossed onto a smooth green sea.

A bugle recording sounded over a loudspeaker: slow formal notes, a medieval herald's horn proclaiming the death of a king. Patterson stubbed out his cigarette on his boot sole, slipped the butt into his fatigue shirt pocket, and waited at parade rest.

He would never be a Schmidt. It meant too much to him to be honest. Schmidt would succeed while Patterson followed all the rules and maybe would not. Succeed at what? He knew he had served his time well. Earned his Wings and an honorable discharge. Schmidt was a pretender, incapable of...of what? He didn't know, and used the stillness of Main Post to calm his feelings of being foolish for serving his time while the Schmidts of the world bucked the system and got away with it.

What's Banuelous always say? "Two tears and a bucket and a hi-dee-ho fuck it."

There was a pause between *Retreat* and *To the Colors* while someone changed the record. The loudspeaker carried the needle noises searching for the grooves, then silence again. In that brief moment, the world within Patterson's view froze. Waiting.

Only the sprinklers tossing their shiny coins carried on.

Patterson's mind seemed empty then suddenly full. Vibrantly alive. *Eight days ago I almost died, and now I'm the center of this reflective universe.* He would not break the stillness; it was too beautiful. *Being alive was wonderful no matter what happened back at the company. No matter what Schmidt did. No matter that Breslin is gone. It wasn't my fault. It just happened; it could have been me just as well.*

To the Colors rapid cadence began. The flag was quickly lowered.

Patterson came to attention and saluted as if he was still a recruit under the watchful eye of Sfc. Wisnewski. Across the street on the outside landing of the three-story brick barracks of 18th Airborne Corps, the two men who had ducked inside slowly moved down the stairs in anticipation of the recording's conclusion.

That would've been him and Breslin. "It's a great day for waterin' sidewalks, Scott." The bugle melody ended with a scratch. Patterson came back to attention and stood motionless, then stepped out, turning off his imagination, walking with military crispness toward the Post Gym where Longstreet Road began.

He was ready for the first sergeant. Ready for the Schmidts of the world. Ready for commands to jump in high wind. Ready for anything. "Perspective," he said aloud. "Right, Scott? Perspective. It was an accident."

Somewhere in the world, the scales balanced out. The Martins got their comeuppance and the Schmidts were caught. He didn't have to worry about it either way. All he needed to do was be a decent human being.

Be like Lt. Margolin. Be like Breslin. He walked faster as if his thoughts—his perspective—pumped him up. "Faster," he told himself. "Gotta go. Gotta be, Airborne."

The sooner he saw Martin the better.

He tucked the shaving kit against his side within the sling, and with the medical records in the other hand, he started double-timing. Slowly at first; it felt good. He hadn't run anywhere for a long time. He could run all the way back to the company and jump on Martin's desk and dare the man to fuck with him. He swept off the soft fatigue cap and tucked it into the sling.

One leg in front of the other. "Hup-two-rip-hore. Hup-two-rip-hore." He picked up the pace. "Your left. Your left. Your left-right-left."

He counted silent cadence. Gotta go. Gotta be. Airborne. Airborne. Airborne all the way.

What Martin did wouldn't mean a thing. He had learned to jump out of planes and run to exhaustion and a million other things. He didn't want to miss a day of his final two months. Key West had to wait, because he would be busy taking everything the sons-of-bitches wanted to throw at him. He was ready. Ready for anything that came down the pike.

"All the way. Gotta go. Gotta be. Airborne."

A slug, son, is a work-a-day, fuck-the-old-lady,
wash-the-car on Saturday dud who'll never know
the nut jinglin' joy of leapin' outta airplanes.

BUCK SERGEANT BOBBY TAPPER
77th Special Forces
Fort Bragg, North Carolina

Chapter 19

In 1960s, the United States shifted the emphasis of its military programs in Vietnam from conventional warfare to counterinsurgency. Training programs already in operation were reoriented. Special Forces teams went to train South Vietnamese Ranger Battalions and U.S. advisors were placed at regimental levels to give on-the-spot advice and assess the needs of individual units.

The quirks of the election calendar would spare Eisenhower from facing the ultimate failure of his Vietnam policies. Within a short time after taking office, John F. Kennedy would have to choose between what he called abandoning our 'offspring' or significantly increasing the American commitment. President Kennedy believed he could deal with Vietnam inexpensively as his foreign affairs priorities were Cold War trouble spots like Berlin and Cuba. His brother Bobby said, impatiently and incorrectly, "We've got twenty Vietnams a day to handle."

The first night back in the company, Patterson issued himself linen from the supply room. When he went to the squad bay, he found his bunk occupied by one of the ten new legs who were pulling company details and drilling with Sergeant McClendon while waiting for jump-school slots. *The hell with it*, he thought, and unrolled a mattress on one of the empty upper bunks at the far end of the squad bay. In the morning, he'd get his footlocker from supply and set up an official bunk, wall and footlocker, but really live in supply. It wasn't late, but he decided to stretch out before going to town.

There seemed to be so much to think about: Terri? *Will I dare go to the Keys in two months? How much is Martin going to fuck with me?* His worry and guilt about Breslin seemed minor now. He fell asleep.

Voices woke him up. It was dark; after lights out. People were jabbering about getting Wheeling on the radio. He recognized Hunter and Williamson's voices. Loud. They'd been drinking. His adrenaline picked up. From under his arm, he watched warily.

"I swear, Sonny, that old first sergeant's crazier than a hound in heat. You know what that…"

Mac Wiseman and the Country Boys harmonized about a two-timing woman who better wake up.

"… old boy told me today?" A boot thumped on the floor.

"What's that?"

"First sergeant says, he says, 'James Lee, y'all keep up soldierin' the way y'all been, I'm gonna make y'all a hard E-Four. A genuine corporal'."

"No shit." Another boot hit.

"I truly believe he wants to make me actin' platoon sergeant." Dog tags jingled.

"We sure as hell could use one with 'Ski gone to the Green Beanies."

"McClendon's doin' a good job. He's a good old boy," said Hunter. Patterson imagined he heard the company clerk's belt keys rattle.

"And the truth is, Sonny, I'm glad the door didn't hit 'Ski in the ass on his way out."

"Ahh," disagreed Sonny, "he was all right."

"Let's have one more in my room 'fore we hit the rack," suggested Hunter.

"Not me, man. I'm beat to all hell. I'm brushin' my teeth and sayin' my prayers."

"Y'all ain't prayed since your first piece of poontang. Come on, one more."

Their voices faded as they headed toward the latrine. Patterson leaned out from his upper bunk to watch them. Just as they went out the doors, he heard something about the first sergeant saying something.

"The first sergeant says this. The first sergeant says that." Patterson stuck his face into the pillow. "Holy fuck, I'm a stranger in my own company."

He swung off the bunk and crossed across the cool linoleum to Williamson's bunk and shut off Flatt and Scruggs and the Foggy Mountain Boys rolling into *Blue Ridge Cabin Home*. He made sure he switched the station, then pulled his sheets off his bunk, picked up his uniform and boots, and headed for the supply room. He might as well start tonight.

The next morning, Patterson stood in clean, starched fatigues with his arm in a sling in front of First Sgt. Billy Martin. The first sergeant had summoned him at reveille and now pounded his index finger on his desk and announced, "My TO&E tells me y'all owe Uncle Sam the price of one M-1 Garand rifle, a field pack, and a shelter half. That's one hundred and sixteen dollars and forty-eight cents. It'll be comin' outta yore paycheck."

Patterson finally appreciated being able to look men like Martin in the eye; if nothing else he had learned that in two years. "First sergeant, I didn't lose that gear. The jump tore it off me."

"It was your weapon, wasn't it? Your pack, wasn't it?"

"It was."

"It was, what?"

"It was, First Sergeant."

"Do y'all have any of it? 'Specially the weapon."

"No, First Sergeant, but it'll turn up at some point. Somewhere. It's got a serial number to track back to the company."

The diminutive NCO impatiently tapped his colored pencil on the glass-topped writing surface and said. "I don't give a good goddamn about serial numbers or if it was split into fuckin' kindlin' wood, y'all are gonna pay for it. Go see Sergeant Webster and tell him I want a statement of charges on my desk in two-zero minutes."

"That's not fair, First..." Patterson could almost hear James Lee Hunter smiling behind him.

"Y'all tellin' yore first sergeant how to run his company?" Martin took off his thick plain glasses and squinted at Patterson.

"No, First Sergeant, I'm just sayin'..."

"Y'all sayin' too damn much. That's a bad habit y'all picked up from that Jew boy lieutenant who royally fucked-up this here company." His voice rose loud enough to be heard down the hall by the drinking fountain and the words ran together. "Remember this here." He touched his six chevrons on his sleeve. "Three-up. Three-down. And-a-diamond-in-the-middle. Get me that statement of charges and don't say another word or I'm goin' to bust y'all for refusin' to obey a direct order and dereliction of duty. My company clerk's my witness."

"I heard everything, First Sergeant," volunteered Hunter.

"Now, get-your-sorry-ass-outta-here."

Margolin was right; he had to watch himself. *Take it and run*, he advised himself, knowing he'd shortly be hearing about giving Steele static in the ward, which he thought was the reason he'd been called out at reveille. Patterson did an about-face and walked out. Hunter, behind his long-carriage typewriter, grinned from ear to ear.

"William," said Sgt. Webster, "it'll be a cold day in Hades when one of my chaps has to pay for anything. Now be a good lad, sign this, and take it up to our benevolent company clerk."

Webster did not explain in detail how he would fix the statement of charges. The general idea was the form would satisfy Martin's thirst for paperwork, but once it reached personnel the personnel sergeant-major, one of the few career Negro senior enlisted men in the 504th and a close friend of Webster's, would slip it into a circular file. Patterson was concerned the favor would cost Webster.

"Perhaps and perhaps bloody well nothing. We'll see. At least, Mr. Atkins, you'll be able to pay your and your deceased chum's car loan off before you're discharged." The light bulb went on for Patterson.

Webster's handsome ebony face beamed. "You bloody well better believe Sergeant Webster knows his economics."

Patterson knew the man was Johnny Starr before Banuelous introduced him. The two men carried Banuelous' footlocker into supply and set it by the wire security door. Banuelous could only use one hand; the other was in a cast.

"Willie, take this OD shit off my records. I'm a man with a lot to do and no time to do it in." He snapped his fingers with his good hand and slapped the counter. He wore sunglasses and his long hair showed on the sides under the fatigue cap. "I'm a short-timin' motherfucker, Jim."

Patterson approached the counter as the two men began stacking field equipment on the counter. Just being in the same building with Starr made him uneasy.

Specialist-Fourth Class Johnny Starr had black hair long enough to comb back like Valentino. His triangular face and inset eyes made him look sinister. Tattooed on his left cheekbone was the Pachuco mark like Banuelous had on his hand between his thumb and forefinger. A thin gold chain with a religious medal hung outside his fatigue jacket. On each thick wrist he wore heavy gold ID bracelets. Starr was the same height as Patterson, except stockier across the chest. He looked...cold? Cruel. How could Terri like him?

"Fuck checkin' it," said Patterson. "You got everything. Bring it around."

"I hear you, *ese*," said Starr, and they swept the gear back into the footlocker and carried it into the caged area of the supply room.

"Hey, Broom. What's the haps?" Since their fight, the corporal and the Pfc. got along well.

Broomfield looked up from his arithmetic homework. A new peacetime requirement dictated every NCO had to have a high-school diploma. Whether or not a man was a good soldier didn't matter. It was an inspired Pentagon maneuver to trim excess. Career NCOs army-wide were scared. Luckily, Broomfield enjoyed learning. "S-O-S. Same old stuff. Gettin' out of the war, huh?"

"Most shosk," said Banuelous, "and thirty-four days early."

Patterson asked, as he efficiently took the various items and tossed them in bins, "How you gettin' out early?"

"They need me back on the farm. I got a letter."

"Hey, *ese*, you said you was never goin' to pick lettuce," reminded Starr.

"You know how I cry. Release me early and they did. I ain't pickin' nothin' but babes." Broomfield wished him good luck.

"Broom duked me out once," he said to Starr. "He liked to tear my head off. I should've gotten you to put the heat on him."

Banuelous laughed and made a pistol with his forefinger and pointed at Broomfield. Starr did not laugh; his look indicated Banuelous shouldn't talk like that.

"What happened to your hand?" asked Patterson.

"Nothin'. It's fake." He swung the wrapped hand toward Patterson. "It'll keep me off KP in Separation. The word is they fuck over Eighty-Deuce cats there."

"Let's go, man," said Starr.

Was he in a hurry to see Terri? wondered Patterson.

"Sign me off, motherfucker." Patterson gave the form to Broomfield who initialed it.

Banuelous took the form and talked about one more stop at the orderly room and he'd be out of there. From the counter, he challenged Broomfield. "You and me. Right now, outside. Buckle to buckle."

"You're crazy, man." The corporal waved him off.

"We showed them who was boss on that run, didn't we, *ese*?" Banuelous said as he shook hands with Patterson then told Starr about them being the only two in their platoon to finish the run during jump school training.

"Tony, don't go back on the block and get fucked up on Vaporub or somethin'," warned Patterson.

"I'm clean as the Pope's pecker. California here I come."

Just as Starr and Banuelous reached the main double doors, Banuelous snapped his fingers and turned like he'd forgotten something. "Johnny, this is the cat that's hot for Terri." Starr looked at Patterson with unblinking eyes.

You motherfucker, thought Patterson, and his weak smile tried to make it look like Banuelous was kidding. He said, "She's good-lookin', but she never talks to no one." Starr just stared.

Banuelous laughed. "I'm just jerkin' you off, wetback." He pulled Starr with him out the heavy steel doors then he stuck his head back in. "Keep chasin' her. See, he don't mind."

Patterson waited for Starr to appear like he was off-stage, his cue hanging in the air. He waited. Waited. No Starr.

The relief he felt was his reward for not foolishly knocking on her apartment door since Breslin died. Starr's appearance guaranteed he'd never dare. Imagine, a cat with a Pachuco cross on his cheek and a gun coming after him. It was like a movie.

Adios, Terri.

On the last day of August, Patterson read his name on the jump manifest for September 2nd. The date coincided with his first day off light duty and just 23 days left in the war. There was no doubt in his mind the rebel company clerk-and-jerk had made sure to add his name.

A Hollywood jump. No gear. Daytime. Like jumping off a school bus—but everyone knew the Hawk never rested.

He wasn't about to beg off. That would be too much satisfaction for First Sgt. Billy Martin and his personal secretary newly acting Cpl. James Lee Hunter. *Fuck them and the horse they rode in on*, that's how he cried.

And there he was, walking from the deuce-and-a-half to the issuing shed. The September heat melted the long runways into shimmering pools of concrete that reminded him of the day Breslin died. There was always something coming from nowhere that would momentarily unlock his memory of not checking Breslin's static line, but now the guilty feeling rarely lingered.

"Jump me every day, motherfuckers," Patterson said aloud to himself as he looked for a friendly face. There were not many men from the company. Sgt. Potter was there and two men he considered new, who were already Spec/4s while he remained a professional Pfc.

He patted himself on the back for keeping his rank and not asking Webster about the promotion Margolin had mentioned in the hospital.

The Spec-Four Army eagle insignia holding arrows of war and an olive branch looked like five-day road kill on Highway 301. Who needed a weird looking bird on his fatigues? Pfc. stood for something. A real rank. Traditional. Everyone got the bird; he remained constant in his desire to not march to the same drummer. Breslin would be proud.

The cavernous interior of the shed muffed the sounds of the men passing through collecting their main and reserve chutes. Dust played in the streaks of sunlight penetrating from huge skylights. The red-capped riggers handed out the chutes with few jokes. Walking through reminded Patterson of a graduation ceremony. Everyone picked up the same thing. He wasn't in a hurry to go back outside, so he stepped out of line to check the parachute's log to see how old it was and how used. He could ask for another one if he wanted to. The thought of hiding in the shed came to mind.

No. No. No. He wanted to go all the way. *All the way, Airborne, Jim.*

He slung the kit bag onto his freshly healed shoulder and headed out the wide doors to the sunlight taxiways stretching like strips of blinding desert. In his mind, he heard the roar of Breslin's plane's engines reversing as they had...

A familiar voice chased his thoughts. Ahead, about 25 yards away in the briefing area, an NCO wearing the green beret of the 77th Special Forces was explaining the day's jump procedures as the chalks passed on their way to chute up. It was Sfc. Richard 'Fuckin' Cocksucker' Wisnewski: Jumpmaster. Patterson's stride quickened.

"We're usin' two C-One-Twenty-Threes today. Should be plenty of room. No grabassin' on the aircraft. The skipper says we're doin' the usual north to south pass over Normandy. We have nine long seconds, so take your time goin' out the door. Get a good body position. Surface wind's about five knots. We assemble here..." His pointer slapped the assembly area on plastic-covered outline of the DZ. "...at the reviewin' stand. Any questions?"

An officer asked about the duration of the flight. "Thirty-forty minutes. These fuckin' guys want to get home as quick as we do." The troops were pleased.

NCOs called out chalk numbers to move the men along. Patterson headed to Wisnewski who was speaking to a first lieutenant also wearing the beret. He was standing respectfully to the side waiting to interrupt when 'Ski saw him.

"Excuse me, sir. Willie, how's your ass?" Patterson stepped up to the two men. He saluted the officer. "Good mornin', sir." The lieutenant returned his salute.

"Sir, this here's Pfc. Willie Patterson of the 'Oh-Four Devils In Baggy Pants. A victim of the bad-ass Nixon Jump."

"Good to see you going back up, PFC.," said the officer, nodding his head in approval. He walked away after thanking Wisnewski for assistance.

"No sweat, sir." Wisnewski and Patterson came to a lazy attention and saluted. Wisnewski jerked his thumb toward the officer's back. "Nervous in the service. His first shot at Jumpmaster. I'm holding his hand."

"How come you're here? I thought this was an 'Oh-Four blast."

"Naw. It was going to be a chopper drop for us, but they scheduled planes when the choppers weren't available. We needed bodies to make it worthwhile, so we spread the word. Corps is here. Sneaky Petes. Division paper-pushers. All volunteers. Everyone's getting in a summer pay jump."

"So I volunteered without volunteerin'."

"Good trainin', Pfc. Hey, sorry I didn't make the hospital. My transfer came up and I just plumb forgot. The lieutenant and I were comin' up."

Patterson told him about Margolin's visit.

"Listen, I gotta get this cluster-fuck rollin'." Several chalks of men waited by the briefing map. "See me at the assembly point. I'll give you a ride back."

As they loaded into the C-123s, Wisnewski discovered he and Patterson were on the same aircraft. The sergeant pulled him from chalk order by his fatigue jacket sleeve. "Stick with me," he said. They were the last two in the fuselage. The ramp sucked shut and the plane's engines powered up. Wisnewski moved the lieutenant and an NCO apart so Patterson could squeeze in. He was fourth in the stick, the closest he'd ever been to the door. Patterson strapped himself into the canvas seat and waited for takeoff.

At the end of the runway, the Fairchild C-123 revved its two Allison turboprops, rattling the troops like a cocktail shaker. A series of spasms ran through the fuselage until the plane began a slow, barely noticeable inching forward. As more power was applied, the aircraft seemed to break from starting blocks and drive rapidly, rattling and screaming, along the runway. Liftoff, as always, took out the bounce and vibrations.

The stubby wheels swung into the belly wells. The two planes were aloft in less than two minutes and 20 minutes later, at 5,000 feet over Sanford, North Carolina, began the 14-minute leg to Normandy Drop Zone. The warm air made the flight rough, but the uncrowded conditions and light equipment eased the usual queasiness. Men stood up and walked around. They smoked if they wanted to. The few who did get sick were the ones who always were sick and knew to stay away from the others.

Ten minutes out, Wisnewski and the lieutenant opened the aft doors. Wisnewski helped the lieutenant lead the chalks through the jump commands. After they stood up and faced the rear of the plane, they followed the familiar litany of hook up, check equipment, sound off for equipment check. The troops had their chinstraps tight. Static lines hooked and held. And waited like anxious thoroughbreds in the gate.

Patterson could not help recalling his last jump with Breslin. He checked and re-checked his static line and that of the man in front of him. His mind replayed the morning he and Breslin had chuted up. They were still drunk from the wine and Terri's loving. They were rich men. Maybe on their way to Key West. Then he didn't check the static line and he knew he'd never forget the small body dangling...

"Come here," ordered Wisnewski, unhooking Patterson's static line and leading him to the door where he hooked him up. The other men had to push back to allow him space. No one complained. "Do what I tell you," said 'Ski. "When the lieutenant commands 'stand in the door,' get a door position like you own it and watch this light." He tapped the shoulder high red light on the forward panel by the door.

"It goes green, unass this heap like it's on fire. I'm comin' out last." He hooked up his static line away from the door toward the tail. "I'll see you at the assembly point and buy you a beer."

Patterson did not like changing his pattern of jumping; it might upset the Hawk. He vowed to do nothing fancy. No running. Good door position. Strong tight exit. No standing landing. The engines sounded like they could rip off the wings and streams of exhaust swirled though the door. The ground seemed a long way down and the late summer green boondocks of Bragg rolled and dipped to the horizon. Patterson really preferred the tail end of the stick. He and Breslin liked to run...

"Stand in the door!" commanded the lieutenant with a seriousness that revealed his inexperience.

Patterson swung his left foot around and shuffled forward until his left foot stuck halfway over the threshold. Arms extended down to press against the frame. The carbon monoxide stung his eyes and the wind tore at his trousers, pulling a trouser leg from his boot. He leaned out to look forward, squinting through the engine blast, to see how far away the DZ was.

Ahead, a rectangle of brown dirt lay melting in the engine's heat. The excitement and sounds behind him made him forget his fear. He waited. For just a moment, he saw Breslin's smiling face as they had chuted up that deadly morning...

Suddenly, Wisnewski shouted in his ear. "This is what it's all about, Willie! Why a man volunteers! Why he puts up with the chicken-shit! This is the Airborne! All the way! Gotta go! Gotta be Airborne!"

As Patterson looked over his shoulder, the light turned green. Wisnewski pushed him and he leaped with all his might, clutching the reserve, arms and legs snapped into a tight body position as if he could pass through the torrent of wind waiting to snatch him. The blast lifted him up, legs first over his head then he fell forward as the force diminished and he faced the ground in a headfirst dive until the canopy flicked open into a wide green circle that caught him and bounced him up and down in the cloudless sky.

It was over. That was it. 21 jumps. If his name came up again he'd tell them to shove it.

He checked his canopy for rips. All he could see were the outlines of the risers and the blocked-out sun. He turned in the sky, looking for other men. Each revolution allowed the sun to warm his face. It seemed he was alone, drifting in the suddenly mute wind.

An Airborne king surveying his conquered territories. He ruled all of Bragg.

"Twenty-three days!" he shouted and wished he could hang in that moment for each one of them.

Self-described young and dumb and full of cum, Buck Sergeant Bobby Tapper of 77th Special Forces drove Wisnewski and Patterson back from Normandy in a Forces Jeep. The short, square, talkative man had a weightlifter's bull neck. Slick aviator sunglasses hid his eyes while his mouth went non-stop as if his words were wheels in a hurry to roll somewhere. On the ride back, Tapper did his loquacious best to convince Patterson to re-up for Special Forces. "Take three and see. Whadda you got to lose?"

"Three years," replied Patterson matter-of-factly.

Special Forces was different. They were beefing up. There was no chicken-shit like the division and training was top notch. "You can't be a slug all your life. The beret is the Army's future. We're hard-chargin', stiff-dicked bastards." He reached back to punch Patterson on the leg. "Try flyin' with the eagles for a change."

Wisnewski grinned and totally agreed with Tapper. He admitted, "He says it better than me—and it's the fuckin' truth."

Patterson insisted they drop him at his car in the '04 parking lot so he could drive to the NCO club. Tapper lent him his field jacket with the buck sergeant stripes so he could get in. The Pfc. got a kick out of pulling into the NCO parking lot and walking in among the Non-Coms like he owned the place. No one gave him a glance. It wasn't crowded. The décor was several steps up from Charlie Company's Enlisted Men's club/cellar/car-port interior. There were two pool tables and a row of slot machines against one wall. The jukebox music was the same. A dance floor. Upholstered booths. Tables and chairs. He found the two men at the long bar, a pilsner glass of beer waiting for him. Wisnewski had the same drink. Tapper only touched orange juice, he was some kind of health fanatic. The two soldiers were arguing about medals.

Both were jealous about Margolin getting the Soldier's Medal, the highest peacetime decoration a solider could earn. Tapper wanted a chest full. He planned to prove he wasn't a slug.

After his first few sips of Schlitz, Patterson asked, "Sarge, what's a slug?"

"If you gotta ask...no...since you're a pal of my buddy 'Ski here who's been in the Army so long he got gigged for buffalo shit on his saber, I'll tell you, son." Tapper may have been two years older than Patterson.

"A slug, son, is a work-a-day, fuck-the-old-lady, wash-the-car on Saturday dud who'll never know the nut jinglin' joy of leapin' outta of airplanes."

Patterson grinned and bought it. "Like today," he said and started a fresh beer, silently toasting himself for the jump.

"In other words, a PFC.—poor fuckin' civilian—who will never in his wildest wet dream be a paratrooper. Always, remember, there's two kinds of people in this world..."

In unison, the three soldiers half-chanted, "Paratroopers and them that wish they were."

Someone grabbed Patterson's upper arm of his injured shoulder. A coarse voice whispered in his ear. "Anyone in here under E-Five best get down and give me ten good Airborne pushups." Patterson flinched and pulled away, nearly spilling his beer. Harry Patton Motz, in a green beret, stepped back and saluted Patterson.

On his uniform were new buck sergeant chevrons. His face had changed; the puffy baby cheeks and folds of neck flesh were gone. He was tan and had gained weight. He actually looked strong.

"Holy fuck," said Patterson. Motz threw a long arm around Patterson and ordered three more beers from the bartender and called Tapper a slug for drinking orange juice.

"How long you been in Sneaky Petes?"

"'Bout three months."

"How'd you get outta Dog Company?"

"Hell, everyone wants to go. We're the future." Motz elbowed his fellow members.

Patterson stood mystified by the glow in their countenances usually displayed by Christian Canteen converts. "Why?" he asked.

"Why, the man asks." Motz stepped close to Patterson and looked around so no one would over hear his secret. "You mean, you ain't heard?" The others huddled around the young Pfc. as if waiting for the punch line of a dirty joke. Patterson had no idea what they were up to. The jukebox stayed busy as more NCOs arrived early for Happy Hour.

Motz confided, "The Forces have found themselves a shootin' war. Just like it's supposed to be."

War? They must be nuts. They had almost gone to Lebanon. He knew Special Forces put men inside the Iron Curtain. "Come on, you're jivin' me."

"You are destined to be a slug, my friend, if you ain't ever heard of Laos or the Perfume River," said Tapper.

"It's in Asia," added Wisnewski, "down near the Philippines."

"You fuckin' NCOs don't know your ass from your elbows. It's fuckin' Indochina," said Motz emphatically, "and we're goin' in with both barrels blazin'."

Ski added they needed good men ASAP. "Jump qualified like you, Willie."

"Any Lifer," injected Tapper, "worth the weight of his beer belly is comin' over."

Patterson asked Motz how long he had re-upped for to transfer in. "Right hand to God as Hollywood used to say, none. But I'm takin' six and another stripe next year. Willie, I wouldn't steer you wrong. Take three…"

"… and see," answered Patterson. He wanted to mention meeting Schmidt, but Tapper slapped him on the bad shoulder a little too hard and said, "Be there or be square."

Patterson kept drinking and shaking his head no. He wasn't staying anywhere First Sgt. Billy Martin might have a leg up on him.

"Right now," explained Motz, "there're Green Berets leadin' patrols even whole companies of local troops. Cats like you and me deep in the jungle. Hell, a man could come back an E-Six or somethin'."

Or something? Dead? "Who's doin' the fightin'?"

"Fuckin' Commies, who else," said Wisnewski who handed Patterson another full glass and took away his half-empty one.

"It's the greatest thing since fur-lined jockstraps," pointed out Tapper.

Motz had more details. "Most of the world don't know it's goin' on. It's our own private little jungle war. Special Forces and helicopters. First time using choppers on big time operations. The honchos don't want to go; there's no publicity and it might be a tad hot for the chaps, as Sergeant Webster would say."

"And you know who's goin'?" asked Wisnewski.

"Who?" asked the three men together.

"Lieutenant Margolin." Patterson gulped his beer to avoid spitting it out. Some went down the wrong way and he coughed hard enough to make his eyes water.

Tapper slapped him on the back and called, "Medic!"

"On my honor as a sergeant first class in the United States Army, it's true." 'Ski explained after Margolin's leave and Ranger school he would join Special Forces. They need good young officers. "He extended and made me promise I wouldn't tell anyone." Patterson needed a fresh drink.

What was the world coming to? Margolin a Ranger and green beanie! Holy fuck. Nothing seemed like it was. Like Schmidt getting discharged. He told them about meeting him at the hospital. Wisnewski and Motz marveled at his escape from the system.

"It still doesn't mean he wasn't an asshole," judged Wisnewski, "and time will prove me right."

"The hell with him, Willie," said Motz. "What're you gonna do when you get out?"

"You mean in twenty-three days?" Man, did that feel good to say while these guys stood around the NCO Club with years ahead of them. *Fuck a bunch of NCO clubs.* He didn't say that.

Wisnewski handed him another glass of beer.

"I might go to college, or maybe to Key West to work. I don't know."

"Man, you're stuck between a rock and a hard place." Tapper wouldn't let a chance like this go by. "There's a war cookin'. Every red-blooded American whoever pledged allegiance to the flag should have his hand in the air beggin' to go. Fuck college, man. That's for slugs who wanna read TV Guides the rest of their lives. They need door gunners today..."

"Extend, goddamnit," demanded Motz. "Extend with me and we'll make history in Saigon. Saigon in Sixty. That's what's happenin'."

In his beer haze, Patterson discovered what he thought was a clever reply. "You cats are forgettin' somethin'. If there's a war, that means both sides are shootin'. You might not come back."

Tapper shook his head and turned away. "Christ, you think like that you might as well get a job herdin' sheep."

Motz leaned over Patterson, as he had a habit of doing after several drinks, and stared into Patterson's eyes. "Willie, I'm gonna tell you somethin' and you ain't gonna believe me, but 'Ski will back me up."

Patterson backed against the bar; it kept him from weaving and put some distance between him and the tall young sergeant. "What's that?"

"Inside. Way down deep inside. You. I mean you. You got the heart of a soldier. I mean the heart of a blood and guts paratrooper." Motz straightened up. "Am I right, 'Ski?"

"Right as rain, young Sergeant." Wisnewski pointed at Patterson with his beer glass. "I've seen it a hundred times if I've seen it once, and I told him that today when we jumped. 'You know, he always was one of the sharpest soldiers in the company.'"

Tapper told everyone they were too drunk to make sense and he couldn't handle another orange juice. He left, forgetting Patterson had on his field jacket. Patterson was glad; the slug had annoyed him.

"Willie, you'd look great in a beret." Motz attempted to place his on Patterson's head.

Patterson ducked away, nearly falling. "Let me alone, you assholes. I'm a goddamn supply rat. I ain't no glory hound. I'm tellin' you right now. I ain't takin' three or six. I ain't signin' nothin'." He pushed off the bar and headed for the men's room.

On his way back, he realized Happy Hour was in full tilt. There were NCO stripes from wall to wall. *Enemy territory,* he thought. *Time to grab hat.* He didn't go back to the bar.

He owed no one and did not have to justify anything to anybody. He was on his way out. Free. The vision of leaving

Bragg captured him more than anything his pals could offer. He went to the parking lot and took off the jacket and didn't even think about getting it back to the brash sergeant. With the door open, he sat in his car smoking as the sun slid toward the Great Smoky Mountains.

Where is it? Indochina? Where in the hell is that? It sounds like title of an old movie. There must be broads and rickshaws and booze and even elephants in the streets.

Cool. But what do I really want? At this moment? What? The tattoo?

He could swing over to Sailor Eddie's and finally get the Wings. If Breslin was with him, that's what they'd do. He could ask the Sailor about his future. "What's a young dude to do, Mr. Sailor?" Should he go back in for another beer? One more wouldn't hurt. Besides, he wanted to tell 'Ski about Breslin's static line. See what he thought. But instead of going back, he leaned against the high seat and enjoyed the humid Carolina dusk. Next time he'd ask him.

There were a lot of things he wanted to do, and he smiled, knowing his last jump was over. He wanted to find a beautiful girl with a Jaguar. To fish in Key West. To take Terri...Damn...Terri. If he had the guts he'd grab her and take her to the Keys like they had talked about. He closed his eyes to think about it. Holy fuck. It was too hot and he was tired.

Patterson fell asleep in the parking lot with the door open.

Chapter 20

In the induction centers, the new recruits face their first major military medical function. It is the humbling mass physical, and it is also one of the final events soon-to-be-civilians endure when they are discharged. The initial examination is a more careful inspection; the military doesn't induct people who might become a burden, so a man has to turn his head and cough. Due to the brevity of the final examination, it is difficult to uncover anything and soldiers hide any symptoms that might detain them. Part of both exams is the always entertaining 'short arm' and 'bend-over' event; the first time in a roomful of strangers is shocking. By the time a man is ready to be discharged, it is SOP. Thirty or forty men in their underwear stand along a line painted on the floor and a military physician, unseen until this moment, enters the room. The enlisted medic orders the men to drop their skivvies and skin it' back. The good doctor walks the line looking closely at scrotums and helmets for unusual swelling, drippings, discoloration, and sores—all signs of venereal disease.

At the end of the line he stops. The medic orders everyone to turn around, bend over, and 'spread 'em and keep 'em that way.' The doctor walks back scrutinizing buttocks and anuses with the hope of sighting gargantuan hemorrhoids and whatever else might pop and drip up or out. No one turns his head and coughs.

"Any complaints, gentlemen?" asks the officer after his stroll.

It is the rare moment anyone volunteers a complaint. In fact, if more closely questioned, they would vigorously deny any health defects. They want out. The Army knows that.

Men pull up their skivvies and sign medical release forms that absolve the Army from any further responsibility. They are now just a pube hair from being civilians again.

Patterson was assigned KP. He suspected the chore was a going-away present from the first sergeant, as he had only two days left in the company.

Through a warped sense of pride, he made sure he pulled pots and pans and performed an outstanding job, singing cool songs and advising Sgt. Potter that he should be awarded a silver four-compartment mess tray medal with an oak-leaf cluster for his efforts. Some of the new men wondered how he could be so upbeat with such a tough, dirty assignment. By afternoon, everyone working around the mess hall knew he was a short-timer. Late in the day, Potter called him into his small office and they sipped shots of Jim Beam. Spec-Four Archie wasn't invited and pouted as he went about his chores. They discussed Sidney the Cook and wondered whatever happened to him. There was a rumor he had re-enlisted. The MP who shot up the mess hall had received three months in the Fort McPherson stockade and planned to stay in the Army. Steele and Potter were his character witnesses.

Finally, Potter toasted Patterson and said. "You're a go-go-good so-so-soldier, Willie. Get the hell outta here." It was still early.

Patterson laughed and saluted the older Lifer. "I'll miss your cakes, Sarge." One day left in the company.

The next morning, immediately after clearing himself from supply, he went to the orderly room for First Sgt. Billy Martin's initials on the clearance form of his 201 file. Those initials would officially and immediately send him to Separation Company. He would be free.

As required, he knocked on the open door. Acting Corporal James Lee Hunter pushed back from his Remington long-carriage typewriter and asked, "What'd y'all want, PFC.?" The first sergeant did not look up from his rosters.

Patterson stepped inside Martin's sanctum without having that weak feeling he used to experience when he first joined the company. He spoke confidently. "I need the first sergeant's initials to clear the company."

Without raising his eyes off the page, Martin snappily replied, "Tell that there boy his first sergeant's too busy. Have him come back after he clears supply." Hunter dutifully and solemnly repeated the first sergeant's words like a court reporter confirming something for the judge.

Patterson refused to argue that he had already cleared supply. He walked out and was halfway down the hall when Hunter whispered from behind, "Hey, how'd y'all like that last jump?" The acting corporal stood by the water fountain wearing a smug grin.

"Piece of cake. Give me another one real fast. I only have three wakeups left, Corporal Suckass."

"Y'all come here and say that."

"You know, a corporal's rank is for squad leaders in rifle companies, not for pussies lickin' the first sergeant's ass." Patterson knew he carried immunity because of Broomfield.

"Y'all is chicken shit."

"Better than eatin' it everyday." Patterson gave him the finger and went to supply to bitch to Sgt. Webster about the first sergeant.

Webster sent him on the laundry run to Main Post. To kill the morning, he sat in the cafeteria smoking, destroying two glazed doughnuts and drinking coffee while watching the civilian girls go through the cafeteria line. On his way back, he stopped in the Main Post PX and bought sunglasses. He wanted to look as smooth as possible his last few days.

When First Sgt. Billy Martin returned to the orderly room after noon chow, Patterson stood by the door. Martin pulled his key chain from his belt and unlocked the door. In a rough manner, he snatched the 201 file from Patterson and went in. Over his shoulder he demanded, "Y'all wait in the hallway and take off those goddamn sunglasses." From his desk, he looked to see if Patterson had obeyed him.

"Now, y'all get in the front leanin' rest position for not bein' in proper uniform. The U.S. Army don't issue no sunglasses."

Here was the moment. Disobey. Defy him all the way to a court-martial. *Fuck him!*

However, Lt. Margolin's words of caution halted his mounting frustration. Patterson carefully placed the sunglasses on the shiny linoleum and extended himself horizontally from the hall into the doorway. "You know, First Sergeant, I was just thinkin' the same thing. How many pushups would *y'all* like?"

He stared up at Martin trying his best to smile, but anger showed. "First Sergeant, I asked, how many pushups would *y'all* like today?"

"Keep your mouth shut, Pfc." He studied Patterson's clearance sheet and leafed through his file. "I believe in my Alabama heart y'all should be in jail. If not for associatin' with them nigra reefer smokers and stealin' U.S. government gas, then for yore attitude toward Colonel Steele in the hospital."

Holy fuck. He knows. Patterson didn't shift his glance. If Martin was going to pile on him, he wanted to be ready.

"That's right, boy. Yore first sergeant knows everything. Don't-ever-forget-it. If the colonel hadn't put in a good word for y'all, me and the sergeant major were gonna run yore ass up the regimental flag pole. We should've done it anyways. Any man who associates with coloreds and poisons hisself with those cigarettes deserves to be...y'all and yore buddy, what was his..."

"Breslin, First Sergeant. The man who died."

"Damn fool did it to hisself."

Patterson strained in his leaning rest position. His fury at the little martinet aided in holding him up. Martin executed a quick swirl and looked over the edge of his desk. He gave a slight nod to Patterson to get up.

"Y'all are headed for a pack of trouble in this here world, boy." He poked two fingers down hard on the desktop. "Y'all can find it right here if I see yore ass around here ever again. I'll have you in the barbed-wire hotel faster than a freight train goin' down hill."

"No sweat, Sarge. I won't be back." Patterson stretched his arms in relief and reveled in the idea Steele had protected him.

"First Sergeant, Pfc."

"First Sergeant."

Martin pushed the 201 file to the edge of his desk. Patterson pulled it off and turned to leave as Cpl. Hunter came in, toothpick in hand, picking his teeth from Sgt. Potter's dinner. The two men bumped. "Watch where y'all goin', Pfc."

"Watch me go, Corporal Nobody."

He kept moving, striding in his spit-shined Corcorans along the highly buffed hallway, his pace quick and light, sunglasses back on, out the double-steel doors and down the concrete steps to jog between Able and Headquarters mess halls and along Grave Street to the EM parking lot. If he could have walked on his hands, he would have.

He was out of the company. Officially on his way. *Two days and a wake-up!* He floated to the Plymouth businessman's coupe. At the lot he turned and faced Grave Street and the modern barracks he had lived in for nearly two years.

He saluted.

In the first formation at Separation Company, Patterson attempted to be inconspicuous by standing in the middle. Among the 60-odd men in the formation, he noticed at least 20 pairs of sunglasses, two slings, and a foot in a cast. He pegged the slings and cast as fakes and the sunglasses as attractions to be selected for details. He slipped off his glasses and shoved them in his fatigue leg pockets.

The first group of names called reported to finance for pay record checks. The second group went on PX detail. The third group stood fast in ranks. That usually meant the powers-to-be hadn't yet decided their fate. There was always a need for help in the busy separation mess hall.

Patterson was in the second group. He recognized the sergeant calling out the names, but didn't know why.

Someone called out, "Hey, Sergeant Cooper!" *Cooper!* The hand-job Lifer who made Patterson cut open his duffel bag the first day at Bragg.

Except he was bigger. Not taller, but softer. He still carried the buck sergeant stripes on the sleeve of his loose-fitting unstarched fatigues and still wore the infantry blue cadre helmet liner low on his brow to look stern. After all the names had been called, Patterson approached him and asked if he had been called. Next to the sloppy sergeant, he felt cool in his starched and tailored fatigues with Jump Wings and the Eighty-Deuce patch on his shoulder and shiny-ass Corcorans that Cooper didn't have.

Cooper checked his clipboard. "Patterson. Yeah. You're over there with the PX detail."

Cooper's pudgy cheeks were now spattered with red veins, his eyes bloodshot and Patterson smelled violent hangover breath. *A true fucking Lifer leg. Doing nothing in the U.S. Army except taking roll for twenty years.*

The country should be on its hands and knees for real soldiers like Wisnewski, Motz, and even Lt. Margolin. And Col. Steele, too. It seemed there was one good soldier for every ten freeloaders or assholes like First Sgt. Billy Martin, who was just another roll-taker no matter how many stripes or colored pencils he had.

"Thanks, Sergeant Cooper," said Patterson, and he joined the small group waiting behind a three-quarter-ton truck destined for the Main Post PX.

A well-padded master sergeant at the PX gave them a quick briefing on how to pack a grocery bag and advised them if they stayed by their assigned counters, they'd all have free doughnuts to carry back. He seemed a sensible individual, like a cool uncle who gave his nephews sips of beer—a man who just wanted the world to go right for his customers.

Patterson already knew to put heavy items on the bottom and light ones on top. As a kid, he had helped with grocery bagging in the Downbeach A & P. There were busy moments and moments to take a Pepsi break by the PX entrance. The men didn't really know one another, so they talked about going home and evaluated the good-looking daughters of the military families coming out of the big store.

Patterson, cool behind his sunglasses, told everyone he wasn't going home. He was on his way to Key West to work the fishing boats. No doubt about it, he was slick. He took a long pull from the new swirl bottle. In 24 hours he would be on his way and no one would...

A familiar voice interrupted his thoughts. He peered from under his soft fatigue cap toward the sliding PX doors. Pushing a shopping cart full of groceries and accompanied by an older hefty woman and two little girls was the best ex-machine gunner in the 82nd Airborne Division.

Horsecollar McBride? The man had staff sergeant stripes on his fatigues and a Third Army patch on his shoulder.

"Mac?" Patterson took of his sunglasses and stood up, Pepsi in hand.

The sergeant looked at Patterson and quickly looked around as if checking on who else might be watching them. When he didn't see anyone but Patterson, he smiled and told his wife he'd see her at the car. As he turned back to Patterson, his countenance changed. His face flushed and doubting lips replaced the smile. He took a moment to shove an un-lit, half-used cigar in his mouth.

That's when Patterson noticed the crossed dueling pistols—the military police emblem—under the Wings on his fatigue cap and pinned on his collar. "Where in the hell did you go?" asked Patterson as he slowly added up the Third Army patch, the MP insignia, and the staff sergeant stripes.

"Here and there," answered McBride, using the cigar to emphasize his words.

"You never came back from emergency leave."

"I moved over to Third Army. What're you doin' around here?"

"PX detail from Separation. I get out day after tomorrow."

Suddenly, all of McBride's '04 tenure ran through Patterson's mind. The sudden appearance and savvy about the military from a supposed Pfc. The best ex-machine gunner in the 505th. The tirades against RAs as he claimed to be a draftee. Not smoking any Mary Jane. Asking where they got it. Never coming back from leave. Never clearing the company. Like that, he had vanished. Patterson said, "You've been here all the time."

"Yeah, I found a home at Bragg, Willie."

That was the old McBride. The wise guy. Patterson's gut tugged at his mind. He said, "Breslin's dead, you know."

"Yeah, that was a hell of a thing."

"Mangiameli got killed goin' home at Christmas." Patterson didn't want to provide updates. He wanted to say something and couldn't put his finger on it.

"I heard."

Sure he heard. Sure he knew who stole gas. Sure he knew where Breslin bought his Mary Jane. Sure he knew Carter and Wise were in jail.

"You're sure as hell a stone cop, ain't you?"

"I hope to shit in your mess kit, I am." He grinned and jammed the cigar into the corner of his mouth.

Patterson's words came out without editing. "You ate cheese on your buddies and poor fuckin' Tommy. You sided with that asshole Martin. You're fuckin' CID."

The cigar came out. "Willie, welcome to the real world." McBride shifted his shoulders as a boxer might and kept his arms ready at his side. "So what do we do? I'm a cop. A good one."

Patterson heard the challenge. The defiance. "You don't give a shit Tommy died and those guys are in jail."

"They were breaking the law," replied McBride, "and Mangiameli was an accident. It's that simple." He returned the wet cigar to his mouth with a 'so there you are' gesture. "Look, I got to be shovin' off. See you later." He turned away with the cart.

Patterson took two quick steps and grabbed his upper arm. He wasn't sure if the older soldier would slug him and didn't care. If it happened, all he wanted was one good punch.

"Mac, you fooled the hell out of us. Lied to us. You know, Breslin always said there was somethin' about you…"

McBride challenged Patterson. "Don't handle the merchandise, Willie." McBride looked him up and down and pulled out the cigar. "I always liked you. You soldiered and treated new men fair, so let me tell you somethin'." He relaxed and seemed to not know what to do with the cigar. "It's a tuff fuckin' world. You either fuck over or get fucked over. All I was doin' was a job. A job that protects the government from bein' ripped off by dudes who think it owes them a livin'."

"You did a job all right. On your pals. There's more to life than fuckin' over people."

"You're young and foolish, Willie. Still innocent even after two years in the green machine." McBride attempted a kinder look. "You show me there's more than that. Make me a believer, but, you know, there just ain't time. I have to go, Pfc." McBride started again.

This man wasn't McBride from the squad bay. He was a non-commissioned officer who might stop Patterson's discharge. He reined in his temper, but when he spoke most of the people close by heard him. "There is more. There's me. And Tommy. And Scott and everyone else who…" His voice grew louder and he didn't care. "… Sergeant 'Ski. Lieutenant Margolin. And Motz. Yeah, Motz. He's twice the soldier you think you are. You walk away, but you'll never get away. You gotta live with who you are! You stole the trust of your bunkies! Best ex-machine gunner your Lifer ass!" McBride continued his journey with the shopping cart. He never looked back.

Patterson held his spot, slowly sipping his drink, afraid to move in any direction because it might be towards the sergeant. No wonder the son-of-a-bitch was always so cocky. He knew he could leave anytime. *There is no forgiving a man without honor.*

And Patterson would never believe there were those who fucked over and those who got fucked over. That would be a sad way to walk through life.

Two years to the day, nearly the hour, he was out. A year ago, a month ago, a week ago, he would have stated categorically the Army could never be that efficient—even bet Sgt. Webster on it. His DD-214 separation form showed only a few decorations, the parachutist's badge, expert with the M-1, and the National Defense Medal. No Good Conduct Medal for Pfc. William C. Patterson, for he had been given an Article 15 and been reduced in rank. He wore only the Wings.

Sixty-three men in their summer khakis were processed with final pay, medical, dental, and personnel forms all in sturdy 10 by 13 white envelopes marked with the large black silhouette of the U.S. Army, an eagle with olive branches in its claws, a symbol once known as the Honorable Service Lapel Button—or the Ruptured Duck—which was worn by World War II veterans who had been honorably discharged. A second lieutenant who looked like a high school senior lectured them on their veterans' benefits and all were invited to a final dinner in the separation mess hall. The offer was roundly booed.

Then he cautioned them about driving safely and reported the statistic that one in ten men separated from the Armed Services were killed or injured driving home. "...and with that, gentlemen, your friends and neighbors thank you for your valuable contribution to the defense of your country." He saluted them.

Many of the troops returned the courtesy, Patterson included. Some men cursed with joy. Others quietly walked away to waiting families. More than a few ran toward their cars. It was as if they not only wanted to escape Bragg, but also one another. In the parking lot, he watched one man strip off his uniform to his underwear as his young wife or sweetheart watched with embarrassment.

Patterson opened the door of the coupe, allowing the September heat to escape while he removed his US and rifle collar insignia, his Wings, blue infantry shoulder braid, and looked around for a trash can. There wasn't one. Maybe he'd toss them out the window as he departed Bragg. But then, just like that, he decided he'd keep the Wings and other stuff. Like Motz said, inside he was really a Lifer. For the time being, he stuck them in the glove compartment. He laughed and climbed into the car.

As he swung on to the main road, he saw Sgt. Cooper talking to the young lieutenant. He felt sorry for the man and said aloud, "Goddamn it, Cooper, shape up. Go Airborne for Christ's sake."

Maybe he should have hollered out the window.

Patterson aimed the ugly Plymouth toward Longstreet Road. A final drive through the division seemed a necessity.

He wasn't in any hurry, because he honestly didn't know where he was going and was avoiding making that decision.

He caught up to a Jump School platoon double-timing along Longstreet. Close-shaven heads called 'whitewalls' confirmed their Jump School status. Men running along Longstreet in formation usually were. They were stripped to white T-shirts, trousers, and boots. Patterson slowed alongside.

Sergeants Barnes and Tate and numerous other Black Hats ran them, taking turns leading the cadence. The men sounded like an aggressive Russian military chorus.

"G.I. brush and G.I. comb!" called out Barnes.

"G.I. brush and G.I. comb!" answered the platoon of shuffling feet.

"Gee I wish I stayed at home!"

"Airborne!"

"Drivin' on!"

Patterson picked up the cadence. He heard their boots pounding the macadam in unison and their strained breathing.

"There just two things that I can't stand/ A bow-legged woman and a straight-leg man."

"Airborne!"

"All the way!"

"Bo Didley, Bo Didley have you heard/ We're gonna jump from a big iron bird!" *Run, you fuckers*, thought Patterson.

"One-Nineteen rollin' down the strip/ Airborne daddy gonna take a trip!"

Patterson's delight in being out made his eyes water as he pulled away and took the left turn on Ardennes, passing Jump School on his left. The tower was empty, but the PLF platforms and aircraft mock-ups were jammed with fresh troops enduring their first week.

It was hard to believe he had ever been there. "Twenty-one jumps ago." And he was 21 years old and wanted more excitement from life. Do something new. Different. What had Breslin said about that first jump? It was like being born again.

"Right, Scott?"

He turned onto Grave Street and passed the company. The building and its contents made his stomach uneasy. He wasn't going to stop. All his good-byes were over. He needed only to pass by to ensure he was leaving. A tremor of loneliness touched him.

There were good times in that building. Good men there. Broomfield. Banuelous. Mangiameli. Lt. Margolin—he still didn't believe the lieutenant joined Special Forces—Wisnewski, Webster, Scott. Holy fuck, Scott. *How many more times will I re-live that day?*

He used the regimental parking lot to make a U-turn and went down Grave again. Past the PX, the chapel, Dog Company, and recalled all those cold, tired mornings at reveille. He turned onto Gruber Road and picked up speed, passing the 504th regimental sign that read, "You Are Now Leaving 504th Airborne Infantry Regiment. The Best Damn Soldiers In The World." Going through Smoke Bomb Hill area, he noticed a lot of men in green berets; 77th Special Forces was growing. If Lt. Margolin ended up there, he and Wisnewski would be a good team.

Bragg Boulevard appeared ahead. Patterson slowed for the light and waited for the green.

He planned to drive down Hay Street, then head for Highway 301 to go either north to Downbeach or south to Key West. He wished he knew for certain which direction. Everything he needed was with him: discharge papers, shaving kit, and Schmidt's radio in the AWOL bag on the back seat. His footlocker rested in the trunk. It held his overcoat, civvies, a set of fatigues, the buck sergeant's field jacket, and the new green winter uniform he did not like and planned to wear in the unemployment line. Plus two new wool OD blankets 'borrowed' from supply. A moment after pulling onto the boulevard, he passed the imposing looking sign with division and corps logos that validated

Fort Bragg, North Carolina, was the Home of the Airborne. He had seen it from the bus his first day there and hundreds of times going back and forth to Fayetteville. Before he headed through Fayetteville to the highway, he had an important stop on the boulevard: cold sober at Sailor Eddie's.

After the tattoo, he'd pick up a six-pack and swing by the Carousel Lounge to see if Terri was around. Maybe he'd dare to go to her place to show her the tattoo. Even if Starr was there. He checked in the rear view mirror hoping to see a brave young man: all he saw was a guy with crew cut. A Pfc. Poor Fucking Civilian.

He could do it. Make her an offer on the spot. "Come on, Terri. Get the kid and we'll go."

Right in front of Starr. Why not?

He had over $1,000 from Soldier's Savings, a month's pay, and cash for unused leave. It would be enough for them to live on until they found jobs. They'd name *their* kid Scott.

Maybe get Lt. Margolin to be the godfather. Wisnewski? There wasn't anyone from home he'd ask. No best friends. No girl friend. His parents would worry Terri might embarrass them.

The same thing waited at home that was there when he left. Waiting for him. Waiting to paint him back into the woodwork as the comptroller's son who owed his job to his father's position and his father owed his kiss-ass job to the mayor.

Man, he might as well be a tent peg. "Right, Scott?" *A dud. A work-a-day slug.*

His best friends were the men he'd met in the Eighty-Deuce. Those who shared two years of 'dress right and cover down/ Forty inches all around' bullshit. And now they were gone. A few dead.

The gravel from Sailor Eddie's driveway splattered on the Plymouth's undercarriage waking Patterson from his reverie. He stopped and looked. Sailor was there. He stood behind the screen door barely visible due to the sun playing on the screen's ripples. The wizard waiting on his mountain-top. Patterson climbed out and walked to the worn wooden stairs. Sailor Eddie didn't move.

Patterson stood still. His khakis warming in the hot sun. The screen opened and Sailor said, "Come in, son. You're my first customer. That's good luck." Patterson took a step up.

Wings are what I want, Sailor. Wings that lift a man and carry him to wherever he wants to go. Wings for freedom, to soar forever like an eagle. Sometime in the past, Breslin had said that. Patterson didn't know where his thoughts started and Breslin's ended.

"The flies are comin' in, son."

Sailor's sleeveless T-shirt revealed the faded reds and blues inked on his arms and shoulders. Patterson vividly remembered the night they all got the chutes on their asses. Little tattoos. Real Wings were different. Sidney the Cook had real Wings. Sgt. 'Ski, too. Even asshole Archie and 10,000 other paratroopers who passed through Bragg. That's a lot...

Wait one, motherfucker, he ordered himself.

Patterson wanted to get away from all that. Two years of discipline. Martin's rosters. And the Hawk circling in the clouds. Patterson looked at himself in his unadorned uniform and saw a different person. Perspective, Breslin had always said. Perspective.

He wasn't going to be like 10,000 other men. He wanted to stand on his own. Face himself. Resist becoming one of those faceless numbers. A comptroller's son. A private first class stuck in the rear rank with a faded tattoo. A common man Hollywood Jack once knew.

The Sailor beamed from the half-closed door with the gentleness of a confessor. "Scared, son?"

A man had to work at being an individual. Patterson wanted a new life with a perspective to know what was right and wrong. He wanted new challenges. From Sailor Eddie's doorsteps, Patterson imagined he saw the whole world and his future. He had learned to run and jump from planes and stand up to the Martins and Steeles of the world. He hadn't fully realized his growth until that moment. He wasn't less than other men, maybe he was more, a professional Pfc. His future appeared unlimited and a tattoo wasn't going to make it any better or worse. He needed no mark for inspiration; he had perspective. Steele had cautioned him in the hospital that a man sometimes had to do things he didn't want to do. Steele was right and had let him off. Maybe the colonel's charity helped Patterson understand what was really important. He wasn't sure, but he knew what he wanted to do.

"Sailor, you're a beautiful cat," he took off his sunglasses and admitted, "but I'm not comin'." Patterson stepped down and headed back to the Plymouth.

"Wait, son!" called Sailor. "I've got a special today. Fifty cents off any design."

Patterson chuckled and climbed into the car. Sailor remained invisible behind the screen door.

Patterson started the engine and laughed at the image of strapping the footlocker to the luggage rack. Where did that idea come from? Breslin? He shifted into first and took a last look at Sailor Eddie's. "I'm gonna forget all this shit."

He popped the clutch and swung onto the boulevard. No more stops. He was on his way. The radio news talked about Communists units in South Vietnam being identified for the first time as Viet Cong. A full-scale battle between South Vietnamese troops and a large-scale guerrilla force occurred on the Plain of Reeds near the Cambodian border this past Thursday. The smaller Viet Cong platoons inflicted heavy casualties on the government battalion. In Saigon, President Diem was...

Patterson jammed the station selector twice before he found music. He grabbed his Luckies from the small plastic dashboard dish held on by suction cups. Taking out his lighter from his tailored khaki trouser pocket required some shifting and digging.

The unlit cigarette hung from his mouth. He pulled out the lighter and rubbed the raised '04 Devil insignia.

There wasn't anything he had to do or not do and no matter how many ways he tried to shape it, the simple bald-ass truth was he didn't want the tattoo. He didn't need Wings. *I am what I am. What happened happened.* There was no wishing for a different outcome. Wishing he and Breslin were headed for the Keys with fresh Sailor Eddie Wings on their shoulders. Wishing for the 1,000th time he'd checked the static line and knowing he'd wish for that forever. Wishing Mangiameli was alive and married to Judy. Wishing Terri was going with him. Wishing he was standing in the door again with that tinge of fear of the unknown, anticipating the joy of being alive, being reborn again and again with each jump.

He shifted the lighter to his right hand and steered with his left. Again, he rubbed the insignia. There were seconds when the pressure of his fingers felt as if every atom of his body was trying to crush the regimental crest. "Forget it."

The lighter lay easily in his palm.

With a quick motion, he spun the flint and lit his cigarette, inhaling powerfully, forcing the smoke out his nose and mouth, then he reached back to toss the lighter out the window onto Bragg Boulevard. Halfway across his chest, he swallowed it in his fist and held it tightly as Highway 301 appeared ahead.

Epilogue

SP/4 ADAM 'ARCHIE' ARCHIBALD: Archie did die young. After being discharged, he worked at various menial jobs in the Pittsburgh area and drank a great deal. Throughout his life he complained he was sick and went in and out of the VA hospital. He died of cancer at 31. In the late seventies there was a government investigation into the high incidence of cancer among veterans of Operation Smoky.

SERGEANT FIRST CLASS LEROY 'BRUTE' BARNES: Served two tours in Vietnam as an infantry platoon sergeant: one with the 173rd Airborne Brigade, the later tour with the 4th Infantry Division. He was slightly wounded during both tours, but never seriously enough to be sent home. He finished his career as a Jump School instructor at Fort Benning, Georgia. He knew it was time to retire when females were allowed in Jump School.

Pfc. ANTHONY 'TONY' BANELOUS: Tony returned to Salinas and after several close calls with the law fell in love and married. He used his GI Bill to attend San Jose State, where he developed an interest in the expanding field of computers. He eventually worked for IBM and quietly raised a family in Alamo, California. They had two daughters.

EX-CORPORAL FRED BROOKES: Brookes returned to the Newark, New Jersey, area after his dishonorable discharge and disappeared.

CORPORAL MARCUS BROOMFIELD: Broomfield earned his high school diploma and stayed in the Army. To advance his career, he abandoned boxing and became a straight infantry platoon sergeant. He deployed to Vietnam in 1965 with the 173rd Airborne Brigade and did a single tour. He retired from the Army and coached boxing in Atlanta boys clubs until his death in 1999.

MAJOR NATHANIEL BYRD: The Chaplain was a career soldier and moved around the country to various posts until he was assigned to the huge hospital in Bien Hoa where he conducted services and spent most of his time counseling wounded men. The position preyed on him and tested his positive disposition. After 18 months, he returned to the states and his family waiting at Fort Sam Houston, Texas, where he retired.

SP/4 SIDNEY 'THE COOK' FOSTER: Sidney re-enlisted after the MP incident and went to Korea where he picked up a VD wart. He became mess sergeant and overlapped with Sgt. Potter during their tours in Vietnam with the First Brigade, 101st Airborne and spent most of his career in Airborne units. He married a Korean bar girl and owns a horse farm in Oregon.

SERGEANT ADRIAN COOPER: He went to Vietnam in 1966 with the Fourth Infantry Division. He took a accidental grenade stomach wound in base camp and was medivaced. He received a permanent medical disability and drank himself to death while an out-patient at the Lexington, Kentucky VA hospital.

CORPORAL JAMES LEE HUNTER: James Lee did his two years and returned to Nashville. He enrolled in the University of Tennessee. Through family and fraternity connections, he became a successful stockbroker and raised a family.

BUCK SERGEANT MICHAEL KENNEDY: The sergeant did make his 20-year requirement for retirement. Prior to discharge, he volunteered for Vietnam, but his poor health kept him stateside. After he retired, he stayed in a trailer park in the Bragg area for easy access to the PX , the American Legion club, and health care privileges. For a few years, he enjoyed driving his truck to the DZs to watch the jumps, then gradually disappeared.

SP/4 NICKY 'MOONLIGHT GAMBLER' LAZOR: Lazor was stopped by the MPs and given a DR for driving under the influence and busted to private. Three weeks later, he was discharged and returned to Calumet City. After five winters of tending bar in private clubs he joined his uncle in Panama City, Florida, and became a hard-working partner in a Chicago Style pizzeria and made amateur porno films.

FIRST SERGEANT BILLY MARTIN: Martin saw the writing on the wall as Vietnam became a major part of the American psyche. He retired early to avoid deployment and remained in the Bragg area working a civilian in the PX system. He died of a heart attack in 1974.

SERGEANT HARRY PATTON MOTZ: Motz became a colonel and retired after 28 years of service. He won a Silver Star in Vietnam as an enlisted man and attended OCS. He did a second tour as a lieutenant platoon leader. During Desert Storm, he commanded a regiment of mechanized infantry. Motz retired to Palm Bay, Florida, where he lives today.

STAFF SERGEANT EDWARD 'HORSECOLLAR' MCBRIDE: McBride went to Vietnam with Army intelligence. He was seriously wounded in Saigon when a VC threw a grenade into the military bus he was riding. It was his third week in-country. After recuperating at Womack Hospital on Bragg, he served his 20 years and worked in the private sector for hotel security in Charlotte.

CAPTAIN CONSTANCE MELBY: Connie served her Vietnam time with the 1st Field Hospital in Chu Lai and married a doctor she met there. Later, they served together at Fitzsimmons Army Hospital in Denver and settled there. After her children grew up, she returned to nursing.

Sfc. TODD POTTER: The mess sergeant stayed in for 29 years. He did two tours in Vietnam as a cook for the generals of the 101st Airborne Division and the Americal Division. He never saw any action, but, as well as he was able, he insured troops in the field received warm meals on holidays.

PRIVATE JACK 'HOLLYWOOD' SCHMIDT: Hollywood followed up on his movie career and, once he lost his hair, he became a producer of low-budget horror films. He made a lot of money in the European markets and enjoyed the Cannes Film Festival every year. Later in life, he became patriotic and liked to talk about the tough times he had when he was a paratrooper in the 82nd. He died in 1995.

COLONEL JACK STEELE: Steele commanded a regiment in the 101st Airborne in Vietnam during 1968. His unit was known for its aggressiveness and he received a Distinguished Service Cross as well as a Purple Heart when his helicopter's bubble was shot out and he was cut by flying plastic. He did a second tour as a one-star general and assistant commander of the 25th Tropic Lightning Infantry Division. After 25 years, he retired and became Head of Admissions at a small liberal arts college in North Carolina.

Pfc. JOHNNY STARR: Starr returned to Los Angeles and never saw Terri again. He worked his way into the Los Angeles Latino mafia and ended up in San Quentin for drug trafficking and attempted murder. In 1982, he died of stab wounds in prison.

SERGEANT BOBBY TAPPER: The talkative sergeant did two Vietnam tours with 5th Special Forces Group. Tapper was highly decorated for various actions. He became a well-known freelance combat correspondent for the networks and stayed behind when Vietnam fell. Once he came home, he never adjusted to civilian life. He married a Vietnamese woman and died of a heart attack in 1987.

Sfc. DAVIS TATE: Tate was killed in action at Tuy Hua while serving with the 502nd Airborne Infantry Regiment, First Brigade, 101st Airborne in Vietnam. It was his second tour. In between tours, he served as a jump school instructor at Fort Benning, Georgia and as cadre at the 'Tigerland' training camp for Vietnam-bound troops.

TERRI & CHRISTIAN: Terri managed to get a job with the Bragg PX system. She married a Vietnam veteran Special Forces NCO. Her son Christian joined the Marines at 18 and was lightly wounded off the coast of Cambodia in 1976 when the Marines re-took the pirated freighter Mayaguez.

Sfc. ANDREW WEBSTER: Sgt. Webster and several other NCOs ran the NCO club system throughout Vietnam from a MAC-V office in Saigon. He was involved in the Army-wide infamous slush fund scandal and received a dishonorable discharge in 1971. He opened an antique business in Tallahassee, Florida and resides there today.

Sfc. RICHARD 'SKI' WISNEWSKI: 'Ski did two tours in Vietnam. He was seriously wounded in the Ia Drang Valley early on his initial tour with the 1st Cavalry. He became a first sergeant and served with the 504th when they were quickly deployed from Bragg to Vietnam during the battle of Hue. After 27 years, he retired and worked on the ramp for Northwest Airlines at O'Hare in Chicago until he retired a second time and moved to Hobe Sound, Florida. He is active in the local VFW. He liked to wear his jump boots on the airport ramp.

CAPTAIN SEYMOUR 'MAD DOG' MARGOLIN: Hanging behind the counter of Ziggy's Deli on Ventura Boulevard in Sherman Oaks is a faded news clipping of Captain Seymour Margolin wearing a green beret. The headline reads "Valley Officer Killed in Vietnam." In 1961, during a night attack against the Minh Long Special Forces camp in South Vietnam, he ran out to assist Sgt. Motz who had been wounded by mortar fire and was killed. He was awarded a Bronze

Star with 'V'. Margolin was one of the first 100 men to die in combat in Vietnam.

Pfc. BILL 'WILLIE' PATTERSON: Willie went to Key West and collected unemployment until he talked his way onto a boat. Hard work, rough seas, and long trips quickly killed the romantic notion of 'wearing leather shit on his wrists.' He returned to Downbeach and painted houses. In the middle of the second winter, he went back to Key West and tended bar and collected the GI Bill while going to Key West Community College. In school, he met his wife and as the real estate market grew in the seventies she became a broker and he was an agent. They were very successful. He named his 27-foot Ericson sloop 'Perspective' and their first child Scott. They retired to Jupiter, Florida, a few years ago.

Glossary

AG: The Adjutant General's Corps. This is the administrative/ personnel branch of the Army. It is considered good duty for those who do not appreciate field training and combat readiness.

Anchor Line Cable: The stiff wire cable that runs aft from the aircraft bulkhead at a seven foot height to hold the static line clips that deploy parachutes.

AWOL: Absent Without Leave. i.e. a soldier is gone without permission.

AWOL bag: A type of gym bag usually carried when going on leave.

Basic: A shortened term for Basic Training, the first 8-10-12 weeks of Army training.

Barbed-Wire Hotel: The basic Army prison on a military post, officially the stockade.

B-12 Parachute: A chute without a static line worn by aircraft crew. It allows mobility within the aircraft and is opened by pulling a D-ring in a free fall.

BOQ: Bachelor Officers Quarters. Where unmarried male officers live.

Brasso: A strong polish used on metal military insignia.

Chalk: A line of paratroopers in jump order. Chalk comes from having chalk numbers on jumpers' helmets in the early days.

Church Key: Bottle and beer can opener before pull-tabs and twist-off tops.

CID: Criminal Investigative Division: the detective branch of the military police. They are often undercover.

Class 'A' Uniform: The dress uniform for parades, guard duty, traveling: khaki in summer, olive drab wool in winter (now a dark green year around).

CQ: Charge of Quarters. The enlisted NCO who watches over the company on weekends and after hours.

Cold or Dead soldier: A cold beer or any empty (dead) beer can or bottle.

Combat Infantryman's Badge or CIB: This highly prized badge is awarded to soldiers who serve under fire. A badge with a star indicates two wars and some individuals have earned two stars.

Deuce-and-a-half: A 2-1/2 ton truck, a workhorse vehicle used to move men and gear.

Daily Dozen: The standard Army exercises 1 through 12. e.g. Side-straddle Hop, Four-Count Pushup, Squat Thrust, and others.

Dear John: An old military nickname for the letter from home that tells the recipient his girlfriend/wife is no longer interested in waiting for him.

DD: Dishonorable discharge.

Dinner: Lunch in the Army, the main meal. Supper is early evening and lighter fare.

Door Position: The stance a jumper makes in the aircraft door. A variation of a swimmer take-your-mark stance. Head up. Hands holding the fuselage. Knees bent.

DR: Delinquency Report. A report for breaking minor post regulations. e.g. speeding, driving under the influence, and whatever else an MP might dream up. The recipient usually is punished within the company with extra duty.

DRO: Dining Room Orderly, the KP who takes care of the dining room, a favorite chore on cold winter days.

Double-time: The command to run…more like a jog in unison with others.

DD 214: Department of Defense personnel form a soldier carries with him when transferring or being discharged. His career is summed up on one or two pages.

1524 Form: A supply request/turn-in form used in the late fifties.

ETS: Estimated time of service. The day a man's obligation is up.

Field strip: Breaking down a weapon into its main components for inspection. Tearing apart a cigarette: tobacco scattered, paper rolled into a tiny ball and pocketed. This avoids cigarette butts in the area.

Four-count Pushup: One: drop to the leaning rest position from the position of attention. Two: the down portion of a pushup. Three: finish the pushup. Four: spring back to attention. Repeat many times. More strenuous than a regular pushup.

Green Beanies: Derogatory reference to Green Berets, particularly before they had proven their worth in Vietnam and future wars.

G.I.: Government Issue. A soldier. "GI brush. GI comb. Gee I wish I stayed at home."

Gig: An imaginary 'mark' meaning not up to par. e.g. shoes not shined, button unbuttoned etc…etc… An insult as in "the man's a walking gig."

Hawk: The unknown waiting in the sky for something to go wrong or maybe make something go wrong for jumpers. i.e. bad luck.

Headcount: The person, usually an NCO or CQ, who tracks how many men eat in the mess hall.

Hazardous Duty Pay: Extra monthly pay for jumping: $55.00 for enlisted men. $110.00 for officers.

Hollywood Jump: A man wears only a web belt with a canteen and first aid packet attached in addition to the main and reserve chutes. Comfortable compared to full gear drop.

Judge Advocate General's Corps: The legal branch of the U.S. Army.

KP: Kitchen police. Enlisted men under the rank of corporal assigned on a rotating basis to assist in the mess hall. At times a difficult, dirty task.

Leg: Anyone, civilian or military, who is not jump qualified. A derogatory term for non-jumping military personnel.

Lifer: A career soldier. It could be derogatory depending on the speaker's tone.

MAC-V: Military Assistance Command, Vietnam. The cover organization for military operations in Vietnam, particularly in the early days.

Mox nixs: An expression derived from the German *macht nichts* meaning it's not important.

Master Blaster: The highest earned status for jumpers: the certification requires a certain number of jumps and flights as a Jumpmaster.

MOS: Military Occupation Specialty. A soldier's job. e.g. Eleven Bravo (11B) = Infantryman.

Mr. 'B' Collar: A raised curved collar on a dress shirt made popular by Billy Eckstine in the fifties.

Moatengator: 10,000 motherfuckers.

MP: Military Police.

NCO: Non-commissioned officers (Non-coms): corporal to master sergeant. The men who make the Army work.

OCS: Officer Candidate School, Fort Benning, GA. Enlisted men train to be officers.

OD: Olive drab. A dull green color that permeates many aspects of military life: Uniforms. Trucks. Buildings. Planes. Blankets. Some say it is the color of a Lifer's blood.

Overseas Cap: A soft dress cap that folds and can be tucked in a man's belt. aka 'cunt' cap because of its shape.

Pinks: Light putty colored twill trousers worn with the formal officer's uniform prior to Army greens. The fabric had a subtle weave of pink thread.

PLF: Parachute Landing Fall. The way to land on a jump. Sideways is best. Feet first. Then knees, hip, shoulder to absorb the shock. That rarely happens.

P.T.: Physical training. See Daily Dozen.

Police Call: Soldiers walk through a specific area collecting trash for disposal.

Queen Anne Salute: A basic rifle drill movement that involves bringing the rifle from a position of attention, over the shoulder and dropping to one knee with the weapon pointing down.

RA: Regular Army. The first letters of a soldier's serial number that indicates he volunteered to join for three years instead of being drafted for two. Sometimes used in a derogatory fashion. e.g. RA12345678

Repo Depo: Replacement Center. The processing center where troops arrive and depart.

Road Guard: The first man in a formation who runs ahead to block traffic coming from a side street. He then returns to the rear of the formation and the next man blocks the next intersection and so on.

ROTC: Reserve Officers Training Corps, usually written ROTC. Campus based organizations that train future officers. Students receive pay while members.

Sam Browne Belt: The old officer's combination waist and shoulder leather belt that went with the three-quarter length chocolate brown jacket. Part of the dress uniform with the 'pink' trousers.

Service Cap: A formal stiff hat with a brim and high peak. Considered a bus driver's hat and not worn by paratroopers. aka 'flying saucer'.

S-4: The official designation for the regimental supply and logistics. S-1 = Personnel. S-2 = Intelligence. S-3 = Operations.

Skosh: Quick. Now.

Smilin' Jack: Heroic comic strip pilot from the forties and fifties.

Sneaky Petes: See Green Beanies.

SOP: Standard operating procedure: normal military activities.

SNAFU: Situation Normal. All Fucked Up. A term describing events going awry.

SP: Shore Patrol. The Navy and Marines military police.

SP/4 or Specialist-Fourth Class: A pay rank (E-4) used to avoid making too many corporals. One pay level above Private First Class (E-3) aka Speedy/4, Spec-Four or SP/4. There is also Spec-Five and up.

Steel Pot: The actual helmet a soldier wears. Inside is an adjustable helmet liner. Often used as a sink, a seat, and a mixing bowl.

Stick: See Chalk.

STRAC: Strategic Army Command: a concept from the late fifties to change infantry regiments to battle groups composed of engineering and artillery units as well as infantry. These units were ready to be deployed worldwide within 24 hours. An adjective to describe an outstanding unit or individual. Sarcastic: Stupid Troopers Running Around In Circles.

Suicide Knob: A small knob attached to a car steering wheel to turn the wheel easier. It was subject to breaking and causing accidents. Finally outlawed and not needed with power steering.

T-Ten Parachute: The standard chute in the fifties: difficult to maneuver and unwieldy on a man's back.

TJ: Tijuana, Mexico.

Top: A respectful and familiar term for first sergeants. Unlike 'First Shirt' *et al.*

TO & E: Tables of Organization and Equipment: All the material including the buildings, lockers, weapons, mess hall gear to run a company, a regiment, a division.

UCMJ: *Uniform Code of Military Justice*: The bible of rules and regulations and punishments for breaking military laws.

US: The first two letters of a draftee's serial number that signify he has only two years to serve his country. e.g US12345678

WAC: Womens' Army Corps. How women served before they were allowed to join the regular ranks.

Westy: General William Westmoreland: Famous Airborne leader from WWII to Vietnam.

White-walls: Haircut required by elite units: skin showing on the sides and stubble on the top.

About the Author

More than a few years ago, Bill won the Samuel Goldwyn Literary Award at UCLA. Immediately afterward he spent a year in Vietnam taking photographs and writing stories about the First Brigade, 101st Airborne. His stories and photos were published world-wide and he earned a Bronze Star. He also served with 82nd Airborne; *Hook Up* is a result of his military experiences. He has written two additional novels based on ex-paratrooper and private investigator Tommy Palmer. Bill grew up at the South Jersey shore and has lived and worked in Africa, Hawaii, and traveled throughout Southeast Asia, the Orient, and Europe. He earned his living as the corporate sales manager for a major international airline and holds a master's degree in Asian Studies. He raised a family close to the beach in Southern California where he resides today.

Other novels:

The Good Seats
Didja' Hear? Danny Devlin's Dead